Flashman's Escape

Robert Brightwell

This book is dedicated to my brother John Brightwell, another Flashman fan.

Published in 2014 by FeedARead.com Publishing

Copyright © Robert Brightwell

First Edition

A CIP catalogue record for this title is available from the British
Library.

Flashman's Escape

Introduction

This is the fourth instalment of the memoirs of the Georgian Englishman Thomas Flashman, which were recently discovered on a well-known auction website. Thomas is the uncle of the notorious Victorian rogue Harry Flashman, whose memoirs have already been published, edited by George MacDonald Fraser. Like his nephew, Thomas has the uncanny knack of involving himself, often reluctantly, with some of the key events and characters of his age.

This packet of memoirs covers the second half of his experiences in the Peninsular War and follows on from *Flashman in the Peninsular*. While it can be read as a stand-alone novel, if you are planning to read both, it is recommended that you read *Flashman in the Peninsular* first.

Having lost his role as a staff officer, Flashman finds himself commanding a company in an infantry battalion. In between cuckolding his soldiers and annoying his superiors, he finds himself at the heart of the two bloodiest actions of the war. With drama and disaster in equal measure, he provides a first-hand account of not only the horror of battle but also the bloody aftermath.

Hopes for a quieter life backfire horribly when he is sent behind enemy lines to help recover an important British prisoner, who also happens to be a hated rival. His adventures take him the length of Spain and all the way to Paris on one of the most audacious wartime journeys ever undertaken. With the future of the French empire briefly placed in his quaking hands, Flashman dodges lovers, angry fathers, conspirators and ministers of state in a desperate effort to keep his cowardly carcass in one piece. This extraordinary account brings together various historical events, while also giving a disturbing insight into the creation of a French literary classic!

As editor I have restricted myself to checking the historical accuracy of the scarcely credible facts detailed in the book and adding a series of notes at the end to provide more information on the characters and events featured.

The memoirs of Thomas's more famous nephew, Harry Flashman, edited by George MacDonald Fraser, are as always strongly recommended.

RDB

Chapter 1

A few miles from Lisbon, March 1811

"So where have you sent my husband this time?" asked Lucy as she pinched out the candle on the trunk that served as a bedside table in my tent.

"Oh, I had to send him to headquarters to see if he could get more boot soles. The men's boots are already in a sorry state."

"Yes, but he is getting sent on so many errands lately that he thinks his new captain does not like him." She giggled and snuggled even closer against me on the narrow cot bed.

"I like Corporal Benton well enough; it is just that I like his wife even more." I put my arm around her and pulled her tight towards me. Apart from the obvious carnal pleasures of being with Lucy, which we had just enjoyed, the shared body warmth on a cold night like this was useful too.

"Will he back tomorrow?" Lucy asked before yawning loudly.

"Yes, I suppose so," I replied gloomily.

It was not the done thing for officers to enjoy the soldiers' wives, but Lucy had been giving me licentious looks since I was first appointed as captain of her husband's company. Benton was a good corporal, if a little too earnest. While Lucy loved him in her own way, he had evidently not been doing enough to please her under the blankets.

As soon as I had looked over the camp followers of my company, she had caught my eye. There were just six official wives on the strength, drawn in a lottery to accompany the regiment when it left England. But since then most of the remaining men had acquired Spanish or Portuguese women. Lucia da Silva was now Lucy Benton, and if they were not officially married in the eyes of the army, they were in the eyes of the men. This was why the philandering captain of Benton's company had to be discrete.

"Do you think we will fight the French soon?" murmured Lucy into the crook of my shoulder.

"I don't know. We have not seen a Frenchman yet and no one knows what state their army will be in when we do catch up with them."

It was just the sixth day of a new campaign which was expected to turn around our fortunes in Spain and Portugal. While we had spent a winter in good quarters behind the lines of the Torres Vedras forts, starvation and disease had finally forced the French to withdraw. Now the British were advancing again.

Aside from Corporal Benton moaning about his various errands, the rest of the men were in high spirits. As with the start of any campaign there was the usual wild optimism of being in Madrid by the summer. Looking back on that time, I thank God we cannot see into the future. For many of those men who laughed and joked about the coming victories would be dead in a few weeks, and those of us who survived often had cause to wish we hadn't.

As Lucy snored quietly into my neck I reflected on recent events. The French had initially thought that they had the British army trapped and besieged, when they drove it towards Lisbon the previous autumn. But as a bitterly cruel winter had set in they slowly realised that the positions had been reversed. First they discovered that the British had built an impregnable line of forts along the Torres Vedras hills. Behind these fortifications we had lived in comfort, either in the forts or the houses of Lisbon, and well supplied with food by ship. Our 'besiegers' soon found themselves cut off from other French armies when the harsh weather blocked the mountain passes, and then the cold, disease and pitiless partisans had steadily taken their toll. Wellington had expected the French to pull back after six weeks but they had scavenged and searched for food to stay for six months. Deserters who managed to reach the British lines had told tales of whole companies wiped out by a combination of starvation and pneumonia, while their accounts of silently murdered sentries and missing patrols showed that partisans and the local population were exacting a gruesome revenge for the brutal methods used by the French to find hidden food.

Many of the British officers had been pressing Wellington to advance against the weakened French for weeks but he had been content to wait. "Let *'General Winter'* do his work, gentleman," he had repeatedly intoned, and it had been one of the harshest winters that anyone could remember. His reluctance may also have had something to do with the fact that he was being entertained by one of the finest courtesans in Lisbon. I know because I introduced him and had spent much of that winter with her sister. You would be a fool to leave either of their beds prematurely. But now that the French had pulled back, the British commander had no choice but to pursue them, taking his army with him.

That meant exchanging a warm house for a freezing tent, although as Lucy shifted against me I had to admit that there were compensations. Life was even tougher for the rest of the company as there were only tents for the officers; the rest had to sleep in the open or under whatever cover they could find. For a British regiment this did not just mean the men. There were a similar number of their women and children, and even a menagerie of animals, mostly goats for milk. There was also a handful of dogs including Boney, my Irish wolfhound, who was curled up just beyond the tent door.

I had been with my new regiment, known as the Buffs, for nearly a week. We had spent all that time marching through the barren Portuguese countryside and for the most part it was a pretty miserable existence. People imagine that when a British army is on the march it is all neat rows of men in red marching in time, with camp followers coming on behind, if at all. Well, it might be if Wellington or some other general is expected, but when the company is marching alone things are rather different.

The next afternoon I scanned my new command, from the dozen men who were marching at our head to the fecund Private Carter bringing up the rear with his wife, babe in arms and two small children. The column must have stretched out a quarter of a mile and that was just our company. Several were limping as there was a serious need for boot repairs; Benton's latest mission was not just to get him out of the way.

My boots were fine, but then I had not been walking. Lieutenant Hervey and I were mounted on decent horses, while a scrawny mule pulled a cart in the middle of the throng loaded with regimental supplies and a handful of tired children. Riding might sound better than walking, but there were disadvantages; especially when it was biting cold and your muscles had got out of the habit of spending a long time in the saddle. After just six days of living out in the open, I was feeling every sympathy for the French. How they could have survived a winter in this freezing wilderness was beyond me. I had lost feeling in most of my body, either through cold or the hard leather of the saddle. The sensation from my nether regions left me wondering if I would ever be able to perform in the bedroom again. I shifted myself in the saddle and felt a searing burst of pins and needles through my bollocks, while my manhood felt completely numb. With Benton back I knew I would have to forgo the arousing massage that Lucy had given me the night before.

The sergeant, noticing my discomfort, called out, "The men could do with stopping for a rest soon, sir. That stone church in the next village could provide some hospitalisation."

I grimaced in pain as I replied, "I think you mean hospitality, but I doubt there will be any of that as we have not seen a living soul since we set out." Every village we had passed so far had been torn down and burnt by the retreating British last autumn to deny shelter to the French. This was the first one we had seen with buildings still standing.

"We should continue until the major calls the regiment to a halt," Lieutenant Hervey said down his nose at the sergeant. "He will want all of the companies to camp together."

"Damn your uncle," I gasped as the pins and needles got worse. "We will stop when we get to that church. It is getting late and I am not walking past stone walls and a roof to camp in the open when it is this cold."

I glanced around me. The army was not marching in a column but spread out across the country. The French had retreated on a broad front, and while scouts monitored their withdrawal, the British army was advancing on an equally broad front. If the French had abandoned cannon and other equipment, Wellington wanted the British to have it. Two more companies of the Buffs were in view on either side of us, but I thought we should be the first to that church.

"Now hold this wretched horse," I called to the sergeant. "I need to get down and walk for a bit."

He held the bridle and for a moment I thought my legs were so stiff that they would not allow me to dismount. But with a grunt of effort I managed to swing my right foot over the horse's rump and drop to stand, slightly bow-legged, on the ground.

"Do you want me to ride your horse up to the church, sir?"

Ensign Price-Thomas was the third officer of the company. Despite being a lad of only fifteen, he had more experience of the regiment than his captain and his lieutenant put together. He had been orphaned as a young boy and raised by his aunt who was married to one of the regimental surgeons. I had planned to let the mare have a rest going up the hill, but the ensign weighed next to nothing and so I nodded my assent.

"Yes, ride up there and make sure our men claim that church before any of those other companies."

7

Not being able to afford a horse of his own, Price-Thomas always took the opportunity to ride someone else's. He was up in the saddle in a flash and was soon galloping the horse up the slope.

"You might have been able to do what you wanted when you were a staff officer, but now you are with the regiment there is a chain of command." Lieutenant Hervey looked down at me from his saddle. "The major will want to know why this company is not with the rest of the regiment when it bivouacs tonight."

"And I am sure you will tell him," I retorted.

For all his talk of chain of command, Hervey did not hesitate to pull family strings with his uncle, the major, when it suited him. Lieutenant Hervey had been acting as company captain over the winter, when he had commanded it almost entirely from the officers' mess. He resented having me dropped in as the new captain above him; but he did not resent it half as much as I did.

I had been sitting comfortably on Wellington's staff, basking in my largely unearned credit. As far as my brother officers knew I had saved the army from ambush at Talavera and then brought detailed intelligence of the French army, all while disguised in enemy uniform. While my work had met general acclaim, a fastidious bastard called Grant had poured scorn on my achievements. He had claimed that to use a disguise was dishonourable. Now that same bumptious little swine had usurped my place in Wellington's favour. He had taken my place on the staff and as a result I was posted to be a line officer in the Buffs.

"The major says that this is the most poorly turned out company in the regiment," continued Hervey. "If Loquacious spent more time inspecting and less time reading, things would be a lot better. The man is an embarrassment. He has no idea what he is saying half of the time."

He was referring to the sergeant who was notorious for trying to improve his vocabulary, not always successfully. Whoever had taught him to read had given him a dictionary, which the man studied with the same enthusiasm that a cleric might use on the Bible. His real name was Sergeant Evans, but when Hervey introduced him the lieutenant gave me a wink and said, "We call him Loquacious after the great Roman emperor." If there had been a Roman emperor of that name I had been asleep in class when they had taught it; but I did know that the word meant verbose and wordy. Judging from the stony, blank look on the sergeant's face as his lieutenant grinned at him, I guessed that the sergeant had also looked up the word himself. I had learnt in India, when I was first reluctantly recruited into the army, what happens when you annoy a good sergeant and I was not making that mistake again.

"He keeps the bayonets sharp and runs a good musket drill," I told Hervey as we walked alone. "The men respect him and that is what counts."

"Well, I think the man is a fool." With that Hervey viciously stabbed his spurs into his tired horse and galloped up the hill towards the church.

I was glad to be left alone with my thoughts. I gave a grunt as I stretched my back to loosen stiff muscles while Boney trotted up alongside and nuzzled my hand. Pulling up my greatcoat collar against the biting cold wind, I reflected on how my circumstances had changed over recent weeks. While my cheeks froze, my innards burned with anger against the man whose success had relegated me to regimental duties.

The worst of it was that I had encouraged Grant to go on the mission that had brought him renown throughout the army. Hell, I had even wagered fifty guineas to tempt him. It was a ridiculous plan and I had been sure that he would end up with a French musket ball between his shoulder blades or captured. Either way he would have been out of my hair.

As the French had started to starve in their encampments, Grant had been whining about the lack of fresh meat and being forced to eat salt beef brought in by the navy. "There are plenty of cattle in the hills to the north of the French positions, guarded by the partisans," I told him. "You can always ride through the French army and up into the hills, to bring some back down past the French again. If you think you can do all that, I would pay to see it."

We had all laughed at his expense that night. No one thought it could be done – well, almost no one. Imagine my surprise next morning when we heard that Grant had seen Wellington to propose the scheme; and that this normally sensible man had offered him a bag of gold to pay for the cattle if he got through.

He left late the following afternoon, wearing his British uniform and on fast horse, hoping to get through the French lines in the dark. Having attempted the same feat less than six months previously, I knew this was no easy thing even in a French uniform. Surely, I thought, the French would not let a British officer ride clean through their lines twice, especially when on the way back he would be bringing livestock past the now hungry men in blue. Several of us rode to see him off and, in my case, make sure he did not back out on the wager. He really did not have a clue what he was doing; he had not even brought a proper map, just some notes on a scrap of paper. I could not help but chuckle at the thought of him riding through the middle of a French encampment as the sun rose the next day.

I wasn't laughing three weeks later when we received reports, sent down the semaphore signalling stations from the forward sentries, that a herd of cattle was approaching. I could not believe it. My friend Campbell and I joined some of the other staff to ride out and see for ourselves. There coming through the first line of fortifications we found an exceedingly smug Captain Colquhoun Grant, with a watchful partisan riding by his side. Behind them were sixty head of cattle with a couple of drovers moving them along. Beyond those a long mule train could be seen lumbering up the slope under a burden of grain sacks, and behind those the start of a flock of sheep, again with more mounted drovers. It was an astonishing sight, especially given that all of it must have been driven through the hungry French army.

As the other officers rode forward to congratulate Grant, Campbell turned to me. "There is something not quite canny about this."

"Not canny!" I exploded. "This smells fishier than Billingsgate fish market. For Christ's sake, the cattle are still wearing their bells. My aged, deaf Aunt Agatha could have heard them coming, so why couldn't the French?" I wasn't exaggerating either: while a few of the bells were made of thin metal, the rest were of the wooden clacker variety, but they still made a lot of noise as the herd moved towards us.

"Congratulations," shouted Wellington to Grant as he rode up. "I must confess I had some doubts as to whether you could pull this off."

Grant glanced triumphantly at me before he replied: "Captain Flashman is not the only one who can pass through French lines." Then he turned directly to me before adding, "And you will see that I have done it honourably in my British uniform."

Several of the spectators shifted uncomfortably at the implication that I lacked honour. Of course it was true: I would do whatever it took to protect my precious skin. I also tried to protect my reputation, but it would not have been seemly to call him out for a duel at his moment of triumph. More importantly, I already had discovered that he shot straight.

"Perhaps the French sentries were too busy killing stray cattle to shoot at you," I suggested with a very fixed smile.

"Ah no," insisted Grant blithely. "We did not lose a single head, did we, Leon?"

"No, *señor*," agreed the partisan as his eyes darted around the assembled company.

"How much did you pay? Are there more cattle to be had?" asked Wellington, looking at the unexpected bounty.

"I still have gold left, sir," replied Grant, holding up a purse with some coins jingling in the bottom of it. "And I saw other cattle."

"That is good news indeed," called Wellington. "But how much a head did you pay?" Wellington, whose mind rarely strayed far from how to equip and feed his army, was already considering a new source of supply. But Grant just looked confused for a moment and then turned enquiringly to the partisan.

"We paid two guineas a head, Excellency," the partisan stated calmly. "But the villagers have sold all of their surplus cattle and the French might not let us through as easily a second time."

Wellington beamed at him. "Well we must be satisfied with what we have, for it looks an exceptional haul." Then he turned to Grant. "Come and show me your bounty and tell me about your adventures." With that Grant rode off with the general, basking in his newfound credit.

"He never struck me as smart enough to pull off something like this," muttered Campbell. "I mean, getting through French lines, persuading all those farmers to sell grain and livestock, organising the herds and then getting it all back under the noses of the French. How the devil has he done it?"

"Of course he is not smart enough," I fumed. "Look at him riding now with Wellington – even if you included their horses, he would still not make the top three for wits. And now I am going to have to pay the whining toady fifty guineas."

As I seethed I watched the partisan called Leon helping to drive the cattle up the road towards Lisbon. He was constantly looking about him and seemed the one in charge, sending one of the cattle drovers back down the column to help with the sheep. That is the real brains behind this outfit, I thought and I resolved to find out how Grant had pulled this off.

That night there were celebrations for Grant's achievement in the officers' mess. No civilians were invited and I had no intention of attending. Instead I roamed the local taverns until I found my quarry. Leon was sitting at a corner table of an inn with a couple of the drovers. I took a bottle of brandy to their table and, uninvited, sat down to join them.

"It is Leon, isn't it? You're the man who came in with Grant, aren't you? Here, let me pour you a drink." While I could speak fluent Spanish, having been taught by my Spanish mother, I spoke to Leon in English, deliberately trying to exclude the drovers as I wanted to get Leon on his own. It worked: the other two men looked apprehensive as the British officer joined their table, speaking in a language they did not understand; they mumbled their excuses and left. Leon watched me with an amused half smile as I poured a very generous measure of brandy into his cup.

"I think you know I am Leon. You are the British officer who was watching me very closely when we arrived. Did my captain not call you Flashman?"

Well, that confirmed my suspicion that Leon was as sharp as a tack. We made small talk for a while. I told him that my cousin was the Marquesa de Astorga and that I had ridden with the partisans the previous autumn to take her back to her husband. I decided not to include in this account that the venomous marquis then tried to have me killed. I told him the creditable parts of my action at both the battle of Talavera and Busaco and how with a few hundred men of the Loyal Lusitanian Legion we had stopped a French marshal with over ten thousand soldiers. In return he told me… nothing. He slipped away from my questions like a greased eel and every time I found myself answering more of his. I kept topping up his glass and ordered a second bottle. But either he was tipping it away when I was not looking or he had the constitution of an ox. The brandy seemed to have no effect at all. Eventually my booze-soaked brain realised that I would have to try a different tack.

"Lishun, old sport," I slurred at him. "I have been ordered by General Wellington to find out how you got all those animals past the French lines. I have orders in my pocket that say you have to tell me." I reached in my pocket and brought out the paper I knew was in there. It was in fact a laundry account from the officers' mess, but it did have the regimental crest printed at the top and looked official.

At first Leon just smiled at me. "I think," he said at last, "that if your general wanted to know this thing, he would just ask my captain." Then he picked up the document I had placed on the table and grinned.

"I was taught English by an Irish monk in a monastery school. I cannot read all of this, but does that not say 'six shirts'?" He passed the account back before continuing. "My captain warned me about you, Captain Flashman. He thinks you will try to find a way to get out of your wager and he ordered me to tell you nothing. But I have asked other people about you too. They say you are a brave man and that you were the Englishman who charged the French battery at Talavera with General Cuesta, something you did not tell me earlier."

I had not mentioned it as I had been screaming in terror at the time, but if the story he had heard was more creditable then I was happy to stay silent while he continued.

"I will tell you some of what you want to know. At night the French retreat to their camps surrounded by circles of watch fires. They hope that these will illuminate any partisans trying to attack. We know the French are hungry and some of my brothers have used cattle bells and sometimes real sheep and bullocks to tempt the French from their circles at night. At first the hungry soldiers would go to investigate but they never returned. The French always found them dead and mutilated the next morning. When we drove the herds through a big gap between their fire circles, the French must have heard, but none came to intercept us. They have learned now never to leave the circles at night. They will have thought it was a trick until they found the large number of hoof prints this morning."

I could easily picture the scene and the frustration that the French must have experienced as the sun rose. With their bellies groaning in hunger, they would have seen how close they had been to plentiful food. They would have felt even worse knowing that the supplies were now in the hands of the British. The French knew we were already well fed and comfortable behind stone forts, while they struggled to survive on land that Wellington had largely stripped of anything that could sustain them.

Leon and I talked some more after that, but I would be a liar if I claimed I had a clear recollection of what he said. Despite my attempts to get him intoxicated, Leon seemed unaffected, while to me the room seemed as steady as a ship going around Cape Horn in a blow.

I paid up my wager to Grant and for the rest of the time we spent behind the lines of Torres Vedras he toadied up to Wellington in a way that would sicken an arse-licking tick. As a result he became Wellington's favourite forward observer. Time and again Grant and Leon went out on reconnaissance rides to see what the French were doing, and most times they came back with useful intelligence. While Grant made sure he got all the credit, I suspected that most of the conclusions drawn from what they had seen were collated by Leon. When the French finally withdrew, you can be sure that Grant was on hand to report on their progress. In contrast I was summoned by Wellington for very different duties.

"Ah, Flashman," he greeted me as I stepped into his rooms. "I take it you have heard of the latest Spanish disaster?"

"If you mean Gebora sir," I replied, "then yes, I have."

The Spanish army had developed a knack of engineering catastrophic defeats from situations that, on paper at least, they should have won. At Gebora they had really excelled themselves. One of the few towns they still held in Spain was the frontier fortress of Badajoz. Marshal Soult had brought his French army to besiege the city. Despite having double the French force, the Spanish army commander sent to lift the siege had withdrawn his men across the large Guadiana River that ran next to Badajoz. The Spanish then occupied some nearby heights, thinking they would be safe. Soult had simply built a pontoon bridge, which was reported to the Spanish commander on the evening before the battle by his scouts. "I will look at it in the morning," he was reported to have replied, but he did not get the chance. The small French force crossed the river that night while the unsuspecting twelve thousand Spanish troops slept, oblivious of the approaching danger. In the morning the French attacked, whereupon the Spanish cavalry promptly ran away. This left the Spanish infantry exposed to the French dragoons and hussars. The Spaniards managed to form two massive squares to protect themselves from the horsemen, but in doing so they made perfect targets for the French artillery. One of the survivors reported that French gun fire had turned his square first into an oval and then an unformed mass, which was forced to surrender. Spanish losses were thought to be five thousand men against an estimated four hundred casualties amongst the French.

"Yes, that is their latest disaster," replied Wellington and then, just in case he was tempting fate, he added, "Well, at least as far as I am aware. Sit down, Flashman," he continued as he settled himself onto a settee by the fire. "Look, you will recall that I asked you to join my staff as liaison officer for the Spanish. You did great service while the independent government existed, but now things have moved on. This latest fiasco shows that little reliance can be placed on Spanish troops and so I really do not need you for liaison." I had a sinking feeling that

14

I knew the direction this conversation was heading and I was not wrong. "I know you, Flashman. You will not want to kick your heels around here with nothing to do. So I have spoken to Colborne and he would be delighted to have you in his division. He has a captaincy vacant in the Buffs, which is now yours. They are part of the new force I am sending under Beresford to relieve Badajoz." He reached across and patted me on the shoulder. "I am sure the Buffs will be at the forefront of any action to secure the area, and I know that is where you would want to be."

Chapter 2

As I walked up the hill towards the little stone church, I saw that the rest of my company had not gone inside it as I had expected. Instead they were gathered around the stone wall of the churchyard, staring at something inside.

"What is it, Sergeant?" I called.

"You had better see for yourself, sir," the man shouted back.

A couple of the soldiers were crossing themselves and there was a look of shock, disgust or naked curiosity on the faces of the others. When I finally got to the wall, I saw a scene of macabre devastation. All of the graves had been dug up; there were mounds of earth and deep holes all around the enclosure. Scattered amongst them were splinters of wood, presumably from where the coffins had been chopped up for firewood, and in the corner was a mound of old bones, some with bits of burial shroud still attached.

While young Price-Thomas watched in silent fascination, his lieutenant was more vocal in his outrage. "Why on earth would they do such a thing?" asked Hervey, looking appalled. "There are much easier ways to get fire wood; there are plenty of trees still around here."

"They were searching for gold, sir," answered the sergeant. "I saw the same in Oporto. The Spanish and Portuguese often bury people wearing gold rings and jewellery, and the French dig up the bodies to steal it."

"The desecrating barbarians," exclaimed Hervey.

But it turned out that this was only the start of the savagery we were to witness in that small village. I guessed that it must have been home to around a hundred people before the French arrived, but there was no one left now, at least not alive. Every house had been torn apart by the French in the search for food. Then they must have turned their attention to the few inhabitants they had found, to reveal any hidden supplies. We found the bodies of three of the villagers hanged from a tree near the church. Two now blackened corpses still dangled from the ropes while the third had rotted so that its remains rested in a heap below a now vacant hoop of cord. They, it turned out, might have been the lucky ones.

In the centre of the village we found two more blackened corpses, one small enough to be a child's. These had not been hanged in the conventional sense but suspended from a high beam by ropes tied

16

around their wrists. Underneath both fires had been lit and the heat had caused the muscles to contract so that the bodies were twisted into grotesque shapes. It was hard to tell from their blackened remains if they had been male or female but it was clear that they had died slowly and in agony. There were murmurs of outrage as the men gathered around the scene, interrupted only by the spatter of vomit as Lieutenant Hervey leaned over the far side of his horse.

"How could Christian men do that?" asked a pale-faced private.

"They were searching for food," I replied. "Most villages around here would have hidden food for their own survival, expecting the French to search the houses. The soldiers must have thought that burning these poor souls would persuade either them or other villagers to reveal the cache." I paused, staring at the awful scene, before adding, "Of course they might not have been the first French troops to raid the village. Other French soldiers could have already taken any cache, meaning that there was nothing left to give."

There was silence for a while as those watching imagined the horror of that inquisition. I had seen that the company was naturally divided into two groups. There were what I judged to be the old hands; they gazed at the scene with nothing more than curiosity. These men had seen such atrocities before, either at Oporto or elsewhere. If they had been on the retreat to Corunna, they may have even carried out some of their own. The other, newer men were reinforcements; they had arrived over the winter while the regiment was in Lisbon. Not accepted into the group of veterans, they tended to look to Sergeant Evans for leadership. These men looked on the scene with horror on their faces, clearly wondering what kind of men they would be fighting.

I felt pretty disgusted about it myself, particularly over what seemed to be a child's body. I had been left hungry and thirsty before, especially when on the run in India, but never bad enough to do anything like that. Mind you, since then I have been left adrift with others in a lifeboat at sea. Extreme starvation and dehydration is a terrible thing. I had hallucinations and came close to cannibalism before I was rescued.

Hervey interrupted any further reflection on the scene by shouting, "I want them buried, and those poor devils hanging from the tree." He turned to the sergeant. "Bury them at once, d'ye hear?"

"The ground is frozen hard, sir, and we have no spades."

"I don't care. I want them buried!" Hervey was nearly shrieking now, his face filled with revulsion at the bodies slowly swinging in the

17

wind. The sergeant turned an enquiring face to me, to see if I was willing to countermand the order.

"Cut them down and put them in the open graves in the churchyard," I told him. "Tip the other bones in as well and then cover them with those piles of dirt. You won't need to dig then."

I left them to it while I went into the little church. It was stripped bare inside, with a black scorch mark in the middle of the floor where previous occupants had burnt a fire to keep warm. There were stone steps in the short tower which served as a lookout and a chimney for the smoke. I went up the turret before the redcoats started to build their own fire. The countryside looked as bleak up there as it did at ground level. I wondered how many more devastated villages like this there were spread across it. Two more companies of the battalion could be seen making their way past on either side of the village some distance away. They would have a long march to find another stone building like the church, as I could see no more from my high vantage point. I hoped wherever Grant was that night he was camping out in the freezing wind, but I doubted it. I still resented my change in circumstances, but at least with the French withdrawing as fast as they could, there seemed little chance of imminent battle.

I turned and went back down the stairs into the body of the church. As I had hoped, some men were already starting a fire in the hearth left by the French. The space was filling with the men, women and children of the company. We had brought our own cooking kettle and rations and it seemed that dinner would soon be on the way. An infantry company at its full complement was a hundred men but that was rarely achieved. There had been around eighty men in the companies at Talavera two years ago but now the average size of a company in the Buffs was just over seventy men. While Evans kept them organised they seemed a sullen lot, with little of the banter that I had known in other units. Mind you, Hervey did not help with his high-handed way of dealing with the men.

They had managed completely without officers for a while during the retreat to the lines and perhaps wondered why they needed Hervey and me at all. The major had hinted that some of the 'casualties' on the retreat might actually have been desertions. Back then morale in the army had been low, and while running to the French would not have been appealing, there was another option.

A cook had deserted the French army, taking around a hundred of the roughest and most rebellious men with him. They had gone up into the hills and taken over an old convent. Well out of the route of either army, they had raided the surrounding countryside, capturing food and women, and settled down to live the high life while the war went on without them. Word of their existence had spread and deserters from both the British and Portuguese slipped away to join them. Soon the French cook, known as Marshal Stockpot, had several hundred men of various nationalities under his command, who dominated the land for miles around their lair.

I wondered if the deserters from my company had ended up with the 'marshal'. If so, they had a grim ending. The French commander Marshal Massena had left them alone to operate behind his lines until they challenged one of his own foraging parties, which, outnumbered and under fire from Stockpot's men, was forced to retreat. Massena then sent a force to destroy the deserters. Stockpot's French soldiers were given a choice: they could either serve in the front ranks in an attack against their former comrades, in which case they would be pardoned, or they would be shot when captured. For the British and Portuguese there was no choice. When the convent was overrun by the French, those wearing red coats or the green and blue of the Portuguese were made prisoner and marched back to the British lines, where they were handed over. Wellington had hanged them all as an example.

If a number of their comrades had been executed then you could understand the resentment of some of the men. Certainly the major sensed the air of rebellion amongst this company, which was why I think he did not make his nephew the captain. He told me that he wanted an experienced man in charge, but he had been deluded by my unwarranted repute. The last company I had commanded had been back in India years ago and I had swiftly learnt that it was best to leave everything to the very capable Sergeant Fergusson. Still, they seemed content to be away from the rest of the regiment now. There were even some smiles as they huddled round the now blazing fire in the centre of the church to get warm. Soon there was a smell of cooking and the chill in my bones started to recede.

Hervey, Price-Thomas and I had taken a corner of the church as our nominal officers' quarters and were making ourselves as comfortable as we could.

"Still want to be camping on a frozen field, Lieutenant?" I asked as I laid out my blanket.

Hervey grunted a non-committal reply and then the door opened and slammed shut to a chorus of groans at the blast of cold air. It was the last of the burial party coming inside for the night.

"Sergeant, are all the bodies and bones buried?" I called.

"Yes, sir, all tidied away."

"You are sure about that, are you?" I asked, noticing some movement amongst the men.

The sergeant followed my gaze and grinned. Boney was weaving his way towards me through the men. He had muddy front paws from where he had been digging and what looked suspiciously like a human thigh bone in his mouth.

"Oh my God!" exclaimed Hervey. "He has got someone's leg. Someone should take that off him."

"I wouldn't recommend it," I replied as Boney settled against the wall of the chapel to gnaw on his prize. "He gets particularly cross if people try to steal his dinner."

"Well, I am not putting up with it," stated Hervey, and he got up and strode purposefully towards the hound.

He has more courage than I imagined, I thought, as I watched him approach the dog. Of course Boney was watching as well and when Hervey was halfway towards him the dog dropped the bone and went down on his haunches, ready to spring. His top lip curled up and he gave a bloodcurdling growl. Hervey stopped in his tracks. After a moment's hesitation he turned, to several jeers from those who had seen the encounter. Despite the cold, Hervey was colouring in embarrassment as he came back.

"I don't know why you would have such a dog," he grumbled.

"Ignore them," I said of the jeering soldiers. "None of them would take the bone off him either. He was a gift from Lord Byron, the poet, and I keep him because once he saved my life."

"How did he do that?" asked Price-Thomas.

"I would have been skewered on the point of a Polish lancer if it had not been for that dog," I told him. "Several stone of angry wolfhound jumping up onto his saddle is inclined to put a lancer off his aim. In fact he has been damn useful to have around on a number of occasions."

Hervey looked dubiously at the dog and then winced as he heard the crunch of the bone between the animal's powerful jaws.

"How did you come to join the regiment?" I asked him. Hervey seemed far too sensitive to be an army officer.

"My uncle gave me a vacant lieutenancy as a favour to my father late last year. The major told me to learn from you, but I am sure he would not approve of us bivouacking away from the battalion."

"Well, we will be more effective tomorrow after a good night's sleep in the warm than if we had spent it half frozen in the open."

Food was served and I tried not to look across too often at where Lucy was settling down for the night with the recently returned Corporal Benton. Despite the lack of female companionship, I am bound to say it was a comfortable night. The warmth from the roaring fire made up for the hard stone floor. There was little privacy in an infantry company and I noticed the odd rhythmic movement and groan from some couples under their blankets. But the children did not cry much; they were exhausted from the day's march. For most of the night there was just a rumble of assorted snores, the occasional quiet bleat of a goat and, every now and then, the crunch of teeth on bone.

The chapel got warm and stuffy so that next morning, when we threw open the doors, the cold air struck us like a physical blow. As we set off again the newer recruits were still indignant over the behaviour of the French towards the villagers; but that was to change during the course of the day. We were following the line of the enemy withdrawal and we saw the first French body later that morning. He must have just dropped from exhaustion on the march and fallen onto the road. His comrades could not have had the strength to get him off the track for he was half buried in the frozen mud. Ruts in his back showed that at least three wheels passed over him, pushing him further into the ooze. We found some of the wheels at midday. They were attached to an eighteen-pounder cannon that had been simply abandoned. They had not even bothered to spike the touch hole.

"We will need to report this to headquarters so that some of our gunners can collect it," I said to Evans as we examined the gun.

Evans looked around to check we could not be overheard before replying. "I would rather not send Corporal Benton this time, sir." He looked me in the eye. "Some of the women are wondering where Mrs Benton disappears to at night when her husband is not on the march. It could get ugly, sir – not for you, but for Sally." He looked up at the sun before adding, "In any event, if I send Benton now he will probably be back before nightfall."

I cursed inwardly, knowing he was right. Heaven knows I am not one to always observe social conventions; why, I have even fornicated in a cathedral during a mass. But I realised that I would have to be a little more subtle going forward. We sent Price-Thomas instead.

Around the gun there were more bones and scraps of hide to indicate that the draft animals hauling the gun had been butchered for food before the men advanced further. Perhaps some locals had found the carcasses after the French had moved, for there was barely a morsel of the creatures left.

Certainly some of the local population were still around; this was proved when we came across more French bodies later that afternoon. There were five of them, all stripped naked, but two buttons found in the dirt were from French uniforms. Their bodies were pitiably thin and they seemed to have dropped out of the march through fatigue. Four had been bludgeoned and mutilated. One of them appeared to have had a cannon ball dropped on his head. Whether this had been done while they were alive it was impossible to tell. But the locals had got creative with the fifth Frenchman, who I guessed had been found alive. They had staked him out spread-eagled on the ground and then built a fire over his genitals.

"Good grief," exclaimed Hervey when he saw the body. "Both sides in this war behave like savage animals."

"It is not so bad between us and the French," I told him. "We each treat prisoners of the other with respect. But between the French and the partisans, as you can see, no quarter is asked for or given."

I could see that he was hesitating about burying those bodies as well, but as we needed to catch up with the rest of the battalion, I forestalled that by ordering the company to advance.

We found the other companies camped out in neat rows that evening and duly took the space allotted to us. As expected I was summoned to Major King to explain my absence the previous evening.

"It won't do, Captain," he berated me. "There is an order of march and it must be obeyed. You were seen by two other companies stopping by a stone church. If they had not reported you, we might have thought you were missing or attacked."

I had already discovered that Major King was a very rule-driven man, but I had thought of one excuse that might serve. "There had been a lot of atrocities in the village, sir – children burnt to death to reveal food hoards, that sort of thing."

"War is a brutal business, Flashman, you should know that by now."

"Indeed I do, sir." I paused before continuing in a more confidential tone. "But your nephew took it quite badly. In fact he insisted in front of the men that all of the bodies be given a Christian burial. I did not countermand the order as I did not want to undermine his authority. But once we were finished it was too late to go on and so we camped in the church." The best excuses are those with a basis of truth and this one I thought would serve perfectly. Hervey would probably unwittingly confirm it if asked about the atrocities.

"Ah, I see," replied the major thoughtfully. "In that case let's say no more about it. Young Richard will need to get used to the realities of war. My sister always was a bit highly strung. Still, he will settle down. Speaking of the realities of war, have you heard the latest news?!"

"What is that, sir?" I asked, noting from the grim look on his face that it was unlikely to be good.

"The damn Spanish have surrendered Badajoz to the French, so instead of relieving the siege we are now recapturing the place. I take it you have been there?"

"Yes, I stayed there with the rest of the army for a while during the retreat after Talavera." I remembered it as a forbidding fortress with the river down one side and thick, tall walls around the rest. When I had been there it had a big garrison of nearly ten thousand men and the best part of two hundred cannon around the walls. "But I understood that they had enough food, sir, and they knew we were coming. Why on earth did they just hand over the town?"

"It seems the old commander was killed and the new one was bluffed by the French into surrendering. Soult certainly did not have enough men to capture the place by force. So now we must besiege the French garrison while holding Soult's army off as he will be bound to disrupt our operations."

The optimism of just a few days ago that we would be pushing back a French army weakened by hunger and disease was fast diminishing. Unlike Massena's forces, Marshal Soult's men had not starved over the winter. Soult had also proved he was a cunning and capable commander. That got me thinking of our own general and I realised that this would be my first army action without Wellington, or Wellesley as he was when I first knew him, in command.

"What is General Beresford like?" I asked.

"Well, he did a good job of organising the Portuguese army," claimed King. "You will soon get a chance to see him as he is gathering his forces. There will be British, Portuguese and some Spanish troops. All told we should have around thirty-five thousand men. Against us the most that Soult is likely to be able to gather is around twenty thousand, so Beresford can afford the odd mistake." As it turned out these were prophetic words indeed, but at the time they gave me some comfort.

The army did gather over the coming days. First our battalion joined another three, to make a brigade of around three thousand men. This was commanded by Brigadier Colborne. For a few days we marched together in a long column. It was still freezing cold but I gradually got used to being in the saddle again. Rarely could we find an intact building to sleep in, and while there were a few tents it was often warmer to sleep outside by a fire where there was at least some warmth. Sometimes rocks would be heated in the fire while dinners were cooked and then, using bayonets, these hot rocks were rolled onto blankets to give extra warmth during the night.

After a few days marching we crested a rise and found some of the other British, Spanish and Portuguese brigades camped before us, under a smog of campfire smoke. Given the smudge in the sky from the fires could be seen for miles, it was surprising that the very next day a much smaller French force of two and half thousand blundered into us. As we outnumbered the enemy by more than ten to one, you might think it would be a simple affair to roll up and capture the hapless French column. If you think that then you clearly have not fought under the command of General William Carr Beresford.

That day was a damn frustrating experience. Previously, as a staff officer, I had been with Wellington and had heard reports from scouts and seen decisions being made. I had known what was happening and why orders had been given. This time I was just a poor bloody infantry officer halfway down the column and nobody had any idea what was happening.

After hearing distant trumpets to indicate that some action was underway, we were ordered to march two miles and prepare for battle. Then we did absolutely nothing. First one hour passed and then two. We heard the odd crash of a cannon but nothing like the sound of a full battle. While other officers fumed at the delay, I was privately delighted. I had no wish to go anywhere near a battle if I could help it. Previously I had some freedom to roam around the battlefield, doing my best to avoid the action. Now I was obliged to lead my men into battle, which gave me much less scope for honourable evasion.

As I had a good glass, King ordered me to ride to the top of a nearby ridge and report on what I could see. I got there just in time to see the small French force pulling back completely unmolested. Meanwhile other British units could be observed scattered around the countryside, also doing nothing. I could make no sense of it.

Then I saw a group of staff officers coming along the ridge, led by an extraordinary character. Judging by the amount of gold braid it had to be Beresford and he was a giant of a man: a full six inches taller than any other officer and broad too, with a chest like an ox. The high collar that he wore combined with his huge chest gave the impression that his head was far too small for the rest of his body. When his little pin head turned in my direction, he glared angrily at me as though I had no right to be on the ridge and I saw that he only had one eye that moved, the other was of glass. I saluted smartly and moved to one side as his large horse thundered past.

As the rest of his staff followed at a respectful distance I saw one that I knew from my early days in the Peninsular.

"Ben," I called to him once Beresford was out of earshot. "What on earth is going on? We have been waiting around here for ages and now the French are pulling back without anyone bothering them at all."

"Hello, Flash," cried Ben D'Urban. He reined in his horse and waited until his companions had ridden on so that we were alone. "Between you and me," he confided, "the general has dithered his way to a defeat. Our cavalry cut off the French escape and captured their guns, but then Beresford worried that there might be another French force coming to their rescue and ordered our men back. Now it seems that there was no second French force and we have let this one escape and recapture their lost guns too."

"He is not very decisive then?" I probed.

"Oh, he is a good administrator, but he does not have much battle experience. His last independent command was the aborted attempt to capture Buenos Aires in Argentina. But Wellington obviously has some confidence in him." D'Urban laughed and leaned forward confidentially. "Although he has given the good general long lists of instructions on how he should conduct the campaign, even including where he should make a stand if Soult attacks."

"Where is that then?"

"A place called Albuera; it is on the road from Seville to Badajoz. Soult would have to come past it to try to lift our siege and it has a ridge from which the army can fight; a good defensive position."

25

It was the first time I had heard the name, which even now, more than thirty years later, brings back memories I would prefer to forget. But at the time it meant nothing and I could easily imagine the battle on a defensive ridge. All of the battles I had seen with Wellington in the Peninsular had involved him hiding his men behind ridges and lines of redcoats beating French columns to deliver victory. Naively I thought I knew what to expect. For the first time we had the advantage of numbers and surely, I thought, we would win the coming action. But I had tragically underestimated Beresford's ability to bring chaos out of order and this time everything would be different.

Chapter 3

If I had harboured doubts over Beresford's abilities from our first encounter with the French they were not allayed over the coming weeks. We crossed the river Guadiana using a flimsy pontoon bridge at the beginning of April. I felt uneasy being on the French side of the river, but we did not see a single Frenchman for over a month. That was just as well as the siege operations were descending into farce.

Daily forced marches were ordered, which often outran supplies, and the hilly stony roads destroyed the soldiers' boots, which had not been in the best state despite Corporal Benton's efforts. It did not help that destinations were often changed at the last minute, as though we were hurrying to no good purpose. While I was fine on my well-shod horse, every evening a long line of stragglers who had fallen out of the day's march hobbled into the camp with blistered and bloody feet. They then had little time to eat, repair boots and sleep before the next day's march.

After days of marching and counter-marching we finally arrived where I had suspected we would end up all along: Albuera. We reached it in mid-April and after all the rushing about we then sat there doing nothing for a month.

Albuera was a miserable place. It had 150 houses and a rather grand old church. But the French had been there before us and it was all now in ruins with barely a roof on any of the buildings. The population of several hundred had been reduced to just an old man and a cat when we arrived. It was down to just an old man five minutes later, when Boney spotted the cat.

We settled in as best we could, stretching what tent canvas we had over the roofs of buildings to make them weather proof and gathering plenty of wood to put fires back in the hearths. The stragglers caught up and those with blistered and cut feet had plenty of time to wonder what the rush had been about. While other captains allowed their men to sit about and do little, I decided to put my men through their paces. Every other afternoon Lieutenant Hervey and Sergeant Evans would take them up on the ridge for musketry drill and bayonet practice for hours. At the same time the women and children would be despatched in groups off to the woods to find firewood and check various traps and snares set for fresh meat.

Oh, I was the proper diligent officer and I was even commended in front of the officers' mess by Major King. He might have been less

27

complimentary if he knew that I spent most of the time my men were exercising doing my favourite form of 'drilling' with Lucy Benton. But it was not just about getting the men and women out of the way so that Lucy and I could have a quiet afternoon together. I was all too aware that when a battle did come, my life would partly depend on how well my company fought. The veterans and recruits were paired together so that the new men learnt how to fight, and I venture that Hervey came to appreciate the skills of Sergeant Evans too. The company was coming together as an effective single unit, and if its captain was able to take advantage of the situation to do some 'bonding' of his own then so much the better.

While I was conducting my own military manoeuvres, things were happening elsewhere. Other British brigades had been detailed to start the entrenchments for the siege of Badajoz. This was back-breaking and dangerous work with the French lobbing out shells to disrupt the digging. Astonishingly only at this point did someone notice that the cannon we had brought with us were not suitable for bringing down the huge walls of the city. Artillerymen were sent off to Elvas, the nearest big British fortress on the other side of the Guadiana, to bring away their largest guns. But by the time they had got them back to the river the pontoon bridge had been partly swept away by the strong current. It took several days to repair and by then Wellington was coming over the bridge with the guns, frustrated at the delay and insisting that the assault on Badajoz start as soon as possible. He disappeared again back to his own army in the north a few days later. From what I learned later from Ben D'Urban, the result of his interference was more dithering from Beresford and feuds between the senior officers.

With suitable guns finally delivered, the bombardment of the city walls of Badajoz started on the eighth of May. It must have been one of the shortest sieges in military history, for they stopped again just four days later on the twelfth. Soult, doubtless monitoring our pitiful progress, decided that it was now time for him to react. He set off with his army from Seville. The poor gunners, who had only just started their work, were told to take the valuable siege guns all the way back over the river to Elvas. Our general was worried that they could be captured if we lost the coming battle. As you can tell from that decision, even Beresford did not have confidence in his own abilities!

I saw our illustrious commander again the day after we had heard that Soult was on the march. He had come to view his designated battlefield and spent the day riding around it, holding a sheaf of papers that seemed to be Wellington's instructions for fighting the battle. His large horse looked like a pony under his great frame, with his feet dangling well below its belly. A group of staff officers rode with him, pointing out various features on the landscape, while he searched for reference to them amongst his papers. At one point they rode near the edge of the village where I was standing and it was then that I saw that amongst the officers with him was Grant. The pompous stuffed shirt could not resist riding over to gloat at my misfortune, followed by the ever-present Leon.

"Morning, Flashman. I hope you are preparing for action, for the French are on their way."

He bristled with self-importance, but as the rest of the staff were still nearby I gritted my teeth and made an effort to be civil. "Yes, that rumour has spread even to us fighting men. Are you still rounding up stray cattle or have they found you something more useful to do?"

"We have just ridden from the outskirts of Seville and seen the French army for ourselves, haven't we, Leon?" He glanced over his shoulder at his guide before continuing. "They are now around eight days' march away with plenty of cavalry, so you might want to practise getting into a square."

"As we told the general," interrupted Leon smoothly, "Soult could be here in a lot less than eight days if he does long forced marches." Leon gave me a meaningful look as though to indicate that is what he expected the Frenchman to do. I just hoped that Beresford's one eye had detected that Leon was a shrewd judge of what to expect, but I doubted it. The man himself turned and barked at Grant to re-join him.

"Captain Grant, when you are quite ready I would be obliged if you would take down some notes to give to Wellington.

"Duty calls, old boy," called Grant with a self-satisfied smile as he rode away. God I hated that bastard.

That evening I was summoned to the old church where General Stewart, one of Beresford's subordinates, gave the more senior officers of his command a briefing on what he thought was happening.

"Gentlemen," he barked at us, "Soult is marching to relieve Badajoz and we stand astride the road he must take to reach the city."

"When will he get here?" someone asked.

"He left yesterday and he could be here as soon as three or four days' time." I was glad that someone had taken Leon's warning seriously. "He will want to come at us quickly to take us by surprise and because he knows that our force is scattered and will need some time to gather. We have two Spanish armies marching towards us to help and General Beresford is gathering other allied units that will rendezvous here. If all goes to plan, we should have a three-to-two advantage in numbers and a strong defensive position on the ridge. Soult will have to decide whether to attack us to go back to Seville, but I think we can be confident that he will not reach Badajoz."

It all sounded very positive and Stewart was a capable man. If Wellington had overall command, I would have shared Stewart's confidence, but I was fast losing faith in Beresford. According to mess gossip he seemed to spend most of his time arguing with his senior men and had now sacked his cavalry commander. He had accepted as a replacement Sir William Erskine, who was a former inhabitant of a lunatic asylum. Mercifully the French were expected to arrive before Erskine could take command.

Major King took the opportunity over the next few days to put the regiment through its paces and I supported him enthusiastically. My life would depend on how quickly they could load and fire, their organisation for rolling company volleys and their ferocity of charge. I was proud that the third company was one of the best in the battalion after the rigorous exercises I had organised for the men... and one of their wives.

I knew I would have to lead them into battle, but once the actual shooting started my position would be behind them and that was where I intended to stay. I was comforted that even the newer recruits seemed to know the drills and for good measure we formed square a few times in case enemy cavalry somehow got behind us.

"The men are shaping up portentously well, aren't they, sir?" opined Sergeant Evans at the end of the second day of battalion drilling.

"Prodigiously well," I agreed. "Are they confident about the coming battle, do you think?"

"Oh yes, sir, the prospect of loot always cheers up a soldier. Deductions take up most of their pay, but any man can get rich on a battlefield."

"He can also get killed or maimed on the battlefield," I reminded him.

"Dead or rich, sir, it is a break from the monotone of being a soldier."

We were walking back to the ruined village, which looked even more depressing in the long shadows of late afternoon. "The *monotony*," I stressed the correct word, "of a soldier's life must be better than that of those villagers. We are generally well fed and clothed, but everyone just takes what they want from them. Where do you think they are?"

"Some will be living in the forest, sir, avoiding anyone in a uniform of whatever colour. We have caught a glimpse of one or two when we have been gathering wood. They are not far away, and will come back when we have all gone."

Battle of Albuera

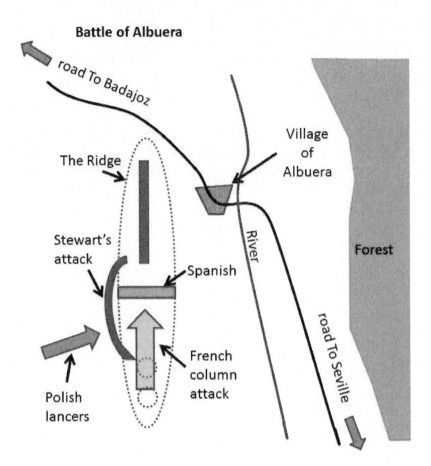

Chapter 4

The evening before the French arrived we moved our bivouac from the village over to the other side of the ridge. The road the French wanted to advance along went right through the little town. So the huddle of buildings was likely to be in the front line of the battle. Encampments were marked out in the fields beyond the hill, but this served to highlight that quite a few were still vacant. The Portuguese cavalry had not reported when it would arrive and no one knew where it was. The Spanish army under General Blake had been expected that afternoon but had not appeared. That was worrying, but of more concern were the absent British forces that were expected to form the backbone of any defence. General Kemmis's brigade was also missing, whereas the large part of the army besieging Badajoz was expected to make the sixteen-mile march from the city that night to arrive just in time for the action.

While some of the soldiers seemed excited at the prospect of a fight, my mood was matched by the low, dark clouds that seemed to be gathering over the battlefield. Nobody seemed clear on what was happening, how many of the French would arrive, where our missing troops were or even if we should fight at all. I discovered that for the last few days Beresford had been seriously debating with his officers abandoning Albuera and pulling back over the Guadiana, effectively leaving Badajoz to the French. All that evening the dithering Cyclops could be seen riding endlessly up and down the ridge that would form the spine of our position. He was still holding the now torn and dog-eared papers from Wellington and staring anxiously around with his one eye for his missing men. Hardly an inspiring sight.

It was a miserable night; not that I would have been able to relax much anyway, worrying what the dawn would bring. There was an intermittent, light rain that made everything cold and damp and we were continually disturbed by soldiers and units blundering about looking for where they should be camped. It was pointless even trying to sleep, and like most of the men I ended up crouched around one of the campfires, trying to keep warm.

"Have you been in many battles, sir?" asked Price-Thomas. He was sitting on a log next to me and tickling Boney behind the ears.

"A few," I replied. Then, mentally, I started to add them up. There had been a crazy shore action at Estepona with Cochrane; Assaye, Argaum and Gawilghur in India; and Alcantara, Talavera and Busaco in the Peninsular. Each had brought its own degree of terror, but this time I thought things might be different. Blake's Spanish force had arrived that night and so it should be the first battle in the Peninsular where we outnumbered the enemy. While our army might be confused and disorganised, the French would also be tired from five days of forced double marches. As I sat warming my hands by the fire I wondered how many of them were still strung out on the march coming towards us. If we could win on the ridge at Talavera when we were outnumbered, we could win on the ridge here, I thought.

Any sense of imminent danger escaped me and in fact I felt strangely complacent. We were in a strong position. I naively believed that not even that bumbling booby Beresford could mess things up, especially with all his written instructions. My men were well trained, fresh and prepared for battle, and as long as the British force from Badajoz arrived on time, it seemed victory was assured.

I put my hand on Price-Thomas's shoulder. "Don't worry if you are feeling frightened; everyone is before a battle. Just do your duty. I have a good feeling about this one; we will be all right."

"That's good, sir." The boy's teeth gleamed as he grinned in the darkness. "And I am not frightened, sir," he added unconvincingly.

Dawn was just before half past four in the morning and so from half past three the army was roused so that it could 'stand to' in case the enemy attempted to attack at first light. As no one was asleep anyway this just meant huddling in a different place behind the crest of the ridge. But we could not take the fires with us and so we just stood there, shivering with the cold. My company stood in the middle of the battalion's line but there was no point in trying to inspect the men. In the darkness I could barely see them. The long lines of soldiers talked quietly among themselves, with the occasional scrape of a sharpening stone as men honed their bayonets to an ever-finer edge.

As the sun crept over the horizon, bugles sounding 'reveille' could be heard from the far side of the valley. They were sounded in our camp as well to an ironic cheer from the men. As the grey light of dawn spread across the sky, not a sound could be heard from the east where the French should have been massing for their attack. I could see Major King and some other officers walking their horses along the crest of the ridge. I mounted mine and rode to join them.

"There were hundreds of French horsemen in the meadow between the river and the forest a few minutes ago," called out King as I approached. "But now they have all disappeared back amid the trees.

34

They must have been there in case we tried an attack across the river. But as they could see no one on the forward slope, they seem to have gone off for breakfast."

"That sounds an excellent idea to me," I replied as my stomach rumbled at the thought. "We are not going to attack and give up the advantage of the ridge and they are not going to attack as probably half their army is still arriving, footsore from a long march."

"They are not the only ones waiting for stragglers," declared King, pointing to our lines.

In the improving light I could now see the leading British units coming from Badajoz, approaching down the road. Our battalion was arrayed in a long line on the reverse slope of the ridge out of sight of the French. The village, with its two bridges over the river, was to our front. A couple of battalions of infantry occupied the village and an artillery battery was set up to cover the two bridges.

"It looks like we will be in the centre of the action," pronounced King grimly.

I looked about. Beresford was moving various Spanish units to our right. Beyond the Spanish the rest of the ridge was empty and at its end stood two small hills. The first was just beyond the Spanish position and the second five hundred yards beyond that. As they were hills on top of the ridge summit they were the tallest points around.

"Should we not have men or guns on those hills?" I asked, pointing.

"We don't have enough men to cover the whole ridge, and if the French attack over the bridges then any men on those hills will not be a lot of use."

Hindsight is a wonderful thing and I confess that I did not think any more about King's use of that little word '*if*'. As no attack at all seemed imminent, the battalion was stood down and my mind turned to breakfast.

The French can be damned inconvenient fellows and I had just been handed a hot mug of tea when the cannon fire started. Over three hours had passed since dawn and we had just been discussing if there would be a battle that day at all. While the sun was now well up in the sky, it was hidden behind dark and brooding storm clouds that promised a deluge before nightfall.

"Stand to," came the call and I just had time to take a gulp of the hot liquid to warm me up before I was forced to abandon the rest. Men kissed their wives and children goodbye, did up belts, checked cartridge boxes and picked up their muskets and started to move to our earlier position on the reverse slope. I tried to ignore the fond farewell that Lucy gave her husband; she was wearing the corporal's greatcoat over a red dress and with her hair blown by the wind she looked particularly fetching. The throng of women and children was calling final reminders to the men to take care, as I pushed my way through to find my horse. Swinging myself up into the saddle, I saw the fighting men of all but one company start to extricate themselves and move up the slope. Each battalion kept one company back to guard the baggage and protect its camp followers. Those fortunate men were already moving forward to strike tents, load carts and try to herd the women and children well away from the scene of any likely action. A handful of women without children followed some distance behind their men up the slope for a glimpse of what was happening, Lucy amongst them.

My company took its place between the second and fourth in the line. The men looked relaxed and confident; it was not a big cannonade, perhaps a couple of batteries of six guns firing on either side, probing defences. As we had done in battles with Wellington, I thought that we would stay on the reverse slope, protected from their guns, until the French launched their attack. In the past we only appeared on the crest as the French struggled up the hill, just in time to destroy them with rolling volley fire. But now Beresford made his first big mistake.

"Battalion advance," ordered King, a call that was echoed by officers and sergeants along the line. Looking along the ridge, I could see that the whole army was moving forward, until we were called to a halt standing on the crest.

It is my belief that Beresford never wanted to fight a battle at Albuera. He had become a nervous old woman fretting at every detail. He had a strong position on the ridge and a big numerical advantage: he had ended up with thirty-five thousand men to the French twenty-four thousand, even though some British units had not yet arrived. I think he wanted to show Soult how many men he did have, to deter the Frenchman from attacking at all. If that was his plan then he had seriously misjudged his man.

Soult was a seasoned and tenacious commander. He must have watched the display with interest and may even have guessed what had prompted it. He was certainly not intimidated, but now he had the advantage of seeing the entire enemy disposition displayed before him. He saw clearly that he was expected to attack across the bridges and how far along the crest his enemy's force extended. He would have seen that it did not reach far enough south to occupy the two small hills that were the highest points of the ridge. He would also have noticed that the troops on the southern end of the allied line were all Spanish.

The victor of Gebora would have quickly seen the potential of attacking from the south. He could occupy the southern hilltops with guns and march his men against the weak Spanish troops who would flee in panic and disrupt the resistance of the British troops further along the crest. With luck he would roll up the entire allied army and once again an emphatic victory would be his. But to do all of this he needed the element of surprise; he needed to get to those hilltops before his enemy had a chance to defend them. So while he sent most of his army south, hidden in the forest, to loop around the bottom of the ridge; he also did what his enemy expected and launched an attack on the village.

Chapter 5

From the British lines it seemed a slow start to the attack. The crest of the ridge was out of range of the French artillery and so we could watch in safety as the scene unfolded before us. The French batteries were concentrating on our guns which were covering the bridges over the river. As we had been given plenty of time to prepare for the battle and our guns were well dug in, they had little effect.

After half an hour of this fruitless bombardment, Soult sent over some of his cavalry. French horsemen cantered over the bridges and through fords to probe at the village. Our cavalry responded with troops of their own, and for the next half an hour there were various inconclusive skirmishes between the mounted men around the village. The British infantry in the village fired their inaccurate muskets at the fast-moving horsemen and had little to show for their efforts.

At one point some of the British horsemen crossed the river to the French side, but in response several brigades of French cavalry moved out from the forest and formed up in their squadrons facing the men in red. Even from a distance it was a magnificent sight. There were thousands of horsemen and their uniforms were a riot of colour. There were dragoons in green, Polish lancers with their strange square-ended helmets in blue, hussars in uniforms of various colours with their dolman jackets thrown over one shoulder and cuirassiers with their metal breastplates reflecting the grey sky above them.

Some of the women who had followed their men up the ridge were now standing in gaps between the companies to see the spectacle for themselves. They exchanged ribald comments with the men on the finery displayed before them. The show of force was enough for our cavalry, though, who retreated back to our side of the river.

"I wish they would get on with it," muttered Lieutenant Hervey, who had ridden up beside me. "It looks like it will tip down soon. It will be difficult firing volleys in the rain, with the powder getting damp."

"Perhaps that is what they are waiting for," I suggested.

But no sooner were the words out of my mouth than trumpet calls indicated that the attack on the village was finally underway. A large French column slowly appeared from underneath the trees on the other side of the valley and started to march down towards the river. We looked for other columns, but there was just one for now. It seemed weak for a main attack, but I wondered if this first column had orders to secure the bridges and the village before the advance of the rest of the army.

We watched as the mass of men came on, with the drummers beating in the centre of the column like the heartbeat of a single creature. A hundred yards down the slope and the drummers gave a double beat and some two thousand men roared out their challenge: *"Vive l'empereur."* It was a sound I had now heard many times before, although it still gave me a chill down my spine. Some of the newer men glanced about them to see if this was normal, but the old hands looked unperturbed.

"Don't worry, lads," shouted Corporal Benton to some of the recruits. "They don't make as much noise when they are running away."

"What do you think will happen, sir?" asked Price-Thomas, walking up to stand near my horse. I noticed that the conversation of the men in the line behind had stilled so that they could overhear the answer.

"Well, there are only two British battalions in the village to defend it and I would estimate six French battalions coming down the hill. So I guess that Beresford will send some battalions down to help defend the village."

But for a while it looked like I was wrong as our artillery put up a strong defence of the bridges and the British infantry already in the village could easily deal with the few French troops that did manage to get across the water.

"It seems the French do not want to get their feet wet," said Hervey as we watched the French move about on their side of the river bank. "The river is only waist deep. They could just wade across without using the bridges."

In hindsight the French troops probably did not want to get themselves killed in what they knew was just a diversionary attack; but eventually they were ordered to cross the river as Soult wanted to draw more British troops away from where his main attack would strike.

Of course the great oaf Beresford swallowed the bait. He ordered our brigade as well as a Portuguese one to advance to the north of the village. For good measure he threw in some Spanish reserve units as well.

Major King rode along our line calling out to his officers, "We are to move forward. Fix bayonets; we will fire a volley and charge at any French who make a stand."

"Fix bayonets," called out Sergeant Evans without waiting for any command from me and grey steel seventeen-inch blades were attached to every muzzle in the company.

"Sergeant, we will advance," I called out, seeing that the company next to mine had just commenced moving, and a solid line of redcoats started to descend slowly down the ridge. There were cheers from the few women still watching, but I was more distracted by the large raindrop that had just landed on my sleeve. I looked up as another drop splashed in my face; the promised downpour was about to start. The men were all loaded, and if rainwater got down the barrels, the powder would get damp and the guns would not fire.

"Sergeant," I called again. "Secure firelocks."

The men came to a halt again as they reached into their pouches for the tompion plugs, which they wedged into their gun muzzles to stop rain getting down the barrel. Then they took large patches of leather or oiled canvas, known as 'cows knees', and tied these over the locks of their guns so that the rain could not reach the priming or dampen the charge. In the short time it took them to complete these tasks the rain had got heavier and there were now damp patches all over my coat. Glancing along the line, I saw other companies had been forced to stop to take the same precautions. I waited for them to finish securing locks and resume the advance before I ordered my company forward, so that the battalion maintained a solid formation.

Along with the other senior officers of the battalion, Hervey and I were riding our horses in front of the line. It was our job to demonstrate courage and leadership to our men by leading the way. When I am only under fire from raindrops it is something that I am happy to do. I could see that we were out of range of the French artillery, and when the actual shooting started officers would retire behind their men so that they did not get in the way of the volleys. I looked over my shoulder to check that the company was keeping in line with the rest. Ensign Price-Thomas was walking behind the line with Boney. Sergeant Evans was shouting orders at men to close up ranks and keep the line straight and everything was clearly under control. I glanced across to the regimental colours. The two flags were being carried behind the fourth company and hung limp in the damp air. Nodding a greeting to Lieutenant Latham of the fourth, I looked past him to see three more sets of flags marking out the other battalions in Colborne's division.

We were halfway down the slope when the French artillery tested the range by firing a salvo at our line. As I expected, all of the balls fell short and barely bounced on the wet turf.

"First three companies support the infantry in the village," called out Major King. "The rest of us to push down to the river."

"Damn," I cursed under my breath as we were one of the first three companies.

Already the other two were changing the angle of their march to reach the buildings, and without any further orders from me my men followed suit. There was a steady crackle of musketry from the ruined buildings and I could see French infantry and cavalry milling about on the far river bank, looking to support their comrades fighting house to house. But the British troops were clearly well entrenched in the buildings and putting up a strong defence. There was no sign of anyone dressed in red pulling back from the narrow streets.

We had gone at least another hundred yards when the French guns fired again. With such a long line and relatively few French cannon, the odds of being hit were low, but not low enough. I did not hear a shout from the men; it was a distant scream from a woman that made me turn around. On the ridge top I saw a figure in a greatcoat and a red dress sink to her knees with her hands held to her face. Glancing back, I saw a body lying stretched out behind our line in the grass.

"Keep going! Close up now," shouted the sergeant as the men moved on.

I turned my horse and the ranks parted to let it through. As I got to the body I dropped down from the saddle. I did not need a close inspection to see that Corporal Benton was dead. A shoulder and a quarter of his chest had been smashed to pulp. I looked up to Lucy still kneeling on the ridge top and shook my head to indicate he was not just wounded.

"You poor devil," I whispered quietly to the corpse. Even though I had been cuckolding him I felt a sadness as I looked into the now glassy eyes. He had been a good man at heart, if a bit too trusting of his wife and his captain. "Don't worry, I will look after her," I told him and right then I meant it.

I turned back to the rest of my men; they were a hundred yards away now and reaching the outskirts of the village. A new crescendo of musket fire indicated that the French were still trying to push into its centre. I was about to remount when I hesitated. The last time I had been in a melee with French infantry, at Busaco, I had found that a soldier with a bayonet had a much longer reach than an officer with a sword. In skilled hands the bayonet would win every time. Benton would do me one final service: I reached down and grabbed his musket before I swung up into the saddle and rode off.

Chapter 6

Hervey was already overseeing the dispersal of the company into the buildings when I reached the village. "Leave your horse here," I told him as I dismounted and tied my mount to a broken roof beam. "The French will try to pick off officers and on horseback you will be a sitting duck. Get yourself a long arm too," I said, holding up my musket, "to make things harder for them."

I looked around for Price-Thomas, but the boy had already disappeared into the buildings, armed with just his sword. The wolfhound was still waiting patiently for me, though. "Come on, Boney," I called. "You can sniff out the French for me." With that I plunged into the tangle of roofless buildings.

Having been bivouacked in the village for nearly a month, I knew its layout well. I could hear my men shouting ahead of me and so I thought the alley I was in must have been cleared of the French. Hervey charged off down another abandoned street and Boney and I were left alone for a moment in the stone maze. I could hear Hervey encouraging the men forward as he pushed through the streets and I added my own voice to the throng. "Come on, men, press on," I yelled, without moving forward myself a single inch.

I had no intention of blundering into a French assault. This was, I thought, an ideal fighting environment for a man with no particular wish to meet the enemy. For with my command divided and unable to see each other, they would simply assume I was with another group. Mind you, it would not do to fall back too far, as I would have to emerge at least in the centre of the village when we had recaptured it.

The village was divided into two halves, with the Seville-to-Badajoz road running through the middle. From the sound of things the British were at least up to the road and so I pressed cautiously on. I had remembered a small roofless house on the main street. It was one of the few with a stone staircase which led up to a window on the first floor. I could leave Boney to guard the door, and while there were no floorboards left, I could perch at the top of the stairs and shoot through the window. Given the ruins of the town, the French were unlikely to be looking up at first-floor openings.

Eventually I reached the doorway and inside found a grim reminder of the battle underway. There were no windows on the ground floor but the light through the open roof revealed two dead British soldiers lying on the floor. They were not from my regiment and must have been part of the original force holding the village. I slung my own musket over my shoulder and picked up one of theirs. There was powder in the frizzen; it was loaded and so was the other. Having commanded Boney to guard the door, I climbed the stairs with my three firearms.

Peering through the window, I saw that the main road formed part of the front line in the battle for the village. I saw some redcoats in houses on the other side of the street but equally I saw three French men try to cross to get into our side. I snatched up one of my muskets and fired at the group, but there was a crackle of fire from many of the surrounding houses. While the men went down I had no idea if I had hit them. Muskets were notoriously inaccurate, particularly with fast-moving targets. This was proved a moment later when three French dragoons rode their horses full tilt down the street. I blazed away at them, as did others, but they all escaped unscathed. I had no cartridge box up the stairs with me and so crouched with my third and final musket, searching for a target.

Boney gave a short bark he normally used to welcome people. I looked down, expecting to see some of my company in the space below, but instead there was a figure in a greatcoat and a red dress.

"What in Christ's name are you doing here?" I asked Lucy.

"They killed my Bill. I want to kill one of them," she stated calmly with an icy and resolute expression on her face. Lucy had lived with the British for two years and had got used to many of our ways. She even spoke English with a country accent. But at that moment I realised that with her eye-for-an-eye, blood-feud attitude, she was still a Spaniard at heart.

"You bloody fool. You will get yourself killed as well if you are not careful." I looked at her standing defenceless in the room below. I was going to give her one of my pistols, but then had a better idea. "Can you load a musket?" I asked, only to receive a very rude expression in Spanish by way of a reply. "I speak your language, remember," I told her, grinning.

"I have been loading guns since I was a girl," she told me. "I was faster than my Bill; we once had a contest to fire three shots."

She certainly handled the two guns I passed back down the stairs confidently. She had already picked up a cartridge box from one of the dead soldiers. In a moment she was spitting the ball down the barrel like an old hand. She could definitely reload faster than me. She had passed me the first reloaded weapon and was just reaching for the second gun when suddenly everything happened at once: Boney snarled, a shot whined away off the stonework just above my head and Lucy screamed.

It was a dismounted French dragoon who had burst through the door. One part of my brain realised that the charge of horsemen we had seen earlier must have been a ruse to get us to reveal our positions. Now they were hunting us down and I had to kill this bastard before one of his mates joined the fight. Boney was already on him, snapping jaws aiming for the man's throat. The dragoon tried to fend him off with his still-smoking carbine barrel while I swung my newly loaded weapon round to fire. But Lucy was in the way. She had snatched up the unloaded musket and with an animal shriek she plunged the bayonet deep into the Frenchman's chest.

Blood gushed from the dragoon's mouth as he swung round to stare in disbelief at the musket, now buried up to the bayonet socket in his body. Then he looked at the woman he knew had just killed him. Lucy was sobbing and trying to pull the gun free but it was jammed in his ribs. As the Frenchman's legs collapsed, he slipped down the wall, dragging the musket from her hands.

"Get back away from the door," I yelled at Lucy. "There might be more so take this." I passed her my spare loaded musket. She took it, but already her bottom lip was starting to tremble at the shock of the last few seconds.

Boney, having sniffed the dying man, looked through the door. He did not growl and so I realised there was no one else outside. For a second I started to relax a little, and then the dog's head cocked as we both heard a new sound. It came from the south. I climbed back to the top of the stone staircase and craned my neck around the gable to identify the source. What I saw was enough to make my blood run cold.

From my higher vantage point I could see over the top of most of the outer buildings of the village and down the side of the ridge occupied by our army. The noise I had heard was the crackle of a new musketry duel. As I stared I could see thousands of French troops pouring from woods to the south and up the unoccupied end of the ridge. They were led by three huge French columns that were already over the southernmost knoll on the ridge crest. Like three battering rams, they were heading towards the Spanish troops at the end of our line, which were hastily realigning themselves to face this new and unexpected threat.

45

I cursed as things fell into place. Now I understood why Soult's attack on the village had seemed so weak. It was merely a distraction, and our giant, one-eyed pinhead of a commander had sent half of his army to block it, while leaving some of his weakest forces to resist the real assault.

"We need to get out of here," I told Lucy, running down the stairs. Everything I knew about the Spanish regular forces told me that the units facing the French attack would crumble in a matter of moments and then there would be a rout along the ridge crest.

After a cautious look down the alley, we emerged from the house. As we reached the next narrow street I stopped and bellowed, "Buffs, fall back on the battalion."

A head emerged from the window of a house overlooking the main street. "What is happening, sir?" asked Sergeant Evans.

"The French are attacking along the ridge from the south. This is not their real attack. Get the men back to the regiment."

"Yes, sir, I will extrude the men immediately."

With that he ducked back into the house and started shouting at others inside, but I was already on my way. I reached my horse and, dropping the musket, jumped up into the saddle. Lucy reached up for me to pull her up onto the horse behind me but I hesitated.

"Wait," I called as I quickly thought through the options of what I was going to do next.

Anticipating the disaster that normally resulted from Spanish involvement in any battle, the safest course would be to turn the horse north and ride for the Guadiana River. Once across that pontoon bridge I would be relatively safe. Lucy was a fine woman, but she would undoubtedly slow the horse down. On the other hand I was fond of her. Did I really want her to fall into the hands of some hairy French hussar? I thought I would risk taking her.

But then, as I looked up and saw the British regiments realigning themselves to face the new threat, another thought occurred. If the British managed to fight their way clear in an orderly withdrawal then my desertion would see me ruined and my hard-won reputation lost. There was also the risk that the pontoon bridge might have been washed away again and French cavalry would be sweeping the countryside looking for prisoners. The allies still had a numerical advantage and lots of strong regiments. If we could not win the battle, I thought we should still be able to fight our way clear. Perhaps the safest course of action would be to stay with the army after all and I would keep my reputation intact.

I reached down a hand and pushed out a foot so Lucy could climb up behind me. I could see that Major King was already riding his horse up the slope to join a knot of officers on the top of the ridge and I urged my horse up the hill to join them.

"Get off when we reach the top and get to the baggage train," I shouted over my shoulder at Lucy. "Tell them to prepare to head north when the Spanish break."

"What will you do?"

"I have to re-join the battalion, but I imagine that we will be fighting a rear-guard action and following you shortly."

The horse reached the crest and I stopped to let Lucy slide off before I approached the group of officers. There was Major King, Brigadier Colborne, Captain Varley, one of Colborne's staff officers, Ben D'Urban and, towering over them all, the vast frame of Beresford.

"How do we know that is the main attack?" I heard Beresford say. "For all we know that is the diversion to draw troops away from the village."

"But they are turning our line," declared Colborne. "We cannot expect the Spanish to hold them for long."

Beresford opened his mouth to say something but I got in first. "Excuse me, sir, but I could see the French attack from a rooftop in the village. The French have committed several thousand infantry to the southern attack. I also saw cavalry and artillery coming forward in support."

Beresford glared at me with his one eye. "When I want your bloody opinion, Captain, I will ask for it," he told me rudely before turning his attention to the others. "We will wait until it is clear which the main attack is before we respond. Gentlemen, good day." With that the great dithering giant rode away followed by Ben D'Urban, who glanced apologetically at me over his shoulder.

"Are you sure it is their main attack?" asked Colborne.

"Yes, sir," I replied, wary now of venturing another fuller opinion.

"I think you are right," replied Colborne. "I will speak to General Stewart and see if he cannot persuade Beresford. In the meantime get the men out of the village and regroup up on the ridge top."

I rode back down the slope towards the village to get my men. They were streaming out of the village now, with Hervey and Price-Thomas organising them into ranks. I saw that the Portuguese division on the

47

other side of the village was sending in more defenders to replace those withdrawn.

"Come on, men," I called. "We are re-joining the battalion and then the whole brigade is reforming on the ridge top."

"Are we going to help those brave Spanish troops, sir?" asked Hervey.

I caught the eye of Sergeant Evans who, like me, grinned at the thought of the Spanish standing long enough for us to join them. "I think it is more likely that we will be fighting a rear guard action after the Spanish have retired from the field."

"Retired," scoffed the sergeant at my choice of word. "They won't be retiring – they will be running. They will be perambulating as fast as their little legs can carry them in a minute."

"Well, they seem to be doing well at the moment," stated Hervey defensively.

To humour him I pulled out my glass to see just how much of a shambles the Spanish line was. "Good God," I breathed as the scene swam into focus. The French had come over the southern knoll in their three columns. Seeing the Spaniards in front of them, they had not wasted time forming line and instead looked to use the columns to smash their way along the ridge top. But to my astonishment the Spaniards were holding them, and doing it well. The Spanish were deployed in lines so they could bring all their guns to bear, unlike the French, who could only fire from the outer ranks. The Spanish also had some artillery pieces in their line which must have been firing canister into the tightly packed French ranks with devastating effect. But in turn the French had now got cannon on the summit of the southern knoll, which were firing to support their troops. The Spanish were taking severe punishment, but standing firm and giving it back with interest. It was probably the finest moment for the Spanish army in the whole war. It was just unfortunate that things would probably have been better if they had run. But I did not know that then and so I turned to the others and admitted, "They *are* holding the French and doing it handsomely."

My view of this military miracle was obscured by what seemed a sudden grey mist. By the time I had put the telescope back in my pocket the squall had hit us too. It was a torrential downpour of rain and hail that stung the cheeks and dropped icy water down the back of my coat.

48

"Come on, men," I shouted above the roar of the rain. "Get up that hill, stopper your barrels and keep your locks wrapped."

It took nearly twenty minutes to get formed up and re-join the rest of the brigade on the ridge top. By then I was soaked to the skin as the storm continued. Most of the men had fired off any charges in their weapons, preferring to march with an empty gun. Drawing a damp charge out of the barrel was a time-consuming business. The Spanish were still holding and seemed to have settled into a battle of attrition with the French. It was hard to see with the rain and the gun smoke, but both sides seemed to be firing away, some eighty yards apart.

Colborne rode past with a group of officers. "Ah, Flashman," he called. "Come and tell us again what you saw from the village."

I rode over to the huddle of officers, wiping the rainwater from my eyes so that I could see them clearly. Saluting, I reported: "I saw several thousand infantry coming up the slope, at least three columns, supported by cavalry and artillery. I am pretty sure that it is their main attack, sir, and the Spanish cannot hold them for much longer." That I thought was the strongest possible hint I could give that we should start to pull back. When the Spanish did eventually break there would be chaos all along the ridge.

A pair of flinty blue eyes surveyed me and I recognised General Stewart, commander of half the British troops, including our brigade. "Of course it is their main assault," cried Stewart impatiently. He stared at the beleaguered Spanish and then seemed to make up his mind about something. "If we don't support them, we will lose this battle. Colborne, I want your brigade to march past the Spanish right flank and along the side of the French columns and then attack the nearest one." He made it sound as straightforward as feeding ducks in the park, but I was appalled. I had re-joined the battalion thinking it would be the safest place in a fighting withdrawal. But now, because the wretched Spanish were being so resolute in their defence, I was being dragged into a counterattack.

I sat aghast for a moment as the implications of this order set in, but Stewart was impatient to begin. He glared at the column of men he was sending in to battle with the same compassion he might have shown for his breakfast boiled egg. "Come along, gentlemen," he shouted over the rain. "We have not got all day; the Spanish will not stand for ever."

I looked around. The Buffs were the lead regiment in Colborne's formation and so we would be among the first into the fray. The men were lined in a column, each company forming two lines with their officers on horseback in front. My company was the third in the column.

"I will re-join my regiment then, sir," said Colborne, who was colonel of the sixty-sixth, which was further back in the group. I certainly did not blame him for moving smartly to the rear; I was wracking my brains for a reason to do the same. How I yearned for the freedom of a staff officer at that moment, but now my place was fixed with my men. I turned reluctantly to join Hervey in front of the two wet and bedraggled rows of the third company.

With Major King beside him, the captain of the first company ordered his men forward, followed a few seconds later by the captain of the second company. I wanted to think of a reason, any reason, not to give the next order, but my mind had gone blank. I turned back to my men. It was hard to see if any looked scared as most faces were turned away from the driving rain. Sergeant Evans stood at the end of the first line while Price-Thomas with Boney was now in the row behind. A few faces now looked up expectantly as I continued to hesitate.

"Advance," I croaked. My throat had constricted through fear and I doubt anyone heard the order. I cleared my throat and shouted much louder to compensate. "Advance, men, forward. Come along there."

We had barely covered a few paces when there was a double flash of lightning, followed by a crash of thunder that made me jump. It did not seem the best omen to march into a pitched battle. General Stewart watched us move off and glanced down at the men following us. I wondered if he was going to stay near the rear of the column; if he did then I would find some excuse to report something to him. Anything would do: I could claim to have seen a fresh attack on the village through a gap in the rain. With such poor visibility and the confusion of battle, they would never find out if it was true. As though the old bastard had read my mind, I saw him turn his mount in my direction and ride towards me.

"I will ride with you, Flashman," he called over the drumming of the rain. "Have you fought in a storm before?"

"No, sir," I replied. I looked at him. He must have been frightened too but he showed no sign of it. He was as rigid as an old maid's starched drawers. I knew what he was up to, though, making conversation to take his mind off the coming dangers. Well, I needed the distraction too, and so I added, "This one is like a monsoon in India, only colder."

"Ah, you were with Wellington in India, were you? I think I recall hearing your name at Talavera too. Well, there will be no need for those heroics today. We just need to keep the men ordered and disciplined so that we cover the whole flank of their column. They won't stand then, attacked on two sides."

We were moving partway down the reverse slope now to pass to the right of the Spanish line fighting the French columns. The rain was reducing casualties; only around half of the muskets on both sides seemed to be firing, with the rest of the men struggling to clear damp powder from fouled gun locks. The ground around the Spanish lines was littered with bodies but they still had plenty of fight in them. As we went past, one of their cannon barked another canister-load of death into the blue ranks opposite.

"Viva!" shouted the Spaniards on the end of the line as we marched past and Stewart raised a hand in salute. Whether the Spaniards were simply pleased to have reinforcements or just glad that the French cannon would switch to new targets it was hard to say. But barely had we appeared around the Spanish than the French cannon started to take men from our column. Two balls whipped through the lines of the first company ahead, leaving trails of broken bodies for the rest of the battalion to step around.

"Close up," called the sergeant of the first company, a cry that was to become all too familiar over the next few minutes.

Stewart was riding calmly beside me as though exercising in Hyde Park and I tried to affect the same level of unconcern while my guts churned in fear. A few moments later I resisted the urge to duck as another ball went whining over my head. There were screams and yells from the men where the ball had landed. I strained my ears and heard another voice calling for gaps in the line to be filled. With relief I realised that it was not Sergeant Evans. The ball must have hit a company beyond mine.

Now, as the head of our formation came level with the front of the French column, I saw a new and more personal danger appear. We were at least a hundred yards away from the side of the nearest French column, and those French soldiers at the edge now readied themselves to fire. At that range and with damp charges they posed little threat, but further along I saw a company of skirmishers, or *voltigeurs*, being advanced to close the range. These soldiers were marksmen who did not fight in ranks, but in a much looser formation. They would be looking to disrupt our attack by shooting officers. I muttered a silent prayer as I glanced across at Stewart. He had seen them but honour demanded that he show no fear and so he continued to walk his horse forward at a steady pace. He was covered in enough gold braid to attract a flock of magpies and even in the rain the skirmishers were bound to see him. The general would be a prime target, attracting musket balls like bees to a honey pot. So why, I silently prayed to the Almighty, did the man have to ride next to me?

Chapter 7

In just a few moments the lieutenant of the first company had thrown his hands in the air and fallen from his horse. "Oh Christ," I heard Hervey mutter to himself. I glanced across at him. He was ashen faced and looking as terrified as I felt. At least, I thought callously, he would provide some cover, being between me and the *voltigeurs*. No sooner was the thought in my head than Hervey jolted in the saddle. "I have been hit," he gasped. His left hand went up to his right shoulder and came away covered in blood while his sword arm hung uselessly at his side.

"Go back, man," snapped Stewart. "You will be no use in that state."

Hervey wheeled his horse away, staying unsteadily in the saddle, and for a moment I felt a twinge of guilt. It was almost as though my thought had caused his injury. If it had then it probably saved his life for he survived the battle. But then I remembered that I was now reluctantly the only person between the general and the *voltigeurs*.

There was a steady crackle of musket fire from the side of the French column, interspersed with the booming of cannon from the French and the Spanish. Most cannon balls went over our heads, but one pitched short and I saw it slam into the horse ridden by the captain of the first company. The animal went down hard but its rider dismounted as it fell, landed on his feet and immediately continued the march while shouting at his men to avoid the still-flailing feet of his animal.

A musket ball whizzed past my head as some of the *voltigeurs* turned their attention to my company and took note of my riding companion. I felt trapped: every fibre of my being wanted to run, but I would be disgraced if I did and quite possibly just as dead. The noise of battle was all around me, firing, screaming and yelling, but strangely muted by the continual downpour of rain. I glanced out to our right but just saw a grey murky field. "What is out there?" I asked the general, partly to make a conversation to distract me from the danger and partly because I realised we would have our backs to this space when we attacked.

"Our cavalry," replied Stewart, "and some of theirs. They will counter each other. That is if they can see…" He paused halfway through his sentence and stared in irritation at his right shoulder. There I saw that half of his golden epaulet had been torn away from his uniform by a musket ball. "Damn and blast them," he grumbled. "Those were a gift from my wife."

I turned back just in time to see a *voltigeur* aim directly at me. I did not even have time to flinch before the powder flashed in the pan of his musket. Mercifully that was all that did ignite as the cartridge powder must have been damp, but it was the final straw for me. I had to do something. I could not ride along like the target in some fairground stall until I was killed. I needed some kind of shield. I wracked my brain for an idea and then realised that I was sitting on it. My horse was half a tonne of shield if only I could find an excuse to get off it and walk alongside.

"Is that movement out there?" I asked Stewart, pointing again into the empty grey field to our right. Stewart glanced in that direction and as he did so I took out a small fruit knife from my pocket and plunged the blade into the shoulder of my horse. Unsurprisingly the mount took exception to this and reared up as I dropped the knife.

"Are you hit, Flashman?" asked Stewart, whirling back round.

"No, sir, but I think my horse is lame," I replied while putting my hand to the newly made wound and bringing it back covered in blood to show the general. "I think I will have to dismount," I added, sliding quickly down from the saddle so that the horse was now between me and the *voltigeurs*.

"Yes, quite," agreed Stewart with, I thought, a degree of peevish irritation. "Well, it is probably time I rode down the column to see how the rest are getting on," he called, wheeling his horse away. The crafty old fox had been using me as a shield too.

That horse undoubtedly saved my life. As we marched along it reared up twice more with genuine musket ball wounds, but it stayed on its feet and kept moving in the right direction. Eventually I heard orders being shouted ahead and Stewart and King rode past to oversee the change in formation. The first company was wheeling around to face left, and as the second company marched past the first it wheeled in turn to join the line. As we marched behind the first and second company lines, we had some respite from the *voltigeurs* and I called Sergeant Evans to the front.

"Four dead and six injured, sir," he reported of the casualties we had taken so far. "Mr Price-Thomas is fine, sir, and your dog."

"Very good," I replied automatically. The casualties were better than I had expected. The first company seemed to have already lost a quarter of their men. "We will be wheeling around left at the end of the second company," I told him. "I would be obliged if you would give the orders."

"Gyrating left, as you say, sir," acknowledged Evans.

While his eccentric ordering caused both Stewart and King, who were nearby, to cock a quizzical eyebrow, the third company joined its fellows without difficulty. This was largely because the men had seen what the earlier companies had done and just followed their lead. The fourth and subsequent companies formed on us to create a new double-rank line facing the French.

Now at last the men could return the punishment that they had been receiving over the last few minutes. As soon as the companies were in position they opened fire on the French. This would normally involve a series of devastating company volleys, but the weather had taken its toll. Only half the muskets in the first volley fired. The other men fell to the rear, cursing as they tried to push pins through touch holes to move damp powder away and sweep away grey sludge in priming pans and replace it with fresh, dry powder from a new cartridge.

Evans had obviously fought in the rain before. "Use the cartridges from the middle of your pouch," he called. "They will be the most desiccated. Here, lad, take this one." He handed one struggling soldier a replacement musket and I saw that hanging from his shoulders he had two more that he had presumably taken from the dead.

"Well done, Sergeant, you seem well prepared."

"It is always best to be expectant, sir," he stated primly. Then, turning to the men, he called, "Come along, lads. Aim at their belt buckles and make those shots tell."

"We have got most of the guns firing now," called Price-Thomas a minute later. He was right. Only three men were still wrestling with the locks of their guns; the rest were getting into the rhythm of firing rolling volleys. Unfortunately the French were doing the same, and while I watched two more men of the company fell. They were pulled to the rear by their comrades. One was wounded in the thigh and was tying a neck cloth around his wound, but the other lay still. Evans looked him over and announced, "This one is mortified, sir."

"I am sure he is, Sergeant." I replied.

"What are we going to do now?" asked Price-Thomas.

It was a good question, as while the Spanish and French had settled into a musketry duel at the front of the column, we seemed to have done the same down the side of the French formation. I peered through the rain down the British line. The Buffs were all in a line. I looked back and saw the forty-eighth were as well, and as far as I could see, the sixty-sixth beyond them. You could make out the different regiments from their colour parties, holding the regimental flags that hung sodden and heavy from their poles. The Buffs' flag was held just behind the fourth company where Major King watched his men from horseback.

All of the regiments were now firing into the side of the French column and getting shot at in return, but nobody was moving. There was only one way this could end and I did not welcome it. We carried on firing volleys for what seemed an age but it was probably only a few minutes. Two more men fell, mortally wounded, and lay bleeding to death in the rain. Then I saw General Stewart riding up the line to speak to Major King and after a moment I heard the order I least wanted to hear.

"Fix bayonets."

All along the line the men reached for their bayonets and carefully attached them to the now hot barrels of their guns, many of which were steaming in the continuing rain. The French could see what was happening and knew what to expect. I saw them fixing their own blades too. Price-Thomas drew his sword and moved forward to join the ranks of the men but I pulled him back.

"Don't be a fool," I told him. "Your sword won't reach a man with a bayonet before he has had the chance to gut you with his blade. Sheathe that sword and get us both a musket and bayonet." Of course I had no intention of actually getting near the French if I could help it, but one had to at least show willing.

This promised to be a most brutal action, for the enemy had nowhere to go. Normally bayonets were fixed when the enemy were on the verge of breaking, to chase them away from the field. But the French we would charge had their own comrades to their rear, the Spanish still fighting the head of the column, and only those at the back of the column had room to escape the charge. The bayonet is an effective attacking weapon but clumsy in defence. Both sides would therefore be stabbing out with it for all they were worth, while desperately trying to parry opposing thrusts.

General Stewart was not looking for a shield now as he rode into the gap between the third and fourth companies. "Come on, men," he called. "We cannot let them stand. See them off the field." With a flourish of his sword he indicated that they should charge and spurred his horse forward to join them. With a roar the men leapt forward to the attack; well, most of them at least.

Price-Thomas, musket now in hand, gave his piping war cry and started to run forward with the rest. He had only taken two paces when his trailing ankle got caught up in the musket strap of the man following him. He fell face first into the now wet, soft mud of the hillside. As he struggled to get to his feet the person who had tripped him fell on top of him, pressing him further into the dirt.

"Dammit, boy, you fell right in front of me," I called indignantly while disentangling my musket strap from the lad's ankle.

"I am very sorry, sir," came Price-Thomas's slightly muffled voice from underneath me.

"Well, it really won't do. I think I have twisted my ankle."

"Sorry again, sir… but could you get off me? I think we had better help with the attack."

"Yes, yes, but I will need you to help me up first."

I rolled away and the boy shot to his feet. He reached down and gripped my hand to pull me up. I soon stood on one leg with an arm gripping firmly around his shoulder, and another perfectly good leg waving in the air. After a moment I started to hobble forward, using the boy as a crutch, and wincing at the imaginary pain. "Go at them, lads," I called encouragingly from a safe distance.

"Shouldn't I run forward and help the men, sir?" asked Price-Thomas plaintively.

"How much practice have you had fighting with the bayonet lad?" I asked.

"Why none, sir. You gave the men plenty of drill with the musket and bayonet, but I have been practising with a sword along with the other ensigns."

"How much drill do you think a French infantryman has fighting with a bayonet then?"

"Quite a lot, sir."

"So what makes you think that a wet, angry French infantryman is going to let an inexperienced fifteen-year-old boy beat him with a bayonet?"

"We have to do something, sir."

"We are, we are managing the men, and if any Frenchmen do get through, we will shoot them. Did you check your musket was loaded?" I asked sternly. I let go of the lad and stepped gingerly forward on my own, using my musket now as a support. I had no idea if mine was loaded either but I knew I had two loaded pistols in my pockets.

"No, it's not loaded, sir." The boy searched in the belt pouch of a nearby corpse for a dry cartridge and set to loading his weapon. I tutted impatiently, knowing that this would make his cold, wet hands fumble the job even more. Just as he was raising the ramrod to push the charge home we heard a cheer from our front and to my astonishment I saw that the first French column was breaking. My joy was short-lived as I saw the second column waiting beyond.

"Come on, men, on to the next one. Keep amongst them," roared General Stewart, providing all the leadership my men needed. It was good to see a general make himself useful for a change, allowing lesser ranks to evade their duty. A damn dangerous duty it was too. As our men surged forward to the next column I saw that a tidemark of bodies had been left behind. Hundreds of them, British and French, lay in a rough line down this part of the ridge where the two armies had fought. At least a dozen of my company were there, some just wounded, others carrying several stab wounds and clearly dead.

"Come on, boy, we need to keep up with the men," I urged Price-Thomas just as he was threading the ramrod back into its brackets along the side of the muzzle. We could not be seen to fall too far behind our men and so I allowed my limp to ease slightly as we moved forward towards the low rampart of bodies ahead of us. Now that the press of men above them had moved on I saw that several were struggling to get up. A French soldier shook himself like a dog and then staggered to his feet, holding a head wound and staring about him. Boney growled at this apparent resurrection. Glancing at the hound and the two officers next to it, the Frenchman turned and stumbled away to the south. Price-Thomas raised his musket but I pushed the barrel back down. "Save that shot for someone coming towards us," I told him.

If the battle with the first column had been brutal, the attack on the second was even worse. The poor French stragglers from the first attack, often unarmed, found themselves trapped between the jabbing points of both British and French troops. They screamed and pushed to get past, through or over the first ranks of the French line, causing confusion that the hardened British soldiers were quick to exploit.

"Go on, go at them," General Stewart was shouting from his horse as he turned and rode down the line of his command towards the next British regiment.

58

I hefted the musket in my hand as we approached the fighting men. There were screams, oaths and yells coming from the heaving and compacted mass of humanity. The French were so pushed in together that few had room to use their weapons at all. In contrast the thin line of redcoats did have room to move and they were thrusting their blades at the men in the sodden blue uniforms. As lightning flashed and the rain continued to pelt down it seemed like a vision from hell.

I looked for the surviving officers of the regiment; two were still on horseback and others were holding their swords and standing behind their men, encouraging them on. One of the mounted men saw me looking around as I strode towards the line and he rode over.

"Why are you not with your men, Captain Flashman?" asked Major King.

"I am just coming up to them now," I replied wearily; we were only ten yards away.

At that very moment the benefit of staying back became apparent as one of our men slipped in the mud. The Frenchman he had been fighting stabbed him in the shoulder and with a roar of triumph stepped over him so that he was behind our line. The two British soldiers on either side of him were both fully occupied with opponents of their own. The Frenchman who had stepped through the gap could see that he only had to kill one or two of the British on either side to create a gap. Then dozens of his comrades could pour through and attack the British line from behind. He turned to face the exposed backs of the British line. Instinctively I raised my musket to my shoulder but the flint sparked down on an empty pan: the gun was unloaded. But before I could even curse, there was a crack of a musket to my left and the Frenchman was falling with a red-rimmed hole right between his shoulder blades.

"What the devil are you doing with long arms? Officers should be using swords." Major King looked down indignantly at us, completely ignoring the fact that we had just forestalled a breakthrough of the line. Without waiting for a reply, he rode on, still muttering to himself about 'irregular behaviour'.

I turned away from him and looked at Price-Thomas, who was staring, ashen faced, at the French body lying on the ground.

"Is that the first man you have killed?"

"Yes, sir," he replied quietly.

"Well, he would have killed you, given the chance. Now go to one of those bodies over there and get some dry cartridges. We both need to reload our weapons."

To keep him occupied, I got Price-Thomas to load both muskets. It stopped him thinking about the man he killed as I urged him to hurry. I had no idea if the pistols in my sodden pocket would still fire and I was keen to get a more reliable weapon in my hand.

If I am honest, the incident had shaken me up too, for it had shown just how flimsy our attack now was. We had started with double ranks of men, but with casualties on the march to make the assault, and then in the musketry duel and finally in the assault on the first column, we were down to a single rank of redcoats along most of the line. There were a handful of officers and sergeants standing behind the line to help fill gaps and stop similar intrusions, but it would not take much for a breach to be made. At one point four or five men did break through together but they breached the line of the fourth company just in front of the group of men guarding the regimental colours. Several of the British sergeants from the colour guard went forward to despatch them with the razor-sharp spontoons they used to protect the colours against horsemen.

I am not sure whether it was the British or the weather which defeated the second French column in the end, as another vicious squall broke out within the storm. Suddenly we were blasted with a gale loaded with thousands of hailstones. You could not look into the wind; you had to turn your back into it. As soldiers on both sides struggled to see and retain their footing, the French decided that they had fought enough. Unless it was hidden by the sound of the tempest, they did not seem to make much noise as they went and I did not notice they had broken at first.

"The French are going, sir," called out Price-Thomas.

I squinted into the sleet and saw a general movement of the men in blue south beyond the line of the darker red coats hunched against the weather. "So they are. Thank God for that."

"Shouldn't we pursue them, sir?"

"Look at the men. They are exhausted, and we haven't got enough of them to take on another column." Now that the French had moved back, it was clearer to see how pitifully few the survivors of the regiment were.

"Close up," called a familiar voice and I saw that Sergeant Evans was among the survivors.

I counted and there were thirty-four men from my company still standing or crouching over wounded comrades. This was roughly half the number we had started the day with. Another tidemark showed the line of conflict with the second column. This time there were more blue-coated than red corpses, with many of those the unarmed stragglers from the first column. A break in the rain showed that the third column was still some hundred yards ahead of us, but like our men most were hunched over to avoid the rain.

Slowly the men heeded the sergeant's call and began to come together in a single soggy line. Looking at the other companies in the Buffs, I saw they were equally ravaged. The British were now a fragile single file of exhausted men, opposed by an entire fresh French column. That is it, I thought. The regiment has fought itself to a standstill; they will have to retire us to the rear now. Little did I realise that the worst was yet to come.

Chapter 8

The squall stopped as suddenly as it started and instead of wind and hail the weather reverted back to just steady rain. Visibility improved and we could now see a large formation of horsemen to our west that seemed to be moving south.

"Are they our cavalry moving to harass the fleeing French?" asked Price-Thomas beside me.

"I hope so; at least they are not heading in our direction." I looked up as a single horseman came galloping up the line. "Ah, here is someone who might tell us. Captain Waller, are those our horses?"

"We are not sure, Flashman. What do you make of them?" Waller reined in beside me and looked at our much-diminished line. "Your men have paid a big price to see off those columns, but it was splendid work, splendid indeed."

I took my glass from my pocket and to Waller's amusement I pulled young Price-Thomas in front of me so that I could rest the instrument on his head for a steady view. "There you are, lad, now you are being useful."

"What can you see, sir?" he asked, moving his head slightly.

"When you stand still all I can see is grey, murky horsemen. They could be anyone, but they now seem to be coming to a halt."

"Captain Waller, do you have a message for me?" Major King was trotting up with Captain Bailey, one of the two captains to retain his horse. The major looked irritated that Waller had stopped to talk to me instead of riding straight for him.

"General Stewart sends his compliments and asks the regiment to stand here, sir, and he will send up reinforcements to help attack the third column. The thirty-first battalion are still in reserve."

"Lucky bastards," I murmured as I continued to watch the horsemen through the glass.

"Very well, Captain," replied King, ignoring me. But then I uttered an oath and he turned, exasperated, in my direction. "What is it now, Flashman?"

"Those horsemen have turned their line and seem to be walking in our direction now."

"Well, if they are French, our cavalry will see them off," claimed Captain Bailey confidently.

There was a crackle as a handful of muskets discharged behind us and one ball buzzed over our heads. The gathering of so many enemy officers had attracted the attention of the *voltigeurs* in the remaining French column.

Without taking my eye from the lens I called out to Evans. "Sergeant, make sure those frogs don't get too close." There was something about the horsemen that seemed familiar, I thought, so maybe they were British. All I could see was a blurred grey silhouette through the rain, but now they seemed to be increasing speed. "I think those horsemen have gone from the walk to the trot," I told the other officers. "They are definitely coming this way."

"Perhaps we should gather a few companies to form a solid line against them, just in case they are French," suggested Waller.

"That would mean showing our backs to that French column," objected King. "General Stewart wants us ready to attack them; I am not changing formation unless he orders it."

There was another crackle of musketry and I looked around at the remaining French column. They had sent forward a dozen *voltigeurs* who were well spaced out. Behind them some men from the main column were also taking some pot shots at us, but at a hundred yards they were not likely to be accurate. Now that they could see their enemy, most of the French infantry seemed to be engaged in checking primings and powder and firing off damp charges to get their weapons ready in the rain for the expected attack.

Evans had got the company well spaced out and was urging the men to kneel like the *voltigeurs* when they were not loading so that they made a smaller target. I nodded approvingly and turned back to find that my telescope rest had walked off and was petting a miserable Boney. The ensign had knelt down next to the dog and put his arm around the animal's shoulders. Boney leant in towards him to share body warmth and I saw that they were both shivering a little. Now that the danger seemed to have diminished slightly I realised that I was freezing as well. My clothes were saturated with icy rain and stuck to my skin.

I heard a yell and looked over my shoulder to see Private Temple clutching a wound on his arm. It did not seem too bad for he took his hand away to pick up his musket. Aiming it at one of the *voltigeurs*, he yelled, "I see you. Let's see how you like this, you bugger," before firing and giving a grunt of satisfaction at the result.

"I think they are Spanish," called out Captain Bailey. He was still staring at the horsemen, who did not seem so distant now.

Without the telescope I could see the grey, undulating line of cavalry. I dashed the rain from my eyes and squinted but I could not make out any colours. I raised my glass again but my hands were shaking with the cold and it was hard to hold the thing steady. Twice the horsemen swam before my eye and once I thought I caught a glimpse of blue but was not sure. The third time I managed to hold the glass steady for a few seconds. They were two hundred yards off in the pouring rain then. At first I had that nag of familiarity as I looked at them. Then one turned his head and I made out the shape of the strange shako and at that moment the rain thinned sufficiently for me to see the little flag at the top of the lance he was holding. I knew them then all right; they were one of the most feared cavalry units the enemy possessed.

"They are Polish lancers!" I shouted.

"Are you sure?" queried King.

"Of course I am bloody sure – I've ridden in the uniform."

Any remaining doubt was resolved by a trumpet call from the approaching horsemen who now increased speed to the gallop.

"Form up to receive horse," yelled Major King to all those about him. But it was too late for that, far too late, and everybody knew it. The ground seemed to vibrate now with the oncoming horses' hooves and men stared in horror at what seemed approaching certain doom… but for me death arrived early.

It was as King gave his pointless order that it happened. I felt a thump in my back and a searing pain in my chest. As I stepped forward to keep my balance I saw a red stain grow across my chest. I stared down in horror, my mind numb. Oh, I had been close to death many times before, but each time I had managed to escape, while those around me fell. Now my luck had suddenly run out. I had been shot in the chest, whether from a *voltigeur* or a lucky strike from the column I did not know or care. All I did know was that shots passing through the torso were invariably fatal. I was done for.

As the world dissolved into chaos around me, the initial horror changed to shock as the implications sank in and then I felt strangely calm. It was almost a serene moment as I realised my time had come. My mind wandered to the people I had killed and the moment of their passing. I wondered almost idly what dying would feel like. For once I seemed relaxed; the tension of surviving had gone. I was still aware of things going on around me, but it was almost as though I was watching myself from a distance. I remember Price-Thomas pulling on my arm

64

and asking if I was all right, and Boney coming over and licking my hand. As the horses thundered towards us Sergeant Evans issued a string of profane oaths, his normal verbal dexterity having deserted him. Men were running all around me; some seemed to be trying to surrender, others running away and just a few preparing to make a fight of it.

The next trumpet call brought me slightly to my senses. It was the sound of the charge: the lancers were just fifty yards off now and lowering their weapons to the attack. Two were aiming at Price-Thomas and I as we stood rooted to the spot, watching them come on. I could still breathe; the world was not going black as I had expected. Perhaps it would not be the musket ball that kills me after all, I thought. Instinctively I reached down and drew my sword; it just seemed right to die with the weapon in my hand.

The lancer aiming for Price-Thomas was fractionally ahead and I can still recall seeing the horseman grin as he crouched over his weapon, aiming it for the centre of the boy's chest. "Run, boy," I gasped as I remembered a moment not six months ago, when another lance was aimed at my chest. But I was not the only one to remember my encounter last autumn with Polish lancers. Boney had been there too and had been nearly shot for his trouble. He was not a forgiving dog and had always been fond of the young ensign. Now, as he saw the lancer approach, he sprang forward, snarling in anger. A look of alarm crossed the cavalryman's face as the dog was already past the now wavering point of his weapon. Price-Thomas threw himself clear and then there was a blood-curdling yelp. The second lancer, who had been aiming for me, had covered his comrade and impaled the dog on his weapon. I felt a white-hot rage burn inside me as I saw Boney writhing to get free. An Irish wolfhound weighs almost as much as a man and the lancer was struggling to clear his shaft of the dog. I managed to stagger forward a few paces. The lancer must have expected us to run away and did not look round, but I was past running. As the Polish trooper looked to his right to pull the weapon free, his horse turned and brought the rider's left side within my reach. I thrust the razor-sharp sword up under his ribs and into his chest. He shrieked in agony and his back arched in the saddle before his horse reared and pulled the body off my blade.

"Look out!" I heard Price-Thomas cry behind me, but I did not have a chance to look round before my leg was knocked from under me. I twisted as I fell and just had time to see Price-Thomas pulling on the first lancer's arm as he tugged his weapon from my thigh. The lancer simply knocked the boy aside and then tried to get his mount to trample me. The horse was whinnying as it moved above me and seemed to be trying to avoid treading on me, evidently a lot kinder than its master. But as the lancer raked his spurs to urge the animal on to new targets a back hoof caught me around the head and for a moment the world did go black.

I came around to a scene of utter chaos. I had been lying on my side but with a struggle was able to prop myself half up on one elbow. There was a burning pain in my chest, my leg throbbed with a gaping hole in it and now blood started to drip into my left eye from a cut on my head, but at least for now I was still alive. I was in the tideline of bodies from the attack on the second column and twisted around slightly to rest against a French corpse that lay face down in the mud. My blood-stained sword lay beside me and Boney lay whimpering a few yards away, but my attention was elsewhere.

Fifteen-year-old Ensign Edward Price-Thomas stood still amongst running soldiers and charging lancers. As its last officer standing, he was trying to gather the men of the third company. "Rally on me, men," he cried, his voice high in fear and excitement. He was waving his word in the air to get their attention. Incredibly one soldier, Private Temple, tried to respond to his call, but he was cut down from behind by a lancer as he ran to his young officer. Price-Thomas just stood there and called again, unsure what to do next.

"Run away, you bloody fool." I had meant to yell the words, but as I inhaled my chest hurt and it came out as a rasping noise. Price-Thomas must have heard something as he looked at me. I remember seeing the surprise in his eyes that I was still alive. I couldn't shout, but now I had his attention I pointed north towards the rest of the British and Spanish forces and managed to croak, "Run." I twisted around to see if he would make it, but almost instantly realised that he had tragically misunderstood my last command. He had run, but not to escape. Instead he headed straight to a furious fight that was underway around the regimental colours. I groaned. Price-Thomas had been with the regiment nearly all his young life. He had been brought up to believe that these two six-foot square scraps of cloth were the honour of the regiment, to be defended at all costs. As I watched my lifeblood seep into the mud, I could not think of anything less important to die for.

There were half a dozen lancers fighting around the two flags. The capture of an enemy colour would normally result in an instant promotion and fame within the army. I could see the sergeants defending the colours with their spontoons. The weapons were designed to bring down enemy horsemen armed with swords; the Poles, with their longer lance weapons, killed them with impunity. Two ensigns held the actual colours and I saw one killed and the flag taken and held aloft by a jubilant lancer. As the trooper tried to ride away with his prize Price-Thomas got in his horse's way, waving his sword in a futile effort to stop the beast. The ensign did not see the lancer riding behind him or probably even know he was there until the lance went clean through one of his lungs and came out of the front of his chest. The second lancer shook the boy's body off his point to lie in the mud. Beyond him the ensign holding the second colour was cut down, but I saw Lieutenant Latham of the fourth company grabbing the flagstaff from the boy's fingers. Two lancers hacked down at Latham with their swords, but still he tried to wrestle the flag away from them and tear some of the cloth from the pole. Incredibly I saw young Price-Thomas somehow stagger back to his feet; his sword still in his hand. He ran a few steps towards Latham and the fight for the colour before more Polish lancers and their horses blocked my view. When they moved away again both Latham and Price-Thomas lay still in the dirt and a lancer was carrying away the pole of the second colour, still with a strip of the precious cloth attached.

You stupid, brave bastard, I thought as I looked at the boy's corpse in the dirt. I might be a coward but I can recognise courage in others. There are some I have known who have not felt fear, at least not until the last. But young Price-Thomas had been frightened; despite that he had still charged into the fray to do what he thought was his duty.

I looked up into the heavens to utter a prayer for both Price-Thomas and myself, as I did not think it would be long before I joined him. My commune with the Almighty was interrupted by a dog's whimper. I looked down and Boney was struggling to reach me. His back had been damaged and he could not use his rear legs properly, but he was half crawling and half scrabbling across the mud to join me. I reached forward and grabbed him by the collar to pull him the last yard to lie beside me.

The exertion caused more blood to come from the hole in my chest. My already soaked shirt, was now a mixture of red and pink. I put my arm around Boney and held him close. He gave a little whine and rested his head on my shoulder. There was a puddle in the ground between our bodies and I watched as blood from my leg wound mixed in the muddy water with blood from the hole in Boney's side.

I was resigned to dying now and I could not think of better company. The battle still raged, but in the distance. There was no shooting nearby and I leant back against the French corpse and shut my eyes. A few moments later I felt Boney's head come off my shoulder and he uttered a low but ferocious growl. Opening my eyes, I saw that soldiers from the French third column had come over and were now looting the dead and taking what wounded they could move as prisoner. They searched the French bodies as well as the British for any valuables, and I saw a group of French soldiers driving some prisoners back to the French lines beyond the southern end of the ridge. Amongst them were two survivors from my own company.

I heard one French soldier crouch near me and rummage through the pack of the man I was lying against. I did not have the strength or the will to object when he turned his attention to me. He removed a ring from my finger and a pistol from my left coat pocket. I hoped he would not find the gold coins that I kept sewn into my belt for emergencies. When he moved to my right coat pocket Boney growled again and his top lip curled up to show his teeth. The soldier thought twice about it and looked on the ground nearby.

"Where is your sword, *monsieur*?"

It had a gold hilt and was one of the most valuable things I owned, but I could not think where it had gone. The last time I remembered it clearly was when I had stabbed the lancer with it. I just stared at the man, puzzled myself as to its location. He looked around at the other men looting the bodies and must have assumed someone else had taken it. He moved on to find some more corpses to search. Boney lay his head back down on my shoulder and in doing so moved his front paw. Beneath it I saw a glint of gold and realised that the dog must be lying on my sword. He had done me one final service.

I think I passed out then for I do not remember any of the rest of the day. From the fact that I am writing this memoir, you will have concluded that I survived. So I should tell you a little of what I missed, which I gleaned from subsequent accounts. The Poles rampaged through three quarters of Colborne's brigade, effectively destroying three battalions. Of the twenty-seven officers and seven hundred and twenty-eight other ranks that had started the day in the Buffs, only eighty-five unwounded men remained. There were various accounts of the Poles striking down those attempting to surrender and misusing prisoners. They were only stopped when they reached the thirty-first regiment, which was still in a column at the end of the Spanish line. The infantry swiftly formed a square to fight the horsemen off. Even then the Poles were not done and some rampaged behind the Spanish line where they found a group of senior officers including Beresford. One charged our commander, and while he might have been an ineffectual general, Beresford could deal with a lancer. He used his immense strength to pull the man clean off his horse and dash him to the ground, where he was despatched by the bodyguard.

Some units of our cavalry belatedly tried to see off the Poles but soon found that they were facing the masters of cavalry warfare. Each lancer had a little red and white pennon flag at the end of the lance. When I had been disguised as a lancer I had assumed that these were for decoration and recognition. But they had a more lethal purpose. As the two groups of horsemen met, the Poles would wave the flags in the faces of the British mounts, causing them to rear and create confusion in the British lines, just as the lance point moved with the momentum of half a ton of horseflesh into the red-coated ranks.

Both sides then launched fresh infantry attacks, and while I lay supine a battle continued to rage all around me. Another stalemate was achieved, but while Beresford dithered several of his subordinate commanders launched a further assault, which broke the deadlock. By dusk the field was ours, but it was a field thickly carpeted with the dead and dying.

Chapter 9

My next recollection was that night. It was still raining and a thunderstorm was raging over the battlefield. I guessed that it was the flashes of lightning and crashes of thunder that had roused me. For a while I was confused as to where I was. As the memories came slowly back I remembered that I had been dying. The chill of that thought closed around me like a cloak. For a moment I wondered if I was already dead, but after trying to move I decided that I remained with the living. There was still a stabbing pain in my chest and I was shivering with cold. Surely, I reasoned, you would not feel cold and pain when you were dead. Indeed, given the life I had led, if there was a heaven and hell, I was expecting to feel things get too hot rather than too cold.

I could only see out of one eye and, reaching up, I found that dried and congealed blood had sealed the lashes of the other eye shut. With my remaining eye I looked down at Boney in the gloomy darkness of the night and touched his side. He had passed on to whatever afterlife awaited animals. He lay damp and stiff beside me with his head still resting on my shoulder. I gently moved it aside so that I could sit up. My leg had stopped bleeding and I pulled open my shirt and looked at the wound in my chest. There was a ragged hole I could put my little finger in just beneath my ribs on the left side. It hurt me to breathe, but at least I was still breathing. Staring about, I saw that there were many more bodies than I remembered. There was now a dead British infantryman lying across my feet who had not been there before. I slowly realised that the battle must have continued, but I had no idea whether we or the French were victorious.

There was a low, continuous murmur of moans and groans from the wounded, interspersed by the occasional high-pitched shriek or shout for help. Somebody nearby was muttering a prayer in French and in the distance a woman was calling out for someone called George. I was staring down the battlefield to my left when the next flicker of lightning illuminated the scene. If I thought the night had no more horrors left, I was wrong. The first thing I saw was a swathe of naked bodies lying across the battlefield. Their white skin shone in the electric light of the storm. Apart from the odd wicked gash, they had been washed clean by the rain. At first I was puzzled: why would there be naked bodies? No one had fought naked. But the next flash of lightning gave me my answer. At the edge of the naked bodies a line of people was moving. There were men, women and even children in local peasant dress. They had sacks and were systematically stripping the dead. But the thing I remember to this day was that, as the lightning flashed to hold the scene in my memory, a peasant woman was frozen in the act of raising a hammer that she must have been using to quell any resistance from one of her victims.

The indignity of being left a sprawled, naked corpse filled me with more anger than the thought of dying at all. I did not have the strength to use my hidden sword but I remembered the pistol that I had managed to keep in my right-hand coat pocket. I pulled it out. The powder would be soaked but I hoped that the act of pointing and cocking it might deter those intent on making me leave this world in the same undressed state as I had arrived in it. I heard a movement to my right and looked around in that direction. Sure enough another of those harridans was working her way over the bodies. This one was alone, and instead of stripping was reaching down and emptying their pockets, doubtless with a weapon ready if needed. I lay back, hoping she would pass by without touching me, but no, she seemed set to travel along the tidemark of bodies I lay amongst.

She was four bodies away when I moved. I sat up suddenly, gasping at the pain this caused in my chest. I raised the pistol and said hoarsely in Spanish, "I have a pistol. Keep away." To emphasise the point I cocked the weapon.

"Oh! Thank God you are alive, Thomas," cried Lucy Benton. She was in the act of throwing herself into my arms when she stopped, her face frozen in horror. I must have looked a sight, half my face covered in dried blood and gaping holes in my chest and leg. She slowly surveyed my wounds, with her eyes coming back to the hole in my chest. She knew what that meant as well as I. "Oh, my poor Thomas. First Bill and now you."

"I am not dead yet," I grumbled.

"No, of course not, and some pull through from terrible wounds." She tried to sound more cheerful but she was not convincing. "I will stay with you anyway." She paused. "So that you are not alone." The unspoken words 'when you die' hung like lead between us.

"Could you get help?" I asked. "Someone to take me to the surgeons."

"Not now," she replied gently. "The few that are left are just exhausted. They battled all day and have just dropped to sleep where they stopped, even in this storm. They will come back in the morning."

The talk of exhaustion made me realise how tired I was. I had used all my energy to make the challenge with the pistol. The rain still beat down around us and I was shivering slightly with shock, cold or both. I remembered the locals still working their way towards us. "Well, you will not have long to wait if those villagers come over here. I think they kill the wounded who resist being robbed of everything."

Lucy looked over at the line of villagers industriously progressing across the battlefield. "We will see about that," she muttered firmly while reaching into her skirts and withdrawing a dagger that I had not known she carried. She marched across to the villagers, shouting at them in Portuguese. I did not understand all of the words, but the gist was that she would cut their throats if they came anywhere near us and her friends, the soldiers, would hunt down every last one of them. The peasants shouted some reply and, satisfied, Lucy came back. "Don't worry, they won't bother us now."

She busied herself amongst the bodies for a while and I realised that she was making stands of muskets around us. Then she rummaged around, finding blankets tied to packs, and stuck them over the bayonets in the musket stands to make a canopy over me. Finally she lay down beside me under the rudimentary shelter and spread more blankets across us. We talked quietly for a while about the battle. I told her how Price-Thomas had died and asked her to tell his uncle. She told me how the battle had been won and held me close. Even though we were both soaked through, slowly I began to feel some warmth.

I must have fallen asleep again for it was dawn when I awoke, a dead dog under one arm and a pretty living girl on the other. As I watched the sun slowly creeping up into the sky, I began to think that if I had lived this long, perhaps I would not die of these wounds after all. It had finally stopped raining and some soldiers were slowly picking their way over the battlefield, looking for comrades and chasing off any of the villagers still working in the daylight. Eventually Lucy saw two men she knew from the Buffs and called them over.

"Take my sword to Lieutenant Hervey and ask him to look after it for me," I told her. "It is hidden under Boney."

A few minutes later I was hoisted up on a stretcher made, ironically, from a broken lance fed through the sleeves of several uniform coats. It was only as I was carried across the battlefield that I realised the true scale of the carnage. The ground was covered with mostly naked white bodies for hundreds of yards. It was estimated that over eight thousand men had died, with at least as many wounded. I remember seeing three wounded and naked men who had dragged themselves to a shallow trench in the mud, probably made by a cannon ball. It had filled with water during the night and they were drinking from the puddle to satisfy their thirst. I was grateful to Lucy, who had found me a canteen to drink from during the night.

My stretcher bearers carried me down to the chapel in the village where the surgeons had set up their dressing station, but I was not seen by a surgeon. One of their assistants had a brief glance at my chest and directed the men carrying me to an open yard behind the church. There I was left with hundreds of other seriously wounded men. Officers were put alongside the wall out of the wind; even near to death rank had its privileges. The rest of the men were laid out all over the yard. There were shocking injuries all about me: chests flayed open by shot, stomachs cut open by bayonets, a head half smashed by a musket butt. The stench of fouled bodies made me gag when I first arrived, but I soon ceased to notice it. What I did see, though, was that hardly anyone from this yard was taken into the church where I thought the surgeons would be operating. Instead padres roamed amongst the prone men with pocket books, taking down last requests, while half a dozen men were fully occupied taking the recently deceased out of the yard to make room for more seriously injured coming in. Finally I realised that this was the open-air equivalent of something I had heard about after earlier battles, a 'death room'. Surgeons, or their assistants, would put those that were beyond hope in a quiet space, where they could pass away in peace. That freed up time to deal with those that they thought they could save. Well, dammit; I was not ready to die yet.

Eventually I managed to catch the attention of one of the passing padres.

"What is it, my boy?" he asked solemnly. "Would you like to pass on a message for a loved one?"

"No, I would like you to fetch Surgeon Price for me." Price was Ensign Price-Thomas's uncle.

"The surgeons are far too busy dealing with the injured to be interrupted now," exclaimed the padre, sounding slightly indignant at the very idea.

I gritted my teeth to stay calm for a moment. Getting angry would not help and I did not have the strength to box his ears. "You may have noticed that I am a little injured myself," I said acidly, but then I thought I would be better served to play on his Christian heartstrings.

"I was with Price's nephew when he died," I explained, trying to adopt a look of God-fearing piety. "He was only fifteen, and as he prepared to meet his maker he begged me as a charity to speak to his uncle for him. With his last ounce of strength he made me give an oath that I would do so." I was wringing my hands at this point like a proper Christian martyr. "He insisted it was the only way he could pass into heaven with a clear conscience. I beg you, sir, let me fulfil the boy's dying wish." It was of course errant bosh – poor Price-Thomas had died alone with at least one lance driven clean through him – but the padre did not know that. The Bible thumper was positively wiping his eye when I had finished and he assured me that he would do my bidding at once.

I sank back against the stone and shut my eyes in relief. In what seemed no time at all a voice was calling out, "Captain Flashman." I looked up and in front of me there was a vaguely familiar cove in a blood-soaked apron with more bloodstains up his arms to his shoulders. The padre also hovered nearby to overhear the conversation. "Lieutenant Hervey has already told me what you…" The newcomer paused before continuing. "… and your dog did to save young Edward. I am much obliged to you. The padre says you have a message for me."

I looked at the padre, who leaned in close to hear the message and nodded at me encouragingly. "Thank you, Padre," I murmured. "If we could have a little privacy…"

"Of course, of course," replied the padre, looking crestfallen and moving away.

I looked the surgeon in the eye and asked quietly, "This is a dying room, isn't it?"

He glanced around briefly at those nearby to check that they were not listening and then slowly nodded.

"Well, I am not ready to die. I want to be looked at by a surgeon."

"What was the message from Edward?" asked Price sternly.

"He declared you were the best damn surgeon he knew and that if I was ever wounded I should ask for you." For a moment I thought Price was going to walk away, but then a sad grin crossed his face.

"I very much doubt he did say that, Captain Flashman, but Edward did speak warmly about you. So for his sake I will examine you. It is only the chest wound that matters; the rest can be healed."

He got down on one knee beside me. I expected him to probe or prod the hole, but instead he moved his head towards my chest and smelt it. He gave a grunt of approval and made me lean forward so that he could smell the entry wound too. "The ball does not seem to have punctured your bowel, and it has missed your ribs. What about breathing – are you coughing up blood?" I assured him I wasn't. "Well, it seems you are in the wrong place after all," he stated at length. Then he beckoned some stretcher bearers and I was carried into the chapel.

I will spare you a detailed description of that charnel house, but after one glance at the buckets of severed limbs and the sweating, screaming bodies tied down to one of the four tables in use, I began to wonder if I had been better outside after all. I joined a queue on stretchers of those waiting to be treated and can honestly say it was one of the most terrifying half hours of what had already been a colourful life.

In battle there was always the chance you would escape unscathed, but waiting there you knew that in a short while you would be hauled up onto one of the blood-soaked doors resting on barrels that served as operating tables in this primitive field hospital. Anyone who tells you that he lay there like a gentleman and had a civilised conversation while his leg was sawn off is a lying bastard. By that point the surgical brandy to numb the pain had long since been used up, as had any opiates. The assistants were exhausted, like the surgeons, and instead of trying to hold down the struggling victims, they had taken to lashing them firmly to the table before proceedings started. Even then the poor devils under the knife thrashed about. I saw one fellow, mad with pain, get a cudgel to the head for his trouble. As he slumped unconscious it seemed a kindness.

By the time my turn came I was gibbering with terror and trying to drag myself back out of the door I had schemed so hard to enter.

"That one next," intoned a tired young man, pointing in my direction.

"I am feeling a little better," I called back hopefully. "Why don't you look at someone else?"

The assistants took no notice and in a moment I was deposited none too gently on the gore-stained planks. Close to I saw that the surgeon, despite the tired eyes and blood-spattered cheek, looked no older than me. He was by far the youngest of the surgeons present and I cursed my luck to get the least experienced man.

"George Guthrie," he introduced himself and held out his reddened fingers. As I reached out a hand to shake it, one of his assistants passed a rope across my chest to start securing me to the table.

"Thomas Flashman." I had started to return the greeting automatically but then as the rope tightened across my chest and my mind flashed to what could follow I began to panic. "No, please," I begged as I struggled to get up.

Guthrie was already surveying my wounds with a practised eye. I found out later that despite his youth Guthrie was the chief medical officer there, having been apprenticed to a surgeon when he was just fourteen. "Belay the rope, John," he said calmly to his assistant. "I might need to turn the captain over." Already his hand was passing over my head and feeling the wound to my scalp. "A nasty cut, but no damage to the skull."

"What is he doing with that blade?" I asked, my voice rising in fear as John, the assistant, moved towards my leg holding a knife he had pulled from his belt.

The answer was accompanied by a ripping fabric sound as Guthrie explained: "Don't worry, he is just cutting the trouser away from your leg so that I can see the wound."

I winced as the blood-soaked cloth was torn away, taking with it some scabs around the hole in my leg. I could not see the actual wound as it was on the back of my thigh but it felt wet, as though it was bleeding again.

"Would you like to sit up so that John can remove your coat and shirt without need of the knife?"

"Thank you." I sensed Guthrie watching me carefully as I struggled to sit up. He did not help but looked closely at how easily I could move different parts of my body. "It is a silk shirt," I explained. "Bloody expensive but I save it for battles. I have heard that silk stays in one piece in a wound, reducing infection – is that right?" The assistant was now reaching for the coat I had shrugged off and was helping me lift the blood-stained shirt over my head.

"That is indeed correct, Captain," agreed Guthrie with a half amused smile. "Unfortunately it is not as good as linen for bandages." As he spoke I heard more ripping of fabric and turned to see the grinning John running his knife straight down the back of my shirt.

"What the devil?"

"I am sorry, Captain," replied Guthrie, "we have long since run out of bandages. But don't worry, you will get your shirt back. And it is not for everyone to leave here bandaged in silk. Now let's have a look at what we have." He bent down to examine closely the star-shaped exit wound on my chest and went through the smelling ritual again. Quite how either surgeon could smell anything with the surrounding stink of blood, guts and shit was beyond me. "You have quite good movement, Captain, the wound smells clean and you are not coughing up blood. You will need some stiches to hold this wound together but let's turn you over."

Between them Guthrie and his assistant helped me to turn over on the broken door table. I felt even more vulnerable face down as I was not able to see what they were doing. I felt Guthrie feeling my leg wound first.

"Just muscle damage," he intoned. "You will need more stitches. You are lucky he missed the bone and the major blood vessels."

I did not feel lucky a moment later when I felt an agonising stabbing pain in my back. I reared up but the assistant pushed me back down firmly on the board.

"What are you doing? That bloody hurt!" I cried out as my cheek was pressed into the blood-stained wood.

"I was just using a probe to pull out some of your jacket that had been carried into the hole by the musket ball. It had scabbed into the wound. I cannot find any of your silk shirt so we must hope that it was carried out with the ball. I just need to cauterise a couple of blood vessels and then we can stitch and bandage you up. Can you lie still for that or do we need to tie you down?"

I lay still, holding my breath when told and sweating as I felt the heat of the cauterising iron move across my back. There was a sharp pain and a sizzling sound as it was used but I did not dare move a fraction of an inch with red-hot metal so close to my insides. Guthrie then put some stitches in my leg and chest and with his assistant started to bandage me in strips of my expensive silk.

"You have been remarkably lucky, Captain Flashman. The ball missed your spine and ribs and seems to have passed between your lungs and your guts, doing little damage to either. Even your liver seems to have escaped its path." I felt a huge surge of relief until he added, "If you can avoid infection, you might just live, but with such deep wounds that won't be easy." While such a diagnosis might seem grim, compared to the imminent death I had been expecting just hours before, it was a big improvement.

"Thank you, Doctor," I said, shaking his hand again.

77

But already his eye was moving to the crowd of men waiting on the floor. "That one next," he called as I stood up from the table.

I still had one good leg and with my improved prognosis felt a lot better than I did before. I thought I could hobble out of the chapel on my own, but quickly discovered that I was as weak as a kitten, probably due to loss of blood. Another orderly helped me put my coat back over my now bandaged chest and guided me out and into a different yard. This one was full of other patients with dressed wounds who had been judged worth saving. Most, like me, were still plastered with caked blood and filthy, but we were alive and we had hope of recovery. I did not want to lie down in the mud and so sat myself on a low section of wall with my bandaged leg stretched out in front of me. A weak sun was shining down and I closed my eyes and turned my face towards it. I felt its warmth on my face and stared at its gold glow through my eyelids, spending a moment relishing the simple joy of just being alive.

Chapter 10

"Captain Flashman, are you all right?" I opened my eyes and there gazing down at me was Lieutenant Hervey. "Well, I can see you are not all right, but er... well, at least you are on this side of the church." He paused, looking embarrassed, and then added in almost a whisper, "They told me you had been taken to the other yard and I have been searching for you there."

"I have been better," I told him, "but at least I am alive. How are you, Richard?" I don't think I had ever used Hervey's first name before, but this did not seem the time to be formal. He was still in the clothes he had fought in, but one sleeve of his coat was empty with the missing arm across his chest in a sling.

"I broke my arm." He took a deep breath and struggled to keep his emotions in check as he sat down heavily on the wall beside me. "It is bloody awful, sir. Apart from us there are only two unwounded survivors of our company: Sergeant Evans and Private Harrison. Most of the rest are dead or taken prisoner. I should have stayed with the rest of you. Others fought with broken arms and worse. They found most of the regimental colour on Latham's body and he had defended it with just one arm."

I had seen this before of course; survivor guilt they call it. I did not feel the slightest guilt for surviving and if Hervey had come seeking sympathy, well, he was knocking at the wrong door. "If you had stayed then the chances are you would now be dead and it would not have changed a damn thing. You would have been just one more naked corpse up on the hill. Anyway the general ordered you back; you had no choice."

"Did my uncle really refuse to form a defensive line against the horsemen, because he did not have orders?" asked Hervey quietly.

"Yes, but it was probably too late then anyway. Was he killed or captured?" I asked, thinking that there was a man I would not miss.

"He survived. He is back in the camp now, organising supplies and burials. General Stewart made it back too."

Mention of camp reminded me that whatever comforts I had were there, including clean clothes and, more importantly, food. My rumbling stomach pointed out that I had not eaten since breakfast the previous day, and that had been interrupted by the start of the battle. Field hospitals then had no notion of what they call nursing now. They cut you, bandaged you and then left you to be looked after by your comrades. At most you might get an orderly doing a round with a bucket of water and a cup. There were three carts roaming the battlefield collecting the wounded for treatment and taking those that had been treated back to their camps. I managed to get a lift on one to where the remnants of the Buffs were gathered.

Instead of a mood of devastation there was a mixture of grief and hope in the camp, and to my surprise six members of my company welcomed me back.

"Welcome back, sir." Sergeant Evans greeted me with a broad smile. "We are 'resurrectionists'. Our numbers keep increasing from those thought dead or missing." Evans led me to a camp chair that had been set by the fire. "Would you like some food, sir?" Cooking on ramrod spits over the fire was the traditional post-battle *plat du jour*: horse, of which there was a plentiful supply. I noticed that the fire underneath had at some point had been fed with musket stocks as I could see barrels and locks amongst the cinders.

"I thought that only two had made it back," I queried, gazing at the extra men sitting with their women and children around the fire.

"They were taken prisoner but escaped, sir," replied Evans. He was about to say more but a woman's voice interrupted him.

"Our boys saw more of our men taken as prisoner, sir, so more might escape and come back." I looked around. It was Nelly Morris, whose man was still missing. She sat with her young daughter on her lap and a gleam of hope in her eyes. Other women missing their men murmured agreement but for others there was just a look of sadness.

"We heard about Mr Price-Thomas, sir," continued Evans. "We will start digging a grave tomorrow." He looked at Nelly. "We might have more men to help then."

The same scene must have played out countless times after my previous battles in the peninsular, I reflected as I chewed on the meat. But being a staff officer, I was insulated. There were no wives and children in the 'family' of staff officers. While we had casualties, they were only a handful at a time and often due to the reckless bravery of some young blood trying to make a name for himself. But this battle had been a mismanaged disaster from the outset. The more I thought about it, the angrier I got. There was Beresford who dithered rather than make decisions; Stewart who was brave but reckless; and King who even when danger was staring him in the face would not react without orders. They had all bloody well survived while thousands of poor sods under their command had died due to their incompetence. It was only when I fought with someone else in command that I really appreciated the cautious but decisive nature of Wellington as a general.

"I hope they are not our muskets you are burning, Sergeant?" I asked.

"No, sir, these are French ones. We have a stack of them. They were easier to gather than firewood when the men were tired."

"Have you checked they were unloaded?"

"Not yet, sir. We thought we did last night but two went off, firing into the mud."

I looked around; Lieutenant Hervey was some yards away talking to one of the newly returned men. "Well, pile on some more and point them in that direction," I murmured. I gestured towards Major King's tent just twenty yards away in the much-reduced Buffs' camp.

"What if one goes off, sir?" whispered Evans.

"Then it will be a tragic accident," I said grimly.

As it turned out three were loaded and one shot went through the major's tent and smashed his commode. My only regret was that he was not sitting on it at the time.

I must have eaten a good amount of horse that day and red wine appeared from somewhere. When I retired that evening to my tent I was feeling a lot better. My wounds still ached but nothing more than that. Lucy came to me that night; with everything that had happened it did not seem to matter now if she was seen. She gently bathed my wounds with hot water and cleaned me up so that I looked a lot more respectable in fresh clothes the next morning. Evans was right: by ten o'clock the company had increased to a dozen men with more escaped prisoners. But Private Morris was not among them.

I left them to dig the grave near where the company had been destroyed. With the aid of a stick I hobbled back over the battleground late in the afternoon for the burial ceremony. There were still mounds of bodies lying around, probably unclaimed French ones, but as they were all naked it was hard to say. Even two days after the battle, survivors were still being found.

I found the men gathered about a shallow grave, just three feet deep. It was a long, wide trench for a dozen men to dig, especially as several of them were carrying wounds and they only had three shovels. We had heard wolves during the night and I did not doubt that many of the graves would be opened by animals once the army had moved on. The dead men lay in a long row, two still dressed and the rest now naked. Price-Thomas's little white body lay at the end, a red gaping hole in his chest and what looked like a sabre cut across his shoulder and neck. At least he would not have suffered long with wounds like that, I thought. Then I saw what lay beside the boy. Boney's body had also been lifted down into the trench and lay with his head on the boy's shoulder as he had died with his head on mine.

"We thought that the dog would keep the lad company, sir," pronounced Evans. "The padre doesn't like it but he stopped complaining when we told him it was your dog and what it had done to try to save the life of the boy."

The padre went quickly through the formal service; it must have been one of many he had done that day. I cannot remember any of it beyond staring at the two bodies at the end of the row. A young boy and a dog lying dead together, when they should both have been running happily through some field. I kept remembering the two of them leaning against each other for warmth just a few moments before they were killed. It just seemed a bloody waste and affected me far more than all the other deserving men in the row. There was plenty of weeping over the others, though, with women and children taking a last look at husbands and fathers before they were covered with earth. Among them was the young Spanish widow of Private Carter with her three young children clutched about her, while Nelly Morris still stared hopefully at the southern horizon.

Once the brief service was over, the men moved forward to fill in their trench. I turned away and caught a glimpse of Sally and smiled at her. I had to try to cheer myself up; I still had a lot to be grateful for. As if on cue Hervey appeared and grabbed my arm.

"I have good news, sir."

"Has your uncle sat on his broken commode?"

Hervey grinned. "No and he is still annoyed over the men's carelessness. It is about Lieutenant Latham, sir. He has been found alive."

"But I thought he was dead? Did they not find the colour on his corpse?"

"It seems that they did not notice he was still alive. He came around last night and managed to drag himself down to a stream for a drink. He had been stripped while unconscious, but he was recognised and taken to the hospital. They say he is in a bad way but that he might live."

"You have checked properly that these are all dead, haven't you?" I asked, pointing at the bodies that were now being covered over. Hervey nodded. "Thank God or Evan's claim that we are resurrectionists will really come home to roost."

I had felt fine all that day, and while the chest wound had bled a little I had taken it for granted that I was on the mend. But that evening I came down with a fever. Lucy looked after me for the first two days, but as I got worse Hervey had me taken back to the field hospital. My chest wound was infected and I was sent by wagon with other wounded the seven miles to the nearest hospital in the town of Valverde.

I came as close to dying then as I think I ever did. I drifted in and out of consciousness and my memories of the next few weeks are hazy at best. Some things that I think I can recall definitely did not happen. For example I hallucinated Wellington, naked but for a flowery dressing gown, writing down detailed instructions for Beresford on how to put on his trousers. Other incidents might have occurred. I recall Lucy sitting beside me and weeping at one point, although if she did visit I never saw her again. One thing, though, definitely did take place, and of all the horrors I had seen in Spain, and you must admit I have witnessed my share, this above all the others is seared in my consciousness. Even now I cannot think of it without clamping my legs together with sufficient force to crack a walnut between my knees.

Two orderlies at Valverde hospital had been carrying me on a stretcher when they were called to help a surgeon with a patient. They put me down on the floor and moved into an adjacent room, leaving the door open so that I could see everything. Initially there was just a forest of moving legs, but eventually my fever-addled braid realised that there were four men trying to get a fifth, who was naked from the waist down, up onto a table. The patient seemed fit and able and was shouting that he had changed his mind, given what followed, who could blame him. As his pleas and begging had no effect, the man started fighting like fury, but eventually the four men overcame him and got him up on the table. They started to strap him down and I saw that there were vertical planks at the end of the short table that they strapped his thighs to. The poor devil was crying and pleading now, offering his tormentors money if they would only let him go, but they took no notice. I wondered in horror if they were going to geld him, and realised that with the business end pointed at me I was going to reluctantly get a ringside view of whatever happened next. I turned away so as not to watch, but found myself drawn back in fascination a moment later. The whimpering had stopped but only because they had jammed a leather pad in his mouth. Then the surgeon leaned forward and made a two-inch cut between his balls and his arsehole. The patient screamed in pain, spitting out the pad, but that was nothing to the primal shriek he gave when the surgeon plunged a couple of his fingers into the wound.

"Hold him still, Ferrers, for God's sake," shouted the surgeon as his patient writhed about despite the tight strapping that bound him. "I think I felt it," he added, withdrawing his fingers as two of the orderlies lay their bodies on top of the patient to restrain him. As his victim continued to shriek, the surgeon plunged his fingers in again, seeming to rummage around with them like a miser chasing the last coin in his purse. I think I passed out after that as I don't remember any more until I woke up in a cot and found the poor sod I had seen operated on lying in the next bed. He was sweating and whimpering in his sleep.

The next morning Guthrie was doing a tour of the hospital. When he reached my bed I asked him about the man still lying unconscious beside me.

"Why do you ask?" enquired Guthrie as he efficiently examined my injuries.

"I saw him being operated on. The orderlies with me had to help hold him down."

"Ahh." Guthrie grinned. "Bit shocking when you first see that one, isn't it?" Without waiting for an answer he continued: "That is Cartwright's kidney stone patient."

"Kidney stones. Are they fatal?" I asked.

"Not immediately, but they are very painful." His keen eyes looked into mine. "If you are alert enough to be interested in such things then I think you are ready to be moved to Lisbon. You can complete your recuperation there."

Three days later I was loaded onto a wagon train for Lisbon. By then Cartwright's patient had died of infection and I had made a decision: if I ever suffer from kidney stones, I will wait until the pain becomes unbearable and then, rather than submit to that surgery, I will blow my brains out with a pistol.

Chapter 11

The passage to Lisbon would have been torture for a fit man, never mind one who had already been injured. I joined another one hundred and seventy wounded men in a convoy of ramshackle bullock carts. The only reason I survived that journey was because I was able to walk some of the way. It was the most miserable expedition I ever endured. The worst cases were laid in the bottom of the carts where their groans and wails as the vehicles bumped over the pitted roads, jarring wounds and fractures, were only partly drowned out by the continuous screech of badly greased wheels. Others, like me, were put on stretchers laid over the sides of the cart. This gave some protection from the jolting but left us exposed to the baking sun. Every so often the end of a stretcher would vibrate its way off the edge of the cart and drop us onto the wounded below.

I was one of the fortunate ones in that I had some mobility and tried to walk a mile or so each day to strengthen my weakened thigh muscles, which gradually started to improve. My head wound was healing nicely but the hole in my chest still seeped blood. It gave me the most pain, particularly when the cart bounced over deep ruts.

Each morning the carts would be searched and invariably there would be half a dozen bodies to bury before we got going. After enduring this for a week I began to wonder if there would be any of us left alive by the time we reached Lisbon. I still had some gold sewn into my belt and decided that I would do better recuperating in some quiet Portuguese town on my own. What clinched it was the sight of pretty young thing passing round a jug of cold well water at one town we stopped at.

"Would you like to earn some gold?" I asked her in Spanish.

"How would I do that, *señor?*" she asked, passing an appraising eye over me. Dirty and unshaven, I was not at my best, but I flatter myself that she saw the potential. There was certainly a flicker of interest in that knowing smile she shot back.

But then some grizzled old man was at her shoulder, asking her what she was about. He glared angrily between the girl and me. "What do you want with my daughter?" he growled. Then his eyes saw the three gold coins in my hand and his expression darkened even further. "Do you think my girl is some common whore that you can buy, you dog?" he roared at me, lunging forward and grabbing hold of my shirt.

"No," I shouted back in Spanish. "Look at me, I am in no state to enjoy a woman." The fist he had swung back hesitated as he surveyed my blood-stained shirt with the bloodier bandage underneath and the cloth tied around my leg. "I am going to die if I stay jolting on this cart," I explained. "I want somewhere I can stay for a month to recover in peace and quiet."

His eyes swung between my imploring face, the coins in my palm, his daughter and then back to me. He licked his lips as he weighed up the risk of letting a strange wounded man under the same roof as his precious daughter and what he could buy with the gold. "One month, *señor*, and then you go," he declared finally. I nodded and he held out a hand for the coins. Once he had them, he reached into the cart and picked me up as easily as a mother taking a babe from a cot. Only then did I realise the huge strength of the man. I was thin, having lost a lot of weight while ill, but he carried me with no effort at all. Given his initial suspicions, I decided against demonstrating that I could walk a short distance without undue difficulty.

He told me that the village was called Arraiolos. It was a poor place with a broken-down castle up on a hill. He walked down a side street and put me down on a bench outside a large cottage and went to speak to a woman feeding some chickens in the yard. Looking around, I saw that the house had a forge in an open-sided shed at the end of the building. It seemed that my new host was the village blacksmith. Already I could hear the sound of the cart wheels screeching on to the next stop in their journey and as the sound receded a sense of relaxation spread over my weary bones. I lay back and shut my eyes until I felt the bench shift slightly and creak as someone sat beside me.

"Do you come from Britain?" the daughter asked. "What is it like?"

I smiled at her open curiosity and opened my mouth to reply. But before a sound passed my lips the woman's voice yelled from the yard beyond. "Maria del Pilar, you come away from that man this instant. You are never to go near him again."

The girl hesitated just long enough to demonstrate some free will before she obeyed. She smiled at me and whispered as she moved away, "I will see you again soon, *señor*." I just grinned for at that moment I really did not have the strength for any amorous pursuit.

In any event her hopes of seeing me soon seemed destined to be unfulfilled as the old man came back and scooped me up and carried me into the cottage. We went through the kitchen and then through the room that served as their bedroom into another bedroom beyond.

There I was laid on a low, narrow bed that I guessed was the daughter's. The old man picked up a dresser of clothes and carried that back out of the door to wherever in the cottage the daughter was now going to sleep. It was the first proper bed I had laid on in weeks and within minutes I was asleep.

I stayed tucked up in that bed for two days, interrupted only by the woman with bowls of delicious soup and bread and use of the jakes pot on a chair in the corner. Occasionally I tried to make pictures from the cracks and stains in the low ceiling that hung over the bed, but for the most part I just enjoyed the peace and relaxation. I even managed to sleep through the loud snoring of the couple in the next room each night and the distant clanging of metal sometimes heard during the day.

On the third morning, though, I decided it was time to get up and stretch my legs. After the wife had brought bread for breakfast, I swung my legs over the side of the bed and staggered a little unsteadily to the door. My chest had not bled for a day and was feeling much better, but my legs needed to start regaining their strength. I walked through the empty bedroom next door and into the kitchen. That was also deserted, but I noticed that a bed had been set up in a store room on the other side of the kitchen. Moving to the outside door, I could see the woman and the daughter working in the fields, but a clanging nearby told me that the blacksmith was at work. I walked slowly outside the cottage and round to the forge.

"You can walk then." The smith nodded at me as he pushed tongs containing some metal back into the glowing coals.

"Yes, I took a lance in the leg at Albuera but it did not break the bone. I was shot through the chest too."

"You were lucky; two men from the village died there fighting." He paused, eyeing me over, before he added, "Any man who kills the French is all right by me, provided he keeps his hands off my daughter."

"I can assure you, sir..." I began, but he cut me off.

"I will only say this once," he growled. "The girl is innocent and pure and I will not have her corrupted. I will geld any man who lays a finger on her and I will do it with my hammer." To reinforce the point he plunged his tongs back into the coals and brought out a glowing orange bolt the size of a man's cock. He put it on the anvil and spoke to me above the sound of the ringing hammer as sparks sprayed from the metal. Clang. "I hope…" Clang. "… we understand…" Clang. "… each other."

I watched, transfixed, as the glowing metal was slowly flattened from the rhythmic beating. As the size of the metal stretched I felt my manhood shrink. The thought of that hammer and red-hot metal anywhere near me did not bear thinking about. "I can assure you, sir," I tried again, "that I just want to get well and get back to the army." I meant it too. I was cut off and alone in that village, and while the girl was pretty, she was not worth the risk.

"Aye, well, just so we are clear. There is a razor and a metal bowl over there," he said, pointing to the corner of the forge. "You can warm some water in the coals to shave, and if you are fit enough, you can help work the bellows."

For the next week or so I helped out with some light work in the forge. Mostly I worked the bellows with either my arm or, using a rope loop, with my legs. I liked the old man. It was through him that I learned of the battle between Wellington and Massena at Fuentes de Oñoro. Like Albuera it had been inconclusive, leaving both armies in a state of stalemate on either side of the Portuguese border. The allies held the fortresses on the Portuguese side while the French held the Spanish ones, and neither side seemed to have the will or resources to displace the other. The smith did not care what happened in Spain; he was just concerned that the French would not invade Portugal again. He told me that during the last French occupation of the region he had sent his wife and daughter into the hills, with many of the other women from the town. "The French tortured and hanged plenty of men from here, but they left me alone. I was too useful for repairing weapons and shoeing horses."

Slowly, as the days passed, I felt my strength coming back. The wife washed my clothes while I borrowed some of her husband's, and with a daily shave I felt I was on the mend. When you look better you often feel better too. I cut myself a suitable walking stick and took to having an afternoon stroll through the village and a glass of wine at the tavern.

Wherever possible I tried to avoid the daughter, and as her parents were of the same mind it did not prove difficult. For several days she was sent away to visit an aunt. It was the day after she returned that things got more complicated. As I came back from my regular afternoon walk I heard a splashing sound from her little room off the kitchen. Instinctively I turned to look and found her washing with the door open. She still had a shift on but it was wet and stuck to her in all the right places. She gave me a coquettish, knowing smile and I realised that the minx had planned the encounter. My mouth went dry as I looked on and tried to remember when I had last been with a woman. Sally Benton seemed a distant memory and I heard a low growl of desire come from the back of my throat. But my thoughts were interrupted by the sound of dull clanging coming from the forge outside. My ardour cooled like a red-hot rivet being plunged into a bucket of water. "Apologies, ma'am," I mumbled before turning back out of the door.

My hands were shaking slightly as I reached the well outside for a drink. By God I needed a woman, but not that one. I was fond of my manhood unflattened. There was a wench in the tavern who might oblige and I resolved to ply her with brandy and try her out on my next visit.

I took my supper in my room that evening. If the daughter was willing to play dangerous games like that, I did not want to give the father any grounds for suspicion. I lay awake later that night listening to the old boy snore in the next room, but for me sleep would not come. Every time I tried to doze my mind would conjure the image of the girl with her wet shift clinging to her most delicious breasts.

When I first heard the noise I assumed it was a mouse or rat scurrying above the plastered ceiling. Then I heard the joists creak above me. Someone was in the attic, and as the snoring from the old man and his wife continued, I could guess who it was.

I stared at the now familiar cracks above my head. Candle light started to shine through three of them that made a triangle shape in the ceiling. Then the centre of the triangle moved to create a hole in the roof. The glow from a candle in the attic illuminated a pair of shapely naked legs that dangled through the hole. They were followed by a rope that was slowly lowered to the floor. Maria de Pilar slipped down the rope with practised ease as I swung my legs out of the bed.

"What are you doing?" I whispered hoarsely. It was a stupid question and one that she did not bother answering with words. Her left hand dropped to my shoulder where I still sat on the side of the bed while she bent down and moved her lips down onto mine to still any further enquiries. My body reacted automatically, my left arm around her waist while my right moved up to cup one of those splendid bouncers. Her tongue darted into my mouth, giving further confirmation that the daughter was not nearly as innocent as her father believed. Any lingering doubts were gone a moment later when her right hand disappeared underneath my nightshirt. In a moment she had demonstrated that she certainly knew how to raise more than just my spirits.

I gave a low groan of pleasure and she stopped kissing me long enough to whisper in my ear, "You must not make any noise or my father will hear you." Those words gave me momentary alarm but a second's listening proved that the snoring in the next room was just as loud as ever. Whether the briefest thought of her father had caused me to flag I don't know, but now her mouth moved down my body. Her tongue could do things that would have earned her a fortune in a Parisian brothel and I was left gasping in silent delight.

She was an artisan of lovemaking, such that I had not experienced since my days in India. Just when I thought I could bear it no longer she pushed me back on the bed and climbed astride me. How I did not burst my chest wound stitches in the next few minutes is beyond me. If Albuera had taken me to the seventh pit of hell then Maria del Pilar took me to the seventh circle of ecstasy as compensation. She might have been the daughter of a blacksmith, but she was a master craftswoman in her own right.

I was gasping for air as she finished, the blood still rushing in my ears. I strained to listen, and despite the noise we had been making, the snoring in the next room went on with the same regular rhythm.

"How did you know about the hole in the ceiling?" I whispered.

"Silly, I made it months ago when this was my room so that I could go out and see some of the boys in the village." I grinned in the darkness. "What are you smiling for?"

"Those boys you were with before," I told her. "I feel sorry for them. Wherever they go in the world, being in bed with a woman is likely to be a disappointment after being with you."

She purred with pleasure at the compliment. "You have been to many countries?" she asked.

"Yes, quite a few. In India they have temples to the art of lovemaking. You could be a high priestess over there."

"I have only been in this village and the surrounding towns. My father made me live in the hills when the French came. I want to travel and visit different countries. Will you take me to Britain and this place called India?"

I grinned and patted her shoulder. "We'll see," I said in the same tone you might use on a child asking for something that you had no intention of giving them. But Maria del Pilar was not going to be fobbed off like a child, as I was to discover later.

We lay in each other's arms for most of that night, before Maria disappeared up her rope and back to her own room. The next morning we studiously avoided each other, assisted in that purpose by her parents, who were clearly oblivious to our earlier liaison.

So began one of the most pleasurable months of my life. During the day I would rest in the sun and take gentle exercise, walking or helping the old man in his forge with the bellows. In the evening an angel would drop from the heavens and take me to paradise. My strength slowly recovered and as it did so we became more adventurous in that tiny bedroom. I recalled various colourful Indian temple freezes and we carried out our own re-enactments, all without making a sound. In fact I got so used to silent lovemaking that when I was next in a brothel the girl complained that I showed her no appreciation. We were fortunate that her parents were heavy sleepers and only once did we wake them. Maria was doing something exquisite with her fingers while I took her from behind and I let out an involuntary howl of pleasure.

"*Señor* Flashman," called her mother, knocking quietly at the door. "Are you all right?"

The door was less than a yard away from where her daughter was bent over the end of the bed receiving the Flashy one-gun salute. I am proud to say that I did not even break my rhythm as I quietly moved one foot in front of the door while I whispered back, "I am sorry I woke you, ma'am. I have cramp in my wounded leg. I am just doing some exercises to loosen the muscles. Best not come in as I am naked."

"I am sorry you are hurt, *señor*," called back the trusting mother. "Exercise as much as you want."

"Thank you, ma'am," I replied, grabbing hold of her daughter's hips and pulling them towards me. "I am sure what I am doing will bring relief."

Of course I was getting over-confident, a state which normally presages disaster. But there was no sign of imminent calamity the next morning when I helped the smith with the bellows. In fact quite the reverse.

"My wife tells me you were in in pain last night," he said between pounding a horseshoe.

91

"Oh, it was nothing, just the old wound settling down," I replied jovially, patting the fast-healing injury in my thigh.

"I am sorry I did not hear you. I am a little deaf after all these years hammering metal." He grinned as he plunged a new horseshoe in a bucket of water. As it hissed and steamed he flexed his huge shoulders. "I have a bottle of muscle liniment if you need it. You are welcome to borrow some. I have to say that I have enjoyed having you here much more than I thought. You are an honourable man and have stayed well clear of Maria. My wife thinks that she has a new boy in the village as she has been very distracted lately."

"Well, you know what young boys are like," I replied airily, happy to deflect suspicion in a new direction. "I have enjoyed staying here too. In fact I was wondering if we could extend our agreement? I have another two coins I could give you."

The smith agreed to a second month without any difficulty at all and so I happily continued my time of daily and nightly exercise. I am bound to say that the liniment worked well too. It stung like a whip stroke, but it had a powerful alcohol in it that brought heat deep within my thigh and the muscle seemed to get stronger by the day.

Chapter 12

It was midway through the second month that things started to unravel. Too much of anything can become tiresome after a while, and Maria was starting to get tedious. It was not so much the lovemaking, which was as creative as usual, but the whispered conversations afterwards. The girl was obsessed with leaving the village. She was constantly nagging at me to help her get away. To get a few days' peace I had even suggested to her mother that if a boy in the village was getting a bit forward, taking her away for a couple of days might be a good idea. But before that scheme could be put in to action Maria launched a plan of her own.

We were lying on my narrow bed after a bout of fornication that would have earned her a standing ovation at Mrs Belmont's House of Pleasure in Piccadilly when she ruined the mood.

"I have not had my monthly bleed this month," she whispered. The blood chilled in my veins. "If you have given me a baby, you will marry me, won't you?" Displaying an appalling knowledge of geography that was only exceeded by her ignorance of my intentions, she added, "You can take me away from here and we can live in a palace in India and go to London for dances."

I had a horrible flashback to a similar conversation when I was just eighteen. I doubted that girl had been pregnant then and I was by no means sure now about Maria. She saw me as a means of escape and might be trying the oldest trick in the book to get me to do her bidding. In any event I was not going to marry her; for one thing I already had an estranged wife in England, a little detail I had not thought fit to mention.

"Is it one or two days' ride between London and India?" she twittered on. "Will we need to go by carriage? Do you have a carriage of your own?"

"Let's wait and see if you are going to have a baby first," I told her. "Your father would be very cross with you if he knew you had been visiting me." My mind was suddenly filled with a vision of a metal bolt getting crushed flat with a hammer. The thought left me quite shrivelled.

"Oh, he won't mind if you marry me," she prattled on in my ear. "I think my father likes you."

I managed to persuade her to keep quiet for a few more days, but she was now so excited about the thought of leaving the village that I did not think she would keep it to herself for long. Just the next morning as I was talking to her father in the smithy she swept past. Instead of ignoring me as usual she gave me a dazzling smile. For the first time in ages a look of suspicion crossed her father's face.

"What has got into her? Why was she smiling at you?" he asked.

"Oh, she was worried about a boy in the village; I mentioned him to your wife. I have had a word with the lad and he won't trouble her again."

The smith grunted his acceptance of this explanation but he still gave me a hard look and I realised that I needed to leave the village without delay. Otherwise it would only be a matter of time before the 'sparks would fly'.

After a somewhat tense dinner with the family I made my preparations and retired to my room. Soon I heard the now familiar sounds of the family retiring for the night. In a short while the snoring began in the next room and then I heard the sound I had been waiting for. Light shone through the cracks in the ceiling, which had widened considerably in recent weeks, and then the patch was removed and the rope was lowered down.

"Darling," I whispered as she dropped directly into my waiting arms. "I have wanted to hold you all day," I lied as I hugged her to me.

"If we tell Papa that you will marry me, we could be together all of the time," she urged in my ear.

"You know, I think you are right about that. Let's tell him tomorrow."

"Really?" She nearly squealed with delight and I hurriedly put my hand over her mouth.

"Shh, they cannot find us like this. They must believe that you are chaste and pure. Do you understand?"

She nodded silently.

"But while we wait, I want to try something new."

"New?" she queried and I could understand her puzzlement. For in the last few weeks we had covered most of the content of the Hindu love manuals and she had taken to every single depravity with the enthusiasm of a glutton in a bakery. She thought we had done all that was possible with the sexual act and she was not far wrong, but I still had a surprise in store.

"Yes, what I am going to teach you is how they make love in the Sultan's harem in Constantinople. They say it is the very best way."

"You are not going to tickle me again, are you?"

94

"Er no, not this time. I want to blindfold you and tie you down to the bed. That way you will not know when I am going to touch you or where. They say it is very sensual."

"All right," she agreed, shrugging her nightgown off over her head and then lying down spread-eagled on the bed. My God, I thought, this is going to be a lot easier than I anticipated. I brought out the cloth blindfold and cords that I had ready and in a minute I had her all tied up.

"Now I need to gag you as the pleasure this technique brings might be too much to stop you crying out."

"Quickly then," whispered the little nymph, even opening her mouth for me to place a small ball of cloth inside to muffle sound. I secured it with another strip of linen around her head.

"Listen carefully now," I murmured in her ear. "The pleasure is increased by waiting. Sometimes the sultan makes the harem lady wait an hour while he watches her body, smells her and breathes on her. You must be patient, my lovely." As I was saying this I was starting to pull on my clothes. I reckoned this could give me at least an hour to get away before any alarm was raised. Perhaps she would not be discovered until dawn. I made a loop in the rope hanging from the ceiling to help pull myself up and was just about to climb up into the roof space, when I looked down on her. That nubile young girl, all willing and expectant... by God it would be a crime to leave now.

Even if I say so myself, I played that body like a concert pianist plays his instrument. I already knew all of her favourite places to be touched and I soon had her arching her back with desire and begging for me through the gag. By then I was in quite a lather myself and set to with the enthusiasm of the desperate and the damned. We had just reached the crescendo of the piece when there was an urgent knocking on the door.

"*Señor* Flashman?" It was the deep voice of the smith and it sounded so close, just the other side of wood plank. "Are you all right? My wife says you have been thrashing about and whimpering in there. Shall I come in?"

"No!" I almost shouted the word as the man's daughter wriggled sensuously underneath me. "Please don't come in. I have had a nightmare, dreaming about the battle. It keeps happening; please ignore me if you hear any more noise."

"If you are sure," he replied and I heard him mutter "War is a terrible thing" to his wife as he stomped back to his bed.

95

That was one scare too many for me; it was definitely time to go. I whispered to Maria to keep still and I would start with her again in a while and she nodded eagerly. I waited a couple of minutes for the snoring to resume and then swung myself up into the roof. Using Maria's candle, I carefully crossed the ceiling, stepping on the beams, until I dropped though the hole in the storeroom that she used as a bedroom. Moving into the kitchen, I grabbed a leather satchel and stuffed it with some bread, a spare shirt the smith had hanging to dry and the bottle of muscle liniment. Then I silently let myself out of the back door. The house was quiet and I imagined Maria still lying on my bed and waiting for my next touch.

I made my way to the main street that ran through the village and there I had a decision to make. As it turned out, my life depended on it. In a few hours the girl would be discovered and then all hell would break loose. The old smith and whatever friends he could find would be in a fever to track me down and exact their revenge. They would expect me to go towards Lisbon, which had been the direction the convoy had been heading when I had left it. But that road stretched up into the hills and there seemed little cover. I wanted to get to Lisbon, but I wanted to protect my manhood from that hammer much more. So I turned east, away from Lisbon, and started a steady jog as fast as my injured leg would go, down the hill to the edge of a scrub of trees that would hide me. Just ten minutes later I knew I had made the right decision.

Instead of hours I had only minutes to make my getaway. I imagine that Maria must have started thrashing about, either because she guessed I had gone or to encourage me to start again. In any event her father must have decided to investigate after all, only to find his naked and blindfolded daughter spread-eagled on the bed. The first I knew of this was a woman's scream, swiftly followed by a roar of rage from the old man. I had nearly reached the trees when I heard him bellow into the night from the village behind me, "Englishman, I am going to find you and kill you for this!"

Well, that was just the motivation I needed to keep moving. It was too dark for the smith to see me from the village and I was soon in the trees. I walked for most of the night, anxious to put as much distance between me and any search party as possible. By dawn I stopped to rest by a river and imagined the smith and his friends riding full tilt to find me down the Lisbon road.

Any sense of complacency evaporated a short while later when I heard the sound of dogs barking. It did not take long for me to realise that they were getting closer and that the bastards were using hounds to track my trail. I was in the river in a moment. It was only waist deep but the current was strong. The water, I knew, would hide my scent but it was impossible to move quickly upstream and away from my pursuers. A few minutes later and I was desperate, realising that I had made a terrible mistake. I had only gone a few hundred yards and I was exhausted. My injured leg was throbbing from the exertion. I could hear men shouting now, encouraging the dogs as they barked and howled while they chased me to ground. At any moment they would burst through the trees and see Flashy standing wet and crippled in the middle of the stream, as exposed as a boil on a tart's backside.

There was a bend in the river and I forced myself round it. As I did so I heard splashing in the distance; they must have reached the spot where I had entered the water. I crossed to the far bank to see if there was a place I could hide there but a flash of movement showed that they now had men and dogs on both sides of the river. They were taking no chances and would pick up my scent again as soon as I stepped onto land. Oh God.

For a moment I was frozen in panic. I had thought I was being so clever, but now it looked like Maria's enraged father would get my cock on his block after all. My mind was filled with a sudden image of that glowing bolt and the sparks as the hammer pounded down to flatten it. I only had seconds left before I was discovered. I would be spotted in the river and I would be tracked down if I left it; what was I to do?

I glanced desperately about me. The bend in the river had undercut some of the bank, causing a tree to come down, which lay partially submerged in the river. I threw myself among the branches, cutting my hands and knees as I scrambled over the wet, slimy wood searching for a place to hide. There was a fork where a bow left the trunk and I dropped into the gap, with a tangle of old branches and twigs half covering me. The water was less than waist deep this near the bank; surely they would see me? I crouched down and scooped up handfuls of the foul-smelling river mud and plastered it over my hair and face and down my front to hide the white shirt. My old army coat had faded to an orangey brown from three summers under the Spanish sun and would not stand out against the river bed. I did not have time to do more before I saw the first dog. It was a youngster, splashing in and

97

out of the stream and playing, while the rest of the pack followed the scent.

I lowered myself into the water and straightened out so that just my eyes, mouth and nose were above the surface. I had to push my arm hard into the mud under the trunk to get a purchase and hold myself steady. As I did so, I felt something slimy wiggle away from my fingers. The dog's barking sounded more distant with my ears under the water and then I could hear men's voices and knew that they must be close.

I only glimpsed the men on the far bank through the branches. There were three of them, all armed with muskets, and I did not know any of them. I thought the young pup had spotted me for a moment as he splashed through the water, heading straight for the fallen tree. But then he picked up a floating stick and turned to carry his prize back to the bank. As I breathed a sigh of relief I saw a wizened old hound sniffing around the exposed roots of the fallen tree I was hiding in. With an easy grace he hopped up onto the trunk and started to walk down it towards me. I realised that my scent must be on some of the branches as I had scrambled over them. The dog stopped and sniffed the air; if he signalled he had the scent, I was done for.

I quietly took in a deep breath and, holding tight to the trunk, I slowly slipped my face underwater without making a splash so that I was completely submerged. I could not see the dog now but I could see its shadow as it walked further along the trunk. It stopped directly above me and I imagined it standing there, smelling the branches and deciding if its prey was near. I lay frozen with fear beneath it. I could hear men's voices on the near bank now, but the gurgling water made it impossible to make out the words. Finally, with infinite slowness, the shadow began to move back up the trunk and out of sight. I made myself count slowly to ten before I brought my face quietly out of the water and opened my mouth wide to take in big, silent gulps of air. Then I twisted my head slightly to bring one ear out of the river so that I could hear the men walking nearby.

"How much further do you think he could get?" asked a man; I was pretty sure it was tavern keeper.

"I'll follow that bastard to the gates of hell itself to get my hands on him," growled the smith.

"But he told me he had a wounded leg; he can't have got that much further."

98

"He told me a lot of things too," snarled the smith. "And right now I don't believe any of them."

"He could have doubled back towards the village when he reached the river, I suppose," mused the innkeeper. "Possibly walking up one of the side streams into the hills."

I could not hear the smith's response as the men continued out of earshot. After all was quiet I slowly sat up in the water and looked about. In the distance I could see the groups of men walking on both banks, all armed and with the dogs bounding in front of them.

I sat on that log in the damn river for the rest of the morning and most of the afternoon. I knew that sooner or later they would come back and I did not want to get out on the bank and leave the dogs with a new trail to follow. Eventually I heard them returning and slipped quietly back into the water. This time they were all on the far bank and seemed to be too busy arguing about how I had given them the slip to take much notice of the ground that they had already covered. Once they were well past I hauled myself up onto the grass bank. I brought the satchel up with me. I was hungry but the bread had been ruined by its long immersion. My feet and fingers were wrinkled from spending too long in the water and I was shivering. But a spell lying in the late-afternoon sun put warmth back in my bones, while a rub from the liniment helped soothe my aching leg.

In case the search party had roused nearby farmers to look for the British 'seducer' I waited until evening to make my move and kept my distinctive soldier's coat in the satchel until it was too dark to make out the colour. I must have made ten miles that night, stopping only to steal some vegetables growing in a cottage garden. The next morning, after a brief sleep under a hedge, I set off again in the same manner. I had planned to march east until I found some unit of the British army, but in the event the army found me.

"That is an officer's coat, English boots too. So how did you get those, my bucko?"

I came to from a doze by the side of the road to find a red-faced British dragoon leaning over me and pulling my jacket from the satchel. "Been thieving from British soldiers, have you?" He looked inside the jacket at the name embroidered inside by my tailor. "So what have you done with Captain… Flashman then, eh?"

I could understand his mistake: I had not shaved for two days, I was wearing the smith's mud-stained shirt and British officers do not normally sleep in ditches. "I am Captain Flashman, damn you," I told him and watched the astonishment cross his face. "And I would be obliged if you would direct me to your commanding officer."

Captain Jennings greeted me warmly. He only had one arm and his hussar uniform was as ragged as mine but he offered his remaining hand to shake. "Captain Flashman, is it? Well, what the devil are you doing out here?"

"I was with an earlier convoy of wounded," I told him, gesturing to the wagon train of injured men that Jennings was escorting. "I was not sure I would survive the journey so I got off and rested up at a nearby town. I am now trying to re-join the army." I stared at the wounded men in the wagons. They looked just as pitiful as the men I had travelled with before, but they all seemed to be wearing cavalry uniforms. "Are these men from Albuera too or has there been another battle?"

"It wasn't so much of a battle as a disaster. A half blind, mad catastrophe called General Sir William Erskine. Do ye know the man?"

"I had heard that he was insane, but I have never met him and did not know he was half blind as well."

"He is so short-sighted he can barely see beyond his horse's arse. He nearly wiped out my regiment and he cost me an arm." Jennings waved the stump before adding, "At least it is not my sword arm. When we get to Lisbon I am going to have a hook made to hold the reins of my horse."

"What happened?"

"The damned idiot advanced us in fog until we found ourselves slap in front of a French division deployed in line with artillery. There were only a hundred yards off but still he could not see them. The adjutant spurred forward and grabbed hold of the bridle of Erskine's horse and started to drag it round while shouting at the rest of us to about-face and withdraw. As the French opened fire the fool was still squinting about him and shouting, 'What are you doing, Partridge? The French are nearby; I can hear them.'"

"What did Partridge do?" I asked.

"Oh, his name wasn't Partridge; Erskine called nearly everybody Partridge. I gather it was the name of his first adjutant and he just stuck with it. The adjutant's name was Major Smiley, but he wasn't smiling then; he was beside himself with exasperation. You hear people say that they have 'had kittens' over some crisis; well, if

Smiley had told me he had shat a cat at that moment I would have believed him."

"What happened next?" I asked.

"Oh, there were all sorts of trumpets of alarm from the French and their cannon opened fire, but the barrels were cold and the first salvo largely missed. The second didn't, though," he said, gesturing to his missing arm. "Did I not see the stupid bastard," he added, "ride past me as the cannon balls came whistling through our ranks, shouting, 'There you are, Partridge. I told you the French were close by.' Bah, Smiley should have just shot him. None of us would have reported it and Wellington would have probably given him a promotion."

Jennings was happy for me to join the convoy and get a lift to Lisbon. Of course such is my luck that my new companions were set to drive straight through the town of Arraiolos, the last place I wanted to be.

"There has been a bit of a misunderstanding over a girl in the town," I was forced to explain to my new friend, who was greatly amused.

"Ah, that explains why you were not wearing your coat when my men found you," he laughed. "Don't worry, I have had one of those 'misunderstandings' myself. We will hide you in one of the carts when we get close to the town."

The next day I was lying on the bottom of a cart covered by blankets and greatcoats as it squeaked and bumped its way through Arraiolos. Through a gap between the planks that made up its side I caught a glimpse of the familiar tavern and standing in front of it was a group of very angry men. In the middle of them was the smith, with a face like thunder.

Chapter 13

January 1812

I won't bore you with too many details of the remainder of 1811 for in truth not a lot happened. I reached Lisbon without any further incident and continued my recuperation. There had been so many officer casualties at Albuera and at Fuentes de Oñoro that there were vacancies again amongst Wellington's staff officers. I think my friend Campbell engineered it for me, but I was invited by Wellington to return to his headquarters. I tooled up there late in the autumn and made a point of leaning heavily on my stick and wincing sometimes as I held my chest to remind people of my wounds. The last thing I wanted was to be declared fit for any exertions.

In truth my injuries were healing well but I quickly discovered that there was no great appetite for an attack amongst the British then. The French had three hundred and fifty thousand men in Spain, to subdue the whole country. That was roughly seven times the British force, but events were happening many miles away that would alter the balance of power. There had been growing friction between Napoleon and the tsar of Russia, and now Bonaparte resolved to put his Russian rival in his place. Troops were withdrawn from all over the French empire, including Spain, to produce a *Grande Armée* for the invasion of Russia. At the same time Napoleon was getting frustrated by the lack of action by his generals in Spain. Massena was replaced by Marshal Marmont, and despite reducing their numbers, the French emperor ordered his armies in Spain to go on the offensive.

As the cold winter approached, the French turned their attention first to the guerrillas and then other Spanish forces operating behind their lines. Daily reports would come in on the movements of French armies and that is when I became aware again of the work of Colquhoun Grant. He was now well established as one of Wellington's best exploring officers. These were a group of men who monitored the enemy while dressed in British uniform, relying on a fast horse for a quick escape. I saw several of Grant's reports written in his meticulous neat hand and they were full of details including numbers of men and guns, routes of march; one even had a report on French morale. Even I had to grudgingly admit that it seemed competent work.

Normally neither side campaigned during the harsh Spanish winters. The roads were often boggy and impassable and the mountain passes were blocked with snow. But Wellington planned to take the French by surprise. They had been concentrating on subduing the city of Valencia and several of their armies had been moved to free up reinforcements for that attack. Reports from partisans and the exploring officers indicated that the two French-held fortresses guarding the main routes into Spain were vulnerable. The first of these was Ciudad Rodrigo which Wellington planned to attack in January 1812.

The weather was bitterly cold but Wellington had spent the early part of the winter amassing a large train of siege guns and strengthening the roads to his first target. The siege began on the eighth of January and by the nineteenth the breaches in the city walls were large enough to assault. The plan of attack worked, despite the enemy laying huge mines in the breaches to destroy the brave souls that made up the first storming parties. Most of the officers leading the assault did so from the front and some paid for their bravery. Two major generals were killed in the attack: McKinnon was blown up by a mine and Bob Crauford was shot through the spine. Colborne, my old brigade commander, took a ball through the shoulder.

But while all this shot and shell was flying about, where was the indomitable Flashy? I hear you ask. Well, all that riding about before the attack in the freezing cold had given me pneumonia. I am proud to say that while the assault was underway I was sitting in a hot mustard bath five miles away and feeling a lot better for it. I had been a coward before Albuera; but afterwards, having seen that being wounded was even worse than I imagined, I was more determined than ever to keep my battered carcass in one piece.

There was the usual sacking of Ciudad Rodrigo after its capture. Our soldiery raged through the place, shooting, raping and looting until they had drunk themselves insensible. I waited until all that unpleasantness had died down before, wrapped in blankets, I made my way to the Montarco Palace in the city where Wellington had set up his new headquarters. That was where I met Grant again.

I had been staying in the palace a week by then and, still unwell, had been given a room of my own. One afternoon I returned from a gentle walk around the town to find Grant standing in my room arraying a selection of washcloths and glass bottles around my washstand.

"Ah, Flashman," he sneered, taking in my red nose and watering eyes. "I have just had to open the window to get rid of your infected air."

"What the devil are you doing in my room? And take all your pots and potions from my washstand. If you think I am sharing a room with you then you can think again."

He smiled in triumph. "You are not sharing a room with me. Your belongings have been moved to share with some captains upstairs."

"What the devil…" I began, but then I noticed that Grant was pointing to the second epaulet on his coat: the bastard had been promoted to major!

"Exactly," declared Grant as he saw the realisation cross my face. "Other majors have been given rooms of their own and I have been given yours. You only had one because you were ill, but now you can share with the other captains. So if you will excuse me, I would like to wash off the dirt from the road."

I cast around for some retort before I left. "I am glad not to be sharing with you. I have never seen an officer with some many pots and washcloths. This room will soon smell like the boudoir of some painted trollop."

"Cleanliness is next to godliness, Flashman. You cannot expect me to wash my face with the same cloth as I wash other parts of my body. You may spend your time in filth and squalor but I do not."

I stormed off at that, not wanting to listen to him prattle on, and at length found myself sharing a freezing-cold attic room with four other captains. But if you think you have got one over on Flashy, you had better watch your back. They say revenge is best served cold, but in this case it was dished with a hot, burning sensation.

It was as I looked at my own paltry collection of toiletries that I got the idea. A washcloth, a toothpick and the old bottle of liniment with just a dribble left in the bottom was not a lot to show for my cleanliness or godliness. But then I remembered that the liniment when splashed onto a more sensitive area of skin burned like an inferno. I waited until the next day when Grant went out riding with Wellington and then slipped down to my old room. There was a clean, soft cloth that I guessed Grant used for his face, but I emptied the last of the liniment onto the other one and folded it so that the thick green ooze could not be seen. Then, to cover the smell, I removed the stopper of one of his bottles of cheap cologne.

Half an hour after Grant had returned to his room nothing had happened and I suspected that my trick had been discovered. Then as Campbell and I were sitting in the officers' mess drinking brandy an animal bellow rent the air from one of the rooms above.

"What on earth was that?" asked Campbell as I grinned in triumph.

"I have no idea," I claimed as innocently as I could manage.

I knew from personal experience that after even the smallest splash the heat from that liniment builds longer and much more strongly than you would think possible. Grant did well staying in his room for another minute, making just the odd whimpering groan. Several had started up the stairs to investigate and were knocking on his door when it was thrown open. A wild-eyed and half-naked Grant charged, pushing all in the way aside. Campbell and I stayed in the officers' mess, but we could hear the cries of those in the corridor outside as Grant pressed through.

"What the devil…"

"Don't push me, sir…"

"You are improperly dressed… are you insane?"

Grant kept pushing through the throng while emitting a regular panting shriek until he got outside.

"Come to the window," I called to Campbell. "This is going to be good."

Campbell got there just in time to see Grant emerge from the front of the building. Still screeching, he ran straight to the nearest horse trough and, to the surprise of two mares drinking from it, threw himself into the icy water.

We joined the throng of officers out in the yard standing around the trough. Grant was only wearing a shirt and was now sitting across the trough with his middle immersed. He was resting there with his eyes shut and ignoring the cacophony of questions that was being directed at him. The water was literally freezing; there were still lumps of ice in it from where the surface had been smashed that morning to allow the horses to drink. Eventually Grant gave a great sigh – the burning sensation must have been extinguished by the icy water – and looked up with still-watering eyes. Someone stepped forward from the group standing around, laughing or exclaiming, and I saw it was Guthrie.

"Come along, old fellow," he cried soothingly. "Let's get you back upstairs in the warm. You are clearly not well."

Grant was pulled out of the trough and an old horse blanket was wrapped around his shoulders. He staggered back towards the headquarters building as though in a daze but as he got near me I could not resist goading him.

"So, Grant," I murmured quietly, "are you still sure that cleanliness is next to godliness?"

He looked up at that and I watched as realisation of what I had done slowly crossed his face. "You bastard!" he yelled as he lunged towards me. "I will kill you for this."

Several officers helped Guthrie pull him back.

"What on earth is he talking about?" asked Guthrie.

"He seems to be raving. I don't think he is right in the head," I replied as Grant thrashed about and yelled to be released. "I was enjoying a drink with Campbell here when I heard him come down the stairs. I just came outside like everyone else."

Guthrie was no fool and he gave me a hard look, but then he shrugged his shoulders. "Well, I will need to give him something to calm him down."

With that Grant was dragged away, still kicking and screaming, and that was the last I saw of him for two months. I don't know whether it was the icy immersion or sharing my room, but after the opiates Guthrie gave him wore off, Grant came down with pneumonia.

It seemed sensible to not to be in Ciudad Rodrigo when the hapless major recovered. The war was moving on, but the place to which it was moving was the last place I wanted to go. Having captured the fortress guarding the northern road into Spain, Wellington now turned his attention to the one guarding the southern route: Badajoz.

Chapter 14

March 1812

We had lost enough men capturing Ciudad Rodrigo, but Badajoz was going to be a far tougher nut to crack. The river Guadiana ran along its northern ramparts and along that stretch it was nowhere less than three hundred yards wide. The town was surrounded by a wall some thirty feet high with a castle and seven smaller bastions built into the walls. Spies had told us that it had rations for two months and plenty of ammunition, while the five thousand men in the garrison had seen off British and Spanish assaults in the previous year. They had spent the intervening months strengthening every aspect of the fortress and laying mines in anticipation of our trench work that would cause carnage in the weeks ahead.

We didn't know about the mines then, but a child could work out that thousands of men would die trying to take the place. By the time I arrived, work was already underway digging out gun batteries and assault trenches. I realised then that I had been fortunate to have been stationed in Albuera during the preparations for the siege the previous year. It was back-breaking and brutal work, not helped by more torrential rain. There was a foot of liquid mud in most of the trenches, which made moving heavy things like siege guns almost impossible. They were often up to their axles in the ooze and had to be hauled slowly over thick planks, which then had to be dug out of the mud to use again.

But you would be a fool to get out of the trenches, for the enemy artillery had plenty of ammunition and knew its business. Countless men lost their lives to a well-aimed cannon ball at Badajoz. I remember the first time I was given a tour of the siege works. The French must have noticed that a group of officers was moving forward and found us a tempting target. Four of their guns fired simultaneously. I had been nervously watching their gun embrasures and saw the first plume of gun smoke before I heard the discharges. I was diving behind some sandbags when the balls impacted. At first we thought no one had been hit as there had been no screams or shouts of pain. But as I pulled myself up from the muddy trench floor I saw Major Thompson's legs lying still over the edge of the parapet. When we pulled him back into the trench we found he no longer had a head.

Eventually the British batteries were established and work began on breaching the walls. But even then the French fought back with vigour. They seemed to have guessed in advance where we would make our assault and had dug tunnels that reached under our trenches. Twice huge mines were blown up under our earthworks, killing many and burying others alive under tons of wet mud. By the end of my first week outside Badajoz, everything I owned was covered in mud and I was plastered in it. As I was not an engineer there was little I could do to help proceedings. I volunteered to take some despatches just to get away and see a green landscape again.

So it was that on my way back a few days later I found myself on the road through Albuera. I had not meant to visit the battlefield, but once I was in sight of that ridge on which I had so nearly died, I felt myself drawn to it. The village was deserted as I rode through but I sensed I was being watched. Certainly some of the villagers had come back as there were signs of repairs to the buildings and some fields had been dug. I did not stop but pointed my horse up the ridge. There a scene of decayed devastation met my eyes. The ground was littered with grey bones, some lying loose on the ground, others protruding from mass graves. In one ditch there had been an effort to cremate some bodies but there had not been enough fuel. The head is the hardest part of a body to burn and a pile of blackened skulls lay in the bottom of an ash-covered pit. I saw the area where the men of my company had been buried, but I could not bring myself to go close to it. I preferred to remember them at peace being buried. I did not want to see that the grave had been disturbed by wild animals like most of the others.

I was in a macabre mood when I returned to the siege works, which was not improved by what I found there. Word had come through that the French were gathering their armies to lift the siege and Wellington had decided to launch the attack without further delay. The assault was set for ten o'clock that night and I cursed myself for coming back a day too soon.

All the talk at the headquarters was centred around whether the breaches were yet large enough for an attack to be successful. Several of the more experienced hands, including an artillery colonel, were insisting that they needed at least another three days to guarantee a safe assault on the city. But with rumours of Marshal Soult approaching from the east and possibly Marshal Marmont from the north, Wellington could not afford to give them that long.

The gunners were still pounding away when Campbell and I rode down to look, from a safe distance. As I levelled my telescope at the city walls I could see that there were already three breaches but only two were big enough to consider. All of our guns were now concentrating on those two breaches, giving the enemy the clearest signal which ones we were planning to use. In front of the wall was a stone-faced ramp called a glacis; this was intended to deflect shot from the bottom of the wall. Normally an assault would not be started until the glacis had also been destroyed in front of the breach. Once a glacis was flattened the gunners could get at the bottom of the fortifications and fill in with rubble any ditch between the glacis and the wall. While it was pock marked with shot holes, the glacis in front of all the breaches was intact, which meant that the lower part of the wall behind it was as well.

"I would not want to be part of the forlorn hope that goes first into those," I declared with feeling. The men first into a breach were volunteers, who were known as a forlorn hope. If they survived then they could expect honours and promotion.

"No, it promises to be a bloody affair," agreed Campbell. "But we took Ciudad Rodrigo with the glacis still intact and so we should be able to do the same here."

"Where will you be tonight?" I asked.

"Wellington has asked me to watch the first assault and then report back to him on how it is going." The brave oaf actually sounded disappointed to be missing out on more of the action. Then he brightened and turned to me. "Why don't you join me? Then one of us can go back with a first report, while the other watches a bit longer."

My first reaction was that I wanted to be nowhere near that assault party tonight. But then I thought that if I did not join Campbell, I could be given a far more dangerous duty instead. Wellington was under the impression that I liked nothing more than risking life and limb on a daring mission. If he knew I was back and available for orders, he might give me command of the forlorn hope as some kind of treat! In comparison to that, acting as an observer sounded relatively safe. We would be standing to the rear and I would volunteer to be the bearer of the first message, which would get me safely away from the action. So I agreed, and if the next few hours turned out to be a living nightmare, well at least I am still alive to talk about them, which is more than can be said for many.

The French would have had to have been deaf and blind not to have known that an assault was coming that night or where it was directed. All day we had poured shot towards the largest breaches. While they had got a little bigger, there was still a very steep pile of rubble leading up to the gaps in the wall that were halfway up its height. Most of the gun fire ceased at dusk when it was hard to see where the shots landed, but one or two continued to deter the French from interfering with these breaks in their defences. Lanterns could be seen moving about on the piles of rubble in front of the breaches as the garrison prepared for the anticipated assault.

If the French were showing lights, they were not the only ones. Our attack force had started to assemble at dusk, when there was still some light, to avoid the deepest puddles in the trenches. But it took ages for the men to work their way forward, slipping and sliding in the mud. Soon countless lanterns and torches could be seen making their way across the muddy terrain. Like a swarm of fireflies in the darkness, they gradually congregated in the trenches dug for the assault. They made an irresistible target for the French gunners, and while they could not see where their balls landed, they kept up a steady fire in the direction of the lights.

I left it as late as I could before we made our way down to the trenches. By then it was pitch dark and the mud in the earthworks was so churned up by the men who had gone before that it was easier and probably safer to walk on the ground above. We had a shaded lantern to show the way and we managed to get to within a few hundred yards of where the men were gathered before we found a trench blocking our route. As I held the lantern over it to see how deep it was a sea of nervous faces stared back up at me.

"Good luck, you fellows," called Campbell cheerily. "Is there a way down?"

The men reached up and helped us into the trench. The sides were slick with wet mud, and once we were in it we could not easily climb back out. We had no choice but to walk along its length. Campbell led the way and was positively jolly with everyone he met, slapping men on the back or shaking their hand and wishing them well. I was sure that he genuinely envied them their chance for glory. We could not see their faces clearly, but most we met were quiet in nervous anticipation. They knew that a good number of them were likely to be dead in the next few hours.

110

We made slow progress through the crowded trenches, but then I became aware of a movement in the men behind us. There were shouts of "Make way!" and I could see people squeezing themselves to the sides of the earthwork to make room for someone important. At first I thought it was Wellington come to take a final look at the preparations for the attack. But then the last few men parted and standing in front of me was the scowling face of Picton. At least this time he was properly dressed in his general's uniform; the last time Campbell and I had seen him face the enemy, at Busaco, he had been wearing a nightshirt and cap.

"You two again, eh," he growled while he surveyed us with his steely blue eyes. He was a frightening figure and even then he made me feel like we were doing something wrong. "What the devil are you doing back here?" he barked in an accusatory tone.

Even Campbell gulped slightly before replying. "We are observers, sir. We are to report to General Wellington on the progress of the attack."

"Well, you are not going to see a damn thing back here. Follow me." With that he pressed past us and, like the red sea parting before Moses, the red ranks parted before Picton. We hurriedly followed in his wake.

"Aren't you commanding the diversionary attack on the castle, sir?" asked Campbell as we splashed along behind the general.

At first I thought Picton would ignore him, but at length he muttered over his shoulder, "Yes, but a diversion must be co-ordinated with the main attack."

In no time at all we were at the forward trenches, with men hissing at us to keep quiet until they saw who we were with. Picton left us then while he went to talk to the commanders of the main assault. Campbell and I found a good position at the edge of an earthwork from where we could see what was happening. We were still some five hundred yards away from the city walls, and while the French must have known that an attack was coming, things were now quiet. All cannon fire from both sides had stopped. The only sign of any activity was the throwing of burning balls of straw into the breaches every few minutes by the French. This was to light the area and check that no one was approaching.

Picton was soon making his way back to his own men and the rest of us stood quietly, waiting for the appointed hour to pass. Even though I was not taking part in the attack, I could feel the tension from

111

those about us. There was a quiet murmur of prayers and the occasional chuckle as people tried to ease the strain with humour. Every so often a man would step out of line to vomit in some corner. The forlorn hope were gathered in the next trench and I guessed that most were now regretting whatever had possessed them to volunteer in the first place. They had seen the breaches before dark and must have known that chances for their survival were slight.

Eventually a church bell clanged the hour of ten, which was the signal to start the attack. With whispered good wishes the forlorn hope started to move forward. There was the odd clatter and oath as the men hoisted scaling ladders onto their shoulders and then they were off into the darkness. More soldiers moved into the now vacant trench to wait and we all listened for sounds that the attack had started. My mouth was dry and I winced as someone in a rear trench screamed and then was reprimanded by some sergeant. It seemed loud enough to be heard in Ciudad Rodrigo, never mind Badajoz, but the garrison showed no sign of alarm. A few minutes later they tossed more burning balls of straw onto the breaches. While they saw nothing of concern, against the light we could make out the silhouettes of soldiers lowering ladders down the glacis into the ditch beyond. Once through that ditch our soldiers would have a hundred yard dash over exposed ground to reach the breaches.

The attack was going better than I had dared hope, but then I heard a crackle of musket fire in the distance. It was the diversionary attack by Picton's men on the castle built further along the wall. There were no breaches there and the poor devils were planning an escalade: running forward with ladders and hoping to get to the top of the walls on them before they were shot or pushed off. There was shouting then from the French covering the gaps in the wall. They were experienced defenders; they knew that the main attack was likely to come in their direction and that we might try a diversion to distract them. More burning bales of straw were thrown down the slopes and this time they illuminated the first few of the forlorn hope climbing up the rubble. All hell seemed to break loose then.

From the breaches there was the sound of musket fire, cannon which must have been packed with canister shot and the individual small explosions of grenades. All we could see in the darkness was a series of flashes and smoke. The onslaught that the forlorn hope had triggered was deafening. I could not imagine anyone surviving, but into this maelstrom was ordered the next wave of the attack. Hundreds of men swarmed past us, resolutely running or marching to what they could see and hear was the hottest of receptions. They had some three hundred yards of open ground to cover, the glacis to climb, a ditch to cross and only then would they be able to climb the rubble slopes towards the breaches in the wall. While most of the French fire was concentrated on those attempting the final incline, other cannon, which had previously been firing at the lantern light, once again belched fire and iron blindly towards the darkened trenches. From the screams, these now also used canister shot and when by chance they found moving groups of men they did untold damage.

Never have I been more grateful to stand safely behind earthworks. A second wave of the attack was launched and then a third, with the poor devils marching resolutely on despite the carnage happening to their front. More burning straw bundles had been thrown down from the battlements but now they just showed that the area in front of the breaches was full of smoke and the flash of charges going off.

"I can't see a damn thing," cried Campbell. "What about you?"

"Just smoke, but we will hear a cheer when they take one of the breaches."

"What if they don't take them?" Campbell asked. "We need to report to Wellington on progress and we have to know how close they are getting and what is stopping them."

I did not reply as I knew what Campbell was thinking. He wanted to get closer to the action; he always did. I stood beside him for a few more minutes and prayed for the sound of men celebrating their victory, because if it did not come, I knew my friend was right: we would have to go further forward.

If anything the sound of firing became fiercer over the next few minutes, and instead of cheering all we heard from our troops was screams and shouts.

"Come on, Flash," called Campbell at last as he got up and started to climb over the rampart.

"How far do you think we should go?" I asked nervously. "We need to be able to get back again with our message."

"Just to the top of the glacis. We will be able to see into the ditch then and the bottom part of the wall. We should be able to make out from muzzle flashes how far up it our men are getting."

I felt a surge of relief as I jumped up to follow him. The massive stonework of the glacis would protect us while we were on it from

French fire. Only our heads would be fleetingly exposed as we peered over the edge and I was planning the briefest of glances.

We swiftly crossed the exposed open ground with Campbell laughing at my apparent enthusiasm as I ran past him. "You are keen, Flash. I thought you did not want to come." As he shouted this another cannon fired and we heard the canister balls splatter into the mud a few yards to our right.

"I just want to get the first report back," I called over my shoulder. "Wellington must be beside himself to know what is happening."

There was another big explosion in one of the breaches which sent a bright flash across the area. I caught a glimpse of Campbell coming up alongside me but when I faced my front again I could hardly see a damn thing. My night vision had gone with the flash and within a moment I had sprawled over a cluster of bodies that had caught an earlier canister blast. Two were still moaning in agony as I pulled myself to my feet and heard Campbell run past me.

"Come on, Flash," he yelled while sprinting towards the bottom of the glacis slope as surefooted as one of his Highland deer. I raced after him, not for the sport, but because once I was on the glacis the French cannon could not reach me.

A few moments later I saw the dark mass loom ahead. Campbell was a few yards further on to my right and I sprinted the final yards across the mud to get a good run up the steep stone surface of the glacis. Soon I was puffing after Campbell as I ran up the incline. I thought we must be nearing the top but Campbell was still ahead and to my right; I could hear his boots thumping against the stone. I gave a final push to catch up with him and then my left foot landed in mid-air.

I did not understand what had happened: one moment I had been on very solid stone with a man ahead of me also on stone and now I was falling through a void. It was too dark to see how far I had to fall and my body tensed for the inevitable impact. I had a momentary fear of being impaled on a stake but then I landed on something soft... but deadly.

It was a wet, seething, desperate mass of humanity, struggling to live in the flooded ditch. The water, I discovered later, was only around five feet deep, but most of those that found the ditch floor that night were at the bottom of the pile and almost certainly dead. While the forlorn hope may have descended into the ditch with ladders, many more of the following troops had either fallen into it like me or been pushed by those coming on behind. When the lip of the glacis had been packed with men, the soldiers had been desperate to achieve the shelter of the ditch which gave some respite from enemy fire.

No sooner had I landed with a wet, smacking sound on the bodies of others than the hands grabbed me. They were pulling me down so that they could rise up in my place. There were screams, yells, awful gurgling sounds, but the thing I remember most was the grasping, scratching, clawing hands.

It was pitch dark down there and the stuff of nightmares. The only way to survive was to stay on the surface. I remember punching out blindly at someone below me who was trying to pull my head under, probably so that he could come up and breathe. I was kicked and punched in my turn. Twice I was pulled under the water, but each time I managed to wrench myself free. After the run and just a few minutes of this constant wrestling and fighting for survival I was exhausted. Eventually I made it to the edge of the ditch and could stand with one foot on the mud beneath, while the other boot found no room amongst the bodies. The side of the ditch was wet and slimy, impossible to climb. But by then my eyes had adjusted to the gloom and I saw that a few yards along men had got one of the ladders against the side. A furious fight surrounded it with men so desperate to get near it and on it that no one climbed more than a few rungs before they were pulled off.

Next to me some tall grenadiers were making another attempt to scale the mud wall. Two had got their backs to the bank and hoisted a third up on their shoulders. A stout corporal stood in front of them and managed to keep the crowd back so that only one person climbed at a time. Two quickly swarmed up the human ladder and then the corporal turned to me. "You next, sir; you are light enough." I slipped twice on the way up and thank Christ I did, for I was just reaching the top when the mine blew.

The French must have packed a huge amount of gunpowder under the breach for it was a thunderous explosion that made the ground shake. The grenadiers collapsed under me and I was pitched once more into the human quagmire below. No sooner had I hit those bodies than we were rained down on by mud, stones and pieces of human flesh. The mine had swept the ground in front of the breach clear and left a massive crater. But it had also blown in the side of the ditch. While some poor souls had been buried under the mudfall, as the dust cleared we saw that there was now a ramp out of the ditch. Soldiers swarmed up the slope towards the breaches and there was a renewed barrage of gunfire from the defenders. Slowly the pressure of bodies around me eased as men made their way towards the new means of escape. There was more yelling and screaming from the breach and the volume of fire showed that the French were still fighting hard.

There was no way I was going closer to the city walls. From being a place of death, the ditch was now the one place that the French could not reach with shot and shell. I could hear the voices of others who were cowering in its dark depths, some muttering prayers, others crying like babies. But most of those that I touched as I moved in the water were floating corpses. As the way cleared I went to the edge of the ramp and peered up at the nearest breach. It was a scene from hell itself, lit by more bales of burning straw. I was just in time to see a determined assault up that final slope by at least a hundred men. Cannon blasted canister shot at them which flattened swathes of men, while grenades and musket fire rained down on them from both sides. If they made it to the top of the pile of rubble in the breach then a horizontal beam studded with blades awaited them. None made it that far and a few moments later all I could see was dead and dying men. I climbed back down into the ditch. I could not escape even if I wanted to. A few had tried the ladders left on the glacis side of the ditch but they were shot down as soon as the defenders had a clear shot. Wellington would have to get his reports on progress from someone else.

Some messages must have got back, though, as twice more assaults were launched by the British. Each time hundreds of men came down the glacis with more ladders and crossed the ditch. Each time there would be a storm of fire and shot and a few dozen wounded stragglers would make their way back to the relative safety of the half-flooded gully. No one got through and jubilant French started to mock us. They knew men were cowering in the darkness and they yelled that we should come to Badajoz, if we had the balls. Meanwhile the impotent survivors around me fumed in shame or anger.

Then, just as suddenly as it had started, the battle was over. Unbeknownst to us, Picton's diversionary attack on the castle had by some miracle succeeded. Those brave fellows had swarmed up ladders, under fire from the garrison, and somehow managed to capture the walls. From there the redcoats had moved to attack from behind the soldiers defending the breaches. The first we knew of this was when we heard shouts and screams coming from behind the city walls and then there were English voices shouting from the breach.

116

"They are running, lads, come on," shouted a soldier who had appeared from the other side at the top of the breach. Any lingering doubt about a trap was dismissed a moment later when the blade-covered beam was torn down, clearing our path to the city.

Chapter 15

As one, the occupants of that ditch came swarming up the recently
formed mud ramp. I had been in the water longer than most and my
muscles were cramped with the cold and my teeth were chattering. As
I finally stood on dry land again I saw survivors coming from
everywhere out of the shadows. There had been hundreds hiding in the
huge mine crater and every large rock or dip in the ground seemed to
exude more dark shadows that quickly climbed up the slope in front of
me. There was an angry roar of rage as they ran up that rock into the
city and even then I could sense the pent-up savagery in them. These
men had seen dozens of their friends and comrades shot down before
their eyes. They had been reduced to hiding from the enemy in ditches
and crevices while the French had ridiculed them. I think many felt
ashamed for hiding and surviving when so many others had died. That
partly explains what followed. They wanted to kill and dominate
others to reassert their manhood somehow. For my part I just wanted
to find somewhere warm and safe.

The slope up to the breach was covered in British dead and dying,
sometimes several deep, and you could not help but tread on some as
you climbed up. Most were long past caring, but twice I mumbled
apologies to the wounded. I could not stop: an icy wind was cutting
through my soaking garments and my hands looked blue with the cold.
Never was a hearth with a warming fire more needed and the city
would be full of them. By the time I was staggering down the other
side of the rubble into the city, I could already hear the screams of the
first women our men had found together with the noise of smashing
doors and windows.

It was nothing out of the ordinary for the time. It was a soldier's
right to sack and loot a city taken by siege and I knew enough not to
interrupt their plundering. As I walked down the first street all the
doors had been smashed open and I could hear the pleading and groans
of the occupants as the redcoats took whatever they wanted. A man
and a woman broke free from a house further down the street and
started to run into the city, screaming for help. They did not get far.
Two soldiers stepped out of the house, levelled their muskets and shot
them both dead. There was nothing I could do. I had looked enviously
in a couple of houses which had fires burning but the soldiers were
feral in their savagery now. They would kill anyone, including their
officers, who stopped them getting what they wanted.

I reached a small square. There was a church to my right; the lock had been blasted away and the door was left, half hanging from its hinge. I could see from the candlelight inside that our men were smashing reliquaries and searching for gems and gold. Next to the church was a plainer building and I could hear screams from women inside. I could not go much further; my scarred leg was agony now. But then I heard someone shout something about brandy. A cheer came from the plain building by the church and I turned towards it. Brandy would warm me up handsomely, I thought, and surely if they had found some barrels in there, they would spare me a cup. I staggered into the courtyard of the building and turned to my left. Through an open door I saw some kind of refectory with long benches and tables and crowds of our soldiers. A corporal lurched out of the door with a cup in each fist. I held up my hand to him and gasped, "Brandy."

"Here you are, governor," he cried, holding out one of his cups. "There is plenty more where that came from."

As I reached for it I glanced over his shoulder to the men inside the refectory. Several of those standing around the nearest table moved and between them I saw a nun being held down on the planks. While I could not see for sure, I was certain she was being raped.

One of the men who had moved turned and saw me staring through the door. I have never forced a woman in my life and the disgust must have shown on my face, for he snatched up a musket and aimed at me. "You keep away, you bastard. They are our women, see."

With that he fired the musket, but it was a wild shot and I heard the ball hit the wall behind me. I had barely any chance to react and was still staring in shock when the corporal whirled round on the soldier.

"Christ, Parker," the corporal yelled. "You nearly got me with that. The officer only wants a drink. Look at him – he is soaking wet. He must have been in the ditch with us." Then he turned to me. "Take no notice of 'im, sir, and have this cup. But it would be best if you did not go inside, sir."

My shaking hands grasped the cup and I drank deeply, feeling the raw spirit burn down my throat. The corporal grinned again and topped up my cup with the other one he held in his hand. "That's right. Now best you go, sir, and forget what you saw here."

I nodded in agreement, my mind as numb as my limbs. I felt sickened by both what I had seen and how close I had come to sudden and unexpected death. I turned to leave as the corporal had suggested;

he was already going back inside to refill his cup. Then I noticed another small building in the courtyard. What really attracted my attention was the chimney: I could see a wisp of smoke coming from it against the night sky. I took another sip of brandy from my cup and staggered towards it. Smoke meant fire and fire meant heat.

By the time I reached the stout oak door I was speculating that it might be a bake house and my mind was filled with images of warm ovens and freshly baked bread. I tried the handle but the door was locked. I could have wept at that point, but I decided that I was not going to give up that easily. I took a step back and charged the door with my shoulder. The door frame that held the bolt must have been rotten as a second later I was sprawled on the floor. I stared about me in wonder. The space was lit by various candles and in the middle of the room was something that spelled paradise for me at that particular moment. The building was not a bake house, it was a bath house, and there in front of me was a hot, steaming bath.

I gazed in disbelief for a moment. The bath was the bottom of a huge wine barrel and beyond it on a platform was a roaring fire underneath a cauldron that must have been used to heat the water. Already my face could feel the warmth while a draught on the back of my neck reminded me of the need to shut the door. I did not want a bunch of drunk or murderous soldiers interrupting my soak and so I looked for something to jam against the entrance. There was a heavy wooden bookcase that now held towels. I managed to drag that away from the wall and tip it against the door. It wedged firmly and I relaxed; no one would get through that door easily now.

A few moments later and I had stripped off my frozen, wet clothes and slipped into the warm water. Sometimes you have to suffer to really appreciate pleasure and I have never enjoyed a bath as that one. I revelled in the sensation of feeling the shivering stop and my muscles slowly relax in the heat.

The water was just starting to cool when I first noticed the noise, a slight grating of wood on stone. There was another upturned bath tub leaning against the far wall, and as my senses started to recover I suddenly realised that I was not be alone. The door had been bolted from the inside and there were no other doors and windows. The person the bath had been originally intended for was still in the room. As the wood scraped against the stone again, I had a pretty good idea where they were hiding.

Having already been nearly killed several times that night, I was not going to be stabbed in a bath by some French soldier or Spaniard, who must now view the British as the enemy. Quietly I stood and got out of the bath. Steam was rising from my warm skin in the cold air and my freezing, wet clothes did not appeal. I drew my sword silently from its scabbard and stepped stealthily across the floor.

Throwing the wooden tub to the floor, I jumped forward, waving my sword threateningly. The girl screamed. I fancy a naked, wet and steaming Flashy standing over any girl, sword in hand, would be an awe-inspiring sight, but it was certainly too much for the young novice nun. She rolled away from me still shrieking and then yelled garbled prayers in a forlorn effort to hold me at bay.

She clearly expected me to fulfil my basest desires on her and so I did. Though I'll venture I took her by surprise, for I was not interested in rape but in more hot water. In Spanish I ordered her to keep quiet and then I told her to stoke the fire and put more water in the cauldron to heat. Her eyes widened in astonishment, but after a moment's hesitation she hurried to do my bidding.

I was walking back to my tub when there was a hammering on the door. "Open up, you damned bitch," shouted one of the soldiers in coarse Spanish. "We know you are in there. Let us in and we will make it easier for you." I realised that some of the soldiers in the courtyard must have heard her scream. To confirm a girl was in the little room she helpfully squealed again and shrank back to a corner of the room.

"Clear off!" I yelled. "The girl is taken."

"Bless me." I recognised the voice of the brandy-drinking corporal. "It's that officer and he has got a bint all to 'imself."

"Not for long, he hasn't," pronounced another.

There was the crash of a musket butt against the wood near the lock and then several thuds as men put their shoulders to the door. The heavy bookcase moved a fraction of an inch until it was wedged against a slightly raised stone in the floor and then budged no more. "Stand back," called another voice and I stepped to one side, guessing what would happen next. Three muskets were fired at the door. I heard the planks splinter, but the door and its bookcase support held firm.

The girl was hysterical now, babbling incoherently in the corner, and I turned and shouted at her to be quiet. The men were cursing and swearing at the stubborn door and I thanked my lucky stars that I had thought to pull the bookcase down when I had first come in. I turned and yelled at the men outside, "It is wedged tight and I have a sword and pistols waiting for anyone who does make it through."

"You have got to come out sometime," yelled a voice, "and when you do we will get you both."

There was a final futile bash at the door and then I heard their footsteps receding. I gave a victorious smile, confident that I could outwait them with the comforts to hand.

"Come on, girl, tend that fire; my water is getting cold."

I lay back in the tub and watched the girl work through half-closed eyes. She was a pretty little thing, and once she had calmed down she kept furtively glancing at me in the bath when she thought I was not watching. I am not sure how many naked men she had seen but I heard her murmur in astonishment when she first saw signs of my growing interest. She blushed then, but she did not stop staring.

I waited until she had tipped in another cauldron of hot water and then I caught her eye. "Didn't you come in here for a bath? Why don't you come in and join me? There is plenty of room."

She looked shocked and excited at the same time. She glanced at the door and I guessed that she was also considering what would happen to her if I chose to leave. After a moment's hesitation she reached down, grabbed her robe and pulled it over her head. Naked as a lark, she stepped into the bath.

The night of the sixth of April 1812 was an awful one for almost everyone in Badajoz. Nearly five thousand British soldiers were killed or injured and fifteen hundred French. After the battle had ended over three thousand Spanish civilians were murdered by rampaging British troops and at least that number of womenfolk were raped or assaulted. In a time when the sacking of a city was commonplace, Badajoz stood out for its brutality and for nearly a day the British soldiers ran riot, completely out of control.

I had suffered in that wretched ditch packed with desperate and drowning men, but I had to admit that there was recompense later that night. Francesca was not quite the novice that her religious title implied. We soon set to washing each other with enthusiasm and then, as the last candles guttered out, we made of bed of towels on the platform next to the cauldron fire. I certainly gave her something to talk about at her next confession. It served to comfort and distract us both. But as we lay quietly afterwards on the towels we could not escape the noise of the destruction of the city. There was a near continuous crackle of musketry, sometimes single shots and at other times volleys. Worst of all, though, were the shouts and the screams of the women. Francesca eventually fell asleep after muttering over and again a Latin prayer that I guessed was for her religious sisters, who were being raped and possibly murdered just yards away.

The morning brought little respite. A glance through one of the bullet holes in the door showed that the soldiers were still in control of the courtyard. Several were lying drunk, but armed, in the corner by the refectory entrance. It was not until mid-afternoon that some sort of order was established in that part of the city. This was heralded by another hammering on the door and a demand that we open up or risk the gallows that were being built in the city's main square. A squint through the bullet hole confirmed that the men were from the provost and we soon manhandled the bookcase aside.

The provost's men would not let Francesca into the convent; the scenes inside were too awful and in any event the rest of the city was not yet completely safe. It took another two days to bring the army completely under control across the city and during that time I had the girl billeted with me in one of the safer parts of town. It turned out I was not the only one of Wellington's staff officers to rescue a nun, or seduce one. Mind you, Harry Smith was foolish enough to marry his!

Chapter 16

I did not see Campbell again until some three days after the assault. He had managed to stay on the glacis and get messages back to Wellington. He actually seemed jealous of the fact that I had inadvertently joined the attack, despite me describing the horror of the ditch. He hinted that he thought I had jumped in deliberately and so we went up to the glacis again in daylight. There we could both see how it had happened. The glacis was not a straight line but zigzagged to match the bastions in the city wall behind. It was clear that in the darkness he had run up a zig, while I had blundered straight off the edge of a zag.

The place had been bad enough at night, but the weak winter sun revealed the devastation and slaughter everywhere. The flooded ditch was packed with British dead, many of whom had started to swell in the water. The crater, where the massive mine had exploded, was still black with dried blood and body parts, while the slope to the breach itself remained thickly carpeted with red-jacketed corpses. For the British, the casualties had been even higher than at Albuera at nearly five thousand men. But instead of being spread over a large battlefield, here they lay in massive mounds where they fell.

"Did you know," said Campbell as we surveyed the scene, "that Wellington actually wept when he stood here the morning after the battle?"

"He is such a cold fish," I replied, "that I don't think I have ever seen him show much emotion. You don't think he will start to lose his nerve, do you?"

"Oh no, he is already planning to divide the army, leaving a garrison here and taking the rest to attack Marmont. The good marshal was marching to help relieve the city and Wellington hopes he can take the French by surprise. Getting the army out of the city will also help re-establish order."

"Well, I will not be sorry to leave here. It always has seemed a grim and forbidding place, but now it stinks of death and decay."

"What about your little nun?" Campbell grinned. "Does she not offer some compensation?"

"She did, but now there is order on the streets again she has decided to return to the convent. No, the sooner we leave, the better for me."

The army started its march north two days later and I made myself look busy tooling up and down the column, but actually doing very little. I tried to avoid Wellington and had not spoken to him since my ride with despatches. I had long since learned that contact with our general invariably resulted in me being dropped into danger. With another battle on the horizon, a very low profile seemed the way to go. But you can't hide from fate and on the third day of the march I received an early-morning summons to report to his tent.

From extensive experience I can tell you that when you get an urgent summons to a general's quarters, it is rarely good news. I speculated on the cause as I hurried across the camp ground. There was no attack imminent, Soult was still in Seville and Marmont was miles away with various exploring officers keeping tabs on him. With no obvious reason to throw Flashy into jeopardy, I wondered if it was a reprimand. Had Francesca's mother superior complained about my behaviour? The young 'bride of Christ' was likely to find our Lord a disappointing companion after demonstrating a growing enthusiasm for the type of protection I could offer. Or was it Grant, had he made a formal complaint? After the liniment incident I had been expecting him to exact some sort of revenge when the opportunity arose. My worst fears seemed to have been confirmed by Wellington's opening words.

"Ah, Flashman, good to see you. I want to talk to you about Major Grant."

"I don't know what he has told you, sir, but I can assure you that I had nothing to do with it."

"What *are* you talking about? Of course you have had nothing to do with it. We think he has been captured."

"Captured, sir?" I asked, quickly taking in this change of events and thinking that good news might come from this type of meeting after all. "That is very unfortunate, sir."

"It is more than bloody unfortunate. He has a huge amount of information about our army and he knows we are marching to try to trap Marmont against the river Agueda. If the French find out, they will slip away and this march will have been for nothing."

"Perhaps he has got lost or is just injured somewhere."

"You may be right, which is why I have sent for you. He was last heard of near Alcantara; you know the area from your time there in 'oh-nine. I want you to go up there and see if you can find out what has happened to him."

"Are the French still in the vicinity?"

"No, they have pulled back; you should be quite safe. I don't want to risk losing another man who knows about our attack. Come back as soon as you know what has happened to Grant."

I was stunned: no reprimand, my nemesis probably dead or captured and a mission that did not appear to involve any danger at all. I struggled to stop a big grin crossing my face. "I will do my best, sir."

"I am sure you will," agreed Wellington. He appeared about to dismiss me and then hesitated. "You know Flashman, if you had wanted to join the attack on Badajoz, you had only to ask. I heard about you *accidentally* falling into the ditch and then risking your life to save a young nun." He grinned. "It is just the sort of thing I would expect from you. Campbell was quite cross when he found you had gone into the city without him. The pair of you are as brave as lions, even though you sometimes try to hide it with these ridiculous stories." I opened my mouth to protest, but then shut it again. What could I say without ruining my credit?

"But," Wellington continued, holding up a finger in warning, "this time I do want you to be really careful Flashman. No unnecessary risks, do ye hear? I cannot afford to lose another man to the French who knows about our plans." He paused, considering. "It is a sad thing but I would rather Grant be dead than captured."

I was not entirely sure, but that last remark seemed to be a hint to kill Grant if the opportunity arose and I could not bring him back alive. While I could not stand the pompous little bastard, I was not sure I hated him enough to kill him in cold blood, especially after what I had already done to him. But this was one occasion when I could give Wellington a truly honest reply. "Don't worry, sir," I told him. "I give you my word that I will do everything in my power to come back in one piece."

Two days later and I was taking in a view that I had last seen nearly three years previously. Then I was newly arrived in Spain and about to take part in an extraordinary action where a few hundred men from the Loyal Lusitanian Legion and some militia from the Idanha a Nova regiment stopped Marshal Victor and an army of ten thousand Frenchmen in its tracks. This was largely achieved when I blew up a span of the old Roman bridge that I now saw stretching out across the gorge in front of me. To my surprise as I looked down on the broken structure I saw a dozen carts and several British officers amongst a group of men that seemed to be working to repair it.

The memories flooded back as I rode down into the valley to speak to the engineers. The French had lined the opposite bank and sent a storm of musket shot across the river, with cannon fire and several assaults across the bridge itself. Things looked different now as I arrived at the end of the bridge. Men were pulling on ropes to manoeuvre a large wooden platform to cover the seventy-five-foot chasm of the missing arch. As I asked for who was in charge, the platform started to teeter on the edge of the existing stone supports. It was a big oak repair that must have weighed tonnes. As it started to tip into the chasm the weight on the ropes increased, dragging the men holding them towards the gap in the bridge. With what seemed infinite slowness the platform fell into the river, to a chorus of shouting and swearing as men tugged on ropes to stop it getting washed away. I looked for the commanding officer and decided that it would not be politic to mention that I was the chap who had blown the bridge up in the first place.

Colonel Sturgeon, who was in charge of the engineers, remembered seeing Grant a week previously. "He passed us on the road here, but there was no reason for him to come to the bridge as he could not get across. He was heading up to Idanha a Nova. He had a guide with him and they seemed to know where they were going."

They next day I followed Grant's footsteps into the small town of Idanha a Nova. Most of the houses were gathered around a square which had a large tavern, always the best place to get information. I strode in, nodding in greeting to the dozen patrons that sat on the benches. The conversation that had been going on died away at my arrival. Several of the men there looked awkward and embarrassed. I wondered if they had been part of the militia that had run away during the French attack after their commander was cut in half by a cannon ball. I did not blame them if they were; I was trying to do the same at the time, but my foot had been stuck fast in a rock fall.

"I am trying to track down an Englishman who came this way a week ago," I announced. "His name was Grant and he had a Spaniard called Leon with him. Do any of you know what happened to them?"

They looked away and shuffled their feet. These men just wanted to farm their land and they had long since learnt that any involvement with men in uniforms invariably brought trouble.

Then one of the men at the back stood up and asked hesitantly, "You are *Señor* Flashman, yes?"

"That's right. Do I know you?"

127

"My cousin Jorge and I sheltered with you behind the same rock when the French started shooting at Alcantara." He looked embarrassed as he added, "We ran away, but you stayed. I heard later that it was you who blew up the bridge."

I remembered them now, although back then I had been too busy to make a note of faces. There had been three of us huddled together behind a rock while musket balls lashed all around us like horizontal hail. It was just the break I needed to get these men to help me.

"I am glad to see you survived." I walked towards him, holding out my hand in greeting. "Let me buy you a cup of wine."

Cups of wine for all present soon loosened their tongues and I swiftly discovered why the men had initially been reluctant to talk. Grant and Leon had been staying in a house on the outskirts of town. They had been captured because someone in the village had betrayed them to the French. When they had gone to bed that night there was not a Frenchman within ten miles of the village, but by dawn they were surrounded.

The French were determined to catch Grant and had thrown a cordon of infantry around the town to stop anyone escaping and more soldiers had systematically searched all the houses. The search had started at the other end of the village, so Grant and Leon had time to mount up and try to charge their way through the cordon. They had managed to burst through the line of troops and were fortunate to escape the shots fired at them. But then their luck ran out as they rode slap into a patrol of French dragoons. Even then they had tried to escape, riding into some trees to the west. But a short while later the dragoons were seen riding back through the village, with Grant in his distinctive red coat amongst them as their prisoner. Of Leon there was no sign.

With the promise of more wine I persuaded the villagers to take me up to the woods where Grant was captured. I thought he might have thrown away notes and maps while he was being pursued, but I also wanted to know what had happened to Leon. If the guide had been wounded then unless he had found some water he would almost certainly be dead now. I organised the men into a line and we stepped through the trees. They were dwarf oaks barely coming up to our heads when we were on foot. Grant, on horseback with his red coat, would have been easy to track.

Half a mile into the woods there was a shout from the other end of the line. When I got there I found the men gathered around a body lying in the dirt. It was Leon. He had been shot in the head and judging from the powder burns on his cheek it was from point-blank range as he lay on the ground. The French had clearly seen him as some valueless servant and had not even bothered to search his body. I did and found a notebook tucked into the waistband of his trousers. Inside the book I found pages of notes and maps, but not in Grant's neat handwriting. The content seemed familiar and then I found a page on French army morale. I recognised some details that had been quoted in one of the reports from Grant I had seen at Wellington's headquarters.

All of Grant's neatly copied reports were taken directly from Leon's notebook. There was also more valuable information in its pages that for some reason Grant had not seen fit to include, probably because he did not understand its significance. I did not know whether to laugh or cry. The French had summarily executed the finest intelligence officer used by the British army. Instead they had taken Grant, thinking he was the man who helped guide Wellington's decisions. The irony was that Wellington had been duped like the French, and he had given Grant all the information that the French were seeking.

We wrapped Leon's body in a blanket and carried it back to the village. There was lots of dark muttering about finding the traitor, but they agreed to arrange for a proper burial for Leon in the church. I burned the notebook. Nobody who mattered would believe that Leon was drafting Grant's reports. Now he was dead it made no difference. A lot of the information was too old to be useful, but it was better burned than falling into the wrong hands.

Two days later and I had caught up with the forty thousand men in the British army as it steadfastly marched to trap the twenty-thousand-strong army of Marmont against the banks of the Agueda. There had been heavy rains in the hills and the strong river current had washed away one bridge. It left Marmont with even fewer options to escape.

"What news do you have?" called Wellington as I pushed open the flap of his campaign tent.

"Grant was betrayed to the French and taken. He was seen being ridden away as a prisoner, apparently unwounded. His guide Leon was shot and killed."

"Damnation. Still, I should not be surprised. I have just received a message from an agent in Salamanca saying that the French think that they have taken an important prisoner." Wellington looked tired and harassed. He ran his fingers through his hair as he continued: "We need him back. He knows too much about our operations. I am sending out a message to all the local guerrilla chiefs offering two thousand dollars in gold to anyone who can bring Grant back to me alive. Of course if the French get wind of that then they will realise just how important Grant is."

"Well, if they cannot get him back then no one can," I agreed supportively. I then took my leave before he thought of any more ways to use my services.

I spent the next two days riding in the rain and through mud with the rest of the army to trap the French. When we were just a day away, the French suddenly discovered how close the British were and made their escape across the remaining crossing point of the Agueda river. Wellington was furious, but it was nothing to his anger when he called me into his tent the next morning.

"Would you believe it, Flashman?" he shouted at me, waving a piece of paper in the air.

"Believe what, sir?"

"Grant has given his parole to the French. I have thousands of bloody partisans trying to help him escape and Grant has given his word of honour to the French that he will do no such thing."

I suppressed a smile. Ever since his food-gathering mission Grant had been one of Wellington's favourites. Guided discretely by Leon, he could do no wrong. Now, just days after Leon's death, Grant was proving that he was not the shrewd operator that Wellington had taken him for.

"Does he not realise how important it is for us to get him back?" Wellington asked in exasperation

"Perhaps he is hoping to be exchanged."

Wellington gave another bark of laughter. "Of course he is, but Marmont is too smart for that. I wrote to Marmont a week ago when he had first gone missing, offering to exchange a colonel for Major Grant if he had been taken. I got a reply from Marmont today very graciously agreeing to my request. But see here…" Wellington picked up another paper from those piled on his desk. "This is another letter dated the same day as Marmont's response to me. It was intercepted by the guerrillas and has just been handed over. It is from Marmont's aide to the minister of war in Paris, offering Grant for interrogation and stressing his detailed knowledge of our affairs." Wellington made a visible effort to calm himself before continuing. "Have you ever faced torture in your adventures, Flashman?"

130

"Yes, it was here in Spain in 1800, but luckily I was rescued just as they pulled the hot knives out of the fire."

"You were most fortunate. I have often wondered how I would stand torture, but I imagine that it is not something that you can judge until you face it. Everyone thinks that they will be brave, but alone in some basement with no hope of rescue…"

"It certainly tests your inner courage, sir," I agreed. "I was not sure how much I could stand." This was not exactly true. I had been willing to tell them anything and everything to avoid the pain, but I was sure they would have tortured me anyway given the chance.

"They are bound to have experts in this dark art in Paris," continued Wellington. "Grant is a brave man, but I doubt that there is a man alive who cannot be broken given time. If he tells them all he knows, it will do irreparable damage. We must get him back."

"Well, I don't see how. He is probably in Marmont's headquarters in Salamanca under the tightest guard. You know how jealously Grant guards his honour; now he has given his parole he will not even try to escape. On top of that if Marmont has promised Grant to the minister of war, he will provide a huge escort to make sure that his prisoner is delivered."

"It is not a job for an ordinary man," stated Wellington and suddenly I felt my blood chill. I had a horrible feeling that I knew where this conversation was going; a sensation that was only strengthened by Wellington's next words. "Do you remember where we first met, Flashman? In India when I sent you behind enemy lines to cause chaos with the Mahratta. You far exceeded my expectations in what you achieved, disguised as a company lancer and then in two Indian armies. Since then you have masqueraded as a French officer at Talavera and as a Polish lancer before Busaco. There was no need to take such a risk, but you are a natural spy."

"But this is different," I tried to object. "The French will be expecting something like this."

"Your experience makes you ideally suited to the task," responded Wellington as though I had not spoken. "And this time you will not be working alone. We have another agent working in Salamanca who can help you." He beamed as though this was the very best news.

I tried to look pleased but my heart sank. The presence of this other agent meant that I could not hide out on some hilltop; I would actually have to go to Salamanca.

"Who is this other agent?" I asked, hoping that he was some disreputable cove who could be persuaded to deceive Wellington into thinking we had done all we can.

"He is an Irish Catholic priest, a professor at the University of Salamanca. No, don't look disappointed, Flashman; he is a good man. He is very shrewd and runs his own network of spies." Wellington paused, his brow furrowed in thought. "Grant has not met Curtis, that's the priest, but he knows I have an agent with a network of spies in Salamanca. If he is made to talk, we could lose many of our informants."

"But Grant has given his parole. He will not be willing to escape." I was starting to get desperate now as I sensed a net closing in around me. "If we cannot break him out..." I paused, judging how my next suggestion would be received. "There are other ways of stopping him talk. Perhaps a local partisan could be paid to do the job."

"You mean kill him?" Wellington looked shocked at the idea, despite the fact that he had ordered countless executions in his time. "You are a ruthless man, Flashman."

"You suggested he would be better dead when we spoke before. It would be a quicker death than one by torture."

"I know what I said before, but I will not be party to the murder of a British officer." Wellington had spoken sternly but then he smiled again. "I think you underestimate your abilities, Flashman. You have not failed me yet, and if anyone can get Grant away, you can. I will give you a copy of the letter sent to the minister of war that you can show Grant. It should be more than enough to persuade him that he is released from his parole."

Chapter 17

Three days later and I was to be found riding through the streets of
Salamanca in the uniform of a French lieutenant. I was cursing Grant
for getting captured and this priest called Curtis too. Why couldn't he
have been the kind of person who would know a cut-throat murderer
for hire? I was sure that there was no way we would be able to get
Grant away. Even if we did get him out of the prison, there would be
guards at every exit to the city. Once his absence was reported,
Marshal Marmont would do whatever it took to get his prize back. He
was not going to write to the minister of war and admit he had allowed
Grant to escape; it could be the end of his career. So once again Flashy
was being forced into the soup.

At least the journey into the city had been much easier than I had
expected. For two days I had ridden the main roads in my British
uniform, but then as I approached Salamanca I went up into the hills. It
was always difficult to judge when to change from the British coat into
the French one and for a while I rode in just my shirt. I did not want to
be seen by any French patrols in a British uniform, but even less did I
want to be found by the partisans in a French one. Eventually I spotted
a company of French infantry guarding a column of hay carts that were
being taken in the direction of the city. I slipped on the French coat
and transferred my pistols and other possessions into the pockets,
before making sure that the red cloth was stuffed well out of sight in
my saddlebag.

The foraging party showed not the slightest concern as a French
officer rode down towards them. I trotted my horse down the line of
wagons and saluted the lieutenant at its head.

"Lieutenant Moreau of the engineers," I called to introduce myself.
I thought being an engineer would raise less suspicion than a line
regiment officer riding alone about the countryside.

"Lieutenant Parquin, as you can see, attached to the
quartermasters." He gestured to the line of carts behind. "Where have
you come from?" he asked more out of politeness than genuine
curiosity.

"Une femme," I replied as though that explained everything, and
for Lieutenant Parquin 'a woman' seemed all the explanation he
needed.

I encouraged him to do most of the talking so that I did not give
myself away. It was not difficult as Parquin liked to talk. By the time

we reached the gates of the city I had discovered that he had had been in Spain a year, that he thought his wife in Bordeaux was having an affair and that his captain was suffering from piles. The captain apparently preferred his men to think it was the clap, a more soldierly complaint, unless of course he had both. The sentries at the city gates watched two officers chatting amiably in charge of a company of French infantry and hay carts and saw no reason to interrupt their lunch by asking awkward questions. They just waived us through. As I travelled under the stone portal, I could not help wondering how easy it would be to pass in the opposite direction.

"Do you know where the university is?" I asked Parquin casually. "I have a friend who asked me to look up a mathematician there." He gave me directions to a palatial baroque building very near the cathedral. There I asked for Don Patricio Cortes, the Spanish name of my contact.

The first time I saw Curtis I thought that there must have been a mistake. Wellington had not told me how old he was and the man pointed out to me looked as ancient as Methuselah. He was sitting on a bench in a quiet colonnaded courtyard and seemed to be asleep. I walked up to him and scuffed my boot on the stone flags to wake him as I asked hesitantly in Spanish, "Are you Don Patricio Cortes?"

The bright blue eyes opened immediately and made me doubt if he had been asleep at all. Without saying a word he studied me carefully from the top of my battered hat to my boots and then replied in the same language. "Who is asking for him?" There was no trace of an accent to his Spanish and I hesitated before replying. If Grant had already been interrogated, this unlikely looking agent could be bait for a trap. I glanced around but there were just two other old men in the courtyard, both well out of earshot.

I took a deep breath and then spoke quietly in English, "A friend from Ireland sent me." Wellington was proud of his Irish roots and this was the phrase that he had apparently used before to introduce men to Curtis.

In a broad Irish accent Curtis replied, "In that case you will be knowing the name of the little place at the mouth of the River Liffey."

I gaped; I had already used the only phrase that Wellington had given me and I had not set foot on the emerald isle, never mind seen that river. "I am sorry… I have never been to Ireland." I did not want him to turn me away and so I added, "Our Irish friend was very keen that we talk. Perhaps I could tell you something else?"

"Not here," he murmured, getting up. "I have been expecting you. You might have a French coat but your boots are English. Let's go up to the observatory; we can talk privately there." He gave me an impish grin and added, "That little place is called Dublin, by the way."

His observatory was a small room at the top of one of the towers. He locked and bolted the door before bidding me to make myself comfortable in his cluttered eyrie. "Take those papers off that chair and sit down. I take it you are here about Major Grant?"

"Yes, our Irish friend wonders if there is a way that we can break him out from Salamanca and return him to behind British lines."

"That is impossible," stated Curtis firmly. "He is being held at the citadel. I called there yesterday to see if he would be allowed to go to mass but he is not allowed out of his cell."

"I thought he had given his parole."

"He has, but Marmont is taking no chances. The guard told me that the marshal has ordered that Grant cannot be allowed out of his cell unless Marmont is present. Apparently he lost a prisoner once before with a forged release order."

"If we cannot get him out, the marshal is planning to send him to Paris, where he will be tortured. I gather he knows someone runs agents from Salamanca. The French will soon start narrowing down a list of suspects."

Curtis stared out of the window for a moment in thought. "Our best chance of freeing him will be when he is moved to Bayonne. It is a long distance and the partisans will help."

I was warming quickly to the old man. He was talking sense. No reckless attempts to break Grant out of the citadel and leaving the partisans to take all the risks was fine by me.

I was just starting to relax when he added, "Is Grant a shrewd man? I am surprised he gave his parole as he must have known that our Irish friend would want him back."

I had relaxed too much for I answered honestly. "He is as dumb as an ox. His guide did most of the thinking for them, but the French shot him when Grant was captured." Then, realising that I might have been a bit too forthright, I added, "But he is very proud and guards his honour with the tenacity of a cat. Whatever Marmont could offer or threaten him with, I don't think he would talk."

"Mmm," uttered Curtis thoughtfully. "Marmont is more subtle than that. As it will take him a while to organise a large escort to Bayonne, I think we need to talk to Grant to find out if he has told the French

135

anything. Remember the French did manage to escape across the Agueda just in the nick of time to avoid the British trap. It will also be good for him to know that help is at hand."

"But how the devil will we do that if he is shut up in the citadel?"

"Oh, I am known in there. I often go to hear confession from the prisoners. Perhaps if you go as my guard they will let us see him."

The last place I wanted to go was to the cells under the citadel. I did my best to talk him out of it but Curtis was resolute. If Grant had talked, we needed to know. Of course if he had talked then the French would be on heightened alert for a mysterious spymaster based in Salamanca. The Irish priest professor with correspondents around the country would be a prime suspect, as would an unknown French officer in British boots, with no papers, trying to vouch for him.

Perhaps rightly concluding that I would not come back if we delayed the encounter, Curtis insisted that we went to the citadel straight away. He picked up a satchel containing communion wine and other priestly vestments and led the way out of the university. For an old man he walked at a good pace and the citadel was not far away. It gave me little chance of thinking of another excuse not to go.

"Don't worry, many people know me here," Curtis murmured in Spanish as we walked through the forbidding stone arch into the fortress.

"That *is* what is worrying me," I replied in the same language as Curtis chuckled. But many of the guards did recognise him and a few who were Catholics greeted him kindly, receiving blessings in return.

With his French lieutenant companion watching sternly on, we were soon conducted not to the cells but up some stairs to another room where the prisoner was being held. We were left waiting in the corridor while the guard went in and announced that a priest was there to hear Grant's confession.

"But I am a Presbyterian," whined Grant and for a moment I thought the idiot would refuse to see us. Then Curtis gently pushed in through the door.

"I am from the Order of Saint Arthur," he declared referring to Wellington's first name in his softly spoken Irish accent. "I am allowed to hear Presbyterian confessions too." The guard stared between the two men, unable to understand what was being spoken.

"That will be all right then," agreed Grant, still appearing confused as to what was happening.

Curtis turned to the guard and gestured to me standing outside. "Perhaps my companion can stand guard on the meeting?"

It was then that Grant noticed me still standing in the corridor outside. "Flash…" he gasped before he could stop himself as his eyes bulged in astonishment. Luckily the guard was looking at me at the time and missed the reaction.

"I will guard them, Corporal," I said sternly to the guard and stood back to encourage the man to leave. "We will knock on the door when we are ready."

The guard seemed happy to have one less job to do and stepped outside the cell. Once I had entered, the door slammed shut and I heard the guard shooting the bolt across.

"What the devil…" started Grant but Curtis held up his hand to silence him. Then the priest started to recite a prayer loudly in Latin as I put my ear to the cell door to check that the guard's footsteps were receding.

"He has gone," I declared as the noise on the flagstones died away.

"I demand to know what is happening!" exploded Grant. He was glaring angrily at me as though it was my fault he had been arrested. Sensing the obvious hostility between Grant and me, Curtis replied.

"Your General Wellington has sent Mr Flashman to visit me to see if we can help you." He spoke slowly and calmly as though quietening an overexcited child and it seemed to work. "Now why don't we all sit down and discuss what is happening?"

There were two chairs in the room, a table and a bed. Curtis and Grant sat opposite each other on the chairs while I sat down on the bed facing the table.

"That is better," said Curtis smoothly. "Now why don't you start by telling us how you got arrested?"

"We were betrayed," cried Grant hotly and the wretch even had the nerve to flick a glance in my direction as though I might be responsible. "We tried to get away but we ran right into one of their cavalry patrols." He paused, seeming sorry for himself, and then added quietly, "They shot Leon. I thought that they were going to arrest both of us, but as they led me away I heard a shot. When I looked he was on the ground covered in blood. He had all of our notes tucked into his waistband."

"We will have to recover those," stated Curtis quietly.

"I have already done it," I interrupted. "The notes have been destroyed."

"Was Leon…" Grant's voice was barely a whisper now. He could not bring himself to finish his question.

"Dead? Yes, he was, but I got the villagers to give him a Christian burial."

"Thank you, Flashman," he muttered dully, staring down at the table top.

"Have they questioned you yet?" prompted Curtis.

"Yes, they have." Grant looked up now, suddenly indignant again. "It was some fat general called Martiniere. But I told him nothing, despite his threats to have me hanged as a common spy when I am still wearing the uniform I was captured in. He was a foul-mouthed bully, but fortunately Marshal Marmont heard about the interrogation and had the decency to invite me to dinner by way of an apology."

Curtis and I exchanged a glance at that. We had both seen the letter from Marmont's office offering Grant for interrogation. Marmont was urbane and polite, but he was ruthless in achieving his goals. I wondered if Martiniere had been used deliberately to shake up Grant before Marmont tried a softer line of questioning.

"Did you like Marmont?" enquired Curtis.

"Oh yes, he was a proper gentleman, a man of honour and integrity," enthused Grant, again giving me a sideways glance. "He gave me his word that there would be no question of me being hanged for a spy as I had been captured in uniform and he gave me an excellent dinner."

"Was this before or after his army escaped the trap at the Agueda river?" I asked the question casually but Grant was quick to take any offence and saw the inference that he might have talked.

"I said *nothing* about the plan, *Captain* Flashman," claimed Grant, reminding me that he was my superior. "And the marshal declared he would not have embarrassed us both by asking about it. In fact he told me that his spies keep him very well informed on what the British are doing."

"Did he tell you what they had told him?" asked Curtis amiably.

"Not a lot, but I don't think they are very good as they overestimated our casualties at Badajoz."

"Did you tell him they were wrong?" probed Curtis.

"Yes, but that does not matter as the battle is over now. We spent much of the time arguing over whether British or French soldiers could march the quickest." Grant paused as though remembering something and then pressed hurriedly on. "But what are you doing

138

here? Have you not heard? I have given my parole and I am to be exchanged."

Curtis briefly caught my eye. It was now clear as day what had happened. Marmont had plied Grant with a mixture of wine and charm. The fool had then confirmed the existence of a plan of attack, the size of army Wellington had left and probably when they could be expected.

Curtis looked down at his fingers before continuing. "Our information is that you will not be exchanged. Mr Flashman is here to arrange your escape back to the British lines."

Grant gave a scornful laugh. "Oh, you would like that, wouldn't you, Flashman? Seeing me dishonoured by breaking my parole; then having me as some kind of trophy to prove that your sordid way of conducting war in an enemy uniform is best. Do you think I have forgotten what you did to me at Ciudad Rodrigo?" he hissed. "You are vile and detestable, Flashman. I would no more place myself in your care than in that of Bonaparte himself."

He turned stiffly to Curtis. "I am sorry, Father. You are clearly an honourable and God-fearing man, but I regret that I know your companion well and he is nothing of the sort. I have given my parole to no lesser man than Marshal Marmont of France, whom I also believe to be honourable. He is arranging an exchange for me in Paris and I have given my word that I will not try to escape before I am delivered to that city."

Curtis looked a little bewildered at the outburst from Grant and so I leaned forward and dropped the copy of the letter from Marmont to the minister of war on the table. "Then you had better read that," I told him. "Your honourable marshal has no intention of exchanging you. He has offered you to the minister of war for interrogation. I will leave you to imagine what that will involve."

Grant paled a little as he read through the lines, but then he saw that the letter was a copy with no signature at the bottom. "This is not the original letter," he cried, glaring at me. "It could just be one of your tricks to get me to do what you want."

"Oh, for God's sake," I exclaimed, now exasperated beyond endurance. "Do you really think I care what happens to you? Would I risk my life by coming all this way into the very heart of Marmont's army unless Wellington had ordered it? They can torture you until your toes curl as far as I am concerned, but Wellington evidently values you much more highly than I do."

"It is true that Wellington wants you back," stated Curtis quietly. "But Mr Flashman cannot break you out from the citadel. He will have to try to help you escape on the journey to France."

"But I have given my word of honour that I would not try to escape before I reach Paris," whined Grant.

I took the letter back and we left him then to reflect on his position, with Curtis promising to return. I knocked on the cell door and after a delay the guard came and let us out without showing any interest in his prisoner's visitors. Grant bid us good day and then sat at the table staring at his hands as he started to take in what we had told him and doubtless review his dinner conversation with Marmont. We were halfway across the courtyard in front of the citadel when Curtis turned to me, his face a picture of curiosity.

"What on earth did you do to Grant in Ciudad Rodrigo that would make him rather face torture than be rescued by you?"

"Oh, you heard him," I exclaimed. "A village idiot has more wits and he is an irritating little toady to boot. Marmont tricked the Agueda plan out of him and he was too stupid to even notice. Why Wellington wants him back is beyond me. It was his guide Leon who did all the thinking and he is dead."

"But what did you do to him in Ciudad Rodrigo?" persisted Curtis, smiling at my attempted evasion of his question.

I sighed. A Catholic priest was hardly likely to approve of such a spiteful act. "I put muscle liniment on his bollock-washing cloth."

"You did what?" exclaimed Curtis, stopping in astonishment.

"Well, he had been given my room and he was damn smug about it. The fastidious little swine was laying out his wash things on my washstand as he threw me out of his new quarters. It seemed appropriate somehow."

"And from his reaction I am guessing he washed with it. The liniment must have burned his balls like the fires of hell."

I grinned. "Oh, it did. He must have tried to wash it off but that did not work. He ended up sitting in the half-frozen water of a horse trough right outside the officers' mess." I chuckled at the memory but Curtis roared with laughter. He was obviously picturing the scene and his thin elderly body shook with mirth. Eventually he had to sit on a low wall to wipe the tears from his eyes.

"I can understand now why he really hates you, Mr Flashman," he gasped when he had got his breath back. "I think I misjudged you," he said, grinning. "You really are a bit of a bastard, aren't you?"

Chapter 18

It took ten days for Marmont to organise a suitably sized escort for Grant. He was required to send a draft of three hundred men back to France to support the reinforcements for the invasion of Russia. To help protect this group against partisan attack, the column was provided with six cannon. There would also be the usual covered supply wagons and in one of these there would be a large ringbolt nailed to the floor. This was to transport Grant, who would be chained to the ring on the floor to stop him escaping or being carried off. The French had learned of Wellington's offer to the partisans. They hoped by keeping Grant hidden in one of many wagons they could reduce the chances of losing their man.

Grant, however, was still adamant that he would not escape until he reached Paris, as he had given his word. He doggedly hung to the desperate hope that the letter I had shown him was a forgery. He was also convinced that his initial impression of Marmont as a man of honour stood true. I knew all this because Curtis had visited Grant twice more on his own after our joint meeting. Curtis thought he might make more progress with Grant alone. But Grant was a stubborn mule who insisted that his word of honour could not be broken. I have no doubt he would have changed his mind when they chained him to the rack, but he did not seem to have the imagination to work that out for himself. Marmont must have been getting reports on his prisoner for he heard about Curtis's visits. When the priest tried to see Grant for the third time he was arrested and questioned.

I had been waiting outside the citadel for him, and as first one hour passed and then two, I realised that something was wrong. I quietly made my way to a tavern opposite the entrance to the university and there I watched a group of soldiers enter and head towards the priest's rooms. They emerged a while later carrying books and a box of papers back to the citadel. It says something about the calm competence of the old priest that I never once considered that he would betray me. Curtis, a doctor of astronomy as well as a priest, was highly respected at the university. I was sure that the search of his room would have been reported to the academic authorities and that the chancellor would be sending representations to Marmont seeking the release of their professor.

Certainly if the French had their suspicions about an accomplice, then the city gates would be thoroughly guarded. The attempted escape of a junior French officer with no papers would only make things worse. It seemed to make sense to stay amongst the crowds within the city walls.

That afternoon and evening I moved between three taverns with views of the university, waiting to see if he would be released. I was playing chess and getting roundly beaten by a young student who looked like he had not yet started shaving, when I saw Curtis walking down the street. With him were two soldiers carrying his papers. The priest looked shaken and tired but he walked erect with his chin held high. He glanced around the square, but if he saw me he showed no sign of recognition. That was just as well as I was not the only one watching him closely. A swarthy little man, who had not been in the bar long, was also studying Curtis. The fellow was following the priest's gaze, trying to see who he was staring at. But when the man looked over his shoulder at me I was busy studying the bottom of my tankard, appearing as disinterested as possible.

A few minutes after the old man had disappeared into a courtyard of the university, the stranger got up and followed him through the arch. I was sure he would be watching Curtis's rooms to note down any visitors. But Curtis was a wily old fox who had been in the spying business for much longer than his pursuers. I knew that there was a secret back entrance to his chambers.

A while later the young sprog across the table shouted "Checkmate!" for the third time in an hour and picked up his board and pieces to look for more worthwhile opposition. I was sitting at the table wondering what to do next when I felt a tug at my sleeve. I looked around and there was a very serious nine-or ten-year-old boy holding out a tankard to me. As soon as I took it he turned and walked quickly away. I could tell from the weight that it was empty, but in case anyone was watching I pretended to take a drink. Everyone in the tavern seemed to be concentrating on their own business and so slowly I took the pot below the level of the table to shield it and put my hand inside. There was a slip of paper; on it was an address and it was signed *'Saint Arthur'*.

The address was an old house in a backstreet near the university. Without a word the old woman who answered my knock gestured to a room at the back. There I found my belongings, which someone must have taken from the room Curtis had arranged for me in his college. I met the old man there early the next morning.

"Ah, Flashman," he called, taking off the cloak and wide-brimmed hat that had hidden his priest's robes. "It is just as well that Grant cannot abide you or you would have been taken yesterday. I only just convinced them of my innocence and I have lived in the city for years."

"Did they not find anything in your rooms?"

"Of course not. I am not stupid enough to leave anything there. But they are very nervous over Grant and his escort leaves tomorrow. I have arranged for you to join it to try to help Grant escape, if he changes his mind."

"I couldn't possibly get him away from an escort that size, even if he was willing," I protested. "We will just have to tell Wellington that his bird has flown." I paused and then added hesitantly, "Unless you are willing to consider another way of stopping him talking?"

"You mean killing him? I am a priest, Flashman. I could not countenance such a sin, even if I thought it was better than the torture that must await him. No, we must do all we can to help Grant see the error of his ways. I am passing the word to partisan groups that Grant is leaving and reminding them of Wellington's reward. In the meantime I have papers authorising you to leave the city and more ordering you to join the force with Grant. It would be best if you join the escort after it has left the city; I suspect that Marmont will be watching it closely while it is here." He passed me some papers and I saw that both orders were signed by General Martiniere.

"Isn't he the officer that threatened Grant with execution?" I asked, pointing at the signature.

"Yes, the orders are forged. Any officer is likely to accept an order from him rather than risk his anger by checking it. They will welcome an extra sword in the escort and see no danger in one additional man."

"But if the partisans attack, they are likely to kill me as a Frenchman, and what do I do if they do not attack?"

Curtis's plan seemed desperate to me, and try as I might I could not see an outcome that would work out favourably for T Flashman Esquire. Either I was to be knifed by a partisan who mistook me for a frog officer, or if the partisans did not attack I was on my way into France with three hundred soldiers and a witless idiot who refused to escape.

"If the partisans attack, you will have to try to stay close to Grant. He will vouch for your identity," stated Curtis with more confidence than I think he felt. Even if Grant did overcome his hatred of me to confirm who I was, it would probably be too late. The partisans were likely to attack at night, shooting and stabbing first, and asking questions later.

But what choice did I have? If I did not join the escort, I did not doubt that Curtis would find out from his spies and report back to Wellington. I still had my British uniform coat but it would be damn dicey deciding whether to use that in a night action, when it was hard to see who was winning. It would be a firing squad for Flashy if the French beat off the attack and I was found in it, and a cut throat if I left it too long to make the change.

Not for the first time in my life, I felt as though doors were being slammed shut all around me leaving me with only one dangerous way forward. My mind raced, thinking of a way out, but all the options I came up with had unpleasant consequences for me. The futility of my situation was highlighted by Curtis's final words after he had wished me good luck.

"What do I do if the partisans don't attack?" I almost pleaded with him.

"In that case you will just have try to reason with Grant to persuade him to escape." Even the priest had the grace to look slightly embarrassed by that response. He knew as well as I did that I stood more chance of teaching a fish to knit.

From a discrete distance I watched the escort march out the next morning. There were six groups of fifty men marching in lines five abreast. In between each group a team of horses pulled a cannon and behind each gun were two identical wagons. Twelve wagons in all and in one of them I knew that Grant would be hidden. Marshal Marmont himself accompanied the escort outside the city and took the salute as they marched past him down the road. For the marching men it was the start of a three-hundred-and-twenty-mile journey through Valladolid, Burgos, San Sebastian and over the border to Bayonne in France.

Chapter 19

With forged papers in the name of the engineer Lieutenant Moreau, I joined the escort that afternoon. There was a knot of mounted officers at the head of the column and I reported to their commander, a Major Lagarde. He looked a capable character, grey haired but his back was ramrod straight with the bearing of a soldier. He accepted my orders and, having noted the signature at the bottom, he simply invited me to join their group. I fell in with some of the other lieutenants behind and discretely examined my new companions.

Marmont had been ordered to send a draft of three hundred men to France and he must have searched for men who would be least useful in future combat. Examining the group of officers and the first section of men, I could see plenty of grey beards. Quite a number had been wounded too; I counted five men wearing eye patches marching in the first section and amongst the officers two had arms missing. I explained to my new companions that I was an engineer and was expecting to be ordered to join the *Grande Armée* going to Russia when I got back to France. Many of the old hands looked at me with sympathy.

"You don't know cold until you have been east of Berlin," grumbled one grizzled captain. "Tears turn to ice in your eyes and the cold air freezes your lungs."

"But," objected the only young officer in the group, "the *Grande Armée* is marching in the summer; they will be back before the winter, once they have taught the Russians a lesson."

The grizzled captain turned to me and nodded towards the young man. "Jerome's uncle is a general who has pulled strings to get the lad on his staff." He looked at the young man. "I hope your uncle has more sense than you and prepares for winter. You can always take things off but you cannot put them on if you do not have them." He turned back to me. "Take my advice, lad, and take the warmest clothes you can find to Russia, whenever you travel." Having been to Russia myself a few years previously I knew all too well that he was right, not that I could admit it then.

The junior officers chatted for the rest of the afternoon, mostly about what they were looking forward to in France, and I joined in. Major Lagarde was a dour, silent man, but he knew his business. He seemed to be constantly scanning the horizon and had a group of riders scouting ahead and on our flanks. He was clearly determined to bring as many of his men through the partisan territory as he could. By evening his scouts had found a plateau of ground on which to camp. The wagons were gathered together, perimeter fires set around the camp to illuminate anyone approaching, and the cannon, loaded with canister, were placed at intervals. Guards were set with a full fifty sentries at any one time. Many of the men might have been old, but they were also practised veterans and set up the camp with ease. I realised that this convoy would not be an easy nut for the partisans to crack as Lagarde was determined that they would put up stiff resistance. I pulled out my glass and studied the surrounding terrain but could see no obvious route to attack. Once the camp had been alerted there was little cover from the French volleys that would be poured into any assault.

I felt confident that there would be no partisan ambush that night but I still needed to find Grant if he was to give me protection when the partisans did appear. No one had mentioned his existence all afternoon. It was only as I walked with Lieutenant Jerome through the wagons that evening that I saw that one in the middle had four sentries around it.

"Are we carrying treasure back to France?" I asked confidentially, gesturing at the guards.

"No," replied Jerome, glancing furtively about him. "We are not supposed to know, but it is a spy. A British spy that we are taking back to France for interrogation."

I did not sleep well that night. Despite Lagarde's precautions, every screech from an owl or bark from a fox had me wondering if it was some partisan signal. As the sun rose next morning and we prepared to get underway again, I desperately hoped that somehow the partisans had managed to spirit Grant away without his guards raising the alarm. But when I looked, the sentries around his wagon were alive and checking on their prisoner.

We set off again in what was to become a regular routine. But that morning I noticed that Lagarde rode down the column and when he reached Grant's wagon he dismounted and went inside. He was with Grant for about an hour and when he rode to the front of the column to re-join us, he looked a troubled man. Over the next few days Lagarde spent several hours with Grant, as did some of his captains, but they kept their own counsel and none of the more junior lieutenants knew what was discussed.

146

We had passed through Valladolid and were on our way to Burgos when Jerome rode up alongside me one morning looking very pleased with himself. If there is one person you can rely on to tell you a secret, it is someone who should not know it in the first place. They are always desperate to prove that they are in the circle of knowledge.

"Moreau," Jerome whispered. "I have news."

"What is it?"

"The spy in the cart is a British officer called Grant."

"So?" I asked.

"You have not heard of him? He is a famous British officer who has often been seen watching our positions. They say he knew more about where our army was than the marshal himself."

"Pah, he probably just had a good guide," I cried dismissively. I was irritated to know that Grant had acquired such an illustrious reputation.

"But you don't understand. He is a British officer and he was captured wearing his British uniform, so he is not a spy."

"Why does that matter?" I asked, not wanting to appear too knowledgeable on the difference between spies and officers.

"He is being taken to Paris, to the minister of war, for interrogation." Jerome looked around him to check we were not being overheard. "You know what that means? It is torture for him but he is a prisoner of war. If the British find out, they might start torturing our prisoners of war. Major Lagarde says it is a dishonourable way to behave."

"Well, I don't see what he can do about it… unless he is willing to let this Grant escape." For a brief moment the thought that the French would do my job for me filled me with hope, but it was soon dashed.

"He can't do that. Some police from the ministry are waiting to collect the prisoner in Bayonne. The major would be arrested if he was found to have deliberately released him. But all the senior officers are upset about it; they say that they want nothing to do with the torture of a brave man."

The probability was that Grant would refuse to escape anyway if they offered him the chance, I thought. Even the partisans would have to carry him away by force, but with two thousand dollars in gold at stake, they would not hesitate to do that. But there was precious little sign of any partisan rescue. Each night we either camped in a town or city with a French garrison or on a carefully selected site as the first night. We had not even seen a partisan, never mind been attacked. In fact we had seen very few Spanish in our travels, as word of our march seemed to travel faster in the local community than our scouts. Whenever we reached a village it was abandoned, the inhabitants hiding with food supplies and anything else of value.

If I was in any doubt of the fear and intimidation that the French inflicted on the Spanish population, I was reminded the day when we reached Burgos. As we marched through the centre of the city I looked up at the massive cathedral with its multitude of turrets and towers. It was a beautiful Gothic building, but the grisly sight above the main entrance was the thing that attracted my attention. A long beam had been fixed above the cathedral door and nailed to it were a dozen round blobs. When we got closer I realised that they were human heads. Visitors to the cathedral would look fearfully up at them and cross themselves as they hurried under this gruesome portal. We found out later that the heads belonged to captured partisans. The local commander, a fanatical Bonapartist called General Hugo, had the heads removed after his prisoners had been killed and nailed to the beam. In France all church property had been confiscated during the revolution and the general had no time for religion. He particularly hated the Spanish church as he rightly suspected that it helped partisan groups.

We found more of General Hugo's handiwork on the outskirts of the city where the bodies of forty men were dangling from a huge gallows.

"The general has promised me that we will not be attacked in the vicinity of Burgos," stated Lagarde with a hint of distaste as we rode past this spectacle. "He claims he has killed all the partisans and exacts reprisals if any of his men are attacked."

"Most of these are too old to be partisans," the grizzled veteran claimed of men little older than himself. But he was right, many were grey bearded; although examining closely I saw two young boys also suspended from the ropes. The officers I was with fell silent as they rode past. They must have experienced, and probably taken part in, atrocities of their own to subdue the Spanish population. But they took no joy from it. The rumours we had heard about General Hugo indicated that he was a man who relished his work. Whatever they had done before, I sensed that these proud French soldiers did not approve of the unnecessary killing of old men and young boys.

While the reluctance of the partisans to attack the column was understandable, it did not help me. We were soon two weeks into the

148

journey and just a few days away from the French border. Grant always had four sentries guarding his wagon, and even if I could get inside and break him free from his shackles, the great booby would probably raise the alarm himself. I had to do something or I would end up in France and conscripted to the Russian campaign for real. It was time to make a break and return to the British lines. If I happened across partisans on the way, I would try to persuade them to attack the column. But unless they were a large group, they would stand little chance against Lagarde's careful preparations and his elderly, but competent, soldiers.

Escaping the column turned out to be far simpler than I expected. The next day we were marching through a partly wooded valley. The column's line of march stayed in the clear pasture and mounted officers were warned to stay away from the trees where we could be ambushed. Other officers were exercising their mounts by riding them up and down the column and I did the same. The difference was that I allowed my horse to ride slightly higher up the slope. When I got to the point where a finger of woodland scrub extended down in the valley I looked about. No other mounted officers were near and the nearest marching troops were a good distance away. I drew one of my pistols from my pocket and cocked it. I took a deep breath and then gave a shout of alarm. I pointed my pistol into the nearby woodland and fired. Several men shouted from the valley below, asking what it was, but I did not answer. I dropped my pistol back into my pocket and, drawing my sword, I charged into the woodland after my unseen prey.

You might think it was foolish to draw attention to my departure like that, but I knew my man. Lagarde was too experienced to allow his officers to charge off unsupported into woods that could be packed with partisans. He had given me orders to stay with the column, and if I was too headstrong to obey them then that was my lookout. I heard the shouting of orders to stand to, but there was no pursuit as my horse cantered into the trees. I got to the top of the slope and slowed to a walk, listening for any sign of action by the column. There was nothing, just the distant tramp of marching feet and a squealing cart wheel.

I wanted to be certain that the whole column was continuing without me; the last thing I needed was some chump like Jerome coming to find me. So when I came to a small escarpment that gave a view of the valley a quarter of a mile ahead of where I escaped, I settled down to wait. With my mount tied to some trees behind I crept forward with my telescope and lay on top of the little cliff. In a few minutes the first section of marching men appeared with the cannon and wagons following on behind. I could see several of the officers, including Jerome, riding along the column and scanning the hillside with their telescopes. I shrank back a little further and checked that the sun would not reflect off my glass. Soon the sixth wagon appeared, the one that I knew Grant was in.

"You poor, stupid bastard," I murmured to myself as I watched him go by. I did not feel any guilt. The idea of getting him away from the French had been mad from the start, even if Grant had been willing to co-operate. It was the damn partisans who had let him down, I reflected. We were constantly hearing of how they raided French supply trains, but they had stayed well clear of this column despite the two-thousand-dollar reward.

Thought of the partisans reminded me of the need to change my uniform. I took out the British coat from where it was pushed at the bottom of my saddlebag and slipped off the French uniform. I swapped the contents of the pockets and pulled on the familiar red coat. I pushed the blue coat back into the saddlebag and prepared to remount. I had one foot in the stirrup when I felt the cold metal circle of a gun barrel press into the back of my neck.

"Nice try, *monsieur*," called a voice in French.

Chapter 20

"Don't shoot," I replied automatically in French, the language the man had spoken. For a moment I thought that there had been a pursuit from the column after all. Had they had just watched me change sides? Then I heard more people moving through the trees and they seemed to be coming from higher up the hill. I tried to turn my head but the muzzle was pressed harder into my skull.

"Keep still, my little tyrant," taunted the man behind me in French. "You will see us soon enough." Then the man called out to those behind him in Spanish. "Look, we have a French officer trying to disguise himself as a Briton. Perhaps he is trying to desert."

"Officers don't desert their armies," called another voice behind me. "They live like kings in them."

"Perhaps that bastard Hugo sent him to find out where he can kill more partisans," declared another voice and that suggestion was met with growls of agreement from several others.

"No," I called out this time in Spanish. "I am a British officer. I was sent to rescue a man called Grant who is travelling in that column. There is a two-thousand-dollar reward from General Wellington if you help me take him alive."

This suggestion was greeted with the sound of expectorating and a loud spit from the man behind me. "We know all about El Granto and his reward," he stated gruffly. "It is just the kind of bait that Hugo would use to tempt us to attack his men in the open. Is that why he sent you, to persuade us to walk into his trap?"

"No, of course not. I am British, I tell you. I can prove it…"

Before I could say any more a rough cloth sack was pulled over my head and my arms were grabbed. As I yelled my muffled protests, my hands were tied behind my back but not before several fists connected sharply with my ribs. I was still yelling that I was British when a gag was tied tightly over the top of the sack, forcing the rough cloth into my mouth and leaving me only able to grunt incoherently. I felt my sword being unbuckled and the pistols being taken from my pockets.

I received another rain of blows when they found the copy of the letter to the French minister of war in my pocket. They could not read all of it but they knew it was in French and that it was addressed to Paris. Then I felt a rope noose pass over my head and for an awful moment I thought that they were going to hang me on the spot. I thrashed and writhed around to get away and they must have guessed what I was thinking for there was more laughter and blows, before I felt the rope pulling me forward rather than up.

They dragged me for what seemed several miles through the trees, yanking on the rope when I tripped over a root and kicking and punching me when I did not move fast enough. I might not have been able to speak, but from what I overheard I gathered that when we got to wherever we were going they were going to hold some sort of trial. There was much talk of a fearsome 'chief' who hated the French and seemed to specialise in getting information from prisoners. Nobody seemed in any doubt of the outcome of my inquisition as the punches kept coming; but at least, I thought, I would have a chance to defend myself. Surely, I reasoned, I could get them to send word to the British to prove my identity. Even this chief would not kill a British officer, especially if there was a chance that Wellington would pay a reward for me too.

Eventually they started to slow down and I could smell wood smoke and human excrement through the sacking. I realised that we were getting close to their camp. Suddenly I felt the rope being removed from my neck and I was pushed forward. The sack was still kept firmly in place by the gag so I could not see where I was going. Then the men made me crouch as though to get through a small opening. They pushed me forward into whatever space it was but my head hit something hard and I fell to my knees, feeling slightly sick. They rolled me through the opening into the area beyond. There was plenty of light coming through the fibres of the sack and so I guessed I was still outside. Was I in some sort of cage? I wondered. I heard the men move away, laughing, as I struggled to get on my knees while my head throbbed with pain. Then I heard something scuffle much nearer.

There was a strange crooning noise and I tried to work out what it could be. Had they left me defenceless with my hands tied behind my back, in an enclosure with a vicious wild animal? No, I could hear the men still moving away. If I was about to be killed by some creature, surely they would have stayed to watch. I tried to shuffle away from the sound but my back was soon up against branches that seemed to have been tied into some form of wall. The crooning noise came closer and then I felt hands touching my face. The fingers pressed into my eye sockets. I thought they were going to try to gouge my eyes and tried to turn away. But then the hands got purchase on the sack cloth and started to tear it.

The hands tore a wide long slit in the sacking opposite my eyes. Through it I got my first glance of the creature helping me. I say creature, for that was what he was then; but from the shreds of uniform he still wore, he must have once been a French soldier. Now he was half naked with long hair and a matted beard. But most disturbing were his wild, rolling eyes and the strange, guttural animal noises he made. I tried to ask for help through the gag, but even though I barely managed a series of strangled grunts, my companion just started to scream to drown out the noise. When I shook my head at him in an effort to get him to remove the gag he shrank back out of my view. Moving my head against the bars behind me, I managed to widen the slit in front of my face. Slowly I managed to draw the top of the sack over my head like a hood and then I saw what had driven the poor devil mad.

We were both in a wooden cage, not tall enough to stand up in, but made of stout branches that were well lashed together and as thick as a man's wrist. It was set in the middle of a circular clearing between what I took at first to be gnarled tree trunks. Then I saw some colour on one and realised that most of the trunks had at least one man nailed to them. The bodies were blackened with age and decay but the one that had caught my eye still had part of his blue uniform coat showing.

Dear God, I thought, I have to convince them that I am not French. I cannot end my days like this: dying in agony nailed to a tree just because I was caught wearing the wrong coloured coat. Little did I know that the crazy events of that day were only just beginning.

I have had the misfortune to stand in various courts in my time, from a drum head court marital, to hearings in the House of Commons. But I have experienced nothing like the trial with the partisans – and that includes a trial by ordeal I endured in Africa. In all of those cases the accused had at least the slightest chance of being found not guilty. I quickly discovered that the verdict in my trial was a forgone conclusion.

"But the chief is always the judge," whined one of the men who came to collect me some three hours later. "I don't see how we can have a trial without the chief."

"The chief would find him guilty as well," claimed another. "Gomez used to be a lawyer so he can be the judge as well as the prosecutor. Now what is he fretting about?"

You can imagine the stifled protests I was trying to get past the gag at hearing this.

153

"Listen here, you French bastard," shouted the second man. "It is better for you that the chief is not here. The chief knows ways to kill a man that will make you beg for a death like crucifixion."

With that cheery thought rattling around my mind, I was picked up and half dragged away. I tried to reassure myself that if this Gomez was a lawyer then at least he was an educated man who would listen to reasoned argument. But as I saw my 'courtroom', I had fresh doubts. It was an old stone barn that was packed with at least two hundred people. There was a roar of rage as I appeared in the door and the crowd surged towards me. I was defenceless with my hands tied behind me and for a moment I thought I would be lynched on the spot. Certainly if the guards had not pushed them back with cudgels, I would have been torn apart without the benefit of any trial at all. I have never experienced such venous hatred from a mass of people, and I speak as someone who has sought election to parliament. They saw me as a personification of the French invader and all the atrocities that the French had committed. I was surrounded by screams and threats in Spanish and some dialects I did not understand, but their meaning was clear.

Eventually the guards started to push their way through the throng, but they did not do a lot to deter several fists that flashed out at my head. They even stood aside for a young woman whose face was contorted in rage as she kicked me in the balls. I was therefore battered, bruised and bent over in agony with watering eyes when I finally made my way into the cleared space which comprised the centre of the court. My hands were untied and I was forced to stand straight against a beam before my hands were rebound on the other side of the pillar. Gazing around as my vision cleared, I could see the barely restrained mob still yelling all around me while more people sat up on the roof joists to get a better view of the coming spectacle. In the centre of the cleared space was a table with my sword, pistols and the damning evidence of my French jacket and the letter to Paris.

A man, whom I took to be Gomez, stepped forward and hammered the hilt of his dagger on the table to call the trial to order. "Quiet, quiet," he yelled. "We are not barbarians; we are not going to tear him apart now." I felt momentary relief before he continued. "We will have justice, proper legal proceedings, and then when he is found guilty we will execute him." A huge cheer greeted this pronouncement and people began to settle down expectantly.

By now the pain in my balls had dulled to an ache and I started to marshal my thoughts. There did not seem to be a counsel for the defence. I guessed that I would have to defend myself and, considering the mood of the audience, I would not be given long to convince them. I had been thinking about this in the cage and I had what I thought was a pretty conclusive case that I was British. Unless they had worn away since I last looked, my boots still had a London maker's mark inside. My shirts and breeches were embroidered with my name for the laundry and this name matched that sewn into the red coat. The only item of clothing I had that was not British was the French uniform coat, and I could explain about my mission. This was surely more than enough to create at least an element of doubt, I thought. At worst, if they were still not convinced, I could suggest that they get a message to Wellington. I could promise a generous reward for my return and the general's displeasure and retribution if I was harmed in any way.

I started to rehearse my brief and effective argument in my head as Gomez opened the proceedings. "This French officer," he began, "was seen riding with the French column that passed through the valley this morning. Where is the man who saw him?"

A wiry partisan pushed through the crowd, "I did," he declared. I recognised the voice of the man who had pushed the gun muzzle against my head.

"The prisoner *claims* to be a British officer," announced Gomez, giving me disappointed look as though I had let him down by not immediately admitting my guilt. "What uniform was he wearing when he was riding with the French column?"

"The French one," replied the partisan promptly while grinning at me. The response brought a cheer of approval from the watching crowd that completely drowned out my incoherent raging from the dock.

"Of course I was wearing the French coat! I was in disguise, you bloody fool." That, at least, was what I was trying to say. But all that came out was a strangled roar as I went red in the face straining against my bonds.

Gomez gave another sad shake of the head at my outburst and pressed on. "And did the other French officers appear to treat him as one of their own?"

"They did," confirmed the partisan to more acclaim from the crowd.

"And when you captured him, was he changing into a British uniform so that he could discover our camp and lead General Hugo's men to destroy us?"

"He was," affirmed the partisan, again still appearing very pleased with himself. This brought a triumphant roar from the crowd. Some of them started waving large knives in the air as though they were ready to hack me to pieces there and then.

I was damn scared. I had not been expecting the fair advocacy of William Garrow but this was ridiculous. With the suggestion that I worked for Hugo planted firmly in their minds, it looked like few would be willing to listen to anything I had to say. But Gomez was not finished yet. He turned to the items on the table.

"Was he carrying this Mameluke sword?" cried Gomez, pointing to the Arabic writing on the hilt. The Mamelukes were Arabic soldiers the French had recruited in Egypt. They had been responsible for a massacre of civilians in Madrid among other atrocities. My sword had been captured from an Arab soldier in India. The affirmative response from the partisan was completely drowned out by another roar from the mob.

Gomez waited for the noise to die down and then held up his hand for complete silence. In the hush he picked up the piece of paper from the table and held it by the tips of his fingers as though it was contagious. If he was a lawyer, I thought, he could probably read French and that wretched document could be my death warrant. "And was he carrying this?" asked Gomez quietly.

"Yes," agreed the partisan, unsure, like the rest of the audience, what message was on the paper.

"This man, who *claims* to be a British officer," proclaimed Gomez, his voice rising, "was carrying a letter from Marshal Marmont to the minister of war in Paris!" There were gasps and exclamations at that, but Gomez was not finished. "A letter that offers the British officer Major Grant for interrogation and torture." He could not have created more of a sensation by announcing I was actually Bonaparte himself in disguise. The fact that I could not have been both spying for General Hugo and taking Grant for torture did not seem to occur to anyone as the room fell into uproar. People were yelling my guilt, shouting suggestions for my death, and now nearly everyone was brandishing a knife in the air. I realised then that I would not get a chance to defend myself, but also that no one would listen to me even if I did.

Gomez walked up to me and gestured at the howling mob. His eyes burned into mine with unbridled hatred as he hissed, "See, Frenchman, like many of your countryman before you, you will learn that you cannot rape and murder with impunity. Justice will be done."

"I'm British," I tried to shout back at him through the gag but he had already turned away. I leant back against the pillar I was tied against, sweating and shaking with fear. I have seen a couple of lynchings in my time and I think the poor bastards must have felt as I did then. It was not about justice, it was about fear and revenge. They had suffered and they wanted to inflict suffering on someone else. Even if they took the gag off to hear my screams when they nailed me up, they were not going to listen to any proof that I was not French. Their bloodlust was up. The Spaniards were notorious for their blood feuds and I was a score that they could easily settle. I stood there with my mind stupified with shock and horror and for a while I could not think straight at all.

Then things got even worse. I gradually realised that a gruesome auction was underway. It was not for money; none of them looked rich enough to have a pot to piss in. It was about suffering, my suffering. They were absolutely arguing over who should hammer in the nails. Gomez had three of the huge cast-iron pins in his hands. God knows how many had been sold before I realised what was happening. I remember that the woman who had kicked me in the balls was arguing passionately that she should have one as the French had killed her father and her son. Another older woman had lost two sons to the French but I gathered she had been given a nail for an earlier victim. They fell to arguing between themselves and a scuffle broke out before the women were pulled apart.

I was still struggling to accept it was happening at all. After all my suffering at Albuera, not to mention all the other battles I had fought in, was I really going to end my days nailed to a tree, the victim of mistaken identity? I was not going to give up yet. "I'm British," I shouted through the gag and then I kept on shouting it, again and again. Surely, I thought, someone would take the gag off to give me a chance to say something to prove I was on their side. "I'm British, I'm British, I'm British."

Eventually my noise cut through the hubbub and heads turned in my direction. But their looks were not curiosity as to what I had to say, more irritation that I had interrupted them.

157

Gomez walked towards me and waved his razor-sharp dagger in my face. "One more word from you, Frenchman, and we will start cutting off your fingers now." To show he meant business he used the blade to nick my cheek just below my eye and I felt the warm trickle of blood down my face.

I am pretty sure I prayed then, as I am inclined to do when things are really desperate. If I did, it produced quick results, for almost immediately a hush fell over the angry mob. I could see heads starting to move at the back of the crowd as the words were spread through the throng: "The chief is here."

Chapter 21

I admit I may have thought sourly of the Almighty at that point. For just when I thought things could not get any worse, he delivered a person that my guards had already told me could give me a crueller death than crucifixion. With trepidation I watched two tall men push their way through the crowd, making a path for someone in between them. Gomez strode forward to welcome his master, probably anxious to ensure he was not punished for taking on the role of judge. Then the crowd parted, and as the chief came into view I knew that my unworthy prayers had indeed been answered.

The chief stared at me with shock and surprise for a moment. Despite my mouth and jaw still being covered by the sack and gag, I watched as recognition crossed her beautiful face. Then I think my legs gave way and I slid down the beam until I was resting on the floor.

"Release him. I know this man" were some of the sweetest words I ever heard. They were greeted with expressions of dismay from the crowd, but I knew I was safe now. I remember staring up and thinking that even in her shirt and riding breeches and with the mud of the journey spattered on her face, Agustina de Aragon was still the most beautiful woman I had ever seen. The last time we had been together was some three years ago in Seville, when I had paid for clothes, weapons and a horse to help her join the partisans. By Christ, I thought, that was the best investment I ever made. Gomez, though, was not willing to give up that easily.

"Agustina, this man is a spy. We saw him in a French uniform riding with a French column and he has letters from Marmont to the minister of war in Paris."

"I know he has been a spy and a soldier, but he is British," announced Agustina loudly for all to hear.

"Perhaps he is a spy for both sides," replied Gomez stubbornly, still making no move to release me.

"This man is one of Lord Wellington's most trusted aides," declared Agustina, turning to the crowd. "He worked with Lord Wellington when he was in India, long before they came to Spain. If you kill him, we will have to fight the British as well as the French. Is that what you want?"

The mood of the crowd was changing, the knives quietly being sheathed and several hostile looks now being directed at Gomez. I would have backed down at this point, but Gomez was made of sterner, or perhaps stupider, material.

"How do you know this is the same man?" he persisted, standing behind his table of damning evidence.

There was a flash of metal and a knife thudded into the wood between his hands. I recognised the thin blade; it was the knife that Agustina wore up her left sleeve. "Because he was my lover," she shouted angrily. "Do you think I do not know the men I have had between my legs?" She took a deep breath to calm herself and added with an icy chill, "Now release him, or you will replace him."

Gomez moved then all right. He clearly took her threat seriously and I began to wonder what Agustina had done to become the chief of this band of partisans. When I had been with her before, she had been known as the Maid of Zaragoza; a national heroine who was famous for firing a cannon that stopped a French attack on that city. She had shown she could manipulate men even then, not least by involving me in an act of notorious blasphemy in Seville cathedral. As Gomez cut the bindings around my wrists and pulled me to my feet I reflected that Agustina must have developed a steely and ruthless streak to command a group of partisans this size.

"Give the captain back his possessions," commanded Agustina to Gomez to complete his subjugation. Then she turned to the large crowd in the barn. "Leave us," she ordered, and the two henchmen that had cleared a way for her into the hall now started to marshal the crowds out of the double doors at the end of the barn.

I put my pistols in my pockets as I watched them leave. Then I looked at Agustina. She seemed to have aged more than the three years which had passed since we last met. She looked thinner, and when she returned my gaze her face looked tired and drawn, although she still managed a weak smile.

"Are you all right?"

"I am now you are here. Things were getting a bit ugly a while back." I tried to sound casual but my legs were still trembling and it had taken me two attempts to buckle my sword as my hands were shaking with what must have been shock. If she noticed, she did not say anything.

"Gomez," she called after her lieutenant, who was now rushing from the room. "I would like you to join us in a few minutes. Bring some food and wine with you." She cocked a quizzical eyebrow at me and then added, "And some maps. I have a feeling that we will need them and your counsel." He nodded, appearing ridiculously pleased to be back in her favour, and hurried away. "Despite what you may think, he is a good man," she declared quietly after he had gone. "His wife and three children were killed by the French. Now what are you doing here?"

"I was going to ask you the same question. How did you end up in charge of these partisans?"

"Oh, I have been in several different groups since you knew me," she replied. "They were all happy to have the famous Maid of Zaragoza in their ranks. I had planned to eventually return to the city, but when I got here the local commander and I became lovers. We were together for over a year. When he was killed they voted for me to take over. My fame brings in new recruits and Hugo hates being beaten by a woman."

She had become tougher, I thought. When we had met for the first time she had cried when she had told me that she only fired the cannon that stopped the French assault because an earlier slain lover had begged her to. Now she mentioned the death of this more recent partner as casually as she might describe her dinner. I had no doubt that she must have seen and perhaps committed some appalling atrocities since we last met; the evidence of the forest clearing proved that.

"Your people certainly have a grotesque way of disposing of prisoners," I pointed out. "It is not something that I would have thought you would have done, but I suppose we have both changed a lot since we last met."

"It was something that they started before my time, but I could not stop it. That would have appeared weak. These men are as tough as iron. For me, as a woman, to lead them, I have to appear even tougher." She looked uncomfortable, as though this was not something that she wanted to talk about, and said more brightly, "What about you? Why are you here with letters to the French minister of war?"

"I have been sent to try to help that infernal nuisance Grant escape, or El Granto as you know him. That was why I was riding in disguise with the column he was in. The idiot has given his parole and refuses to escape, and anyway they guard him around the clock. I had been hoping a partisan group would attack; that was why I left the column to find one. Unfortunately your men found me and drew their own conclusions as to my mission."

161

"We cannot attack a column that size; we would lose too many men. They would probably still get Grant away if we tried. Where are they taking him?"

"To Bayonne and then on to Paris."

She looked thoughtful for a moment. "Bayonne is in Basque country. That would be the place to get him."

"What is Basque country?"

"The Basques are a people that live on both sides of the border; there are lots of Basques here. They are a proud mountain people that don't see themselves as either French or Spanish. Inside France the French will think that they are safe and may drop their guard. They certainly won't use three hundred men to take Grant all the way to Paris. But if we can capture him in Bayonne we can soon get him away across the mountains. With Wellington's two thousand dollars in gold to share with those that help, we will not be short of volunteers."

I loved the way she used the word 'we'; my spirits were rising already. These Basque fellows could take all the risks and deliver the doubtless protesting Grant to me. Then I would return to Wellington with a suitably enhanced tale of my endeavour, the hero of the hour. Meanwhile Grant's reputation would be tarnished by capture, his parole and probably by him whining about being rescued with his honour ruined. I chuckled at the thought. "If your men have to hit Grant to get him to come with them, that will be absolutely fine," I offered happily.

Agustina looked puzzled. "But you will need to go with them to find Grant and help plan the capture. My men can hardly march into a French barracks and start asking questions, but you can in your French uniform."

I gave her my most winning smile. "But I thought we could renew our old friendship while your men are away. I could lend them my uniform; surely some of them speak French?"

She reached out and held my hand. "Maybe tonight," she smiled. "But tomorrow you go with the men. They are not proper soldiers and don't understand about saluting and ranks. They would soon give themselves away."

Her jaw had a determined look when she had finished speaking and I could sense that she was not used to challenges to her commands. What she said made sense too, for at that moment Gomez returned with some maps followed by a girl with food and wine on a tray. I watched Gomez cross the barn; his manner could best be described as furtive, shoulders slightly hunched and not soldierly at all.

Agustina explained to him the plan while I tore into the bread and guzzled the wine. I had not eaten or drunk anything since breakfast with the French early that morning and I was famished.

"I would like you to go with Captain Flashman," Agustina declared to Gomez. "You know the Basque contacts we have in France. Take six trusted men."

Gomez shot me a dark look then. Whatever his mistress thought, I sensed that he was yet to be convinced of my loyalty. Agustina, who missed little, noticed the glance.

"If you go with him, you will be able to see for yourself that he is not working with the French and that he is a British spy."

She smiled happily at this resolution to Gomez's concerns, while he looked at me as though he found me as trustworthy as an angry scorpion. We spread the maps out then and I traced the route that the column was planning to take to Bayonne. It was the fastest route over good roads but Gomez knew another we could use where we were less likely to encounter French troops. Mounted on horses, we were set to reach Bayonne at the same time as the French.

"It is settled then," pronounced Agustina firmly when the planning was done. "Gomez, select your men and have them ready to leave at noon tomorrow. In the meantime, Captain Flashman and I can catch up on old times."

I took the half-drunk jug of wine and two cups with me as we made our way to the woodland hut that was the home of my favourite partisan *generalissima*. My body was battered and bruised from the beating I had taken in the courtroom, but there were no serious injuries. Now the recent danger was past and the shock was receding, I felt that familiar joy of just having survived another brush with death. Inside the hut, as she lit some candles, I saw hanging on the wall the medal that she had been given by the Spanish government for saving the city of Zaragoza. She had been wearing it the first time we met. Agustina followed my gaze

"A lot has happened in three years. Did you think of me during that time?"

"Of course. After what we did in Seville cathedral, people keep reminding me or hinting at it. I am still not sure if you enhanced my reputation or ruined it." A priest had promised to blacken my name after we had made love in a dark corner of the huge building during a

163

midnight mass. But the British and Spanish had fallen out on strategy shortly afterwards and there had mostly just been muttering behind my back.

She giggled. "I am sorry I tricked you into entering the cathedral. But if it makes you feel better, no mass I have been to since has been as pleasurable."

"I should hope not."

She looked beautiful in the candlelight and I stepped across and took her in my arms, crushing her lips on mine.

"My my," she gasped, laughing when she could breathe. "We are not in a cathedral now, you know."

"Really?" I growled back. "Because I was thinking we could have our own very special holy communion right here."

We were at each other then, tearing off clothes, desperate to renew the passion of former times. It was one of the best communions I have ever had. The sacrament was given and received at least twice before we lay naked and sated in her bed, drinking more wine. I reached over with my cup and splashed some red wine between her breasts.

"Behold the blood of Christ."

"Thomas, don't be blasphemous," she cried, smiling and wiping it away. "You might be a Protestant but I am a good Catholic girl."

"I know a priest in Seville who would disagree. But he is wrong: you are a *very good* Catholic girl."

"Why, thank you, kind sir. But my men are Catholic, and while I have had my disagreements with the Church, I think I still am too. I go to mass when we can get a priest to come up here."

"Well, your next confession should be interesting."

"Mmm, yes. If I have to do a penance, I might as well make it worthwhile. Perhaps I can perform a Christ-like miracle on Lazarus here." With that she reached down and started to caress my resting manhood, which began to respond instantly to her touch.

I pretended to ignore her act of resuscitation while I sipped more wine. "You must have over a hundred fighting men here and their families. How do you survive?"

"Oh, there are deer and boar in the forest and farmers sell or give us food. We get supplies from enemy columns, but we generally attack small ones so that we can be sure that there are no survivors. That way it takes much longer for them to realise that the convoy is missing and has not been diverted elsewhere."

"Aren't you worried about French attacks?"

164

"We have to move camp sometimes and we have people in all the towns where there are French forces who will warn us if an attack is planned. We had messages about your column over a week ago telling us it was on the way." She paused. "There now, you see? Lazarus has risen and come back to life. I have performed a miracle." With that she leaned down and gave 'Lazarus' a kiss.

"You are a very wicked woman."

"Yes, that is what they say about me," she purred, running her fingers up my chest. "Oh, I forgot to tell you. Remember when we met before, I had vowed to kill the Frenchman who had refused to help me and let my little son die when I was in prison?"

"Yes," I agreed, recalling that she had been captured briefly by the French when Zaragoza finally fell.

"Well, I found him. He was one of the guards in a supply column we captured."

"Did you kill him or was he already dead from the attack?"

"Oh, I killed him. He had let my little son die in agony over seven days and so I did the same to him. You have to use a hot knife to cauterise the wound or they will bleed to death too quickly," she claimed matter-of-factly. "I put out an eye, cut off some of his fingers and toes, gelded him and then burnt his cock before slicing his guts open towards the end." She listed the injuries with the same dispassionate manner that a quartermaster might use counting off supplies. The casual way she spoke about such horrors sent a chill down my spine, while my imagination conjured up such graphic images that my ardour was soon cooled.

Watching your child die must be awful, but to inflict that torture on another human being in revenge seemed monstrous to me. My mind struggled to reconcile the beautiful woman I had known and had just made love to with someone who could do such a thing. I know she had to appear tough in front of her men and she had probably seen far more brutality in the war than me, but the Agustina I had known before had definitely changed. I tried to rid my mind of a picture of her standing over her naked victim with a glowing hot iron in her hand. To try to distract myself I looked across at her naked loveliness. There were those now familiar curves and a face that looked warm and loving. There was not even a hint that she could be capable of such atrocities. As I watched she raised herself up on one elbow, but then frowned and looked a little disappointed.

"Oh dear," she exclaimed. "Lazarus seems to have died again."

Chapter 22

Agustina understood that talk of gelding and burning was not ideal foreplay to get me in the mood, and I confess that I never felt entirely comfortable with her afterwards. That is not to say that I was immune to her considerable charms and persuasive skills. Like a well-run monastery we continued regular communion during the night, observing the services of Matins and Prime, and we would have enjoyed the communion religious houses call Terce at mid-morning if someone had not knocked on the door. It was Gomez, ostensibly come to check on arrangements for the journey, but probably because he did not like me getting too close to Agustina.

A short while later and I was mounting my horse alongside Gomez and five other swarthy cut-throats. I saw then what Agustina had meant: they could no more have passed as soldiers than my Aunt Agnes. I was in my British uniform with the French coat once more in the saddlebags. Word had got round the camp that our mission involved earning the two-thousand-dollar reward and quite a few came to see us off. There was no cheering, though, and most looked damn sheepish when they caught my eye, remembering that they had been baying to crucify me just the previous day. Having given me a long, lingering farewell kiss in her room, Agustina was more formal in front of her men, wishing us all well before we set off along a forest track.

We had gone just a few miles when we reached a crossroads and Gomez pulled his horse up to a stop. I had already decided that I was set for a tedious journey as the man had ignored half my questions about the route and had given short, unhelpful answers when he did speak. Still, that was better than his companions, who pretended to speak only Basque so that they could ride in a group together behind me. Now, though, Gomez did turn to talk to me.

"Hand over your pistols," he ordered curtly.

"What is this?" I responded indignantly. "You know I am a British officer and that I am on your side."

For a moment I wondered if it was Gomez who was a French spy and the story about his lost family was just a cover. But then I heard hammers cocking behind me and turned to see the other Basques all with pistols or carbines levelled in my direction. I realised that I did not have a choice and slowly reached into my pockets to withdraw the weapons.

"You can keep your fancy sword," continued Gomez, "but when I am riding in front of a man I do not trust, I do not want him to be able to shoot me in the back."

"Oh, for God's sake, there are six of you. How am I supposed to kill six of you with two pistols? And anyway, your chief has told you that she knows me as British from three years back."

"Agustina might trust you, but I do not. From what I hear you have spent time wearing many different uniforms and I wonder where your true loyalties lie. If we get back here with Major Grant then I will give you your pistols back and apologise. But until then my men and I will be watching you closely."

I suppose I should have been glad that they let me keep the sword, but if we had happened across strangers, it would have seemed odd for an officer to be seen without such a weapon at his hip.

With comrades like those you can imagine how joyless the journey was over the mountains. Everywhere I went, even to the privy, one of the Basques would be watching me. We often stopped at little villages in the hills. They would all talk Basque so that I could not understand and often I could tell that they were talking about me. From the hostile looks, whatever Gomez and the others were saying it was not favourable.

One morning after about four or five days of this icy camaraderie, Gomez called me over.

"We are in France now," he announced. "From now on you wear this." And with that he threw down on the dirt my French coat that he had taken from my saddlebag. As I shrugged the blue cloth over my shoulders, the look of dislike from the villagers intensified. Despite being in France, the French army was clearly not popular with the Basques.

We picked up a local guide on the French side of the border who took us north via back roads and footpaths where we were unlikely to meet any genuine French soldiers or French authorities. Just to be on the safe side Gomez had one of his men ride scout ahead, and often we would leave a man back to check we were not being followed. Eventually, after two days of this furtive travelling, we crested a hill early one evening and saw a large town some miles ahead of us and a stranger sitting under a tree.

Gomez pointed at the city and announced, "Bayonne," before spurring on to talk to the stranger alone. The rest of the partisans and I rested just below the crest of the hill so that we would not stand out on the horizon. After some minutes Gomez came back and announced that the French column was approaching the city several miles to our east. We rode along the ridge for a while until we could see the main road. I reached into my pocket for my telescope and studied the dusty little snake that seemed to be moving along it. The sun was low in the sky behind me but there was enough light to show that they were still moving along in six blocks comprising infantry, a cannon and two wagons in each segment. As far as I could tell the infantry detachments looked roughly the same size as when I had last seen them. At the front I could just make out a group of horsemen. I felt a touch of admiration for Lagarde, who seemed to have brought his men cautiously, but unscathed, through hundreds of miles of partisan territory. He would have probably cursed me and my stupidity, thinking I was the only casualty of the journey.

"The city gates of Bayonne shut at dusk so they will camp at the town of Villefranque tonight," said Gomez. He turned to look at me. "They will enter the city tomorrow morning and you will enter just afterwards. Jorge and Hernando" – he gestured at two of the Basques – "will come with you. Find out when and where Grant is travelling to Paris and let them know. They will get a message to the rest of us."

"Where will you be?" I asked.

"The river L'Ardour runs through the centre of Bayonne. There is only one bridge leading north. To get to Paris, Grant must cross it. We will be waiting on the Paris road." He gave me a guarded look before adding, "You do not need to know precisely where."

I just sighed in response; I had given up trying to convince them that I was on their side. They were clear that they would only trust me when I had proved my loyalty with actions rather than words. Gomez had explained once on the journey that the three worst defeats the partisans had suffered were after informers gave information to the French. "Everyone has their price," he had told me – not always money; sometimes it was a threat to torture or kill a loved one. He did not trust anyone any more and "especially not bastards with a French uniform in their saddlebags". There was, consequently, the usual frosty air around the campfire that evening as the Basques made their final plans together and probably debated whether I would indeed betray them.

The following morning Gomez and all but two of the Basques set off to ride ahead and prepare an ambush on the Paris road. I took a more leisurely approach, boiling the last of my tea over the campfire

168

and gnawing a crust of bread for breakfast. Jorge and Hernando watched my every move as though even by making tea I could somehow be signalling to the enemy.

As the sun climbed into the sky we rode towards the city and from another hilltop watched Lagarde and his men approach Bayonne. There were huge walls around the city that would have looked star shaped if viewed from above. One by one the columns of men, cannon and wagons entered under a huge arch in the fortifications and disappeared from view. I watched carefully with the glass. There were sentries at the gate but they did not interfere with soldiers. They only approached civilians; they seemed to be charging a tax on goods taken into the city.

"We go now," insisted Jorge, mounting up.

Soon we were riding down to the main road approaching the gates. There were poorer houses and hovels outside of the city walls which would be sacrificed in any attack. The paltry size of these dwellings made the huge stone walls of the city look even larger. Closer to, I could see that there were also half-flooded ditches in front of the walls while cannon seemed to bristle from every embrasure. It would be a formidable place to capture, I thought. The gate house was massive with two sets of gates. While only half a dozen soldiers were visible, I did not doubt that more were garrisoned in the stout towers on either side of the entrance. The Basques had dropped back now and were helping a woman drive some geese towards the city as though they had come together as a group. I had no papers: Lagarde had kept the orders to join his column and I had burned the damming letter from Marmont in a fire; it had caused me enough trouble already. If challenged, I had planned to say I was a straggler from Major Lagarde's column, but in the event no deception was necessary. The guards barely gave a lone French lieutenant a second glance. I watered my horse at a stone trough beyond the gates while I waited for my Basque shadows. After the old woman had paid her tax on the geese, they followed me into the city. Making sure that they had seen me, I remounted and started to walk my horse through the crowded streets, searching for a sign of the wagons and cannon that had travelled from Spain. I thought that they would be in or near the citadel and so I headed towards the centre of town. I had nearly got there when I heard a voice calling.

"Moreau, Moreau! My God it is you. Moreau, over here!"

For a moment I did not realise that the voice was calling me. I had not used that name for a week. But then I looked round and saw Lieutenant Jerome running towards me.

"Moreau, we thought you were dead. Lagarde would not let us ride after you as he thought it was a trap. Come, man, come down from your horse so that I can greet your properly."

Jerome had grabbed hold of my horse's bridle and was beaming up at me. I had no choice but to smile back and dismount.

"It is good to see you, old friend," I cried, throwing my arms around him. Over his shoulder I caught a glimpse of Jorge glaring at me with suspicion.

"You must come with me into the tavern," called Jerome enthusiastically. "Everyone will want to see you, especially the major. He said losing you was the one thing that spoiled the trip."

The young lieutenant was already pulling me towards the door of the tavern. I only just had time to tie my horse to a post before more of my former comrades tumbled out to see what the disturbance was. There was much exclaiming then about how they thought I had been lost and how pleased they were to see me. After the frigid companionship of the Basques, I was genuinely touched by the warmth of their welcome. It was not hard to return their greetings with enthusiasm. Quite what Jorge made of the hearty reunion I could only imagine.

Eventually I was pulled inside the tavern and a cup of wine was pressed into my hand. Then the crowd cleared in front of me and Lagarde appeared, beaming with pleasure. He grabbed my shoulders and kissed me on both cheeks to the delight of those watching.

"I am so pleased to see you," he cried. "I thought we had lost you back there to a partisan trap. I hope you understand why we could not risk searching for you. What happened? Why did you charge into the woods?"

"Of course I understand," I replied, "and you were right: it was a partisan trap. I was a chump to fall into it, but at least I got away again."

Of course after that they all wanted to know what happened. So I gave them a story that I had started to make up the moment I saw Jerome, for an explanation would obviously be needed.

"I thought I saw a partisan in the trees and so I shot at him, but he ran off. He seemed to be on his own, so I chased after him. But once well into the trees a whole line of partisans appeared between me and the column, forcing me to ride deeper into the forest. They must have been planning an ambush, which I had disturbed."

"How did you get away?" asked Lagarde.

"I rode deep into the forest to get away and got lost. Then I spent several days trying to get out while avoiding partisan groups that were living among the trees. I was nearly caught once, but got away. Eventually I made it back to the road. I have been following on behind you ever since and now I have caught you up," I declared, smiling happily. "Have you been here long?" I asked innocently.

"We arrived this morning," cried Lagarde. "Here, let me get you more wine. Do you need food? There is ham and bread on that table."

I made my way to the food while glancing about at the throng in the tavern. I wondered if they had brought Grant with them for a farewell drink before they handed him over, but there was no sign of him. Still, I was at least among the people who could tell me what happened to him, although I had to be subtle about it.

I pulled on Jerome's sleeve. "What have you done since you got here? Have you found any lodgings yet?"

"Not yet. The men and most of the carts have gone to the citadel. Then we came to the tavern to celebrate our return home to France. Here, pass me some bread, will you?"

"It is good to be home among friends," I agreed. I had noted that he had said *most of the carts* and wondered if that included the one Grant was in, or was he already on his way to Paris in it? As casually as I could, I asked, "What happened to that English spy? Is he in the citadel?"

Jerome had been in the act of stuffing bread into his mouth when I asked the question, but now he almost jumped, as though startled. I thought I had somehow given myself away by being too keen to ask the question, but Jerome started peering over his shoulder as though he had something to hide. Then he beckoned for me to join him in a corner of the room. "You must not mention the English spy to anyone," he whispered when I was standing beside him.

"Why not? Is he dead?"

"No. You remember he was to be tortured despite being captured in his uniform and giving his parole?" I nodded, still confused as to what was happening. "Well, when we got here there was no one from the ministry of war waiting for the prisoner." That, I thought, was not surprising given that I knew the despatch from Marmont to Paris had been captured. They might have sent a duplicate message, but that could have suffered the same fate.

"So what has happened to this prisoner?"

Jerome glanced around him again to check we could not be overheard. "The major and the captains used to ride with the prisoner and thought he was an honourable man. They feel it dishonours us if he is tortured." He paused as a pot boy walked past us collecting empty cups, leaving me almost beside myself now with curiosity.

"So what has happened to him," I asked again.

"Lagarde says our orders were to deliver him to Bayonne, which we have done. It is not our problem that the ministry of war agents are not here to collect him. So we have let him go."

"You have done what?" I gasped, astonished.

"It is a matter of honour," stated Jerome defensively. He clearly thought I disapproved of their action. "But you must not say anything about this or the ministry will blame Lagarde for setting him free. He will say that he delivered the prisoner to Bayonne and let the people here argue about what happened." Jerome gave a deep sigh before adding, "It probably will not matter, though, because the prisoner is refusing to escape. He says he has given his parole to travel to Paris. Lagarde has explained that he will be interrogated and tortured, but the man refuses to break his word."

"He is a damned fool," I replied with feeling.

"Yes, but Lagarde says his honour is now satisfied. It is up to the prisoner to make his escape."

"Where is the prisoner?" I asked as casually as I could manage, while my mind reeled at this unexpected change in fortunes.

"The last I heard he was still in his cart in one of the central squares."

I could not believe my luck. It sounded like no ambush would be necessary. We just had to grab Grant from the wagon. If he put up a struggle, we could take turns punching him. I grinned at the thought. Perhaps it would be easier to take him in the wagon out of the gate. One of the Basques could easily pass as a wagon driver, and with a French lieutenant riding as escort few people would ask questions. If they did, I could explain that Grant was an English prisoner who was to be exchanged with a French one. I was still considering the possibilities when I realised that Jerome was looking at me expectantly and I hurriedly rewound what he had been saying in my mind.

"Share lodgings with you? Of course, I would be happy to. And don't worry, I will not say a word about the other matter. Now after a morning in the saddle and all this wine, I need the jakes, so I will see you in a minute."

I went out of the back of the tavern into a small yard where there was a latrine against the wall. Ignoring that, I turned into a narrow alley which took me back out onto the street. I looked up and down but could see no sign of my Basque shadows. Damn, I thought, the one time I need them and they are not here. My horse was tied right outside the tavern windows; I would have to leave it for now. I was just heading up the street towards the centre of the city when I heard a voice behind me.

"Did you enjoy spending time with your French friends?"

I turned and saw Jorge standing hidden in a doorway. I walked over to him so that we could not be overheard. "I was doing my job and getting information," I hissed at him. "Now why don't you do yours and get a message to Gomez to say that Grant has been abandoned in a wagon in the city. He is in a square somewhere. We have to find him before someone else does, or he does something stupid."

I turned and continued up the road to the citadel. When I reached it there was nothing in the square in front of the gates and everyone who entered the fortress was being questioned about their business by the guards. I pressed on towards the bridge and found nothing in the next square either, but there was a large stone arch leading to another open space and there I did find what I was searching for.

I saw the lone cart as I was walking under the stonework. Its canvas covering was still tied down tightly over the support hoops and so it was impossible to see if anything or anyone was inside it. The wagon had been left in the middle of this new square under some trees to provide shade for the horses as well as the vehicle. But once I was through the arch I realised that I was not alone. A half troop of dragoons were gathered in a corner of the square, near one of the buildings which appeared to be a hotel. It would have looked more suspicious to turn back having seen them, and so, taking a deep breath, I carried on walking towards the wagon. I was dressed as a French lieutenant, I reminded myself; there was no reason that they should be suspicious of me. Having calmed myself, I looked across at the horsemen and nodded in greeting to the lieutenant commanding the thirty men. He just nodded back and returned to inspecting his

173

troopers. Behind the horsemen outside the hotel was a shiny, black open-topped carriage. Someone important was about to leave.

I was nearly at the cart now. I just hoped that Grant was still inside. I walked round and pulled myself up onto the driver's seat so that I would be hidden from the horsemen behind. Having had a final look round to check we could not be overheard, I called out quietly in English, "Grant, are you there?"

"Yes, who is that?" came a disembodied reply from behind the cloth.

"It's Flashman." I turned and started to untie the cord holding the covering behind the driver's seat.

"What are you doing here?" asked the voice.

"I've come to check that they are serving port and nuts with your cigar," I muttered irritably as I pulled open the fabric. There I saw Grant sitting miserable and dejected on a bench in the middle of the cart. At his feet was a pile of chains and manacles that Lagarde must have taken off before he abandoned his prisoner. "Why do you think I have travelled all this way across Spain and into France in an enemy uniform?" I hissed at him. "I am here to help you escape and you damn well will escape regardless of any paroles or promises, do ye hear me?"

His chin came up at that and he looked at me stubbornly. "You don't understand about honour, Flashman. I have given my word that I would not escape before I reached Paris."

I took a deep breath, trying to keep calm. Tempting though it was to bludgeon the idiot with whatever weapon came to hand, such activity would probably attract the attention of the horsemen outside. So instead I tried to reason with him.

"Yes, and in exchange for giving your word you doubtless expected to be able to travel freely instead of being chained in this cart for weeks. Marmont's treatment of you has invalidated your parole. Even your French guards think you should escape and have set you free. In any event Wellington has ordered you to escape. He does not want you tortured and giving away details of his spy network."

"I would never talk, even under torture," he exclaimed hotly. "I know my duty."

"Nobody knows what they will do under torture," I told him scathingly. "Wait until they have broken every bone in your hands and feet, burned you, perhaps cut bits off and are then racking you until the pain is so bad that you are begging them to kill you. See how you feel about your precious honour then."

Grant just glared at me sullenly.

"So forget about promises and Paris," I continued. "I have got some friends in the city who will help get you back to British lines. Just wait here while I fetch them and then we will go." I looked about the interior of the cart; the cover completely hid the inside. "In fact we may take the cart as well. Now wait here until I get back."

Without waiting for a reply, I slid back out of the cart and dropped to the ground. Having, I thought, talked some sense into Grant, I now had to find the Basques so that we could get out of the city. I walked back to the main street I had been on before and stood for a few minutes in the square outside of the citadel. Several streets passed through this square, and so instead of chasing about the city I stood on the base of a statue of some local dignitary so that I could be easily seen and waited for the Basques to find me. It did not take long; five minutes later Jorge was studiously gazing at the inscription on the base of the statue while talking quietly so that only I could hear.

"Have you found him?"

"Yes," I murmured, bending down to check on the fit of my boot as though it were pinching. "He is still in the cart. I will lead you to it. I will get in the cart with him so that my former comrades do not see me and you can drive the thing out of the city. We will say he is a prisoner being sent for exchange. Have you sent a message to Gomez?"

"Yes, *señor*," he replied. I looked up at that. It was the first time that any of the Basques had called me *señor*. I sensed that the surly man was grudgingly impressed with what I had achieved. Perhaps finally he was starting to believe we were on the same side.

"Good, now follow me. I will go first and get in the cart. You follow on behind and drive it out through the city gates."

I straightened up and started back the way I had come. I did not look back, but as I turned to go through the stone archway I caught a glimpse out of the corner of my eye of Jorge walking about a hundred paces behind me. The cart had not moved and I had taken several paces towards it when a voice called out in English.

"Ah, there you are, Lieutenant." It was Grant's voice calling out from the front of the hotel building. I turned and just gaped at the vision in front of me. Grant stood there out in the open in his British uniform while beside him, standing companionably, was a French general.

"You should stay closer to your charge, Lieutenant," warned the general in French, smiling. "I nearly had him arrested before I discovered he was an American."

"The general is going to Paris," declared Grant with a note of triumph in his voice. "He has kindly agreed to let us accompany him."

Editor's Note: Incredible as it may seem, Grant's release in Bayonne and his journey on to Paris and many of the events that follow are confirmed by various historical sources. Further details can be found in the historical notes at the end of the book.

Chapter 23

I was beyond speechless at these revelations. I was frozen to the spot, and while my mouth opened and shut a couple of times no words came out. What Jorge must have thought seeing my expression I cannot guess, but he had the sense to stay out of the square. "What... How..." I tried, speaking in English before words failed me again.

"You should speak in French, Lieutenant," Grant warned in that language. "The general does not speak English. May I introduce to you General Souham?"

I was still lost for words as I took in the rapidly changing circumstances, but at least I had the presence of mind to come to attention and give a sharp salute. Souham took my inability to speak as due to being overwhelmed in his presence.

"Don't worry, lad," he said, walking over and offering a hand to shake. "I was once a private in the old royal French army. I know it is the sergeants and you junior officers that do most of the work." I shook his hand and he led me towards Grant and the carriage beyond. "Where will you be going when you get to Paris, sir?" he asked Grant.

"Oh, I suspect I will get orders when I reach the city," explained Grant airily. "And I must thank you again for your generous offer of transport."

"Think nothing of it. My adjutant has heard all my stories at least once and has few good ones of his own to tell. It will be good to have someone new to talk to on the way."

With that I found myself steered towards the shining landau carriage... and Paris beyond. I wracked my addled brain, but I could not think of a way to slide out of this one. With the dragoons mounting up in front and behind the carriage, a run for it was also out of the question. The general and Grant took the forward-facing seats while the adjutant, who introduced himself as Gaston, and I took the seats opposite. The coachman cracked his whip and we moved off.

I sat there, feeling like I was in a daze, as I watched the buildings pass by. Grant refused to meet my eye and contented himself asking the general about Bayonne. One person who did meet my eye, though, was Jorge, who stood in a doorway watching the carriage drive past. With the general sitting opposite me I could not make any signal and had to just stare blankly back.

Within a few minutes we were crossing the bridge, which was a damn rickety affair. The original stone bridge had been swept away by floods years before and a temporary bridge had replaced it. The noisy wooden roadway was suspended between some of the original stone supports of the old structure and some anchored boats. The flimsy construction had already been cleared of other users so that the general and his escort could have an uninterrupted passage. It was as we reached dry land again that I saw Gomez. He was standing amongst the crowd forced to wait to use the crossing. I saw him look scornfully at the general and then curiously at the man in red beside him. When his gaze switched to me sitting opposite the general, his jaw dropped and then his face was suffused with rage.

Thinking back, I can see things from his point of view. He had been convinced I was false from the outset, a French infiltrator only pretending to be British. Now, instead of rescuing Grant as planned, he saw me sitting opposite a French general who was carrying Grant away to Paris with a guard of dragoons.

"Flashman, you treacherous bastard," he roared in Spanish. Then he had the audacity to raise one of my own pistols against me.

The carriage was already picking up speed as the gun fired. Pistols are notoriously inaccurate at any range and I thought I would be safe, but this ball managed to smash the top of the carriage door. As this was just inches from me it was one of the truest pistol shots I have seen against a moving target. Gomez did not have long to appreciate his marksmanship, though, as a second later a dragoon's carbine shot him in chest. More guns fired as several more of the Basques tried to make a run for it, when they would have been perfectly safe if they had just stood still and looked innocent. I watched in horror as two more of the partisans were hit and the crowd waiting to cross the bridge dissolved into chaos and panic.

"What did he shout?" asked the general, who had half stood in the carriage and was now kneeling on his seat to see what was happening behind us. "It was in Spanish," the general continued. "I understood 'bastard' but what is a 'flashman'?"

Grant stayed silent but caught my eye. He must have realised that those men were some of my accomplices and that they had died as a result of his decision to head north.

As no one else offered a suggestion, the adjutant spoke up. "Perhaps a flashman is another one of their words for the French."

"Come on, leave them," roared the general, waving for his escort to break off the pursuit and re-join the carriage. "So," he called, turning and slumping back down in his seat, "apart from the American here, we are all flashmans." He paused and grunted. "Well, that cove looked furious, so it is bound to mean something foul."

"Quite so," agreed Grant, now recovering his spirit. "Probably a dishonourable and treacherous creature. You certainly would not want to be called a flashman." He shot me a spiteful glance and I came within an ace of denouncing him as a wanted British prisoner there and then. The only thing that stopped me was the fact that I would be arrested instantly too.

"Oh, I am sure that there are worse things than flashmans," I claimed coolly. "The Scots for example."

Grant bristled at that; he was immensely proud of his Scottish heritage. But Souham got in first. "Ah, I think you have faced their Highlanders, have you, Lieutenant? Damn brutal creatures, aren't they?"

"I have come across them, sir, yes," I agreed. In fact I had commanded a company of them in India, and so I spoke with some authority on the subject. "They fight like tigers but they stink."

"Stink, eh?" The general laughed. "Well, I never got that close to one. Still, I would not say that in front of Marshal MacDonald, but he is on his way to Russia now."

With Grant glowering at me, we settled down to the journey, the general happily regaling us with his adventures. He had been born into poverty and joined the royal French army as a boy, serving as a private for eight years before the revolution. By the time we met him, he had been a general for nineteen years with a string of victories behind him. It never occurred to the general to question our intentions. After all, why would an escaping prisoner try to reach Paris, the centre of the enemy empire? But he did have a curiosity, particularly about America, and that was nearly our undoing. The closest Grant had ever been to America was a posting in the Caribbean. It was just as well that the rest of us in the coach had not even been that far.

"I must say," said Souham as we bowled through the French countryside that first afternoon. "I am surprised that the American army fights in red. Did that not cause confusion when you were fighting the British?"

"It does, sir," agreed Grant, taken by surprise. He said no more, and while the general looked at him expectantly, Grant just stared at the floor of the carriage. He was clearly unable to think of anything more to say on the matter.

The general was just about to ask how this confusion was avoided when I decided to speak up. "I imagine that they have soldiers in all sorts of uniforms, like us. In the French army we have men, Hanoverians and Swiss I think, who fight in red coats. I have not seen them but I imagine that causes confusion too."

"Yes," agreed Grant, latching on to my lead. "We have men who fight in all sorts of colours." He paused, plainly racking his brains for some fact that would add more authenticity to this lame confirmation. "And we have the savages of course; they fight in brightly coloured war paint and are festooned with feathers and tiger and leopard skins."

"Really?" enquired the general. "I had no idea that they had tigers in America."

"Oh yes," confirmed Grant, warming to his theme. "We have lions and tigers, and buffalo the size of elephants for them to hunt. No man starves in America as there is always plenty of game to eat and good land for farming too."

He went on at length, extolling the paradise that he claimed was the land of his birth. We all sat there taking it in, and if the Frenchmen believed every word, I was not sure what was true and what wasn't. I thought Grant must have heard something about America from his time in the Caribbean islands, while I had not been further west than Lisbon. He did make it sound a fantastic place, but as I discovered later his grasp on the flora and particularly the fauna of this new land was not exact. I remember Gaston, the adjutant, interrupting at one point to ask about snakes. Someone he had met in Spain had been to the Spanish colonies in America and claimed that the snakes had rattles on their tails so that you could hear them coming.

Grant instantly dismissed this as nonsense. "How," he asked, "could the serpent hunt if its prey could hear it coming?" He laughed at the adjutant and suggested that he had been the victim of a tall story. I confess that at the time I thought Grant's dismissal made sense. It was only years later that I was to discover the hard way that he was wrong.

If you are going to flee as a fugitive across a country then I can heartily recommend an enemy general as a travelling companion. As members of Souham's party we were given the finest rooms in every coaching inn we stopped at and the best food and wine available too. Even if the French had been searching for a missing fugitive, and there was no sign that they were, we would have been beyond all suspicion. If it were not for the fact that we were travelling in precisely the opposite direction to the one I wanted to go then things would have been perfect. Twice I tried to get Grant on his own so that we could talk in private, but each time he ducked away back to where people were standing. He knew I was livid with him, but now I was committed to travelling to Paris as he had wanted. To try to escape or do anything to raise suspicion would only land us in deeper trouble.

For most of the journey we stayed on the safer topic of the war in Spain. It was something we all knew a lot about, even if Grant and I had to try to remember to see things from the French perspective. Souham had been fighting the Spanish in eastern Spain and sported a nasty scar above one eye, incurred when his division had routed a Spanish army twice the size of the French force. He had followed the war against the British but had not seen any of it. I remember describing the horror of Albuera from the imagined perspective of a French officer. Grant talked about being taken on a reconnaissance ride to see the British army marching after Badajoz fell. He seemed to be describing the scene he must have witnessed before he rode away and was captured. But for the most part Souham talked about his earlier campaigns.

Grant and I encouraged him by asking questions and prompting more tales. There was less chance of us giving ourselves away if the general was talking. But the stories of his rapid promotion during the chaos of the revolution and the early Napoleonic campaigns were genuinely fascinating. Despite his humble beginnings and lack of education, he had a sharp strategic understanding. I was not surprised to learn later that when he returned to Spain and commanded an army against Wellington he manoeuvred cleverly to force the British army back some two hundred miles without the need to fight a battle.

The roads from Paris into Spain were among those that Napoleon had ordered straightened and tree lined so that he could move his troops quickly around his empire, with some protection from the sun and wind. While the days were hot, there was not yet much shade from the very young poplar trees that lined many of the new, fast roads we travelled along.

Several times we passed semaphore towers that could transmit messages from Paris to Bayonne and the Spanish border in a matter of hours. One was relaying a message as we passed it. A man with a telescope was watching the next tower in the chain and calling out the signals to his colleagues, who with ropes controlled the huge signal arms at the top of the structure. I could not help wondering if a message about Grant had already overtaken us. But we would not have long to find out. With Souham's tales to keep us entertained, it seemed no time at all before we were approaching the outskirts of Paris.

Chapter 24

Souham was travelling to his home at the north of the city and so I asked him to leave us near the Tuileries, the old royal palace gardens which were now a public park. It was a place I remembered from my only other visit to Paris back in '02. I had no idea if there even was an American embassy in the city, never mind where it was. I told Souham that Grant would want to find some lodgings and rest from the journey before reporting to his superiors. As the old boy was keen to get home to his family he did not press me with questions. After brief handshakes and good wishes for the future all round, Grant and I were left standing on a street in the middle of Paris as Souham and his carriage disappeared around a nearby corner.

Without the influence of a general to speed our progress and allay any suspicions, I suddenly felt very alone and exposed. We were now in the absolute heart of enemy territory, with no friends or allies and no means to get back to England or Spain. On top of that, my companion was a wanted man and an idiot who insisted on wearing the uniform of France's most notorious enemy.

I suspected that his American persona would fall apart like a loaf in sea water as soon as we met anyone from that country, and there were bound to be some Americans in Paris. What really made my blood boil was that we were both in this dire situation because the buffoon had given his word to a French marshal who had planned to betray him anyway. Feeling the rage start to build in me again, I turned away from Grant and walked through the gates of the Tuileries. There was a bench screened from much of the park by rose beds and hedges and I walked towards it, needing to find a space to think. Grant made the mistake of following me.

"Look, Flashman, I know you did not want to come to Paris. But as you know it was a matter of honour for me and well, now we are here, I think honour is satisfied."

"Well, that is a weight off my mind," I muttered in a tone of sarcasm that was entirely lost on Grant.

"It is for me too," he agreed, smiling. "In fact now I think we can try to escape… Oof."

There is something eminently satisfying about punching someone really hard in the solar plexus. Watching their eyes bulge as they double over in agony, then there is that gasping sound as they try to

183

get their breath. The best part, though, is that they are incapable of interrupting as you tell them what you *really* think of them.

"Yes, your honour is a *huge* comfort to us all, isn't it?" I whispered hoarsely at him in English, heedless of any passers-by who could be watching. "I am sure that you will find it immensely helpful when they are pulling out your fingernails and breaking your bones. As you are screaming for them to let you die, having given away all of Wellington's agents, at least in your last babbling moments of agony you will know that you have kept your honour."

I glanced up and saw two Parisian ladies standing in a gap between the rose beds, appearing alarmed at the scene before them. "An English prisoner. He has eaten some bad mussels," I explained, gesturing to Grant, who had by now sunk to his knees and was still bent double, gasping for breath.

"It must be very bad," exclaimed the younger one while her companion smiled in amusement.

"Don't be naive, Beatrice; he punched the prisoner," stated the companion as she walked past. "Food poisoning does not stop you breathing." At that she glanced over her shoulder to give me a smile, clearly not minding a British prisoner getting roughed up.

I waited until the pair had disappeared around a corner and turned again to Grant, who was by now trying to get back to his feet. I kicked his legs from under him, sending him crashing back to the ground.

"You think this is all about you, don't you?" I snarled. "What use is your honour to me, standing in front of firing squad when I am found in an enemy uniform? Did you use your brain at all before you marched up to Souham's coach?"

"You can't…" Grant gasped between breaths, "hit me… I am senior… to you… Oof!"

Having proved Grant wrong, I left him writhing on the ground and strolled off through the park. Once I had outdistanced the groaning and retching sound behind me, it was a pleasant sunny day. I walked across the park until I got to a bench where I could watch the boats going up and down the Seine and the people walking on the opposite bank of the river.

When I was last in France I had spent most of my time with other British people here to enjoy the sights during the brief peace treaty of Amiens. I had met an old French general who had served in India and might have helped us, but that was ten years ago. I had no idea if he was still alive or in Paris, and I could not remember my way to his house even if he was still in the city. Scrutinising the people going about their business, I saw that my French lieutenant's uniform could be a blessing or a curse. It was a curse if I was caught in it for I would be shot as a spy. But it was a blessing as the perfect disguise if I was not caught. Virtually every man I could see was in some uniform or clothing relating to his occupation. Had I been in civilian clothes I could still have been shot for a spy, but I would have stood out far more.

I reached down and touched my belt. Since Albuera I had restocked it with a dozen gold guineas and that seemed the only positive in my situation. I could not stay in Paris as sooner or later I would be caught and executed. So I had to try to make my way back to safety. The shortest route was north and across the Channel to Britain. But with the navy blockading French ports and the English Channel to cross, it seemed unlikely that I would get home that way. This left trying to retrace my route back to Spain. Without a general's carriage and escort to speed my progress through roads and checkpoints it would take weeks. As well as the French, I would also have to deal with the partisans if any of the Basques survived to report my apparent treachery. Even if I eventually returned to Spain I would then have to make my way across the occupied half of the country before I reached safety. I looked up as the two ladies I had seen earlier walked along the path in front of my bench. The older girl smiled at me and nodded over my shoulder. "Your prisoner seems to be recovering, *monsieur*."

I looked behind and there staggering towards me was Grant. He had his hat in one hand and he was holding his stomach with the other. He was still breathing heavily and he had a tuft of grass stuck in one of his epaulets. I shook my head in dismay. Getting across France and occupied Spain would be hard enough on my own, but with Grant it would be impossible. I turned back to face the river as he walked up to the bench and sat down at the opposite end from me.

"Look, I know you are cross with me," he began. "I understand that, but we have to work together if we are to get out of here."

"Really? I was just thinking that I would do rather better on my own."

"You can't do that," he cried, sounding alarmed. "Wellington sent you to rescue me; what will he say if he finds out that you abandoned me in Paris?"

"That assumes that you live long enough to tell him."

"What do you mean?" asked Grant. "Are you threatening to kill me?"

"Of course not. I may be a lot of things but I am not a cold-blooded murderer. I meant that you would not last a day in this city in your British uniform without my help. You will be arrested and eventually they will tie up the British major that has appeared in Paris with the one that has gone missing in Bayonne. You will not get the chance to get a message to Wellington."

That gave Grant something to think about and he sat there silently for a full minute before he spoke again. "What you say may be true, but if they do capture me then they will find out about you too." I looked sharply at him at that and he hurriedly continued. "I am not saying that I will deliberately betray you. That would be dishonourable. But they will know that I must have had help to get here so quickly from Bayonne. If their torturers are as good as you say, it will not be long before they are talking to Souham and finding out about the French lieutenant who travelled with me."

I had to grudgingly concede that he had a point. If descriptions of me were circulated with a reward to all the towns between Paris and Spain, I would stand no chance at all of escaping. Whether I liked it or not, Grant and I were still bound together.

"Well, you will have to get rid of that British uniform. Everyone will notice you wearing that."

"I will not," insisted Grant hotly. "I would be shot as a spy if I were not in uniform."

"You bloody idiot, you will be tortured to death if you are caught wearing it. At least a firing squad is quicker."

"No," declared Grant flatly. "It is matter of honour; I must wear my British uniform. Anyway claiming to be an American seems to work. If Souham believed it, others should as well."

His jaw was set and I knew by now that on matters he perceived as pertaining to his honour he could not be shifted. For a moment I considered punching him again, but instead I got up and began to wander along the river bank. To stand any chance of getting out of the city, never mind France, with Grant in his uniform we were going to need some help. I thought back to my last time in the city and tried to remember anyone who might assist us. I desperately tried to recall the route to the old general's house but it would not come. Grant had started to follow dejectedly in my footsteps and I turned to face him.

"Do you know anybody in this city that might help us?"

"No, I have never been to Paris before."

I turned away in disgust and stared out across the skyline of the city. In front of me I could see the Île de la Cité, the island in the middle of the Seine that was the oldest part of the French capital. On it I could just make out the Conciergerie, the old prison that I had visited on my previous trip. There is every chance I could be a prisoner in it this time, I thought. I gazed further along and saw the twin turrets of the Notre Dame cathedral beyond.

I looked back at Grant. "What about wearing something over the top of your uniform, then perhaps we can travel by night and..." My voice trailed away as a nagging thought crossed my brain. It was as though I had an idea but it was tantalisingly out of reach. I turned back and looked across the river. "Notre Dame," I exclaimed. "That is it."

"What is it, what about Notre Dame?" asked Grant, coming up and staring across the river.

"Three years ago," I explained, "after the battle of Talavera, the battlefield caught fire. Many wounded of both sides were trapped in the long, dry grass as the flames approached. There were lots of us trying to pull them to safety and one of the men I saved was a Frenchie. He told me that his father was an organist in Notre Dame. In fact he offered me a concert if I was ever in Paris."

"But we don't want a concert," queried Grant, puzzled.

"Of course not, but if he feels indebted to me for saving his son's life, he might help us get out of the city."

"Or he might be a fervent Bonapartist that sees us arrested," pointed out Grant.

"Do you have any other ideas?" I asked impatiently and Grant just shrugged in response. "It is the only plan we have. You can sit at the back of the church while I talk to the organist. If I am arrested, you can still try to get away."

It was, I thought, a tenuous chance. The man I rescued had a wounded leg. He could have died before he told his father I had saved him, or the organist could have been dismissed or moved on. There were a hundred reasons why it might not work, but when it is the only option you have, you cannot stop the hope soaring. It was something to pursue; without it the chances of survival were looking bleak indeed.

We made our way across the Pont Neuf Bridge onto the island and past the forbidding walls of the prison. They seemed to emanate a chill despite the sunshine in the rest of the city. We hurried past the gaol and wove through the streets towards the huge twin towers of the cathedral. A few minutes later and we were standing in front of them. The ancient building looked tired and rundown, and various street sellers in the square outside were hawking food and trinkets. But plenty of people were passing through the large open doors as we joined them.

"God, it looks awful," Grant murmured as he looked around inside.

"Remember to speak French," I hissed. "After the revolution all religious buildings were stripped of anything of value and this one was turned into a temple of reason. There was a fake mountain built in here and statues to goddesses of truth, liberty and philosophy."

"How do you know all this?"

"I was here before as a tourist in 'oh-two, and a guide told us about it. Napoleon gave the building back to the Church, but there is no money to restore it to its former glory." I looked about the bare walls for any sign of organ pipes. "Let's hope that there was still money for an organ and music." It took a moment before I spotted the pipes under a round window on the west side of the church. "Wait here," I told Grant. "I will look for the organist."

When I got close, I saw that the organ itself was high on a platform but the seat was empty. Glancing around to check that no one was about, I climbed up the steps to the platform to look at the instrument. It was well looked after and there was no dust on any of the keys. There was even a pile of music scores on a little table beside the bench that the organist must sit on. The organ was obviously still in use and so I would just have to wait until an organist appeared. I turned and started to climb down the little ladder back to the ground.

"What are you doing, *monsieur*?" called a voice sharply. "You are not allowed up there. The organ is a very valuable instrument and must not be damaged."

I turned and there was a pinch-faced priest glaring at me. "I was seeking the organist," I explained.

"We have several; which one do you want?" challenged the cleric.

I had no idea who I wanted but knew enough that when lying it was always best to stay as close to the truth as possible. So I opened my arms in a sign of submission and tried to appeal to the priest's goodwill.

"I am sorry, sir, I do not know. As you can see I am a soldier, and three years ago I saved the life of a brother officer at the battle at Talavera, in Spain. He had been wounded and when the battlefield caught fire I managed to drag him out of the path of the flames."

The priest looked slightly mollified but asked, "What has that to do with our organists?"

"I cannot remember the man's name but he told me that his father was an organist here. In fact he said that his father would be pleased to play for me should I ever be in Paris. I am not here for a concert, but as I was in the city I thought I would enquire to see if the man I saved had survived."

"I see," mused the priest. "Monsieur Lacodre had a son who was wounded in Spain."

"That could be him," I replied. "Was it at Talavera?"

"I have no idea but I can send a boy to get him. He does not live far away. Why don't you wait here?"

With that the priest bustled off and I sat down on one of the benches. I tried to think back to my brief meeting with the wounded officer; was his name Lacodre? It was strange: I could remember his face well and even that we had joked about him not having a sister he could introduce me to, but his name was a complete blank. Even if it was Lacodre then there was no guarantee the organist would help us. I would have to make sure we were somewhere private when I explained what we wanted. That way we would have some chance to escape before he could raise any alarm.

I sat there in the light from a nearby stained window rehearsing in my mind how I would remind the man of the service I had done his son and subtly pressure him to help us. I had been sitting there for some ten minutes when I noticed a slight disturbance at the entrance of the cathedral. A tall soldier had walked in, followed by an elderly couple who were nearly running to keep up. The man quickly scanned the congregation, and spotted Grant sitting there in his red coat facing the altar. The soldier grinned and started walking directly towards Grant. Even if the officer had not been limping heavily, I would have recognised him for the man I had saved. I got up quickly and strode to intercept him; but he reached Grant first and stared down at him in confusion.

"You are not the man I was told about. What is this?"

Grant looked up in surprise at being challenged by the Frenchman and noticed various other members of the congregation turning to stare at him.

"I think I am the man you are looking for," I called from a few yards away as I rushed up.

"Yes… yes, you are," agreed Captain Lacodre hesitantly, taking in the man he knew to be a British soldier now wearing a French lieutenant's uniform. He looked from me to Grant in his red coat and then back to me again, obviously trying to work out what on earth we were doing in the capital city of our nation's fiercest enemy. His gaze encompassed the curious faces watching this encounter and he gave me a rueful grin. "I think perhaps we should talk in private. Would you like to come back to my parents' apartment?"

We walked back the few hundred yards to *chez* Lacodre with Madame Lacodre hugging and kissing me once she understood that it was me that had saved her son from the flames and not Grant. The old organist barely uttered a word. He just strolled along beside us, slightly bemused and puffing on his pipe. Inside the apartment the woman fussed around finding wine and getting us bread and cheese. Then, once we were settled around the table, Lacodre looked at us expectantly. "Perhaps you had better tell us what this is all about," he suggested.

We gave them the edited highlights: how Grant had been captured and had given his parole. That his guards had freed him in Bayonne when they learned he was to be tortured and that I had been sent by the British to get him back.

"But why did you come all the way to Paris once your guards had released you in Bayonne?" asked Lacodre, confused. When Grant explained about his precious honour Lacodre shook his head in dismay while the father muttered to his wife something about Grant's sanity.

"The point is that we are here now and we need help to get home," I declared. "Is there anything you can do to help us?"

"It is impossible!" exclaimed the old man. "There are patrols all over the country searching for men who are avoiding conscription or trying to get out of the invasion of Russia. You would need papers to prove you are not deserters just to get out of the city." He looked imploringly at his wife. "The government will be looking for these men. If Jean helps them, he will be arrested – we could all be arrested. *Mon dieu*, people have already seen them with us in the cathedral. We are already in danger…"

"Calm down," snapped his wife as the old boy worked himself into a state. "Do you think this man," she cried, gesturing at me, "worried about the danger when he charged into the flames to rescue our son?" As it happened I had been on the verge of abandoning their son when I spotted a gap to safety through the smoke and flames, but now did not seem a good time to mention that. "If he had not shown courage," she continued, " Jean would have been burned alive. We owe him the life of our son; we are not going to abandon them."

"From the sound of things the ministry will not know you are missing yet," suggested Lacodre to Grant. "They might not realise you are missing until Marshal Marmont sends another message to find out what information has been gathered from the interrogation."

"Exactly," I agreed to help calm the old man. "And even when they do find out, they will assume Grant slipped back over the border into Spain. They will never think he was idiotic enough to continue on to Paris."

"They might," protested Grant. "They know I am a man of hon… ouch." Grant glared at me, rightly guessing who had kicked him under the table.

"We are trying to reassure the organist," I murmured at him in English, "that there is little risk in him helping us. If you cannot say anything helpful then keep your damn mouth shut."

The old man glared at me suspiciously as he had not understood what I had muttered to Grant. "It does not matter," he announced at last, "because you still cannot get out of the city without the right papers and you cannot hide here. We can give you some food and some money and then you must go."

"Wait," replied Lacodre. "They might be checking the roads but they do not search all of the river barges that leave the city. I have a cousin Marcel who owns a barge. It runs down the Seine from Paris to the canals that join with the Loire. Then sometimes he goes all the way to Nantes on the Britany coast."

My heart soared. Here was help indeed, and it sounded so simple. Instead of travelling by night and hiding by day in hedgerows, risking capture at every step, we would float downriver gently to our destination, with plenty of time to hide among the cargo if anyone tried to board the vessel. Of course life is never that simple, as we were to learn.

"What could we do to escape when we reach Nantes?" I asked.

"There will be ships there who will be trying to run the British blockade of the port," explained Lacodre. "My cousin will know some of the captains. If you go in one of those, they will take you to safety. If the ship *is* captured by the British navy, well, you will be saved then too."

"That is an excellent plan," I cried, feeling a great weight lift from my shoulders. Rarely had I known my fortunes change so fast. Just a few minutes ago we were trapped in an enemy capital, with no means to escape, and now we had what sounded like a comfortable and well-thought-out plan. "When can we meet your cousin?"

Lacodre's face dropped. "Not for a while. I saw him a few weeks ago and he was heading south; I am not sure how far. But sooner or later he will be taking a shipment of wine back to the river quay here in Paris."

"But that means we could be trapped in Paris for weeks waiting for him to return," I exclaimed, dismayed.

"And you are not staying here while you wait," insisted the old man firmly.

"Can we get a message to Marcel, asking him to come quickly?" I asked.

"Barge men carry messages for each other and pass them over on the river but they are not secure. Anyway Marcel makes his living from the boat; he must deliver his cargo or he will not be paid." Lacodre looked at me. "The barges are not fast. Even if he is heading to Paris now it will take at least a week or two for him to get here."

"So we have to find somewhere to hide for a few weeks?" I asked, feeling the hope start to subside.

"What about the old chapel in Madame Trebuchet's garden?" mused the old woman. "People have hidden there before."

"Are you mad?" shouted the old man. "Think of who she is, what she is. We cannot afford to get involved with her, especially with men that the government will soon be hunting down."

"Who is Madame Trebuchet?" I asked with a growing sense of unease.

"It is best you do not know in case the worst happens," stated Lacodre quietly. "What you do not know you cannot tell. Another cousin, Anna, is a maid in her house. It is a big rambling building, part of a former convent, with a huge garden. At the bottom of the garden is a half-ruined chapel which has been used to harbour fugitives before."

"And what happened to the last fugitive?" enquired the old man before answering his own question. "He was arrested, and how Madame Trebuchet escaped arrest and imprisonment is beyond me."

"You think she betrayed the fugitive?" asked Grant, alarmed.

"No, no," replied Lacodre, raising his arms to calm the growing tension. "The man was her lover, a former French general who had been implicated in a plot against the emperor. She was distraught when he was arrested; there is no question that she betrayed him. She still visits him in prison."

"Why wasn't she arrested then?" demanded his father.

"I don't know, but Anna is convinced that Madame Trebuchet did not betray anyone." Lacodre turned to me. "It does not matter, for you should not see Madame Trebuchet and with luck she will never know that you are hiding at the bottom of her garden. The chapel cannot be seen from the house. Apart from Anna, who can bring you food, no one should see you at all."

A short while late Lacodre was leading us south through the streets of Paris. With half a million of the French empire's soldiers marching on Russia, there still seemed a lot of uniformed men about. Lacodre explained that soldiers had been brought in from other parts of the empire to give a show of strength and normality in the French capital. I imagined that this was the reason that the soldiers who had escorted us from Salamanca had been summoned. There were dragoons, hussars, infantrymen and gunners all strolling the streets. But on closer inspection, most looked past their prime or sporting wounds.

Grant still walked along wearing his British uniform and while he got the odd sideways glance as there were two French officers with him no one intervened. The idea that an escaped British officer would stroll brazenly around Paris was so preposterous that no sane person would consider it a possibility. With a myriad of uniforms worn across the empire, perhaps most who saw him assumed that he was from one of the Swiss or Hanoverian regiments. Only one person showed any hostility: a suspicious old matron with a ribbon stall. Grant simply raised his hat to her and called, "Greetings from America," and her expression lifted at once.

"Long live George Washington," she cried in reply.

The old convent had been called the Feuillantines and it was off the Rue Saint Jacques in the southern half of the city, just a few hundred yards from a large park called the Luxembourg Garden. Lacodre left us by a locked gate in an alleyway at the back of the house while he went around the front to speak to his cousin. It was by now a pleasant and warm afternoon. Grant and I sat down against the wall in the shade of a tree that was growing over the stonework.

"What do you think of this Trebuchet woman?" asked Grant.

"If her lover has been imprisoned by Bonaparte then surely she is not a supporter of the emperor. Perhaps she will just turn a blind eye if she thinks someone is living in her garden."

"Unless she thinks she can win favour for her lover by turning us in," said Grant with one of his rare astute thoughts.

"Possibly," I agreed.

We fell silent then as a marching band started up nearby. It got steadily closer and so we walked to the end of the alley and watched it pass by. More grey-whiskered men, but they knew how to play. The tunes were not familiar to us but they were rousing anthems. A crowd followed the band along the street, some singing along and others cheering when a new refrain started. The sight of so many happy people and the jaunty music made me almost forget I was in the enemy capital. I could not help tapping my foot in time to the music as I watched the band march by. Then I felt a hand clap me on the shoulder.

"Come away," whispered Lacodre. "The police often follow the bands to check that any men who look like they should be in the *Grande Armée* have got exemption certificates."

I glanced around but no one seemed to be watching us as Lacodre led us back up the alley. This time the gate was open and we walked into the very overgrown garden. Lacodre bolted the door after us. "The house is a hundred metres in that direction," he explained, pointing away from the wall. "Now let me show you the chapel."

He led the way between some bushes until we emerged further along the wall in a small graveyard. Standing amid the gravestones was the chapel. It was a Gothic medieval affair with a stubby bell tower at one end and the door at the other. The door end had partly collapsed but the roof looked sound over the rest of the structure.

Lacodre led the way inside and a young woman was waiting for us. "This is Anna," Lacodre introduced his cousin and turned to her. "And these are the two gentlemen I told you about."

The girl looked anxious and twisted a cloth nervously in her hands. "Please, *monsieurs*, you must be very quiet and very careful. Madame Trebuchet's young sons are home from school and they sometimes play in the gardens."

"I am sorry," added Lacodre. "I did not know they would be here, but we have nowhere else to hide you. If you can stay out of sight all will be well. Anna will bring food for you once a day. There are some blankets left on the altar and an old cot bed behind it. I will let you know as soon as we have heard from Marcel."

With that Lacodre and the girl took their leave, the girl still whispering anxiously to her cousin as they walked away and clearly not happy with the arrangements.

Chapter 25

Three days later and Grant and I were bored out of our skins and getting on each other's nerves. Twice we had heard the boys playing in the garden and had slipped out of the chapel to hide in some very thick undergrowth along the garden wall. The second time the brats had played for hours while I was nearly eaten alive by ants, which had a nest near where we were hiding. Eventually the boys were called in for tea and Anna arrived a short while later with a cloth-wrapped parcel of food for us. She was a plain creature, but if she had been willing, she could have helped me pass the time more pleasurably. Instead she rebuffed all my advances.

"Get way with you," she cried, slapping away a grasping hand. "What would my husband say when he comes home from Russia to find me carrying another man's baby?"

"How do you know he is not helping himself to some Cossack wench?" I goaded. "Come on, just a little cuddle."

But she was having none of it. She seemed to view my company as some form of contagion and Grant was little better. He barely spoke to me either unless he had to. He still resented me punching him when we first arrived in Paris. Grant had persuaded Anna to get him some books from the library and now he spent most of his time reading up in the bell tower. I made him give me a book to read, but it was some treatise on philosophy that soon sent me to sleep.

After three days in that garden with an existence that resembled the life of a Trappist monk, I was desperate for diversion. I was in Paris with half a million French men marching to Russia. That meant half a million French women missing male company. Surely I could find just one that would welcome Flashy's attention. To start with I worried about the risk of being caught either by those that might be searching for us or those just looking for deserters. But as the days passed frustration overtook my fear, until on the third afternoon I could stand it no longer. Shaved and smartened up as best as I could, it was time to leave my self-imposed monastery.

I had already heard the marching band pass down the street at the end of the alley. Having given it time to reach the Luxembourg Garden I slipped quietly out of the garden gate. When I reached the street few people seemed to be about and so I forced myself to walk slowly and casually towards the park. It was a warm day and as I walked through the park gates it seemed that half of the city was taking its leisure there. Two thirds of those promenading around the flower beds and the band stands were women, and oh what women!

There is something about Parisian ladies that you don't find anywhere else. Paris has always been known for its fashions, but in my experience since the revolution there has been a licentious recklessness to them as well. As I learnt to my cost during my previous visit, it even infects girls visiting from Britain.

I started to wander around that park, feeling like a bee in a honey pot. There was at least a score of veteran soldiers taking advantage of the female company. Some had one girl on their arms and some had two. All had broad grins showing through their grey whiskers. Flashy, I thought, if you spend tonight alone, something is seriously wrong with the world.

I was so busy weighing up likely companions that I almost did not spot the policeman heading towards me. He wore no uniform, but as I glimpsed him out of the corner of my eye he stood out as the only man in the park who did not have a female companion. He was fifty yards away but, worryingly, he was walking straight in my direction. Affecting not to have seen him, I turned away and walked towards some bushes and trees that had been arranged to form a woodland glade. I was cursing my stupidity now. Of course I would stand out compared to the other soldiers; I was twenty years younger than most of them. As I disappeared from the view of the policeman behind the bushes, I started to run. If I was caught without an exemption certificate, the best I could hope for was an armed guard to the Russian front. I had been to Russia and had no wish to go there again.

I had gone twenty yards when I spotted my deliverance ahead. Lying half hidden in the long grass ahead was a couple and judging from the rhythmic movement they were fully focussed on each other. I would probably have missed them entirely had it not been for the meticulous tidiness of the moustachioed infantry officer, who had hung his jacket up on the branch of a tree. I swiftly moved across to them on the balls of my feet, trying to make no noise. Any sounds I did make would have been drowned out by the grunting of the old boy, who had found a filly half his age. Glancing down, I saw that she had her eyes closed, perhaps to imagine that the man on top of her was her husband. Right then I did not care if she was picturing being mounted by Bonaparte himself; all I was interested in was searching the soldier's coat. I found what I wanted folded in one of the pockets, a certificate of exemption in the name of Henri Lafitte. I grabbed it and disappeared into the deepest undergrowth I could find.

I had to move slowly to avoid making a noise and so was still in earshot of the amorous couple when they were discovered by the policeman. Give a man the right to interfere in the lives of others and they become right officious bastards and this policeman was no exception. I felt sorry for the old boy as he was rudely interrupted mid-ride. His companion screamed as he was hauled off her and then there was shouting as the old soldier insisted that he had an exemption even if he could not find it.

"Look at me," he roared at the official. "I am fifty-four years old and have been a soldier all my life. I carry eight wounds, most earned in the emperor's service. I have an exemption; it must be in the grass here somewhere."

The petty bureaucrat was having none of it. "The emperor needs all the soldiers he can get," he insisted. "No exemption and I have to take you back to the barracks where they can check the details."

After much more yelling and what was probably a fingertip search of the long grass they had been cavorting in, the old boy was hauled away. While that was happening Flashy, now with his certificate securely buttoned in a pocket, was disappearing through the trees to sample the delights of the park in safety.

As it turned out the women found me rather than the other way round. I was just doffing my hat to a very pretty blonde who seemed to be chaperoned by her mother when a voice called from behind me.

"So you have taken the day off from beating British prisoners?"

I turned and there were the two ladies I had met in the Tuileries gardens when we had first arrived in Paris.

"It was food poisoning," I reminded them.

"Of course," agreed the older girl with a knowing smile. "That is what I told Beatrice when we saw you."

"No, you didn't," objected the younger woman indignantly. "You said he had punched the prisoner."

"Well, as long as you do not think we are British prisoners, you are welcome to accompany us around the park," offered the older girl. "You are much younger than the other soldiers here," she pointed out as she ran an appraising eye from the top of my head to my boots. "I am Claudette, by the way," she introduced herself. "This is my cousin, Beatrice. Once we have listened to all the bands we will have to walk Beatrice home. Then if you are *very* attentive," and here she squeezed my arm encouragingly, "I might allow you chaperone me home as well." I almost growled in anticipation at the final sentence for the look in her eye left little doubt as to what my chaperoning duties would include.

You can imagine I attended their every need that afternoon, finding them chairs by the bandstand and regaling them with modestly told tales highlighting the courage of my new persona, Henri Lafitte. They did not seem to notice my ignorance of the words to popular songs played by the bands or that some of the martial deeds I described had been achieved by the British rather than the French. The crowds were drifting home and I was close to boiling in anticipation when another of those infernal policemen intervened again.

This time I did not see him at all until he stepped out from behind a bush, where he had clearly been waiting to intercept me. It was a different policeman to last time, but my relative youth was obviously attracting their attention.

"My apologies, ladies, but I am afraid I must detain your companion." He held up a card that had an impressive embossed crest. "I am sure you will understand," he added with a note of menace.

The girls backed off immediately, alarm in the eyes of Claudette; she evidently wanted nothing to do with the authorities. "Of course, of course. Perhaps we will meet you again, Henri," she added, before pulling her cousin away and walking swiftly down the path.

"Come back," I called after her. "It is all right; I have a certificate of exemption." I was unbuttoning my pocket as I spoke, but the girls did not look back and just hurried away.

"Well, well," exclaimed the policeman as he studied the certificate. "Henri Lafitte. By the strangest coincidence a gentleman of exactly that name claims he lost his certificate in this very park earlier this afternoon. And here you are with a certificate in that name and appearing far too young to be awarded any exemption."

"It is a common name," I protested. "I imagine that there are lots of exemption certificates in the name of Henri Lafitte."

"I am sure you are right, sir, but fewer, I think, for soldiers that appear to be as fit and able bodied as yourself."

"I have been wounded, badly wounded, serving the emperor," I protested. For the first time in my life I was grateful that I had been shot in the chest, for now I saw that there was no alternative but to show him the wounds I had received at Albuera. "Look at my chest," I insisted, pulling open my shirt. "I have another wound in my thigh if you want to see that."

The policeman's jaw dropped in surprise as he caught sight of the large star-shaped musket ball exit wound scars in the middle of my chest. *"Mon dieu,"* he murmured and he actually reached forward and stroked one of the lines to check that they were real scars. "I am amazed you lived with such a wound," muttered the policeman, with a note of reverence in his voice now. "My apologies, sir," he said, handing me back the certificate. "But you understand we must do our duty."

He walked away, leaving me to do up my shirt with slightly trembling hands. That had been a close call. Without the wound he would have arrested me for certain. I looked around but the two girls were out of sight and the park was emptying as evening set in. It looked like I would sleep alone that night after all, but for the moment I was just glad to still be at liberty. I made my way back to the alley and through the gate into the garden. There I found a reception committee of Grant and Anna waiting for me.

"Where have you been?" they chorused.

"Don't you realise how dangerous it is on the streets?" persisted Anna, seeming genuinely frightened. "They are picking up all sorts of people for the army. If you are arrested, we could all be caught. You don't know what you are doing."

"Don't worry," I replied, putting my arm around her waist. "Look, now I have a certificate of exemption, and when I was stopped, the policeman looked at it and let me go."

"You have already been stopped by the police?" She sounded horrified as she stared at the certificate I held out for her.

"Where did you get that?" enquired Grant, but I ignored him.

Anna's body felt warm and yielding to the touch, reminding me of my earlier desires. "You worry too much," I told her as I moved my hand up to cup her breast. "Now why don't you let me help you lose all that tension?"

I did not see her hand before it slapped my face hard. "You are a dangerous fool! You have no idea what risks you are taking," she shouted, pulling herself away. But then a look of malevolence crossed her features. "But if you really want a woman, I will send Clothilde, the dairy maid, to see you in the morning." With that she picked up her empty basket and stalked off back through the garden.

Grant demanded again to know where the exemption had come from. When I told him, he had the effrontery to accuse me of taking unnecessary risks and endangering our escape. This from a man who had dragged us all the way to Paris on a whim. We fell to arguing again, and while Grant might have had a point I was not going to admit it. I reminded him that without me he would almost certainly have been caught wandering around in his red coat, and would now be strapped to a table having his fingernails pulled out. He raged back and eventually stormed back up the ladder into his belfry to spend the night with his books.

He was still snoring up there the next morning as I sat on the chapel steps gnawing on a crust of bread for breakfast. It had been a chilly night and I was sitting back against the stonework with my eyes shut, soaking in the warmth of the early morning sun. Suddenly I heard footsteps coming through the trees. I was just judging whether I had time to run and hide in a nearby bush when what can only be described as an awe-inspiring sight hove into view. If the woman had been two hundred pounds lighter, she might have been attractive. But she wasn't and she wasn't. This, I realised, must be Clothilde, the dairy maid that Anna had promised me the night before. My jaw must have dropped in astonishment as I took in the sight and when she saw me she gave me a cheery wave and a smile.

"Hello, my lover," she called in a strong country accent. "Are you the man that Anna promised me?"

As she approached I realised that her bulk was not all fat; there was a waist behind her dairy maid apron and her forearms were as broad as my thighs. She was taller than me and had hands the size of shovels. I did not doubt that if a cow in the dairy gave any trouble, she could tip the poor creature on its back. The force she could bring to bear on any man reckless enough to get between her legs did not bear thinking about.

"Er, no," I replied hesitantly, desperately thinking of a way out of the situation. Any amorous intentions I had harboured the previous day had melted away. The thought of any congress with this amazon frightened the life out of me and I don't mind admitting it.

Suddenly the perfect solution to my dilemma came to mind. "You must be Clothilde," I greeted her. "The man you are seeking is resting up in the belfry." I gave her a warm smile. "He might be a bit reluctant to start with," I confided. "As he is very proud of being a gentleman and would not want to be seen to be taking advantage of you."

She chuckled at the idea that someone could take advantage of her. "That is a shame, dearie; I was hoping it was you." As she walked past me, she gave my cheek a pinch with enough force to bend a horseshoe nail. Then she whispered, "Perhaps we can get together once I have seen your friend upstairs."

I smiled wanly with half of my face; the cheek she had pinched had gone numb. Then I watched her go into the chapel. She moved surprisingly lightly towards the bottom of the belfry and only broke one rung on the ladder as she swiftly climbed up the tower. I heard Grant's startled gasp of pain as the trap door was thrown open; it must have hit him in the confined space of the little tower.

"Flashman... who the devil are you?" he cried in pain and surprise.

"It's Clothilde, silly. Now come here and don't be shy."

"Get off me you mad... fnfnfn." I imagined that the rest of the sentence was cut off as his face was pressed into her enormously ample bosom. He was still putting up a struggle, though, as I could hear his boots scraping along the floor. Then there was a shattering crash that sent dust and cobwebs down from the underside of the platform.

"Now you lie quietly while I take off my shift," Clothilde cooed at him as Grant must have lain stunned and in pain.

"Please leave me alone," I heard him wail.

I laughed in delight; it was about time the pompous prig got taken down a notch or two. I resumed my place sitting in the sun, lying back against the wall with my eyes closed. I was going to enjoy listening to this, but I would make damn sure I was out of sight before the giantess descended that ladder.

"There now, what do you think of those?" I heard her say. "Go on then, you can hold one of them if you want." I pictured those huge breasts being dangled in Grant's horrified face and was not surprised to hear a howl of despair that seemed almost animal in origin.

As the cry of torment finished, there was the sound of a twig snapping nearby. I opened my eyes to find myself gazing at a fresh-faced young boy standing just a few yards in front of me. He was frowning at me but then he asked simply, "Who are you?"

"I'm Henri," I told him. "Who are you?"

"I am Victor." I recognised him as one of Madame Trebuchet's boys that we had glimpsed earlier in the week. Well, there was no chance to hide this time, and in any event Grant's wailing seemed loud enough to wake the rest of the household. "What is that noise. Can I go and see?"

"No, no, you cannot go up there." Those sights would scar the memory of an adult, I thought; God knows what they would do to an impressionable child. I tried to think of something that would frighten the boy away. "There is a nasty, old, one-eyed hunchback living in the bell tower and he does not like children."

"Why is he making that noise?" the boy persisted.

"He has fallen in love with a beautiful, very light ballerina," I told him. "But the ballerina does not love the hunchback and so he is crying in despair."

The boy considered this for a moment and may have even believed it, but then we heard Clothilde's voice again.

"Now why don't you suck on one of these bubbies and stop all that noise." The howl was suddenly cut off and a muffled gurgling noise resumed as she added, "Let's get these britches off you."

"That is Clothilde. She is not a ballerina," announced the lad perceptively. "What are they doing?"

"Never mind that, what are *you* going to do today?" I asked to distract him.

"My mother says I must write a letter to my father." He wrinkled his nose in distaste at what he obviously viewed as a tedious chore.

"Where is your father? Is he marching to Russia?"

Before the boy could reply we were interrupted by more noise from the belfry. First there were loud gasps for breath, as Grant must have got his face free from the flesh that had been pressing against it. "For the love of God, get off me, woman... I'll pay you, just get off me... No, don't touch me there... I am a British gentleman, dammit – you cannot do this."

"Ah, he said you might worry about that," Clothilde cooed back. "You just lie back and relax. You will enjoy it."

"He said?... Flashma–!... fnfn..." Mercifully the cry was cut off at this point as more flesh was pressed into Grant's face.

"The hunchback does sound very cross," declared the boy, before adding, "My father is a soldier, but he is not in Russia; he is in Spain."

"Really? I was in Spain too."

"It is a horrid place isn't it? We all went to visit Father last year."

"Your father must be a senior officer if he can arrange for his family to visit him."

"Yes, he is a general," the boy replied.

"General Trebuchet." The name did not ring any bells with me. "Is he fighting the partisans rather than the British soldiers?"

"His name is not Trebuchet; that is my mother's name. His name is General Hugo."

"General Hugo," I repeated softly as the morning air suddenly felt several degrees colder. Now earlier events made more sense: the reluctance of Lacodre's father to be involved, Anna's fear and her shouting at me that I did not understand what I was doing.

The boy interrupted my thoughts. "Do you know my father?"

"No. I have heard about him of course, but we have never met." My mind was suddenly filled with an image of the great Gothic cathedral at Burgos where Hugo had nailed partisan heads over the entrance. "You will have to ask your father to decorate this chapel when he comes home. He probably has some interesting ideas for it." The boy looked puzzled at the suggestion, but my mind was already turning to his mother. If she had visited her husband in Spain last year then they must still be close. If she was as rabid a Bonapartist as her spouse then he could come home and find our heads nailed over the lintel.

"Should I tell Father about the hunchback?" the boy asked.

"I think not. In fact I think it is best if you do not mention anything you have seen or heard this morning to either of your parents. It should be a secret."

"All right, I will keep it a secret," agreed the boy, appearing very pleased at having such a responsibility.

In a flash of inspiration I added, "Promise me you will keep it a secret, on the emperor's life."

"I promise on the emperor's life," the boy replied solemnly.

"That is good," I told him. "But if you break that promise then the emperor might die and you and your parents could be arrested for treason."

The boy's eyes widened in alarm. "I won't tell anyone," he promised me again. Then, with a glance up at the bell tower which was emitting more half strangled wails, he walked away back through the bushes while I slumped back down against the wall.

One thing was for sure: we could not stay any longer at the Feuillantines house. I had no idea how well a small boy could keep a secret, but I guessed it would not be long before he let something slip. Even if he did manage to keep quiet, Madame Hugo might notice food disappearing into the garden with Anna. Unless she was deaf, she probably had also heard the cries of Grant and Clothilde carry towards the house in the quiet morning air. But where could we go?

The original idea of escaping upriver and down the canals to Nantes seemed a good one. Surely Lacodre's cousin Marcel was not the only bargee to take illicit passengers. I still had the gold in my belt; perhaps we could buy our passage with someone else. That was the best plan I could come up with. I thought that we would be best to get to the docks at night when there were fewer officials to ask awkward questions. In any event, if I was bringing Grant, we could not leave now; he was rather occupied. The floorboards at the top of the bell tower had now developed a very regular creak as several hundred weight of flesh moved above them, accompanied by a faint gasping whimper. There was no way I was going to be found when Clothilde came back down that ladder and so I slipped away to the garden gate.

Chapter 26

I wasn't in the mood for the park. The grunting and groaning from the top of the bell tower accompanied by the sound of flesh slapping on flesh was quite disturbing. It conjured images in my mind that drove away any carnal thoughts. I was much more concerned with Madame Hugo and the reliability of young Victor. As I slipped away down the alley I wondered if the boy was even then blurting out his secret or if the general's wife was at that very moment walking through the garden to investigate the strange noises from the chapel. What would she do if she discovered that fugitives were hiding in her garden? Almost certainly she would summon the authorities, like a good little Bonapartist, and then when I returned I would be arrested.

So should I go back at all? Having delivered Grant to the tender mercies of Clothilde, even I would have felt a heel sliding out on him without any warning. More importantly if he was arrested, he was bound to talk, willingly or unwillingly. He knew about the plan to escape upriver. Once the authorities had that information, they would search every boat to find me.

On the other hand, little Victor had looked alarmed when I had made him swear on Bonaparte's life. Perhaps he would keep his mouth shut, at least for a day, which was all we would need.

Instead of going to the park, I walked around until I could see the front of the house. Finding an abandoned old news sheet, I sat down on a nearby bench and pretended to read. I was a hundred yards away from the house, but if Madame Hugo summoned the authorities I would know about it. Then I would at least have a chance of getting away.

I must have read that news sheet twenty times. Even now I can recall that the headline was about the French army crossing the river Vistula in the new Polish kingdom. There were also claims that the Russian army was fleeing in terror at their approach. Clothilde left the house an hour after I took up my surveillance. I shrank back into some bushes, but she walked off in the opposite direction. I spent the rest of the day sitting on that bench, apart from a few short walks to renew the circulation in my buttocks. Not a single person left or entered the house apart from the dairy maid. Eventually the sun began to set and, offering my heartfelt congratulations to young Victor on his discretion, I got up and walked slowly back round to the garden gate.

It had gone dark by the time I quietly approached the little chapel again. I saw against the night sky that was something sticking out of the top of the belfry. As I got closer I realised that Grant had pulled the ladder up into the bell tower so that he could not be disturbed again. Half of it was now pointing into the sky from one of the shuttered windows. At least that indicated that he was still there, and as the garden was quiet, hopefully he was alone. I cautiously entered the building and looked around; it appeared undisturbed from my last visit, a half-drunk cup of water still on the altar.

"Grant," I called quietly up the tower. "It is me, Flashman. We have to get away." I waited but there was no reply. "Grant, you bloody fool," I called in English. "I know you are up there. You pulled the ladder up after you." Still there was no reply and for a brief moment I wondered if he had done something stupid like kill himself. Surely Clothilde was not that bad? But then I heard him move on the platform above me.

"Flashman, you are an absolute swine. I know you sent that… that… monster up here. I will never forgive you for that, never, you hear?"

"Yes, I hear you, and I am sorry," I lied. It had been a choice between him and me, and there are some things and people I will not 'do' for king and country, Clothilde being one of them. "Listen to me. Madame Trebuchet is General Hugo's wife. Do you understand what that means? As soon as she discovers we are here, she will turn us in for certain. It will be the rack for you and a firing squad for me. We have to leave now and try to get a boat by ourselves."

"How do I know that this is not another of your damn tricks? You would sell me out in a heartbeat to save your own precious skin."

"Maybe I would," I answered honestly. "But ask yourself this: if I was going to hand you over to the French, why would I be sneaking around on my own in the dead of night to do it? It would be much easier to wait until daybreak, get some soldiers and shoot you down." I grinned to myself in the darkness and then suggested something that would really horrify him. "Or I could find another ladder and get Clothilde to go back up there to flush you out."

"You wouldn't!" cried Grant, aghast at the thought.

"Just think about what I told you and then come on down," I replied. "We need to get moving." I was happy to give him a few minutes to mull it over, because when he did even someone as dim as Grant would realise that he had little choice.

I stepped out of the church into the moonlit graveyard that surrounded it. My stomach rumbled in protest; I had not eaten anything since breakfast and there was no food on the altar, which was where Anna normally left it. There was a vegetable garden near the house. I was just wondering if I had time to raid it or hope for something better than raw vegetables at the docks when one of the gravestones moved. Well, it did not move as much as elongate, as a figure stood up behind it.

"So you are British," stated a woman's voice I had not heard before. She spoke in French and I wondered how much of my conversation in English with Grant she had been able to understand. Certainly she was on her guard: her arm was extended towards me and something metallic glittered in her hand.

It had to be Madame Hugo, I thought. She was brave or foolish if she was going to try to arrest two soldiers alone with just a pistol. My eyes darted around the other gravestones for movement in case she had any accomplices.

"No, my lady," I replied in French, searching for an excuse that would buy us some time. "We are Hollanders on our way back from Spain to join our emperor in Russia. Your husband, the general, agreed we could stay here, but it seemed too late to disturb you. We thought we would just camp in the chapel for the night. I apologise if we caused you alarm."

The response to this long and rambling explanation was brief: the metallic click of a pistol being cocked. She was still six yards away, shooting me from there would be a challenging shot in the dark. Unless it was a rifled barrel I stood a good chance of diving for cover and surviving. That at least was the logical response but my mind froze on the thought of another ball of lead smashing its way through my flesh. I could not steel myself to make the move and I felt beads of sweat break out on my brow as she spoke again.

"You are Captain Thomas Flashman and your companion is General Wellington's chief spy, a man called Grant. Anna has told me everything." I glanced around us again, expecting to see soldiers emerge from the shadows. Surely she had not come alone if she knew who we were.

"I am sorry, Madame Hugo, but you are mistaken..."

"Do not call me Hugo," she interrupted. "My name is Trebuchet. And you need not look around for soldiers. I have not come here to arrest you. I am here to help you."

"Help me? I don't understand." I must have stood and gaped as my mind tried to keep up with this extraordinary turn of events. "Are you not married to General Hugo?"

"We are separated," she snapped, "and that is none of your business. What does matter is that you have been betrayed. There has been someone watching the house all day. They will probably arrest you as soon as you try to leave."

"If you mean the French soldier sitting on the bench down the street, that was me," I explained. "I thought *you* were going to betray us when I found out who your husband was."

She was silent for a moment and I saw her eyes glitter in the moonlight as she looked about us. Then the pistol slowly lowered. "I think we should talk," she said quietly, "and we would be more comfortable in the house. Why don't you get your companion down and then we can go inside? I can help you, but I think that you can also help me."

I wandered back into the chapel, feeling bewildered. "Grant, listen to me," I called up in English. "Madame Trebuchet is outside. She knows who we are and she is offering to help us. She wants us to go up with her to the house." Even as I uttered the words I knew they sounded ridiculous. Grant was bound to object, not that I blamed him.

"But you said that Madame Trebuchet is the wife of General Hugo."

"Yes, she is, I think, although she says that they are separated."

"How can you trust her!" exclaimed Grant. "She married Hugo. He did not become a fanatic overnight. She is bound to be a fervent revolutionary."

"But she came here alone. She would have brought soldiers if she just wanted to arrest us. And anyway I have been watching the house all day; she has not sent for any soldiers."

"She must have seen you watching the house. She will have sent for soldiers as soon as you left your post. I'll wager she has promised to deliver us to them to save troops trampling over her rosebushes in the night. You will be arrested the minute you step foot in the house." He paused and then added, "You go if you want, but I am staying here. I will jump before I let them take me alive."

He had a point, I thought. Why would a French patriot help a British spy, and what help could she possibly want from us? Things did not add up, but my gut told me that if she was playing us false, she would have brought some armed men into the garden with her as

209

insurance. God knows I am not one to put myself into danger, but as she knew all about us, we seemed to have little choice.

"Where is your friend?" she asked as I returned to the little graveyard.

"He does not trust you," I answered bluntly. "He will stay here until I come back."

She did not seem too alarmed by this development and simply gestured towards the house with the pistol barrel. We walked together through the shrubbery, initially without speaking. She did not point the pistol at me, but held it loosely in her hand, pointing at the ground. She saw me glance across at her and look at the weapon.

"Do not worry, Captain Flashman, I will not shoot you unless I have to. We both have to trust each other." She did not say any more and I was not sure how to respond, so I stayed silent.

As we got closer to the house a door opened and I saw Anna framed in the light. We entered what seemed to be the scullery and for the first time I could see the features of Madame Trebuchet. She was, I thought, around forty, not a classic beauty, but her big eyes captured your attention while a firm jaw gave her a determined air. She returned my inspection and smiled.

"I see that you are the man who was watching my house all day. I take it you are hungry," she continued as we walked into the kitchen. "I heard your stomach rumble in the graveyard." Without waiting for a reply she turned to Anna. "Bring us some game pie and a bottle of the Burgundy; we will be in the library." The maid looked more frightened than I had ever seen her before, but nodded and turned to start preparing the supper.

A few minutes later and I was settling myself at a table while Anna laid out a large helping of pie with some pickled vegetables.

"I trust I can put this away now," declared Madame Trebuchet, showing me that she was putting the pistol in a desk drawer. "I am hardly likely to feed you and then have you arrested."

I washed down a mouthful of food with some of the red wine. "I still don't really understand what is happening. What is it that we can help you with?"

"I will come to that presently," she replied, settling herself into a chair. "But first tell me this: does your General Wellington trust you? If I was to help you get a message to him, would he believe it?"

"It would depend on what the message was. I have known the general for ten years, and I think he trusts my judgement, but ultimately he always makes up his own mind on things."

"What about your colleague, Major Grant; he is a more senior officer?"

"Oh, Grant is just a reconnaissance officer. He has not known Wellington for long. He is not a proper agent, which is why Wellington sent me to rescue him."

"I see," said Madame Trebuchet thoughtfully. She stared into space for a while, considering what I had told her, and then she turned to me. "If something important happened in France that Wellington had been warned about, would he be able to stop the war?"

"Stop the war?" I repeated, barely able to believe what I had just heard. If I had been confused as to what was happening before, now I was dumbfounded. It took me several seconds to gather my thoughts sufficiently to answer her question. "Well, I suppose he could suspend fighting by the British in Spain, but he has no influence on the Russians or the Austrians. What important happening are we talking about?"

She took a deep breath before replying. "We are talking about a change of government in France."

I think I might have pinched myself at this point to check I was not dreaming. "You mean you are a royalist?" I gasped, astounded that she could be the complete antithesis of what I had expected.

"Of course not," she snapped. "I am a republican. We want to return France to the ideals and principles of the republic, the people voting for their government."

"But it can't be done," I objected. "The French soldiers I have met are all loyal to the emperor and I have seen the people cheering the soldiers in the streets. They would not support another revolution, especially if Bonaparte brings them more victories and spoils after beating the Russians."

"You are wrong. The plan comes from an army general, one still loyal to republican principles. Many French people are proud of their republic and what it stood for. They have watched with disgust as we have replaced a king with an emperor. The names might have changed, but the tyranny is just the same. When a second republic is declared and they see that power is being returned to the people, they will rise up and defend their rights."

"And do you think Bonaparte and his supporters will just let them take his power away?"

"The republic will be declared when he is deep into Russia; his key supporters will be arrested and replaced. The plans are already made. By the time he hears he has been overthrown it will be too late. If we can agree a peace with Wellington then we can bring the French armies in Spain back into France to defend the new order. Bonaparte and his family will be declared enemies of France and exiled."

"Good God," I breathed as I took this in. It was turning out to be an extraordinary evening. What she was proposing would bring Britain victory in Spain and probably an end to the war with France. "And you want Grant and me to write to Wellington to let him know about this plan?"

"Yes, but not until you meet the general who is going to create the new republic. I am going to take you to see him tomorrow."

Instead of returning to the chapel, Madame Trebuchet, or Sophie as she now insisted I call her, offered me a room in the house. While Grant lay curled up on his hard wooden platform, I reclined on a comfortable mattress with embroidered coverings; but I hazard to guess that Grant slept better than me. My mind was in a whirl at the revelations of the evening. It was scarcely believable that Grant and I could play a role in changing the government in France and consequently the political situation around the world. We would be feted across England and I imagined the honours that would be heaped on us: peerages, the thanks of parliament and pensions.

Britain would be the dominant power in Europe as France would almost certainly fall into a civil war between the republicans and the Bonapartists. I was not at all convinced by Sophie's claims that the country would slip peacefully into a benign republic, bringing order and peace to the country. The original French republic had been a chaotic and bloody affair and I was doubtful everyone would welcome it back. Even if some generals would support the new order, others would stay loyal to the emperor. The French army would be split and would waste its energy fighting itself rather than France's neighbours.

With advance warning of what was happening, Wellington would let the French army withdraw from Spain as he would see as easily as I could the chaos that would ensue in France. Some of the French army units in Spain would support Bonaparte, others the republic, but the British objective of liberating Spain and Portugal would have been achieved. Doubtless Britain would look to snap up other French possessions to take advantage of the situation. All this because Grant and I, people Wellington trusted, had happened across the plotters in Paris. It was an incredible chance.

I must have slept a little, but as soon as it was light I got dressed, slipped from my room and went down to the chapel. Having assured himself that Clothilde was not in the vicinity, Grant lowered the ladder and came down from the tower. He was unshaven and looked haggard, but he brightened up as we sat behind the altar and I whispered to him everything that Madame Trebuchet had told me the previous evening.

"But our government wants to put the French king back on the throne," he protested.

"It doesn't matter. Once the Bonapartists and republicans have fought themselves to a standstill, they will probably let a French poodle sit on the throne, never mind the king, if it means peace."

"Will we have to stay in Paris and provide Wellington with reports on the plot as the preparations are made?" asked Grant.

I hadn't thought of that. I had no wish to stay in France, especially if the plot was not going to be activated until the *Grande Armée* was deep into Russia. That could be several months away and in the meantime we risked firing squads and torture.

"If Sophie, I mean Madame Trebuchet, and the plotters have a means of getting written messages to Wellington, perhaps they can help our escape too," I mused.

Then we both sat back in silence, thinking about how we had a part to play on the world's stage and the glory it promised. Little did we realise that we were just bit part players in a drama of which we were then completely unaware.

Chapter 27

There have been several times in my life when what had seemed sensible, well-thought-out plans turned out to be unmitigated disasters. The defence of a hill fort against Pindaree bandits in India had been one; trying to outrun a Zulu impi on horseback was another – but for sheer certifiable lunacy the plans for the second republic in France take some beating.

My initial high hopes for the scheme were dashed almost from the start. When the carriage that Sophie Trebuchet had ordered pulled up outside the house, I saw that it was open topped so anyone could see who was inside. I had expected to be taken out of the city to a remote headquarters of the conspirators or at the very least through a maze of streets and alleyways so that we could not be followed. Instead I was told that we were visiting a rest home operated by a Doctor Dubuisson not far from the centre of Paris.

"That is where General Malet is living," announced Sophie.

"Is he the general who will establish the new republic?" I had been hoping for a general I had heard of or even a marshal of France, but Malet was not a name I was familiar with. My disappointment may have sounded in my voice.

"He is a great general of France," declared Sophie defensively. "Once a rival of Bonaparte, but he refused to bow the knee to the tyrant and is now forced to live in the rest home."

"He is lucky he is not in prison," I muttered.

"Oh, he was," declared Sophie proudly. "He was arrested for his involvement in another plot to overthrow the emperor, but he used his influence to secure a release to the rest home."

"You mean he has done this before?" I was astounded. "Surely the authorities are already watching him?"

"Oh no, they allow him visitors freely and no details are taken of those that see him. You should not underestimate the arrogance of Bonaparte and his minions. They think they are quite safe. Bonaparte has been emperor for nearly eight years and his ministers, relatives and marshals are too busy squabbling amongst themselves. The minister of war and the minister of police hate each other and most of the ministries have their own agents who spend their time spying on their rivals."

Sophie was right up to a point. No one stopped us entering the rest home, which was a large, rambling affair, and no one asked for or checked our identities. But as Sophie led me along a corridor on the first floor a man stepped out from a side room. I guessed he was the good Doctor Dubuisson.

"Madame Trebuchet, a pleasure to see you again. I am sure that you will brighten the general's day. And you have a companion, a soldier no less…" He beamed at me expectantly and held out a hand in greeting.

"Captain Henri Lafitte," I muttered, reluctantly shaking the cold and clammy hand. It was the only identity I had a document to support.

"Well, I am sure you will find the general in good spirits," the sawbones announced with a satisfied smile and then he stepped out of the way and allowed us to continue down the passage. It had been smoothly done but I guessed that no one visited the general without some sort of interception.

"I don't trust this place," I whispered to Sophie as we walked along. "Somebody might be eavesdropping on the general's room. I would be obliged if you do not give the general our real names, just say we have a code Wellington will trust."

"Of course, if that is what you want," she whispered back. "But I think you are wrong. They have forgotten about him and soon they will pay the price."

A moment later she knocked on a door, which was thrown open by a wild-eyed cove. He looked to be around sixty, but may have been slightly younger. His powdered wig and knee britches that were long out of fashion, gave him the air of an aristocrat; not something you would think would be popular in a republican France. As Sophie introduced me as her friend Henri Lafitte, he made a great show of hospitality. He offered us the two chairs in the room and glasses of water, the only refreshment he had. Mine had a dead fly floating in it and so I left it on the windowsill.

Sophie and the general spent some time on pleasantries such as the weather and the health of her children, which gave me the opportunity to observe him. Given that he was in a rest home I had half expected him to be slightly deranged; but apart from his eyes, which never settled on anything for more than a second or two, he seemed well balanced. He made some reference to a quote from Plato and so was clearly well educated, his hands were steady and he seemed open and welcoming. Eventually he took his seat on the side of the bed and looked at us expectantly.

"I have brought Henri because I think he will be able to help us," declared Sophie quietly. "You told us that it was vital we disengaged our army from Spain before any forces could return from Russia. Henri can help us. He knows Lord Wellington and believes Wellington will trust him. I thought he could write to Wellington with some warning of what is going to happen so that the British support the withdrawal of our troops."

The general turned to face me, his eyes locking briefly onto mine and then darting about my body before returning to my face. "How well do you know Lord Wellington, Henri?"

"I met him ten years ago in India. I did him a good service there and since then I have met him in Spain several times."

"India?" queried the general, smiling. "We did not have many French soldiers in India, but there were plenty of British ones. The leather of your boots is also not cut in the French style. No, no, don't try to explain; it is better for us that you know Lord Wellington well. I judge you know him better than any French officer."

I had started to interrupt him, mentioning my boots were battlefield loot, but then lapsed into silence. He was certainly observant, but any hope I entertained of shrewdness was dashed a moment later. "How will you execute your plan?" I asked.

"Ah, the simplest plans are always the best," he replied, getting up. Then he bent down and pulled an unlocked trunk from under his bed. With a grunt he hauled it up and placed it on the mattress before throwing open the lid. "Look, I have now got my general's coat." He showed Sophie a blue army coat adorned with plenty of gold braid. "We will get more coats for the others. Someone else has got my sword, as I am not allowed to keep that here."

Sophie smiled with delight at the sight of the garment, but to me he sounded more like a schoolboy planning a breakout to a local inn than a man planning a revolution. Things did not improve when he started showing what he kept beneath the coat.

"We will wait until Bonaparte is deep into Russia and then we will announce that the emperor is dead and a new provisional republican government has been appointed. Look, here are some of the proclamations." He passed me an undated document announcing the death of Napoleon and the appointment of a new provisional government. It had various stamps and seals on the bottom, but how genuine they looked I could not judge.

"But surely his supporters and those in power will insist that he is still alive?" I asked sceptically.

"Oh, the first step will be to secure the Paris garrison; you see here is an order signed by the new provisional government, putting it under my command." He handed me another official-looking document before continuing. "Then we will release key prisoners who will support the republic." He handed me more papers.

"That one is for the release of Victor Lahorie, another general," stated Sophie. "He used to live in your chapel before he was arrested, but now he will be the new minister of police."

That, I realised, must be Sophie's former lover, but I was more concerned with the wild optimism of the plan. "But surely the incumbents in these roles won't give up their power that easily?"

"As soon as the prisoners are released," Malet explained, "they will be sent with a detachment of the Paris garrison to arrest their predecessors. By lunchtime republicans will hold all key positions of power. The Bonapartists will be arrested before they even know a coup has happened. Once we have secured our position we will issue a declaration to the people to announce the return of their beloved republic."

I shook my head in disbelief as he rummaged in his box, bringing out arrest warrants and release papers, all undated but bearing seals and stamps. The whole plot was laid out in detail for anyone to see, in an unlocked chest, kept under a bed in a nursing home.

"How many people know about the plans for the new republic?" I asked, and before he could answer I could not help myself from suggesting, "Surely you should at least keep a lock on that box?"

"The general knows what he is doing," reprimanded Sophie, but Malet held up a hand in submission.

"Our British friend is quite right to challenge us." He turned to me. "Very few people know about our endeavour. I learned that lesson from my first attempt to overthrow the emperor. We were discovered because too many people knew about the plans. This time only a core of trusted people knows what will happen and only I know all the details."

"But it is all in that unlocked box," I protested. "You must leave this room sometimes, and anyone can read through the papers."

"You are right," agreed the general. "My box does not have a lock. Sophie, my dear, would you be kind enough to bring some chains and a padlock when you next come? But, Henri, don't worry: the authorities have quite forgotten about me. So, do you think that your friend Wellington will support the new republic?"

"He will," I confirmed without hesitation. "Wellington is no republican but you are effectively offering him the liberation of Spain with no further British casualties. I am sure he will suspend hostilities if the French army retreats into France."

Malet looked delighted and actually clapped his hands with joy, but it really should not have been a surprise. As well as the liberation of Spain, the British commander would envisage the chaos that would follow in France. But Wellington was an old hand at plots and intrigues, and if I was a judge, he would not put much credence on this one until it happened.

We took our leave shortly after that with me wondering if my security suggestion had in fact made the situation worse. If Malet was right and the authorities had forgotten about him then several yards of chain around a box under his bed might attract their attention. On the other hand, I found it strange that a known conspirator had been released from prison at all.

On the way back Sophie could barely restrain her excitement, but managed to avoid giving any details of their scheme with the coachman just a few feet away. Once back inside the house she hugged me and announced that Grant and I would be heroes of the new republic. Her two boys in the house came to see what all the noise was about and it reminded me of the huge risks she was taking.

"How often do you visit the general?" I asked when we were alone again.

"Oh, at least once a month. I help him get messages out to some of the others."

"Then surely if the plot is discovered, you will be arrested too. Are you not worried for yourself and your children?"

"No," she declared simply, before adding, "I have protection. They cannot arrest me."

"What do you mean?" I asked. "Surely if you try to overthrow the emperor, they will detain everybody."

"They would certainly arrest most of the conspirators, but the minister of police will do everything in his power to ensure that I am not taken into custody. He knows that if I am arrested, he will be too."

"I don't understand. Is he a friend of your husband?"

"The minister of police is a man called Savary. He likes everyone to think he is a committed Bonapartist, but a few years ago he was aware

218

of a scheme to overthrow the government by some of his former commanders. It was the plot Victor Lahorie was convicted for. Savary wrote to Lahorie, mentioning the plot, before it was discovered. I have the letter and Savary knows it. If the letter were revealed, it would show that Savary was once a traitor to Bonaparte. That is why he will make sure that I am not arrested."

It sounded tenuous protection to me but I did not argue. Imperial politics was a volatile affair with ministers plotting against each other. Savary could easily be replaced in his role by the emperor or even be killed during the attempt for the second republic. Then if the Bonapartists regained power, she would have no protection at all. I thought it unlikely that the plot would stay secret long enough to be activated. But if it did, I also had doubts that the people would flock to the new republic.

"If the French army is released from Spain," I asked, "are you sure that most of them will serve the new republic? Surely some, like your husband, will take their forces to support the emperor?"

"My husband will certainly stay loyal to the emperor," she answered with disdain. "His republican principles have long since been bought with the baubles of rank and privilege. But many of the common soldiers will join us, particularly if we promise them peace." She smiled at my look of scepticism. "You are British. You do not understand France. We have been at war with one country or another for twenty-five years; we have run out of fit young men. For the Russian campaign they have swept the hospitals for walking wounded, conscripted young boys and re-enlisted old soldiers who had been retired. The country is being bled dry and the people want their surviving sons and husbands to come home." She paused and added, "Although in my case I am happy for my husband to stay away with his mistress."

"How did you meet your husband?" I asked. "You do not appear to have a lot in common."

"Oh, we did originally. He was a young soldier sent to defend the republic against a royalist uprising in Brittany and I was a member of one of the few republican families in the region. Initially I was attracted by his drive and ambition; back then it was dedicated to serving the republic. But now he sees more opportunities with the emperor and his ambition has driven us apart."

As I was to discover a short while later, General Hugo was not the only one to suffer from excessive ambition. When I finally got to tell

Grant about the events at Malet's nursing home, his eyes lit up with delight. He was still imagining being heaped with honours and glory as we brought peace to Britain and chaos to its main enemy.

"Calm down," I told him. "Remember what I told you of the plans being kept in an unlocked box. The chances are that the plotters will be arrested long before they get the chance to implement their plot."

"But this is vital intelligence to get back to Wellington," he protested. "Even if it has only the slightest chance of success. There is no risk to us as the British will only act if the plot is successful."

"There may be no risk to the British army," I pointed out, "but we are still stuck in Paris, now in a nest of the most amateur conspirators. If they have not been already, they could get discovered at any moment. We still need to make our escape."

"But should we not stay here to liaise with the new republican government when it is formed?"

"You still don't understand, do you?" I persisted in exasperation. "The odds are that there will be no republican government, and when the plotters are discovered, the police will be searching for anyone involved in the conspiracy."

"But you told me that Madame Trebuchet had some kind of protection!"

"It *might* protect her, but it would not save two British officers found to be involved in the plot. Especially if the authorities were already searching for those officers to torture or shoot them as spies."

Still Grant seemed reluctant to move away from what he called the 'fulcrum of history'. I think he imagined himself helping to lead the revolution that would bring down the French empire. In the end as we could not agree we set to writing our own separate messages for Wellington that would be sent together.

Sophie asked us to include some phrase or expression that would prove that the letters had come from us without duress. I did not see Grant's letter but I do not doubt that it was full of optimism and hope about the coming republic and what this would mean for Britain. I took a more cautious line and told Wellington that the general in charge of the plot had all the strategic acumen of Dowlat Rao Scindia, a Mahratta prince we had both known in India.

When Grant and Sophie asked me about this, I explained that Scindia was a particularly astute Indian commander. Grant looked suspicious but Sophie was delighted. In fact, as Wellington well knew, Scindia spent most of his time too addled with opiates and exhausted by concubines to take any sensible decisions. That, I thought, would help our commander make a more reasonable assessment of the chances of success. I may have been wasting my time, though, as Grant might have destroyed my letter before it was sent. Years later I was talking to Wellington's secretary, and while there are records of the general receiving correspondence from Grant in Paris, there is no record of anything from me at all.

Chapter 28

We had not used any of the plotters' names in the letters and only signed off with our initials, but if the letters were being sent together and with my Indian reference, I was sure that Wellington would guess who they came from. However he might not be the only one to read them. I had no confidence that the security of the conspirators' communications was any safer than the contents of the unlocked box under Malet's bed. If the authorities did see the letters then it would not take them too long to match up the 'CG' on one letter with the missing Colquhoun Grant.

Malet judged that there were still two months before Bonaparte would be deep enough into Russia to initiate his plan. Unlike Grant, I had no wish to be in Paris when it happened and could not wait to get away. I paced anxiously around the garden, waiting for news from Lacodre and his wretched barge-owning cousin. Several days passed and we were all getting tense. Even Sophie had started to worry whether a gang of road menders that had appeared at the end of the street were actually watching the house. To make matters worse, Grant had taken himself off one afternoon in his British uniform to watch a passing parade of soldiers, using his notebook to record all the regimental numbers that passed him. He could not have made himself more conspicuous, but claimed that when he was challenged by people they believed his American officer story. I threatened him with Clothilde if he ever left the garden without me again. Judging by the way the colour drained from his face at the thought, I was reasonably sure he would not stray again.

It is easy to speak after the event, but back then I was getting a growing sense of unease. We seemed to be continually piling one risk on top of another until we had a stack of dangers that was bound to collapse on our heads. First we had broken Grant out of captivity, which meant that sooner or later his absence would be noted and a search started. Then Grant had led us to the heart of the enemy capital, which was swarming with Bonapartist officials hunting for deserters. We had no idea how willing Lacodre's boat-owning cousin would be to take us. Not all the Lacodre family was supportive and I was mindful that the old organist would give us away in a heartbeat to save his family. I could be arrested if my stolen exemption paper was ever properly checked, and the buffoon Grant had now paraded himself in British uniform on the streets. Finally we had embroiled ourselves in a half-baked plot against the emperor of the French. It was touch and go whether the scheme would be uncovered due to the careless security of Malet or the vigilance of the French authorities, who were no slouches. Our luck was bound to run out sooner or later, and my guess was sooner.

We spent a fair bit of time in the house now, with Grant usually to be found reading in the library while 'Uncle Henri' spent some of his time with the boys, playing games and teaching them card tricks to pass the time. This meant I was also spending more time with Sophie, and a couple of times I felt that she was giving me more than a casual glance. Initially I had dismissed the idea of having a play at this older woman; it would be a further complication to our already precarious situation. But as the days passed the thought started to play on my mind. I found her deep, soulful eyes increasingly attractive and became more aware of the still-shapely figure under the empire fashions.

The final twist was that Grant seemed to have become completely besotted with her. He gushed about her enthusiastically when the two of us were alone, but became tongue tied and stammering when she showed him any attention. Sophie was amused by the affect she had on him and once asked if he really was a British intelligence officer. She took to kissing us both goodnight on the cheek, which caused Grant to blush furiously. While the gallant major still insisted on sleeping in his tower, I took the opportunity to move into the house.

By the fifth day, the confinement and forced civility were becoming a strain. Sophie had spent the last three nights sleeping in the same room as her youngest son. Ironically little Victor was having nightmares about a love-struck hunchback. During the days I had tried to teach the boys cricket, but they kept making up their own rules. Sophie often tried to include me in card games with the boys, but if we had to play some strange version of 'snap' one more time, I would feel a strong temptation to bludgeon them all with their improvised bat.

I decided that whatever the risk, I had to get outside the house and have some time to myself. After breakfast I brushed down my French officer's hat and coat, checked that my conscription exemption was in the pocket and quietly slipped out of the garden gate.

I walked down the alleyway and onto the road. It was a busy time of day with people bustling about and hawkers and fruit sellers displaying their wares. I stood and watched for a while and saw nothing unusual. Then I wandered up the road to where I had stood to watch the front of the house. Again there seemed nothing suspicious. While the road was busy with traffic, no one seemed to be taking an undue interest in the Trebuchet property. Satisfied that I was safe, I turned towards the park; at least there the policemen knew me as a wounded veteran and should leave me alone.

There was the usual array of females promenading around alone or in groups, but while I would normally have found them diverting that morning I was not in the mood. I went and sat on a bench in the corner of the park where I was unlikely to be disturbed and enjoyed the solitude while I brooded on our predicament.

I had been there half an hour when I noticed the man in the dark coat. He was some way off and talking to a group of ladies, but he seemed vaguely familiar. Then I remembered where I had seen him: he had been buying fruit from a seller when I had emerged from the alleyway. It was just a coincidence, I assured myself, but to be sure I got up and walked around the park to a new bench near one of the park gates. If the man approached again, I planned to slip out of the gates and disappear in the maze of streets beyond.

The dark coat did not appear. But now I was more alert, I did notice a man in a brown coat glance more than once in my direction as he slowly walked past. Again this could be purely coincidence, but then as Brown Coat disappeared around a bend in the pathway I saw Dark Coat coming the other way. More significantly the two men completely ignored each other. That was unusual; when a stranger passed on the same path a man would normally doff his hat or make some form of greeting, even if it was only to wish the other a good day.

The hair on the back of my neck was starting to tickle, indicating that danger was at hand. I decided to take no chances and got up and headed towards the gate. Several carriages with their drivers were parked at the entrance to the Luxembourg Garden, awaiting passengers, and I walked swiftly past them. I thought I had got clean away when two burly men came up behind me and, grabbing me by the arms, pitched me up into the back of what turned out to be a covered prison wagon.

"What the devil do you think you are doing?" I protested, trying to get to my feet. "I am a French officer and I have an exemption certificate"

The brute who had followed me into the vehicle merely stepped forward and kicked me over onto my side. "Stay still," he grunted, glaring down at me. I saw he wore some form of official uniform.

As I lay on the floor his partner shut the door behind him. I was trapped in what was effectively a horse-drawn wooden box with some bars across the small window in the door. I stayed down while a chill of fear ran up my spine. Something told me that this was not how they would normally deal with a deserter. The man had the calm confidence of a professional ruffian, and if the two in the park had been tailing me then they were likely to be police. But what the hell did they know?

If they only suspected me of dodging conscription and possibly stealing the exemption paper then I could expect prison and a forced march east. But if they suspected anything about the plot then I was in much more trouble. If they knew who I really was then it was the firing squad for sure.

My speculation was interrupted when the carriage door opened and the dark-suited man stood in the doorway. He jerked his head to indicate that the guard should leave and then stepped up in his place.

"Look, I think there has been a mistake," I started to protest. "I am a French officer and I have an exemption paper…"

"Silence," he barked down at me. "You will say nothing at all until you meet the minister. Your life depends on it." Then, as an afterthought, he added, "What did you say to the guard?"

"Just that I am a French officer with an exemption," I said hoarsely as my mind spun with the new information.

"Good," he grunted, settling on to one of the bench seats that ran down either side of the box. He raised his cane and banged the roof twice and with a jerk the carriage moved off. I half got up and settled onto the opposite bench. I was apparently going to meet a minister of the French government and that certainly ruled out being treated as a deserter. If my companion was a policeman then that meant I was meeting the police minister and suddenly I thought I understood a little more.

If I was meeting the police minister called Savary, he was the one that Sophie was able to blackmail with the letter. Perhaps he had found out I was staying at the house and was about to put the frighteners on me to find the letter for him. That would explain why he would not want me to say anything to his underlings. I relaxed slightly at the thought. If I was right then they knew nothing about the plot and I would be released to do their dirty work. I would be under constant surveillance, but that was probably no different to the last few days. We might still be able to slip away for a barge under cover of darkness.

The noise of the carriage suddenly had an echo as we went under an arch and then pulled up in a courtyard.

"You will be left in an anteroom until the minister is ready to see you," explained my companion as the door to the prison carriage was thrown open. "You said you had an exemption paper? Give it to me." He held out his hand and reluctantly I handed over the only identity document I possessed. The man put it in his pocket and gave me a final warning as he stepped down from the carriage. "Remember, do not say a word to anyone."

I stepped down into the courtyard and the two ruffians grabbed me by the arms. Ignoring the grand main entrance to the building, we headed to a smaller door and up a narrow staircase until we were on the second floor. There I stepped out onto an opulent corridor with busts of generals and paintings of battles along the walls. A pair of immaculately smart sentries guarded a room at the far end of the passage. Before we reached the soldiers, the ruffians opened one of the side rooms and I was ushered inside. There they left me, turning the key in the lock as they went.

I sat in that room for two hours and spent most of that time considering my predicament. If it was Savary, he would want as few people as possible to know about the letter. Even if I found it for him, he would probably want me to disappear for good. My mind ran through myriad different scenarios, none of them good. The best I could hope for was a forced march to the frozen wastelands of Russia, but most ended up against a cold stone wall in front of a firing squad. I cursed my impetuous nature. What wouldn't I have given to be still in the garden and playing cricket with the boys. But if I was right then I had already been under surveillance and would have been picked up whenever I next left the house.

Finally I heard the key in the lock and an immaculately dressed army captain gestured that it was time for me to leave. Without saying a word, he led the way along the corridor towards the door guarded by the soldiers. Knocking first, he opened the door and led the way into an expansive, well-lit office. At the far end was a large ornately carved desk, which almost dwarfed the man behind it.

"Your guest, sir," announced the captain, gesturing me to a chair opposite the desk. Then he turned sharply and left the room.

I sat and looked at the man I took to be the minister, who returned my inspection. He was in his late forties with thick, curly hair which was starting to grey at the temples. He had the look of a politician rather than a soldier, with fashionable side-burns and clean, manicured fingers. Despite his general's uniform, I suspected he had never fought a military campaign. The closest he had come to a battle was probably the paintings of them on his office wall. I shifted uncomfortably in the chair as he gave me a slight smile. It was not a warm gesture, probably similar to the expression a cat might give a mouse before killing it.

"So you are Captain Henri Lafitte," declared the man, waving my exemption paper in his hand, "even though you are only wearing a lieutenant's uniform." There was a note of sarcasm in his voice that indicated a reply was not required. Despite the danger of the situation my muscles relaxed slightly; he would not have used that name if he knew my English one. "I have to say," he added, glancing down at a note on his desk, "that you are looking remarkably well for your fifty-four years, Captain."

I opened my mouth to say something, but could not think of anything useful to say and so shut it again. I could not prove any other identity without landing myself more deeply in trouble. If by some miracle I was here just for desertion, it was probably the best I could hope for.

"You have no defence then," the man accused sharply. "While other citizens of France loyally serve their emperor, even though they are old or wounded, a young, fit and healthy man thinks he can malinger and even claim the sympathy rightly earned by others." His voice rose in anger as he spoke and I realised that I would have to say something or he could have me ordered to a firing squad there and then.

"I have served my emperor," I replied at last, "and suffered wounds in his service."

"Really," responded the man derisively. "I have spent the last weeks sweeping the sick bays of the army for reinforcements, sending men with hands, feet and eyes missing back to the front line. Yet you stand complete before me and claim to have a debilitating injury."

For the second time recently I had cause to be grateful for my earlier wounds. I remembered the effect my scar had made on the policeman and with fumbling fingers I reached up to my shirt and pulled it to reveal the wicked star-shaped musket ball exit wound in my chest. "I was shot through the body and I have another hole in my leg. I cannot march far without coughing up blood," I lied. "To go all the way to Russia would kill me."

The man gave a grudging nod of acceptance as he stared at my wound. "So why did you not get a certificate of exemption for this wound if it is that bad?" he asked.

"I tried but I was refused." I remembered Sophie telling me about the hostility between the minister of war and the minister of police and decided to try to appeal to it. "I did not want to cause difficulties for the police, but you must know that the ministry of war will not listen to reason. They allow hardly any exemptions."

The man behind the desk smiled wolfishly. "Who do you think I am?" he asked quietly.

"*Monsieur* Savary, the minister of police," I suggested hesitantly, fast coming to the conclusion that I had just made a very bad mistake.

"No," the man said, still smiling. "I am Henri Clarke, Duke of Feltre, the minister of war and, as you rightly say, I allow very few exemptions."

"I am sorry, *monsieur*," I apologised abjectly. "I had not wished to cause offence."

"Nor have you," he responded briskly while watching me closely. He must have seen the uncertainty play across my eyes as I reassessed the situation. If he was not the police minister then what did the minister of war want with me? He surely did not personally interview every deserter; there had to be something else. If he did not know I was British then there was only one other obvious possibility and the thought turned my guts to jelly.

Almost as though he could read my mind, Clarke now spoke again. "Last week with Madame Trebuchet you visited citizen Malet in his rest home. Why did you do that?"

"Sophie, I mean Madame Trebuchet," I replied, thinking fast, "asked me to accompany her. The general is an old friend and I think she visits him regularly." That, I thought, was safe enough: Sophie did visit him regularly, and if they had been watching the old lunatic, they would know that. But I had made a slip and Clarke was quick to pounce.

"How did you know he was a general?" asked Clarke. Then, before I could answer, he casually added, "Did he show you the uniform in his trunk?"

Mention of the trunk brought beads of sweat out on my brow. Had they overheard our conversation or intercepted the letters? How much did Clarke know? "Trunk, what trunk?" I managed to gasp, but the horror must have shown on my face and Clarke laughed in triumph.

"I know all about Malet and his conspiracy and I know that you have seen inside the trunk. The mastermind of your little scheme told one of the orderlies that a French officer had suggested he get a chain to secure it."

"Dear God," I muttered in abject dismay, slumping back in the chair in defeat.

"You seem surprised at your leader's ineptitude," declared Clarke, enjoying himself now. "Did you know that this is his third attempt to overthrow the government? The last time he shut the doors of Notre Dame, trapping the congregation, while he climbed on a monument and declared that the emperor was dead and announced the new republic. You should be impressed; in comparison this is a much more thorough affair."

"But why don't you arrest him?" I asked, bewildered.

"Arrest him? We are the people who set him free." Clarke saw my puzzlement and explained: "His plots have no chance of success, but he is useful in attracting others opposed to the government."

"I swear to you, sir," I protested vehemently, "that I am not in any way opposed to the emperor. I had no idea about the plot until I visited the general."

Clarke held up a hand to still any further protest. "What is your relationship with Madame Trebuchet?"

I hesitated, wondering what else he knew. His people had tracked me to her house, so he knew I lived there. "We are lovers," I told him. "She is giving me somewhere to live while I try to sort out a proper exemption."

"And what is your role in the conspiracy?"

"I have no role," I insisted immediately. "General Malet suggested I could be one of his aides but I have not accepted. I want no part in the scheme at all."

"Did you know that General Lahorie, who would be police minister under the new republic, was also a lover of Madame Trebuchet?"

"I had no idea. By God, sir, she has played me for a fool!" I tried to sound outraged at being duped by my lover into helping her free an earlier companion. "I will leave her at once and I can assure you, sir, that I will have no further contact with any of them. In the circumstances, perhaps I should risk the journey to Russia after all," I suggested hesitantly.

"On the contrary," pronounced the minister firmly. "You will carry on exactly as before and offer to be an aide to Malet."

"I don't understand."

"It is quite simple: I want the plot to proceed and for a few hours to be a success. I of course will escape arrest and lead the forces that round up the conspirators. Amongst their papers we will find documents implicating a number of individuals who currently have imperial protection. Your job will be to tell me when the uprising is about to happen and to hide papers that I will give you in the homes of the conspirators."

Suddenly it all became clear. This Machiavellian minister was using Malet as bait to attract conspirators. But as well as those daft enough to become involved directly with the plot, he also planned to use the scheme to attack other enemies. I was to be his agent and an inconvenient witness to his treachery. I had no doubt that Clarke would ensure that I was killed when the brief republic was overthrown, but I had to pretend that I was taken in by his scheme.

"If I do as you ask, what will happen to me?"

"If you do a good job then you will be sent to Russia, so that you are out of the way while the investigations are undertaken. You can take your time getting there as the emperor may well be on the way back by the time the plot is revealed." He looked at me sternly. "But if you fail in any way, I will have no choice but to round up the conspirators and you will all be executed for treason." He paused and then added, "And if you are thinking of tipping off your fellow accomplices and making a run for it, remember that you and the house will be watched day and night. You are not the only spy I have in this conspiracy, and if your reports differ from those of the other informers, you will also be arrested."

I knew then that I was stuck fast in his web of intrigue, but at least I would be able to walk out of the ministry. That was more than I dared hope just a few minutes ago. "I see, sir. I accept," I declared solemnly.

"Accept? Of course you bloody do. You don't have a choice, unless you want to be shot now." I got up to leave but he waved me back. "Wait, you will be wanting this. The police will not dare challenge that one and they should keep out of your way." He handed me a stiff sheet of parchment. Staring down I saw it was a new exemption certificate, made out to 'the bearer' and displaying the ministry crest with the signature and seal of Clarke himself.

Still in something of a daze, I walked out of the office. The man in the dark suit was waiting for me in the corridor. He guided me down a grand staircase to the main front entrance. There he made me wait for a few minutes while he spoke to some of his colleagues, probably to arrange my surveillance. I used the time to peruse the announcements pinned to the wall. There was a wide range of notices and posters, some announcing promotions, others detailing changes to brigade structures as well as miscellaneous announcements.

I almost missed it, but just as I was turning away I saw a pamphlet with a drawing of two faces on it. They seemed vaguely familiar. Under the heading 'Wanted' the notice announced the escape of the notorious British agent Major 'Colquin' Grant, believed to be travelling with a French officer using the name of Moreau, pronounced a traitor of France. Five hundred francs was offered for our capture with dire threats of punishment to anyone harbouring us.

Chapter 29

The man in the dark suit signalled I could go and one of the ministry's most hunted men stepped back out onto the street. Once in the sunshine I paused to take a deep breath. I was at some form of liberty again. Certainly I was a wanted man trapped in a mess of conspiracy and blackmail, but a short while earlier I had been expecting to take that breath in front of a line of men loading muskets. I had faced worse dangers before, and while it seemed certain that sooner or later some people would face a firing squad, I was going to do all I could to make damn sure I was not among them.

I tried to adopt a casual stroll as I sauntered down the road, apparently unaware of those watching me. The dark-suited man did not bother to try to hide as he followed me at a discreet distance. At the next junction I saw the brown-suited man also watching from a side street and there were probably others out there that I did not recognise. Clearly Clarke did not trust me an inch, which was fair as I did not trust him further than I could spit a hedgehog either. They seemed to expect me to make a run for it and that was exactly what I was planning to do, but I would have to tread carefully.

At least for the moment I was safe. I had a genuine exemption certificate that would frighten off any policeman and the plot was not due to take place for months. Maybe I could lull them into a false sense of security. But when we did make our move they would know within hours and then they would be out for us with a vengeance. They certainly did not suspect me of also being the infamous Lieutenant Moreau, but if they ever found out about Grant's existence in the house, it would surely not take them long to put two and two together.

That got me wondering who else Clarke might have spying on the plot. I could not believe that Sophie was a Bonapartist agent. Surely she would not have split with her husband if she was that committed to the emperor. She also seemed genuinely passionate when talking about the republic. The only other candidate in the house was Anna, but she knew about our real identities, which Clarke manifestly did not. I was about to dismiss the idea of her as a spy when I remembered that if she revealed our real names, she would also incriminate her cousin. Perhaps she only gave them limited information to protect her family.

I decided to be wary of her as a precaution, but the person I really could not trust with information was Grant. It was not that I thought him a spy; it was just that I knew he was a dangerous idiot. He was convinced that the plot would bring him fame and glory and he was bound to blurt out that it had been betrayed. He would probably press to activate it immediately and want to arrest Clarke himself.

My best chance, I decided, lay with me keeping quiet about the meeting with Clarke and acting as normal to all concerned. I just had to buy some time until Marcel, the boat owner, finally appeared and then we would have to try to give those watching us the slip.

A short while later I walked up the alley at the back of the garden. As I approached the garden gate I looked back and could see the dark-jacketed agent settling himself on a bench in the street at the end of the alley. I had no doubt that someone was also watching the front of the house. If they maintained this level of vigilance then getting past them would be a challenge.

"Where have you been?" Grant demanded imperiously as soon as I approached the chapel.

"I needed some time by myself," I told him, glancing around to check we were alone.

"You can't just go off on your own now," he rebuked. "We are involved in affairs of state. The future of this nation depends on us, Flashman, on our courage and determination to succeed."

France really was doomed then, I thought. "For God's sake, keep your voice down," I told him. "Let's go up to the belfry. We need to talk in private."

Grant looked intrigued as he followed me up the wooden ladder to the platform at the top of the bell tower. I slammed the trapdoor shut and we both sat on the straw mattress he used for a bed.

"Listen carefully," I whispered at him. "I went out for a walk and while I was wondering about I saw a noticeboard. It had a wanted poster for you and Lieutenant Moreau, your travelling companion. There were drawings of us and a description of you with your red coat. They must have spoken to General Souham because they are searching for us in Paris."

"Posters of us all over Paris," breathed Grant, with a note of pride to his voice. "We will be famous. But we must stay hidden until we are ready to declare the new republic."

"No," I whispered back. "It is even more important that we leave, but we must do it carefully at night so that we are not seen. As soon as we hear from Lacodre we have to go together."

"But I want to stay and help create the new republic," Grant whined like a petulant child. "Think of the recognition we will get if we help stop the war. If we are on a barge or back in Spain when the republic is declared then our moment is lost."

"You are right, I suppose," I acknowledged, pretending to consider his point of view while I planned a new angle of attack. Thoughts of glory were driving him and so the threat of disgrace would turn him. "But what happens if we are captured before the republic has been declared? You are very distinctive in your red coat and Sophie says that everyone in the city is a potential spy. Think who knows we are here: Lacodre, his parents, Anna, Clothilde, the boys – any one of those could accidentally say something to someone that could lead to our discovery."

"Yes, but..." Grant started to object, but I held up my hand to stop him and then held a finger to my lips. I had heard a scraping sound in the chapel below. I reached forward and threw back the trap door, which fell back on the platform with a bang.

Anna stood at the bottom of the ladder, one foot on the first rung. She stared up with what I thought was a mixture of guilt and alarm. "I was just coming to tell you that I have brought your food," she announced, gesturing at a covered basket that she had left on the stone altar.

I looked down at her with growing suspicion. "Thank you, Anna. We will be down presently."

She turned for the door and I watched her walk out of the ruined end of the building. Then I shuffled over to the slatted sides of the bell tower to watch her walking away towards the house.

"You surely don't suspect Anna as a spy?" exclaimed Grant.

"She does not normally come up the ladder to tell us about food," I reminded him. "Normally she just leaves it on the altar and goes. Right now I don't think I trust anybody." I turned back to him. "We might not be betrayed by a committed Bonapartist; it might be someone who is being blackmailed by the authorities. Or little Victor might tell a friend at school about a man with a red coat who lives in his garden. There are a hundred ways we could be betrayed."

"Yes, but even if we were captured, we would not talk."

"Everyone talks eventually. They might use opiates so you are not thinking clearly or drive you mad with pain until you say anything to make it stop. You are right: the republic is the most important thing," I lied. "Imagine if we were captured and the French government proclaimed that we had betrayed the plot. They would claim that our evidence resulted in the arrest and execution of the conspirators, people like Sophie. Is that what you want? The British press and society would decry us as the greatest villains, betraying those who had tried to bring peace and prosperity."

Grant's eyes opened wider in alarm as his previously imagined glory turned into ignominy and condemnation.

I pressed on. "We have already sent our despatches to Wellington. If the plot succeeds then we will share in the glory, and if we can make it back to Britain or Spain, we can be sure that the messages got through."

Grant sat there for nearly a minute, thinking this through, and then he looked up. "You are right, Flashman," he conceded. "The republic is the most important thing and we must do all we can to protect it."

Having convinced Grant not to show himself in public again and to leave as soon as we had heard from Lacodre, I headed back up the garden to the house. Anna gave me a strange look as I passed through the kitchen. I wondered again if she was a spy for Clarke. If she was, she might have been informed that I was also working for Clarke. She might be just as worried about me betraying Lacodre as I was about her revealing our true identities. It was an absurd situation in that neither of us could trust or talk openly to the other without being certain of their treachery. If Anna was just inquisitive or had been asked to watch us by Sophie then it would be fatal to admit that I was being blackmailed by Clarke.

The mistress of the house, however, seemed to have no such suspicions and happily told me that she had arranged for a length of chain and a lock to be delivered to Malet's room at the rest home.

That evening I tried to play cards with Sophie and the boys. My mind was not in the task. I could not help but wonder what would happen to them once Clarke moved against the conspirators. Even if Savary was trying to help her, it would surely be impossible for him to protect her if she was up to her neck in a plot to overthrow the emperor. She seemed certain to face the guillotine, but at least the boys should be saved and given to the custody of their father. While Sophie and her sons laughed with delight at the turn of the cards, I sat there feeling increasingly morose.

I was more convinced than ever that we had to escape. There was no way I was going to play a part in Sophie's downfall or implicate other innocent victims for Clarke. I had grown fond of Sophie and the boys over the last couple of weeks, especially little Victor, who seemed to have a powerful imagination. He would often sit beside me and ask me to tell him tales of the war in Spain.

What is this? I hear you cry: Old Flash getting sentimental and chivalrous? Not a bit of it, although of course I would have been sorry to see poor Sophie lying face down underneath the 'national razor' as it was known. In this case, while Sophie did not know it, our interests were completely aligned. If I was forced to plant papers incriminating others in her house then she would be further implicated in the republican scheme. Equally, I knew full well that the minute I had planted those documents, I would be a dead man. Clarke would not take the risk of me being used by one of his political opponents to reveal his involvement in the conspiracy. But it would be no easy task for Grant and I to escape both our friends and our enemies to make it to that barge.

Even if we did manage to get away, I wondered what would happen to Sophie. Clarke would not give up on his plan of using the conspiracy for his own ends. Perhaps someone else would plant the incriminating documents and our escape would make no difference to Sophie's fate. I pondered if I should simply tell her that the plot had been betrayed; but she was bound to tell Malet and that was as good as telling Clarke. The minister would then have us all rounded up and executed without delay. My imagination was filled with an awful image of staring down into a basket waiting to collect my head. I shuddered with horror at the thought and then, taking the brandy bottle with me, I slurred my apologies and retired for the evening.

I awoke the next morning with a thick head and what felt like a furry tongue. For a few blissful moments I lay enjoying the sound of the birds and the early-morning light shining through the half-drawn curtains. Then, like a black cloud, the memories of the previous day filled me with gloom. The walls of the room seemed to close in and I felt more ensnared than ever before. I had been in prisons and cells before and faced some grim prospects, but here there were so many layers of intrigue and confinement that it seemed almost impossible to break free. I got dressed and went outside, but there was no escape there as I remembered I was due to report to Clarke's men at the start of each day.

I made my way through the bushes in the garden, avoiding sight of the chapel. I slipped quietly out of the gate and walked down the alley to the street. The man in the brown suit was sitting on the bench across the road, unshaven and slightly dishevelled as though he had been on duty all night, and perhaps he had. I walked across and sat next to him.

"What news do you have?" he demanded curtly.

"Not much. I told the minister everything I knew yesterday." I paused, thinking that there was one piece of information that I could safely give them as they would find out for themselves shortly. "Madame Trebuchet has sent General Malet a chain and padlock for the box under his bed." Glancing across at him, I added, "I presume you people can pick the lock?"

The man looked at me with contempt. "Yes. But find out where she bought it in case we need an identical lock."

I got up and started to walk away. The lock probably had the maker's name stamped on it; the man was just trying to exert his power over me. I had walked several paces when he spoke again.

"Wait," he called, and I turned to face him. "Who is the second deserter staying at the house?"

I paused momentarily in shock before I managed to utter, "Second deserter? There is no second deserter." It was a poor lie and we both knew it. The man smiled at my reaction.

"We will find out who it is, but it would be better for you if you tell us."

"I have no idea what you are talking about," I responded more convincingly, but the damage was done.

I turned and walked away back up the alley. My heart was pounding. The hunt was on and this time we were the foxes. I could almost hear the call of the horns and the baying of the hounds as I went through the garden gate. It would not take them long to find out who Grant was. Someone had talked, and once they had a description of a man in a red uniform, they would soon link it to the missing British officer hunted across the city. There could be no more delay or prevarication: we would have to leave that night, whether Lacodre's cousin was ready or not.

Needless to say he was not ready and Anna was damned icy about it when I asked her that afternoon. I have little recollection of that day beyond wandering around the garden in an increasing state of funk as I considered the risks we would have to take over the next few hours and what would befall us if we failed. That afternoon I went to Grant and told him that we had to leave that night. I explained that I had seen men watching the front of the house and with the wanted posters we could not afford to delay any longer. He took this surprisingly well and said he would be ready. If he had harboured any doubts, he had only to go to the front of the house where one of Clarke's agents could clearly be seen sitting on the stone bench I had used to watch the house. I had still not worked out precisely how we were going to escape without being spotted, and as evening fell I found myself turning once more to the brandy bottle for solace.

"What are you doing sitting here by yourself?" asked Sophie when she found me in the library.

I looked at her with a mixture of pity and shame at my complicity in her fate. "Come here and join me for a drink," I suggested, patting the seat on the sofa beside me. I reached across to the side table and poured a generous measure of spirit into a second glass and passed it across.

"What has got into you?" she persisted. "For the last couple of days you have been really miserable."

"I am homesick," I admitted and then, with an unplanned burst of honesty, I added, "and I am frightened about what will happen next."

"You poor thing." Sophie laughed and put her arm around my shoulders and pulled me towards her so that my head rested on her shoulder. I found myself staring down at her smooth breasts and for the first time noticing the flowery scent that she used.

"You don't understand," I cried, sitting up again. "Grant and I have to go soon. Yesterday when I was out I saw a wanted poster for us. The police are searching for us. It is too dangerous for us to stay here. Too dangerous for us, for you and the republic," I slurred.

"Ah, so that is what you have been worrying about." She smiled again and as I took another swig of brandy I realised that she was still a striking woman. "There is no need to get upset; your friendly barge owner should be here any day. Then you will sail peacefully across France to Nantes. It is a beautiful city; I was brought up near there. The coast is rife with smugglers. You are bound to find someone to take you to a friendly port."

"It is not that," I said miserably. "Well, not just that."

"What then?" she prompted, before adding, "Pour me some more brandy. It looks like I have some catching up to do."

"I am not just frightened for me, I am frightened for you too."

"Don't be frightened for me. I have told you before that I have protection. If the plot fails, the minister of police will not let me be arrested." She took a gulp of spirit and as her eyes burned brightly she added, "But the plot will not fail. In just a few weeks the second republic will be born and once again the spirit of *liberté, égalité* and *fraternité* will be alive through France."

"No, it won't," I insisted, suddenly feeling a sense of abandonment. "The government knows all about the plot and in a few weeks you will all be arrested and facing execution." I grabbed Sophie by the shoulders and looked her in the eye. "You have to believe me. If you are caught trying to overthrow the emperor, there will be nothing that Savary can do to save you, even if he wants to." Sophie stared at me in surprise as I added lamely, "I just don't want you to end up on the guillotine."

She leaned across and I felt her brandied lips gently kiss mine. "You really care, don't you?" she whispered, sitting back. "What makes you say these things?"

I realised with a start how close I had come to simply blurting out everything and took another swig to hide my dismay. "It's Malet's damn box," I told her. "Why would they release him from prison if they were not going to keep an eye on him? I am certain with every fibre of my being that the authorities have looked inside it."

"Why have they not arrested Malet then?" asked Sophie.

"Because they want to see who else will become involved in the plot; they are using Malet as bait. It is what I would do if I was a Bonapartist." Christ, I thought, I really could not make it any plainer without introducing Clarke as a character witness. But just to drive the point home further I went on. "And it is not just that. Last night I had a dream, a nightmare really. Ministers were using the plot to round up their enemies as well as the conspirators. You, Malet and dozens of others were waiting by the guillotine. The blade kept rising and falling, rising and falling. It was awful. I have never had such a vivid dream. It seemed like a premonition. I want you to promise me something."

"What?" She looked tenderly at me and one hand reached out to stroke my cheek.

"I want you to promise that before the plot starts you will take the boys to some safe place in the countryside and that you will not return to the city until you have heard that the second republic has been declared."

"I promise," she whispered softly. "I also promise that I will never forget you, Thomas Flashman." At that moment she looked beautiful in the candlelight and I suddenly realised that I had not wanted a woman this much for quite some time. I reached forward and cupped one of her breasts with my hand. "What are you doing?" she asked quietly.

"I am upholding revolutionary principles," I told her. "In England this would be known as taking a *liberté*. I am rather hoping that you will be offering me some *fraternité*."

Chapter 30

There was plenty of *fraternité* that night; in fact we fraternised ourselves to exhaustion. There was even some *égalité* as we both took turns on top. I guessed it was some time since Sophie had been with a man and for me it was a splendid way to release the tension that had been building up over the last few days. We were interrupted once, when we could no longer ignore Anna's less than discreet hammering on the library door to remind Sophie that the boys were going to bed. She went up to kiss them good night while I fortified myself with more brandy and took the bottle with me to Sophie's bedchamber. There we renewed our very personal tribute to revolutionary principles. I well remember Sophie sitting astride me with her splendid breasts bouncing in front of my face, urging me with republican zeal to use my senatorial staff to bring her to liberty. There is a reason that the French statues of the revolution are often bare-breasted women: with bouncers like those ripe for the grabbing, you are not going to waste time thinking of the principles relating to constitutional monarchies.

I awoke in the middle of the night with another sore head and a bladder bursting for attention. Sophie was snoring quietly beside me with her arm draped across my chest. I gently slid out of her nocturnal embrace and staggered across to the corner of the room where I had seen the chamber pot earlier. I had half-filled it when I was hit with the sudden recollection of what I was supposed to be doing that night. Instead of bedding the lady of the house, I should have been making my escape with Grant. I muttered curses to myself as I pulled back one of the window drapes and looked out. It was still dark with no hint of light in the eastern sky. From the light of the quarter moon I could just make out the bushes in the garden below. There was still time to make our move.

I turned back to the bed and saw Sophie's naked body illuminated in the moonlight. For a fleeting moment I wondered if I could postpone our escape until the following night, but then I remembered the smug face of the man in the brown suit. With wanted posters, Grant flaunting himself watching the nearby parades and somebody talking about the second man in the garden, it was astonishing that they had not arrested us already.

I got down on my hands and knees and started to collect my clothes. I was soon dressed apart from my coat, which was still in the library, and my sword, which I had kept in the chapel. I went across and kissed Sophie lightly on the cheek. As I turned away I saw the brandy bottle on the bedside table. My head was throbbing, but I was also thirsty and I thought a little 'hair of the dog' would not hurt. I took a deep swig and then I slipped from the room.

In the library I found my coat where it had been discarded in our fumbling embraces, but before I left I remembered that Sophie kept her pistol in the desk drawer. It was the one that she had used when we first met. I went across the room and, fumbling in the darkness, I found it with a powder flask and a bag of balls. I pocketed them in my coat and followed a passageway that led out into the garden.

Would Clarke really have people watching the front and back of the house night and day? I wondered. The only way to find out was to look, but if they were there then they would be alerted to our escape. Night was the obvious time to make a run for it and Clarke must have thought that I would consider it. I decided that they probably were watching the house and so we would have to find some other way to escape.

As I walked down the garden, I knew that it was surrounded by a stone wall one and half times the height of a man. To my right the wall ran along the main street; a man could stand on the corner and watch both the street and the alley. To my left, the wall separated Sophie's garden from the ones of neighbouring properties. That seemed the way to go, if we could get over the wall.

I reached the chapel, found my sword and whispered up to Grant. There was no reply but he had to be in the bell tower because he had pulled the ladder up with him. He did that every night, even though Anna had promised that Clothilde would not come back.

"Are you there?" I whispered hoarsely again, a little louder this time. I did not want to use his name in case a spy was in the alley near the chapel. Still no response, but listening carefully I could hear his deep, regular breathing. A more drastic approach was clearly required.

I walked to the ruined end of the chapel and found a rock the size of an apple. Then I walked into the base of the tower again and hurled the stone to the underside of the platform Grant was sleeping on. There was a yell from Grant that must have been heard by anyone in the alley. This was immediately followed by a muted yelp from me as the rock fell back and cracked me on the shoulder.

I heard the creak as the trap door opened. "Who is there?" he whispered down.

"Who do you think?" I rasped back. "And for God's sake keep the noise down."

"I did not think you were coming. Anna told me that you were playing games with Sophie and it looked like you would be at it all night."

"Well, I am here now, so let's get going."

There was a scraping sound as Grant started to lower the ladder through the hatch and that gave me an idea as to how we would negotiate the garden walls. In a couple of minutes Grant was dressed in his immaculate and highly conspicuous British uniform. He had a few possessions including some borrowed books in an old sack and to this I contributed the now nearly empty bottle of brandy. It was, I thought, not the best planned escape. With the wanted posters of us around the city, Grant in his distinctive clothes had to be out of sight in daylight. That might mean lying low somewhere, but I had not thought to bring any food from the kitchen. There was no time now: we had to get moving.

I don't know if you have ever staggered half drunk late at night through an overgrown garden holding one end of an eighteen-foot ladder? It is not easy, especially when the person at the other end is asking awkward questions.

"I still don't understand why we could not just have gone through the gate," persisted Grant. "They can't know we are here or they would have arrested us. That is why they are putting up posters."

"I am telling you, I saw someone watching the front of the house," I snarled back as I wrenched the rungs out of the branches of some unseen bush. "If they are watching the front then they will be watching the back." Grant slipped as he half fell into a flower bed and I grimaced as the side of the ladder dug into my newly bruised shoulder. "We just need to get through this garden and a couple beyond and then we can get out onto the street without anyone seeing us."

Two startled birds squawked and flew up from a nearby tree and I prayed that whichever agent was watching the back of the house was either deaf or asleep. As my boot splashed into the edge of an ornamental pond and Grant cursed over some other obstacle, it seemed we were well past any idea of stealth. Eventually we found the next stone wall, half overgrown with ivy. We leaned the ladder against it and I swiftly climbed up it. Swiftly, that is, until my foot reached for the rung that Clothilde had snapped off. Suddenly I found both feet dangling in the air and the bridge of my nose smacking into another rung as I clung on. With eyes watering, I regained my footing and climbed to the top. There I swung a leg over the wall to sit astride it while Grant climbed up.

"You might have told me about that missing rung," I hissed at him as I rubbed what would soon be another swelling.

"I thought you knew about it," he replied sullenly and he swung astride the wall on the opposite side of the ladder.

We hauled it up between us and tipped it so that it led to the new garden. There at least we had some luck: the considerate owner had turned most of their garden to plain, unobstructed lawn. We moved swiftly across it and over the next wall into the third garden. That also seemed relatively clear, and we were halfway across that when we heard the dog. I caught a fleeting glimpse of a large, dark, snarling shape flitting towards us across the grass.

"Let go of the ladder, Flashman," Grant called out. "I will try to hit him with it."

I released my grip on the wood and stepped smartly back so that Grant was between me and the dog. If he wanted to tackle the creature, he was welcome to it. I saw the black shadow close on us and heard the swish of the ladder as Grant swung it in the direction of the animal. There was a thud and a yelp from the creature, but before I could celebrate our success the other end of the ladder came out of the darkness and clouted me around the head.

For a second I lay stunned on the ground, wondering how much more of this escape attempt I could survive. Then Grant was pulling at my arm. "Come on, Flashman, there is a gate in that far wall."

I staggered to my feet and started to run after what seemed a blur of several Grants as they approached a kaleidoscope image of gates and walls ahead of us. I was feeling nauseous now and my vision had only just started to settle as I saw Grant reach the gate and fumble at the bolt. Then I heard a snarl nearby and felt sharp teeth closed around my forearm. I wrenched my arm free to the sound of ripping cloth. The animal was swung to one side and I just managed to get through the gate before it could attack again.

As Grant pulled the gate shut I looked around. I genuinely expected to find a group of Clarke's agents roaring with laughter at out ineptitude, but the alley was empty.

"Come on, Flashman, we had better get away."

With the dog still snarling on the other side of the wooden panel I staggered after my red-coated comrade down the alley. We were moving away from Sophie's house, and once the dog had stopped barking I couldn't hear any sound of a pursuit. Eventually we came out on a darkened street.

It took me a moment to collect my thoughts and assess my injuries. My shoulder was still painful and I could feel a lump growing already across the bridge of my nose. My sleeve was ripped but there was only a light graze on my arm. On top of that my head now throbbed from a combination of the alcohol and concussion from the ladder. In contrast, when I looked at Grant, he seemed as immaculately dressed as when we had left.

"Shall we go?" he suggested brightly. "I think the river is this way."

I squelched along in his wake with one boot still waterlogged from the pond. Mercifully the sky showed no sign of the coming day, so that while you could make out we were in uniform from the moonlight glinting off swords and buttons, it was almost impossible to make out the colour of the cloth. It was a short walk to the river, where we saw boats tied up singly or several abreast along its length. We headed for the thickest congregation of craft with me uncomfortably aware that this could well be the hardest part of our escape.

Chapter 31

Despite my injuries, the climb through the gardens was the less risky part of the night. Now we had to take a chance with an unknown boat captain. If he was a Bonapartist or fearful of the authorities, he might turn us in, especially when he saw the colour of Grant's uniform. But if we were lucky and he was greedy then there was a chance we could get away.

"How are we going to persuade the captain to take us?" asked Grant as though this thought had only just occurred to him.

"I have some gold sewn into my belt."

"You never told me that before," he bleated.

"You did not need to know before," I muttered.

I paused in a doorway and removed my belt. It never did to show people where you kept your gold and how much you had left. There were twelve golden guineas in the belt and I removed six of them and put them in my pocket. Fixing the belt back, I checked that the pistol was still in my pocket and then gestured to where a large pile of cargo was gathered at the end of a pier.

"Let's try over there," I suggested.

Despite the hour there were several shadowy figures moving about; none of them, I suspected, involved in legal activities. We walked between some bales of cloth and suddenly found ourselves facing three dark shadows who whirled around at our appearance. A knife glittered in the moonlight as one snarled, "What do you want?"

I held up my hands to pacify them and show we were not holding weapons. "We are not here on duty," I spoke quietly. "We are looking for a boat to take us upriver and then to the coast."

The man grunted. "Some more who don't want to go to Russia, eh?" It seemed we were not the first to try this route. He gestured up the pier. "Try the last boat on the left, the *Nantes Lilly*; he will take passengers for the right price."

Grant and I walked up the jetty. I looked back over my shoulder to check that none of the men we had spoken to were moving off to fetch the authorities but they seemed more engrossed in whatever illicit business they were conducting. This was turning out to be much easier than I expected. I should have realised that most of the river captains made at least some of their income from smuggling.

We found the *Nantes Lilly* tied up where she had been described. There was no one on deck and so I stepped over the rail and knocked on the cabin roof.

"Who is it?" called a voice.

"Passengers," I replied just loud enough for him to hear.

A hatch slid back and a middle-aged head appeared through the opening. His eyes narrowed as he took in our uniforms and swords in the dim light. I glanced again at the eastern sky; a dim light was just starting to appear on the horizon but it was still too dark to make out the colour of Grant's coat easily. "You are officers," observed the head. "It costs more for officers. Where do you want to go?"

"We are officers who want to go to Nantes without anyone asking questions," I told him. "We can pay in gold, British gold guineas taken from the battlefield. Three guineas for each of us. You get them when we get to Nantes."

"No, I want them before you step aboard," insisted the head.

"Two now, four when we arrive in Nantes. But I will show them to you so that you know we have them."

The man grunted his acceptance and opened the side hatch so that we could step into the cabin.

"When do we leave?" I asked, stepping down.

"First light on the tide... hey, what is this? He is British." As Grant had stepped down towards the cabin the light of a candle inside had illuminated the colour of his coat.

"He is one of the Hanoverians fighting for the emperor; they fight in red like the British."

"Ja, I am ze Hanoverian," confirmed Grant in an appalling German accent.

The boat captain looked suspiciously at Grant, but I distracted him by showing him the six gold coins in my hand and then giving him two of them.

"I want all of the money now," persisted the captain truculently. "I need it to make some... investments." By which he undoubtedly meant smuggling

"Not a chance," I told him. "If we gave you all the money now, you could just turn us in and keep it." I paused, considering. We would have to trust him to some degree. It would not do to make him an enemy when right now we depended on him. I gave him a third coin. "Half now and half when we get to Nantes."

He gave a grudging nod of agreement.

"Are you alone on board?" I asked.

"No, my son is with me." As he spoke the captain moved what had seemed a fixed cabinet to reveal a hatch underneath. He pulled the hatch open and a nervous teenage boy stared up at us from the shallow space under the deck. "We saw you coming and thought you were from the harbour master. Lucien is seventeen, and if they found him, they would conscript him." He looked down at his son. "It is all right, boy. They are here for passage to Nantes."

The captain turned to me. "I have to go ashore to conduct some private business." He patted the pocket in which he had put my gold. "If any officials come, join Lucien in the space under the decks until they leave. He has a string to pull the cabinet back over the hatch; no one will find you down there."

Grant and I sat in the cabin facing the little window that showed anyone coming down the jetty. It was not quite dawn and we were cold and tired, but neither of us could sleep. I thought we had an hour or two before our absence was noticed and I was desperate to have the ropes cast off and be sailing upriver by then.

"Do you think we can trust them?" whispered Grant in English, staring at the young boy who busied himself getting us cups of a very decent wine and bread for breakfast.

"What choice do we have?" I asked. "I think he would have taken his boy with him if he was going to play us false."

It was a tiny cabin with most of the boat dedicated to cargo. Eventually the boy ran out of things to do and sat nervously beside us. I talked to him in French to pass the time. He had been born on the boat, his mother had died eight years ago and he and his father made a decent living, half from cargo and half from smuggling. Light slowly began to spread across the sky and just as we started to make out the colour of things outside the old captain could be seen coming back up the jetty. He had a piece of paper in his hand and he looked furious. I sensed things were not about to go well.

"Take back your British gold and get off my boat," he thundered as he entered the cabin, throwing the gold coins on the table. "Go on, get off! We cannot afford to get involved with people like you!"

"What on earth do you mean?" I asked. "You were perfectly happy to help us last night." I glanced out of the cabin window. We could not leave the boat now; it was too light. Grant's red coat would stand out like a whore at a royal reception. Everyone would remember seeing him.

"Hanoverian my arse," roared the captain, throwing the paper on the table. It was our wanted poster. "You are enemies of the state," he raged. "Do you have any idea what happens to people like us that get mixed up in the state's business? I am taking enough risks keeping Lucien out of the army. They would execute us for helping you." He took a breath to calm himself before finishing: "Now get those British coins and yourselves off my boat."

Grant had gone pale and had started to get up, but I reached into my pocket and pulled out the pistol. I cocked it and put it to the startled head of Lucien, who was still sitting beside me. The boy had been staring wild eyed between the other occupants of the cabin and the poster on the table, but now he paled in horror. "You are right, we are desperate men," I told his father quietly. "This is why I will kill your son if I have to."

"Flashman, you can't! That is murder," cried Grant, whom I could see from the corner of my eye standing at the end of the little table. I had no intention of killing the boy, just to get the captain to do what we needed. I kept my gaze on him and watched the anger disappear in an instant.

"Please, no," pleaded his father, a look of anguish now crossing his face. "We just want to be left alone."

"Then all you have to do is go on deck, cast off and sail up the river as planned," I told him. "We don't want to hurt you or your son, but we have to leave *now*." I reached into my pocket for the exemption and put it on the table. "You get us to Nantes and your son can have that. No one will try to conscript him again."

The captain reached forward and picked up the paper as though it was a venomous snake. Carefully he unfolded it and gave a gasp of surprise when he saw the signature. "It is signed by the minister himself," he breathed.

"That's right; this is a political affair, one minister against another. If you turn us in, you will be right in the middle of it, whether you like it or not." I smiled at him and moved the pistol a few inches back from his son's head. "So go on deck and cast off, would you? There's a good chap."

The captain stared between us from the paper in his hand to his son, Grant in his red coat and me. He clearly did not know what to believe, but his son's safety was his priority. Without another word he dropped the exemption on the table and climbed up on deck. All three occupants of the cabin silently watched through the portholes as he moved about the deck, untying ropes and hauling the big sail up the mast. It was only halfway up when I saw that we were slowly moving away from the jetty. He handled the boat well on his own; soon the sail was sheeted home and the captain was at the tiller, steering through what was fast becoming a busy waterway.

"You can leave us now," I told the son, uncocking the pistol. He leapt from the table like a startled rabbit and ran on deck to join his father. I sank back on the bench seat. "That was close," I breathed. "There was a moment back there when I thought we would never get away from that jetty."

"Where did you get that gun?... You wouldn't have shot the boy, would you?"

"I got the gun from Sophie and of course I would not have shot the boy. I have no idea if the gun is even loaded."

Grant leaned forward and picked up the exemption. "This looks very realistic. Is it one of Malet's forgeries?"

I was an idiot then: I should have agreed that it was. But now we seemed out of imminent danger I could not help showing off. "No, it is genuine, given to me by the minister himself."

Grant sat and gaped at me for a full thirty seconds before he could speak. "You have met the minister of war?... How?... When?"

"A few days ago," I admitted offhandedly. "I was arrested and he wanted me to spy on Malet and the other conspirators, which was why he let me go and gave me that. He also wanted me to plant papers to implicate some of his enemies in the plot."

"You betrayed the plot to save you own skin?" accused Grant, appalled.

"Of course not. The minister already knew everything about the plot. He was the one who released Malet to attract other conspirators. As I had suspected all along, they had seen the documents in Malet's trunk."

"But you agreed to spy on the conspirators for him?"

"When the alternative was a firing squad, of course I did." I gestured around the cabin. "As you may have noticed, we are not staying around to spy on Malet or plant documents."

"But what of the second republic?" he cried. "It is betrayed, Bonaparte will not be overthrown and we will not bring an end to the war." Grant was seeing his dreams of fame and glory collapse in ruins.

"It was never going to happen," I reminded him. "The minister of war was really behind the whole thing to attract those opposed to the regime and implicate his enemies."

"Have you told General Malet that he is being falsely played? And what of poor Madame Trebuchet?"

"I couldn't tell them or the minister would have found out; he had other informers. They would all have been arrested and executed. The minister already has enough evidence in that trunk. But I…"

"So Madame Trebuchet," interrupted Grant, "that dear, precious woman who provided us with hospitality and succour in our hour of need, is left ignorant of the trap closing around her head!" Grant was now working himself up into quite a passion. "You do not know this, Flashman, but I greatly admire that lady and her courage to bring an end to the war. But now she is abandoned because you have behaved like a…" He paused, thinking of a suitable condemnation. "… like a viper in her bosom."

I laughed at him. The pompous prig had barely spoken to Sophie, and if he was honest with himself, he was much more upset over his lost dreams of glory than Sophie's fate, not that he could admit that. "I was a lot more than a viper in her bosom," I told him. "And I fancy you would have admired the lady even more if you had bedded her. She was a skilled and enthusiastic mount, that one."

"You didn't?" gasped Grant. He stepped back as though I had slapped him.

"I did, and because I had a genuine liking for her and the boys, I have convinced her to be out of the city when they attempt to raise the second republic. It will give her a chance to get away when the plot fails."

"You are an evil and despicable man, Flashman," persisted Grant. "You have no honour, and I think you have spent so long in that French uniform that you have forgotten which side you are on. We had a chance to end the war and bring glory to Britain. Instead you have betrayed our allies in the basest way."

"You bloody fool," I roared at the ungrateful bastard. "If I am such a traitor, just think where you would have been without me. Right now you would either be dead or in some basement screaming every secret you know. Meanwhile Sophie would be a sitting duck for the minister's scheming. If we do get out of here, it will be no thanks to you." With that I got up and stormed out of the little cabin. I preferred

251

the company of a man whose son I had recently held at gunpoint to my countryman.

Chapter 32

The journey across France should have been a pleasant affair; the weather was fine most of the time and there was no hint of any pursuit. For the first few days I worried that Anna might have talked about our planned means of escape. Every time we passed a town I expected squads of troops searching every boat, but there was nothing. The boat was only searched once at roughly the halfway point. But we had barely settled in the secret compartment when the captain was pulling the hatch open again. He explained that it was a cursory inspection, with a small bribe in smuggled goods paid to get the guards to turn a blind eye to other contraband.

Considering our introduction, the captain had been quite reasonable. That first morning when I had gone on deck he had asked if he could borrow my pistol. I sensed that this was a test of trust, and as I could not shoot anyone without attracting unwelcome attention, I handed it over. He cocked it, pointed it over the side and fired. The lock clicked harmlessly without discharging a ball. The captain nodded, satisfied, and handed the weapon back. We both thought it was unloaded, but when I looked later I discovered that there was powder and a ball in the barrel, there was just no powder in the priming pan.

Leaving our distinctive jackets below, Grant and I spent most of our time on deck, although the barge crew needed little help to sail. It was certainly the most peaceful journey I have ever had across an enemy country, with friendly waves to other boatmen and those living near the canals. There were only two beds on the boat and the little cabin had barely enough room to swing a rat never mind a cat. We settled into two watches so that all could sleep. I was with the captain and Grant was with the boy, Lucien. The boatmen did most of the work, but at least, having had a year in the navy years ago, I knew how to haul up the sail and tie off a rope when required. Most of the time our duties consisted of helping to open and close lock gates.

It took us nearly three weeks to get to Nantes and Grant barely spoke to me at all during that time. I did not miss his company. The one time we did have a conversation he haughtily informed me that he would be writing a report once we reached England. He told me he would be certain to include an account of my treachery and deceit. I was not unduly worried: Wellington had been furious he had given his parole and he would be livid to hear from Curtis that Grant had refused to escape and had gone on to Paris. Wellington was a pragmatic man and would not consider the journey to Paris a matter of honour at all, especially as he knew Grant had seen the letter from Marmont to the minister of war. Our general would be far more concerned with the risk that Grant could divulge all the information he knew under torture.

To any rational person I had gone well beyond the call of duty in accompanying him to the French capital and organising his escape. The more Grant cold-shouldered me and stared at me in his condescending and contemptuous manner, the angrier I got. Increasingly I came to wish that I had left him behind for his inevitable arrest and torture; a spell on the rack was just what the ungrateful wretch deserved.

As my mood darkened so did the weather. By the time we reached Nantes even the canal was choppy and angry storm clouds scudded across the sky. We had made it across France but a big obstacle still remained.

"What chance do you think we stand of getting out of France?" I asked the captain as we stood on deck, sailing towards the city docks.

"A better chance in this weather," he replied, hunching under an old army greatcoat as a squall of rain brushed over the boat. "In fact this storm might work in your favour."

"Why is that, fewer guards about?"

"Yes, but more importantly the British blockading squadron will be blown off station. That means that a few of the faster trading ships might make a run for it."

"Would you be able to help us get a passage? You must know a lot of the captains." I hesitated. I did not want my next words to sound like a threat. "It would be better for all of us if Grant and I were not found in the port." The captain looked at me warily and so I added, "We would not say anything voluntarily, but I was sent to stop Grant getting interrogated. They will torture him if they find him and a man can say anything to stop the pain."

The captain nodded slowly in understanding. "I will speak to some of the captains. Do you have any more gold?"

I took off my belt and removed the remaining six coins so that he could see that there were no more left. "That is all we have, but we don't mind working during the passage too." In fact I would be delighted to see Grant being started with a rope's end to do some menial work for a change.

We docked a short while later and the captain set off into the rain with his bills of lading and to see if any passage could be arranged. He had explained that nearly everybody in the city was involved in trade, legal and illegal, and in most cases they were involved in both kinds. People were used to turning a blind eye as smuggling was a way of life.

As the storm lashed down Grant and I sat with Lucien in the tiny cabin. Very little was said as Grant and I stared stonily at each other, while Lucien busied himself caulking some leaks in the cabin roof. Even though it was the middle of the day, the dark sky, now interrupted by flashes of lightning and thunder, made it seem as dark as dusk. Eventually, during a prolonged flash of lightning, we caught a glimpse of the captain making his way back to the boat. A short while later the hatch was thrown back, soaking us with rain, as he climbed down into the cabin.

"I have got you a passage," he announced, "but you need to move quickly. It is on an American barque that is planning to leave on the next tide."

A few minutes later and Grant and I were running up the canal docks towards the adjacent port for seagoing ships. We were both soaked through to the skin in moments, but because of the torrential downpour few other people were about. Those we did see were huddled against the weather and taking no notice of us. Grant's coat was now dark with the water and we probably both just looked like grey figures through the rain. We were aiming for a big shed on one of the wharves that had a white 'LV' painted on it. It had doors at one end facing the canal moorings and at the other end it opened out on the dock for ships. We reached the door facing the canal and pulled it open a few inches. This was the riskiest part of the journey: if people were inside, we would not be able to make the rendezvous.

The shed was empty, illuminated by a couple of lanterns fixed to supporting beams. In their dim glow we saw what the captain had told us to expect. There was a pile of crates and sacks in the centre of the shed, but to one side lay a row of barrels. They looked like brandy barrels but their real purpose was for smuggling, usually silk. The captain had explained that the tops of the barrels had not been coopered in the normal way. They were hinged so that cargo, or in this case people, could be hidden disguised as wine. All we had to do was chalk two 'x's on the lid of two barrels and climb inside. Then we would be rolled onto the American barque right under the noses of the harbour authorities. We both ran to the barrels. I found an empty one and I felt in my pocket for the stub of chalk that the captain had given me to make the marks. Grant was already sliding into his barrel.

"Chalk mine too, Flashman," he ordered curtly before slamming his lid shut.

I raised my hand to make the marks, but then I suddenly stopped. Until now I had been obliged to protect Grant because if I didn't it would increase the risk of me being caught. But once I was on that ship I would be away safely to a friendly port or captured by a friendly navy. It would not matter to me what happened to Grant. In fact with Grant promising to make trouble for me when we did get back to the British, it would be better for me if he did not make it. But could I really abandon a comrade, even one as annoying as Grant, in enemy territory when rescue was at hand?

"Flashman, have you chalked my barrel yet?"

"I am just doing it now," I replied. I scratched the wood with my fingernail so that he heard a mark being made. I was still uncertain if I could really just leave him in the warehouse and I stood there with the chalk still poised in my hand. Then Grant made up my mind for me.

"You know, Flashman, I will have to write that report. But don't worry: I will also include how you helped me in my escape."

The damn nerve of the man: how I helped *him* in *his* escape. I could see now how the report would be written: the gallant Grant risking all for his country with the snivelling traitor Flashman stabbing him in the back. This was a man who had risen to glory entirely on the back of his guide Leon's efforts and not once had he given the man any recognition. It was clear that he was now planning to exploit me in the same manner. Well, to hell with him, I thought, as I moved away.

They would be expecting two barrels and so I looked down the line until I found one with some sack-wrapped bales in it. I put two chalk 'x's on that and them moved back down the line to my barrel and gave that the same markings. I was just getting in my cask when Grant spoke again.

"Are you still there, Flashman?"

"Yes," I said, glancing again at the blank end of his cask.

"Do you think the crew will be surprised when we climb out of the barrels?"

"Oh, I am sure that there will be lots of surprise when the barrels are opened," I told him. "Now keep quiet as I think I can hear someone coming."

Epilogue

I cannot recommend a barrel as a means of transport. It was hard work keeping my feet and back braced against the sides as it was rolled along, and whenever we hit a pothole I was nearly sent flying. The continual rotation was also making me feel queasy. Once we were outside, the sound of the rain, thunder and the grind of the barrel against the road seemed very loud. But listening carefully I discovered that the man pushing my cask was French. He was complaining about having to work in the rain. From the way he spoke about the crazy Americans wanting to sail in this weather, he was clearly not part of the barque's crew.

Just when I thought I could stand the jolting no longer I felt the barrel lurch in a sideways motion and realised that it was being swung in the air. I have seen ships loaded many times and could picture my barrel being rolled onto a cargo net that was then hoisted into the air by a rope from one of the ship's yards and lowered into the hold. There was a thud as I landed on board and I could hear more voices talking in the background. Then a voice was very close at hand speaking quietly.

"Stay still and silent. There are still a load of Frenchies in the hold. We will get you out when we can."

I seemed to sit in that barrel for an age and I cracked the lid open slightly so that I could get some fresh air. The storm was so severe that even in the harbour there was a swell that kept planks and lashings creaking together. I was not going to do anything that risked discovery this close to salvation. A few weeks ago, when I had sat in Clarke's office listening to his threats and plans, it seemed impossible that I would be here now. But I had made it. With luck when Grant discovered that he had been left behind, I would be long gone. Let him see how *his* escape would go then, without me to help.

I knew we had cast off when the rocking motion changed. Instead of swaying from side to side my barrel was now swinging at a diagonal angle. That is it, I thought: we are free from French soil; and from the strength of the wind, there could be no turning back.

When I was finally released from my barrel by a grinning American tar, we went straight over to the second barrel that they had brought aboard. I had to feign dismay to find it full of a dozen bolts of silk. The sailor beamed in delight at the valuable booty.

"We have to go back to that warehouse," I cried to play my part. "My companion must still be there in another barrel."

"Can't do that, mate," said the sailor. "We are already shooting the ship through the harbour entrance."

I ran up the ladder onto the deck and was nearly knocked flat with the force of the wind sweeping across the harbour. Even under just top sails the barque was accelerating across the harbour, followed by shoals of white-capped waves. I went to the rail and stared aft. I could still just make out the warehouse as there was a 'LV' on the front as well as the back. Inside there somewhere Grant must still be crouched inside his barrel, waiting to be rolled onto the ship. I wondered how long he would wait and what he would do next. I might have felt a twinge of guilt then as the warehouse disappeared behind a squall of rain and spray.

The Indians believe in something called karma, meaning essentially you get what you deserve. There may be something in it, as Grant's journey home ultimately turned out to be a lot easier than mine. He did manage to escape France a few weeks later. After further adventures along the coast, he got a fishing boat to take him out to one of the blockading British ships and there he was rescued. He never did write his report though, as by the time he got back to London the Malet scheme had already enjoyed its brief moment of glory. Indeed, the selfish bastard never mentioned the part I played in keeping him alive to anybody. Wellington did refer to despatches he had received from Grant while we were in Paris, although the details of those despatches were kept secret.

Incredibly the second republic did exist for a few hours. Dressed in his general's uniform, Malet persuaded some of the Paris garrison to support him, while his forged documents secured the release of republican comrades including Sophie's lover, General Lahorie. The conspirators arrested several officials including Savary, the minister of police. For nearly a day Lahorie sat in the minister's office as the new republican minister, issuing decrees and prison releases. Clarke of course made sure he escaped arrest by the new republic's troops, and soon vigilant officers realised that they had heard from the emperor after the date of his death given in Malet's proclamation.

The conspirators were swiftly rounded up, with the exception of Sophie. I never discovered if she did leave town when the republic was declared, but it seems that Savary managed to protect her after all. For the rest of the plotters, and some innocent parties implicated by

Clarke, little mercy was shown. Malet and eleven others were executed by firing squad a few days after the attempt. I heard later that the game old duffer even directed the firing squad himself. Certainly the soldiers seemed sufficiently impressed to aim elsewhere. Once the smoke was cleared Malet was left still standing and untouched by lead. He ordered them to reload, shouting, "You have forgotten me," while a mortally wounded Lahorie at his feet gasped, "Me too, for God's sake."

Of course I knew nothing about all of these events to come as I introduced myself to the ship's captain. Initially he paid me little attention, concentrating on getting his vessel out of the harbour in the middle of a storm. I was told to lend a hand on the braces and be damn smart about it. The barque was called the *Mary Ellen* and it moved through that tempestuous sea with the speed of a porpoise. The strong easterly wind had scattered the British squadron and blew us well out into the Bay of Biscay. For the first twelve hours I spent on that ship I was cold, wet and usually hauling on some rope or another. It sounds a miserable existence but it wasn't, for every minute took me further from France and closer to safety. The *Mary Ellen* had been designed for speed and it was exhilarating to work with the crew to make it race through the waves. I had been in some fast sea chases years before when I had sailed with Cochrane in the navy, but I had never sailed as fast as then. As the storm eased we pressed on more sail and positively flew along.

As the sun rose on my first full day at sea I felt a hand clap me on the shoulder as I sat, exhausted, with two other seamen, sheltering from the spray.

"The old man wants to see you," advised the man I knew as the master's mate. "He is in his cabin, aft."

I stepped over to the hatch and lowered myself into the gloom below. Mostly by feel, I worked my way back until I found the door to the stern cabin. I knocked and a hoarse voice called out, "Enter."

The 'old man' was not that old, probably in his early fifties, with a weather-beaten face and steely grey eyes. "Help yerself to coffee, sir," he offered, gesturing to a tray of breakfast on his desk. "The bread is still fairly fresh and there is some butter."

"Thank you, sir," I replied. Realising that I had not eaten for hours, I helped myself to a large hunk of bread and a cup of coffee. Sipping the hot liquid, I discovered that it also contained a generous slug of brandy.

"So you are my passenger," the captain continued. "I am sorry we missed your friend. You had better have this back." He pushed the three guineas for Grant's passage across the desk. I looked up in surprise and he continued: "I am an honest man, sir. I won't take what I have not earned, especially when I have acquired some very valuable silks by mistake." He chuckled. "I pity the poor captain expecting those and finding your friend instead."

"Do you think he might have got away on another ship then?" I asked.

"He might," agreed the captain. "We were not the only ones planning to take advantage of the storm." He grinned again and held out a huge hand to shake across the desk. "I am Captain Henry Sawyer, from Boston. I have not yet had the honour of your name."

"Captain Thomas Flashman, late of the British army in Spain, but escaping from France to avoid being a prisoner of war or worse."

"Aye," said Sawyer. "But you are wearing a French uniform and I heard you travelled from Paris. I think you must have a good tale to tell, sir, and we have a long distance to travel. Help yourself to more coffee and tell me how you come to be on my ship."

So I told him, all the creditable bits apart from the details of the Malet affair. New England people are hard to impress but I think I managed it. Several times he rocked back in his chair and exclaimed. At the end he told me he was quite glad Grant was not on his ship as he sounded an ungrateful squab. In return he told me that his ship was bound for his home port of Boston, which would take three to four weeks to reach. From there he advised there were usually plenty of ships going either to straight to England or Canada from where I could get passage home.

Just a few weeks later and I was sailing along a coast with familiar names like Falmouth, Truro and Plymouth on the chart. I was not off Cornwall or Devon in England but Massachusetts in New England, heading towards Boston harbour. It was a busy port and no sooner were we tied up to the quay with the gangplank down than the usual group of harbour officials could be seen coming towards the ship: half a dozen men including, I guessed, the harbour master and several uniformed men whom I took to be customs and excise people.

"Henry, good to see you back," shouted their leader. "Was it a good voyage?"

"Very satisfactory, Caleb," responded the captain. "I will bring you the manifests from my cabin presently. Come aboard, come aboard."

"Any passengers?" asked the man called Caleb as he shook the captain's hand.

"Just this fellow," replied the captain, gesturing me to join their group. "Let me introduce Captain Thomas Flashman. Ignore that French coat; he is actually a British officer. You must hear his tale, Caleb; it is quite incredible."

"Really?" answered Caleb, shaking me by the hand. "It sounds intriguing."

"Oh, it is," enthused the Captain. "This fellow was sent by Lord Wellington himself to rescue another officer who had been captured by the French. He had to masquerade as a French officer and escape partisans to do it, but he finally got his man. Then, would you believe it, they ended up in Paris hiding from the French in their own capital."

"We were not spying," I interjected. "Just trying to avoid capture and being made prisoners of war."

"Yes," agreed the captain. "They travelled from Spain to Paris and then managed to travel from Paris to Nantes, all with the other fellow insisting on wearing a British uniform."

"What happened to this other fellow?" enquired Caleb.

"He seems to have been put on a different ship," I explained.

"Well, sir," said Caleb, "I congratulate you on escaping France. You certainly went to great lengths to avoid being captured, which makes my next duty more regrettable." He turned to the uniformed men with him and said, "Grab him, lads."

"What the devil is this?" I shouted as the men reached out and grabbed my arms, one of them sliding a manacle over my wrist.

"Caleb, what is happening?" demanded the captain, also clearly taken by surprise.

Caleb held up a hand for silence. "Gentlemen, I have to announce that Captain Flashman is a prisoner of war."

"You surely have not allied yourselves to the French?" I asked, appalled. I could not understand it: why would the United States enter the war now on the side of France? If they had, why had we not heard something in Paris?

"No, sir," announced Caleb. "The United States has declared war on Great Britain, and you have just admitted to being a British officer. After hearing only a little of what you have been through, it is my sad duty to tell you that you are now a prisoner of the United States of America."

Historical Notes

Albuera

Flashman's account of the battle of Albuera and the events that preceded it align closely with other historical accounts. For those wanting to read more, the book *Albuera 1811* by Charles Dempsey is recommended. It was the bloodiest battle of the Peninsular War and many agreed with Flashman that the battle was hopelessly mismanaged by Beresford, resulting in higher casualties. Beresford himself was distraught over the dead, missing and wounded in his initial despatches to Wellington. Indeed Wellington had these despatches rewritten to make it sound more like a victory before they were submitted to parliament. Later a pamphlet war started between Beresford's supporters and detractors, of which there were many, highlighting his shortcomings in the campaign. While Beresford was publicly exonerated from blame, he never held independent command in battle again.

Ensign Price-Thomas, just fifteen, really did exist and did die in the manner described by Flashman. Below is an extract of a letter Captain William Stephens of the Buffs wrote to his surgeon uncle:

I cannot refrain from tears while I relate the determined bravery of your gallant little subaltern, who fell on the 16th instant, covered in glory; and it must in some measure alleviate the grief I know you will feel at his loss, to know that he fell a hero.

Stephens goes on to explain that he saw Price-Thomas try to rally his company in the midst of the attack by the Poles when his captain had been injured. "Rally on me, men, I will be your pivot," the boy is quoted as shouting out. Any rally he achieved was short-lived.

Sources also confirm the extraordinary tale of Lieutenant Matthew Latham, who went to the aid of another fifteen-year-old ensign, Charles Walsh, who was trying to defend one of the regimental flags against the lancers. Latham lost his lower arm to a sabre cut, but still fought on to rip most of the colour from the flagpole despite receiving further sabre blows, including one that severed his nose and part of his cheek. Walsh survived and was taken prisoner, later confirming what happened to Latham, who was left initially for dead. The flag was found on his body the morning after the battle, but it was not until the following day that Latham was found to be still alive and treated. Latham's story has a happier end than you might expect. The much maligned prince of Wales, later George IV, referred Latham to a noted surgeon called Joseph Carpue for treatment at the prince's expense. Carpue used a pioneering skin graft technique to give Latham a new nose from skin taken from his forehead. Latham re-joined the regiment in 1816, when it was part of the allied occupation of France after Waterloo. Ironically he married a Frenchwoman and retired from the army in 1820 to live with her in Normandy. He died in 1865.

To give some idea of the scale of the casualties, below is an extract from another letter written by a Captain Arthur Gordon describing what happened to some of the officers in the Buffs. In this he refers to lances as pikes.

I shall endeavour, however, to give you some facts respecting the First Battalion of the Buffs: Captain Burke is killed, Captain Cameron shot in the neck, wounded in the breast with a pike and a prisoner. Captain Marley was wounded twice in the body with a pike, badly. Captain Stevens was shot in the arm, was a prisoner and made his escape; Lieutenant Woods had his leg shot off by a cannon ball; Lieutenant Latham's hand is shot off, also part of his nose and cheek; Lieutenant Juxon is wounded in the thigh with a pike, Lieutenant Hooper shot through the shoulder, Lieutenant Houghton has received a severe sabre cut on the hand and through the skull; Lieutenant Herbert is dead; Ensigns Chadwick and Thomas are also dead; Lieutenants O'Donnell and Tetlow with Ensign Walsh were wounded and made prisoners, they have since escaped and joined... I was stabbed at the time with a pike in the breast, in the back and elsewhere and the enemy's cavalry galloped over me.

Interestingly the above account does not list any bayonet wounds incurred by the officers, indicating that, like Flashman, officers stood back from the bayonet duels, where they would have been disadvantaged with just a sword.

The appalling eighty-five per cent casualty rate for the Buffs is confirmed by historical sources. For the battalion as a whole six hundred and forty-three were killed, wounded or missing from a total of seven hundred and fifty-five men at the start of the battle. In Price-Thomas's company only a private and a sergeant survived unscathed. There were similar numbers for the other two battalions of Colborne's division that were routed by the Poles. The Buffs were indeed referred to as the resurrectionists in the days after the battle as many of the one hundred and sixty-one missing men escaped their captors and joined the one hundred and twelve initial survivors.

As well as the battle itself, Flashman's descriptions of the life of a company on the march and the horrendous aftermath of the battle are also confirmed by historical sources. British casualties are estimated at over four thousand, approximately forty per cent of the total British force deployed, although, as noted above, some regiments saw double this number. The French are thought to have lost some six thousand men, roughly a quarter of their original force. French wounded left on the battlefield were also at a much higher risk of being murdered by the Spanish in the course of looting that was inflicted on all nationalities.

George Guthrie

George Guthrie was the senior surgeon at Albuera and at one point he had over three thousand wounded in his care with just four wagons to transport them. He was twenty-four at the time of the battle, having been apprenticed to a surgeon aged just thirteen. He passed his surgeon's examination aged sixteen and was immediately posted to be a regimental surgeon for a unit being sent to North America. Some of his notes from the battle survive and confirm that men recovered from some astonishing injuries given the limited medical knowledge of the time. This includes a soldier who had a musket ball pass straight through his body as Flashman experienced, and whose wounds finally healed.

It is not known if this Guthrie was any relation to the surgeon called Guthrie that sailed with Cochrane on the *Speedy*, whose adventures are detailed in *Flashman and the Seawolf*. However, biographical information on George Guthrie indicates that there were other surgeons in the family so it is entirely possible

Badajoz

The capture of Badajoz was a brutal affair that was a source of both pride and shame for the British army. While Albuera was the bloodiest battle of the whole Peninsular War, given casualties across the French, Spanish, Portuguese as well as the British, Badajoz was the bloodiest event in the war for the British army alone. There were four thousand six hundred and seventy casualties of which three thousand seven hundred and thirteen fell during the storm of the breaches.

The battle took place largely as Flashman described. Casualties were appallingly high as the attack was made before the breaches had been properly developed. More than forty separate assaults were made at the breaches. The diversionary escalade assault on the fortress which ultimately helped capture the city was an extraordinary feat of courage and daring.

As Flashman recounts, the French took to taunting their opponents, which served to enrage the survivors when they were finally able to enter the city. In an age when the sacking of a captured city was commonplace, the brutality shown to the citizens of Badajoz sickened even contemporary observers. Some officers did what they could and Flashman mentions Harry Smith who married a nun he found in Badajoz. The fourteen-year-old girl, Juana Maria de los Delores de Leon, had certainly sought shelter in a convent, but she was not a nun. She married Smith just a few days after the battle, and despite this briefest of courtships they appeared to live a long and happy life together.

Ironically given the nature of their meeting, this girl has a personal link to a later famous siege. She travelled to South Africa with her husband and with fellow officer Ben D'Urban. All had a part in developing that country and all three had towns named after them. Ladysmith was the scene of a notorious one-hundred-and-eighteen-day siege by the Boers of the British-held town in 1900.

Colquhoun Grant
Grant is another of those extraordinary characters from history whose real-life adventures seem too farfetched to appear in a historical novel. He was the tenth child of a family of minor Scottish nobility and joined the army aged fourteen. Helped in his career at first by several of his siblings, he came to the attention of Wellington for his extraordinary gathering of cattle and supplies from outside Torres Vedras. With the help of local guides, he managed to transport a large herd of cattle, sheep and draught animals carrying grain unmolested through French lines. He subsequently earned acclaim as an exploring officer. It is known that Wellington greatly valued his services and later appointed Grant as head of intelligence for the Waterloo campaign. It is perhaps significant that without Leon to help him Grant did not cover himself with glory, as the French army caught the British completely by surprise as they approached Waterloo. The only description of Leon in Grant's biography comes from one of his contemporaries. He states that the guide was "a Spanish peasant of fidelity and quickness of apprehension." His evident intelligence would tend to support Flashman's interpretation of events.

Colquhoun Grant was captured by the French on the fifteenth of April 1812 just north of Alcantara, near the town of Idanha a Nova, with Leon summarily executed on the spot. His parole was signed on the eighteenth of April, the same day that floods washed away a bridge that would have been an escape route for Marmont's army. At around this time the French suddenly accelerated their movements, with the French infantry crossing the Agueda through a ford as soon as receding floodwater made it passable. Marmont consequently escaped Wellington's trap, although there is no written evidence that he gleaned any information from Grant.

Wellington was alarmed and disappointed to learn that Grant had been captured and then that he had given his parole – effectively a promise not to escape. Wellington wanted him back at all costs and offered local guerrilla forces a prize of two thousand dollars in gold if they could recapture Grant and return him alive. Copies of the letter Wellington received from Marmont offering to exchange Grant and one dated the same day from Marmont's office to Paris offering Grant for interrogation still exist. These would only have heightened Wellington's desire to get Grant back, and he would have used all resources at his disposal, including Flashman and Doctor Curtis – who is also known to have visited Grant in Salamanca.

Grant's journey from Salamanca to Bayonne started in the middle of May. Grant's biographer states that the men commanding the escort were uncomfortable that an officer who had given his parole and behaved honourably was being handed over to the ministry of war. They obviously knew what would await Grant when he reached Paris. When the convoy reached Bayonne there was no one from the ministry of war to meet them as the despatch had been intercepted. It seems that the officers commanding Grant's escort deliberately abandoned him in a square, to give him an opportunity to escape.

Grant's extraordinary choice to continue on to Paris is one of the most bizarre decisions of the war. He could easily have escaped back across the Pyrenees and with guerrilla support stood an excellent chance of re-joining the British army without delay. There was no good reason for proceeding to Paris as he had no contacts in the city. If he did travel on to Paris with General Souham, as he claimed, then he was either extraordinarily daring or equally reckless.

Grant maintained that he stopped in Orleans on the journey and 'divined' some individuals opposed to Bonaparte, but even his admiring biographer finds this hard to believe. Clearly Grant must have had some assistance to make contact with those who would be willing to help him in Paris. Flashman's account gives an explanation of how this happened and why he became involved.

Most of the information on Grant's time in Paris comes from a diary kept by his brother-in-law of the stories he was told by Grant. It is known that Grant definitely reached Paris and there are records of messages that Wellington received from him sent from that city. Unsurprisingly given the nature of their parting, Grant appears to have made no reference to Flashman at all in stories to his relatives.

As Grant did not leave any written records of his own, the second-hand accounts of his time in Paris do vary. There are some claims that he spent as long as nine months in the city, leaving in spring 1813. But Napier, who was in the peninsular at the time, claims he was back within four months of being captured. The timing in Flashman's account is aligned with that of Napier.

After Flashman lost contact with Grant, it is known that he found his way further down the coast. He made claims that he had contacted a French marshal with Scottish connections for assistance during this journey, but this is unlikely. The two marshals with Scottish/British links, Macdonald and Mortier (who had a British grandmother), are both known to have been on active service in Germany at the time. Grant ultimately escaped by hiring a fishing boat to take him out to sea where the British navy was blockading French ports. On his second attempt he succeeded.

For more information on Colquhoun Grant his biography *The First Respectable Spy* by Jock Haswell is recommended. It is, however, written in a rather hero-worshiping style, which clashes heavily with the opinion of Grant held by Flashman.

Doctor Curtis
Patrick Curtis appears in other novels on the Peninsular War, notably the Sharpe series, because he was a real and important source of information for Wellington. He was born in Ireland in 1740 and served as a parish priest until his late thirties, when he started to travel through Europe. When Flashman met him he was seventy-eight and a professor of astronomy and natural history at the University of Salamanca. He was known in Salamanca as Don Patrico Cortes and he had established a network of agents which extended across occupied Spain. The French had arrested him as a spy in 1811 but he had managed to convince them of his innocence. As Flashman describes,

he was also questioned over his visits to Grant, but again was released. His cover was blown when the British captured Salamanca. Wellington was keen to meet him and it became known that he was a British agent. When the French subsequently recaptured the city, he was forced to flee.

He returned to Ireland after the war and initially lived quietly on a pension awarded for his services in the peninsular. Then, in 1819, he was offered the archbishopric of Armagh and titular primacy of all Ireland. He continued in that role until he died in 1832 aged ninety-two. During that time he did much to secure the Catholic Emancipation Act, which was passed by the British parliament in 1829.

General Souham

Grant's biography confirms that he did start his journey back to Paris from Bayonne by posing as an American officer and sharing a carriage with the French general Souham. Other sources also confirm that the general was returning to Paris at this time, having been granted three months' leave. It is likely that this leave was later curtailed as in June Marshal Marmont was wounded at the battle of Salamanca and Souham was recommended to replace him.

Souham had started his career as a private in the royal French army for eight years before the French revolution offered opportunities for advancement. Souham quickly demonstrated sound judgement and leadership, and by 1793 he was a general of a division during the Flanders campaign. When his commander fell ill he assumed command of a French army that went on to beat a larger British and Austrian army at the battle of Tourcoing or Turcoine. He took part in various other campaigns before being wounded at the battle of Vich, when his army overwhelmed a Spanish force twice its size.

Returning to Spain to take over from Marmont in the late summer of 1812, he found the British at Burgos and in Madrid, threatening to complete the conquest of the country. Skilful manoeuvring of his forces to the north and Marshal Soult's to the south threatened to cut off the British army from its supply routes and safe havens in Portugal. As a result Wellington was forced to withdraw his army some two hundred miles to the Portuguese border, roughly where he had started the campaign at the beginning of that year.

He is a largely forgotten, but very capable commander. After Napoleon's abdication he returned to the royalist cause, which rewarded him with various honours. He retired in 1832 and died at Versailles in 1837 two days before his seventy-seventh birthday.

Agustina de Aragon

Agustina will be familiar to readers of *Flashman in the Peninsular* as she also appeared in that book. She first found fame when she fired a cannon during the siege of Zaragoza. The shot was fired at a critical moment during an attack by the French and resulted in the Spanish saving the city from their assault. The city was later captured and Agustina was taken prisoner with her young son, who died in captivity.

Agustina escaped from the French and was used by the independent Spanish government to promote resistance to the French. They widely publicised her achievement and she had various portraits painted, including one by Francisco Goya. Later she joined the partisans and fought with them for the rest of the war. Some accounts of her life state that later in the conflict Agustina left the guerrillas and went on to become the only female officer to serve with the British army in the artillery during the Peninsular War, achieving the rank of captain at the battle of Vitoria. However, Nick Lipscombe, author of *Wellington's Guns* and a leading authority on the Peninsular War, advises that she definitely did not command a gun in the British army. After the war she married a doctor and settled down to a quiet life living in Zaragoza. She died aged seventy-one.

The Hugo Family

For more information on the parents of Victor Hugo and their activities during this period the excellent biography on Victor Hugo by Graham Robb is recommended.

General Leopold Hugo met his future wife, Sophie Trebuchet, when he was sent to put down a royalist uprising in Brittany. While Victor Hugo himself sometimes described their encounter in romantic terms, implying that his mother was a royalist and their love overcame political differences, this is not correct. His mother was from one of the few committed republican families in Brittany. Her grandfather worked with the notorious revolutionary Jean-Baptiste Carrier who drowned prisoners in the Loire when the guillotine could not execute them fast enough. Her aunt Louise was Carrier's mistress and one of Sophie's closest friends.

From his revolutionary beginnings, General Leopold Hugo became a committed Bonapartist and army officer. Having had three sons, he and his wife grew apart, partly due to her refusal to follow him to his various postings. He ruthlessly put down partisan activity in Spain and, being no admirer of the Church, did nail the severed heads of executed partisans over church doorways. His family visited him in Spain in 1811 and would have been aware of the fear and hatred that the French presence in the country generated. As an indication of how committed a Bonapartist General Hugo was, he held the town of Thionville in France, close to Luxembourg border, for his emperor after Bonaparte's return from exile on Elba. He only surrendered this final outpost of imperial France on 13 November 1815, some five months after the battle of Waterloo.

Sophie Trebuchet, as she preferred to be called when Flashman knew her, did live in a house in Feuillantines off the Rue Saint Jacques in Paris. She was forty in 1812 and her youngest son, Victor, was ten. There was an old chapel at the bottom of the garden where she had harboured her lover, General Victor Lahorie (young Victor's godfather), for several years. Lahorie was almost certainly involved in the planning of the Malet conspiracy as he was one of the key conspirators that General Malet first released. Sophie was likely to have been involved in the plot too, taking messages between the two generals. Her husband also complained that she was spending large amounts of unexplained money at this time. But while the other conspirators were rounded up and shot, she escaped punishment. She claimed to the restored royalist government in 1815 that she owed her survival to information she knew that guaranteed the protection of the minister of police, Savary.

Whether Flashman's explanation of the noise Grant made with Clothilde played any part in inspiring Victor Hugo's classic *The Hunchback of Notre Dame* will never be known. It has, however, been pointed out that the cathedral in the book, with its multitude of spires and turrets, bears little resemblance to the clean lines of Notre Dame. Commentators have suggested that Victor Hugo might have had Burgos cathedral in mind when he wrote the book. Ironically his father demolished three of the pinnacles and a famous stained-glass window in the cathedral when blowing up the fort and part of the town prior to a withdrawal.

The Malet Conspiracy

The attempt to establish the second French republic occurred largely as described by Flashman. Despite being a known opponent of the regime which he had tried to overthrow in the past, Malet was released from prison on condition that he lived in Doctor Dubuisson's rest home. The forged documents to facilitate the plot were kept in a box under General Malet's bed. In spite of this low level of security, the plot was initially successful. Malet, with a couple of accomplices, managed to convince the commander of the Paris garrison that Napoleon was dead and that a new republic had been declared. Then soldiers were sent with release notices for other conspirators including General Lahorie, who went on to arrest the minister of police and replaced him in his office for much of that day.

Clarke, the minister of war, led the efforts to supress the plot and arrest those responsible. While he certainly took advantage of the plot to attack some of his enemies, we only have Flashman's account that he was a prime instigator of the conspiracy. By the end of the day most of the conspirators were under lock and key and others, including the commander of the Paris garrison, were also under arrest due to their complicity in the plot. A brief trial was held before the conspirators were promptly executed, possibly to deter Napoleon from conducting a more thorough inquiry into how the plot was developed. During the trial Malet claimed full responsibility and insisted that no one else was involved. The verdict for the conspirators seemed to have been decided before the trial; most of the defendants were refused access to legal counsel and twelve were sentenced to death.

As Flashman describes, Malet conducted his own firing squad but was completely missed by the first volley. He was obliged to order his executioners to reload and fire again. According to contemporary accounts he used his last breath to shout *"Vive la liberté!"*

Henri Clarke, minister of war and duke of Feltre

Clarke, born of Irish parents, was a shrewd political operator who survived various governmental changes in France. His father was an army officer and initially Henri followed in his footsteps. Commissioned first in the royal army, following the revolution Clarke continued to serve in the cavalry and despite Flashman's opinion he did see some action. However, he soon spent more time involved with politics and was an early supporter of Bonaparte, from the time when Napoleon was just the commander of an army in Italy. He was made minister of war in 1807 and held that position until Napoleon's abdication in 1814.

He sought favour with the new Bourbon government, and when Napoleon returned from Elba, Clarke abandoned his old boss and threw in his lot with the king. His reward was to be reinstated as minister of war, a role he held until 1817, and later a marshal of France. He earned the enmity of many of his former comrades by pursuing the purges that the Bourbon government instituted against other Bonapartist officers.

Thank you for reading this book and I hoped you enjoyed it. If so I would be grateful for any positive reviews on websites that you use to choose books. As there is no major publisher promoting this book, any recommendations to friends and family that you think would enjoy it would also be appreciated.

There is now a Thomas Flashman Books Facebook page to keep you updated on future books in the series. It also includes portraits, pictures and further information on characters and events featured in the books.

Also by this author

Flashman and the Seawolf

This first book in the Thomas Flashman series covers his adventures with Thomas Cochrane, one of the most extraordinary naval commanders of all time.

From the brothels and gambling dens of London, through political intrigues and espionage, the action moves to the Mediterranean and the real life character of Thomas Cochrane. This book covers the start of Cochrane's career including the most astounding single ship action of the Napoleonic war.

Thomas Flashman provides a unique insight as danger stalks him like a persistent bailiff through a series of adventures that prove history really is stranger than fiction.

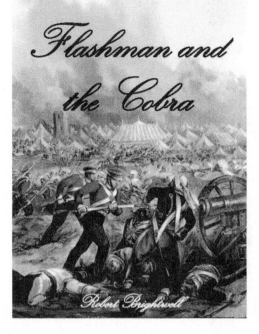

Flashman and the Cobra

This book takes Thomas to territory familiar to readers of his nephew's adventures, India, during the second Mahratta war. It also includes an illuminating visit to Paris during the Peace of Amiens in 1802.

As you might expect Flashman is embroiled in treachery and scandal from the outset and, despite his very best endeavours, is often in the thick of the action. He intrigues with generals, warlords, fearless warriors, nomadic bandit tribes, highland soldiers and not least a four-foot-tall former nautch dancer, who led the only Mahratta troops to leave the battlefield of Assaye in good order.

Flashman gives an illuminating account with a unique perspective. It details feats of incredible courage (not his, obviously) reckless folly and sheer good luck that were to change the future of India and the career of a general who would later win a war in Europe.

Flashman in the Peninsular

While many people have written books and novels on the Peninsular War, Flashman's memoirs offer a unique perspective. They include new accounts of famous battles, but also incredible incidents and characters almost forgotten by history. Flashman is revealed as the catalyst to one of the greatest royal scandals of the nineteenth century which disgraced a prince and ultimately produced one of our greatest novelists. In Spain and Portugal he witnesses catastrophic incompetence and incredible courage in equal measure. He is present at an extraordinary action where a small group of men stopped the army of a French marshal in its tracks. His flatulent horse may well have routed a Spanish regiment, while his cowardice and poltroonery certainly saved the British army from a French trap.

Accompanied by Lord Byron's dog, Flashman faces death from Polish lancers and a vengeful Spanish midget, not to mention finding time to perform a blasphemous act with the famous Maid of Zaragoza. This is an account made more astonishing as the key facts are confirmed by various historical sources.

CPSIA information can be obtained at www.ICGtesting.com
Printed in the USA
BVOW08s2015190815

413998BV00002B/98/P